Fantasy
Both 2026

FATED REBIRTH

A DARK FANTASY ROMANCE

RENO R. MIST

POSH PANGOLIN PUBLISHERS

Fated Rebirth, A Dark Fantasy Romance

Please note that the story, all names, characters, and incidents portrayed in this production are fictitious. No identification with actual persons (living or deceased), places, buildings, and products is intended or should be inferred.

Every effort has been made to trace or contact all copyright holders. The publishers will be pleased to make good any omissions or rectify any mistakes brought to their attention at the earliest opportunity.

Copyright © 2026 by Reno R. Mist

First Edition: March 2026

All rights reserved. No part of this publication may be reproduced, distributed, or transmitted in any form or by any means, including photocopying, recording, or other electronic or mechanical methods, without the prior written permission of the publisher, except as permitted by U.S. copyright law.

Book Cover: Jordan Paige Studio
Character Art on page 376 (ebook): Killer Laurent
Editors: Heartfelt Editing and Rattle the Stars PR

ISBN: 979-8-9989053-2-2 (Ebook)
ISBN: 979-8-9989053-7-7 (Paperback)
Library of Congress Control Number: 2026903806

For permission requests, contact PoshPangolinPublishers@gmail.com
For author information, please contact Reno.R.Mist@gmail.com or visit https://www.renormist.com

My Readers
Mi Lectores

Hello, my beautifully depraved and chaotic *lectores*[1],

I'm so excited to welcome you into this gloriously messy world of divinity, darkness, and desire. If you're here because you love dark romantasy (or dark fantasy) filled with morally grey characters, feminine rage, and a little vigilante justice for abusive men... I know *exactly* why you picked up this book. And trust me... no judgment here. Not even a little.

I like to stick with a theme in all of my books. This may feel repetitive for those who follow me but I cannot express how important this is to me so before we dive in, let's make sure we're on the same page about triggers and boundaries. Consent matters—not only within the story, but in your reading experience too. Some themes ahead may intrigue you; others may hit harder than expected. Please remember: it is always valid to pause, step away, or stop entirely if something becomes too heavy.

A quick heads-up: this is a long read. *Fated Rebirth* is book one in a duology within the Heretical Gods Series, so you're just beginning the journey. And if you enjoy this world, you may also want to explore my *A Second Circle Entry* novellas. These shorter works are meant to entice and entertain while expanding the hidden masquerade of magic

---

1. readers

and supernatural beings that serves as the backbone all of my books. Plus there are going to be a ton of easter egg reveals in them!

I've taken creative liberties with the mythology and folklore woven throughout this story. And while I am of Hispanic and Italian descent, any errors in language, spelling, or translation are entirely my own, I swore an oath never to throw friends or family under the bus.

Below you'll find content warnings and thematic notes. Consider this both your warning label and your safe word rolled into one.

Minor spoilers ahead.

While this is a romantic fantasy, I can say with confidence this is not a light hearted romantasy. It is a bold, gritty, and tragic tale with moments of harmony threaded through the darkness. Archetypes include: rags-to-riches, underdog, slow burn female rage, dismantling oppressive structures, and overcoming the monster.

The story may feel tragic at times as our characters are repeatedly pulled into danger by forces beyond their control, rarely allowed peace without a cost. It also leans unapologetically bold: Rowan and Violet speak their truths, make dangerous choices, and accept the fallout of getting what they want.

At its heart, this is an underdog story. Both Rowan and Violet begin with the odds stacked mercilessly against them, only to be given a second chance at rewriting their fate. There's also a subtle rags-to-riches thread as neither had much in their former lives, and rebirth places them in worlds of greater privilege, power, and peril.

Fated Rebirth blends urban fantasy with romantic fantasy and that can sometimes feel heavy, especially with today's political environment. Expect high stakes, slow-burn tension, found family, frenemies-to-lovers heat, and neo-noir worldbuilding.

Negotiated consent and boundaries are central to this story. Themes of exhibitionism and voyeurism appear throughout. This story contains themes that may be triggering for some readers, including grief and death, animal disembowelment, explicit sexual content, references to sexual assault, mentions of past abuse, and strong language.

If you notice a missing trigger that could help protect another reader, I would be endlessly grateful if you'd let me know through my website so I can update the list.

With all that said... welcome in. I hope you enjoy the descent.
With love,
Reno R. Mist

BOOKS BY
RENO R. MIST

Star-Cross'd Fates Series
One More Chance, A Redemption Novel*
Before We Belong*

Heretical Gods Series
Fated Rebirth, A Dark Fantasy Romance

A Second Circle Entry Series
Captured Prey, A Primal Play Novella*

For those interested in a custom short story with Second Circle, sign up for my newsletter
Newsletter Sign Up

*These stories can be read as standalones

Contents

Dedication	XIII
Prologue	1
Violet	
1. Chapter 1	9
Violet	
2. Chapter 2	19
Rowan	
3. Chapter 3	29
Violet	
4. Chapter 4	39
Rowan	
5. Chapter 5	55
Violet	
6. Chapter 6	63
Rowan	
7. Chapter 7	71
Violet	

8. Chapter 8　　　　　　　　　　　　　　　87
   Rowan
9. Chapter 9　　　　　　　　　　　　　　　95
   Violet
10. Chapter 10　　　　　　　　　　　　　　107
    Rowan
11. Chapter 11　　　　　　　　　　　　　　113
    Violet
12. Chapter 12　　　　　　　　　　　　　　119
    Rowan
13. Chapter 13　　　　　　　　　　　　　　125
    Violet
14. Chapter 14　　　　　　　　　　　　　　133
    Rowan
15. Chapter 15　　　　　　　　　　　　　　139
    Violet
16. Chapter 16　　　　　　　　　　　　　　143
    Rowan
17. Chapter 17　　　　　　　　　　　　　　157
    Violet
18. Chapter 18　　　　　　　　　　　　　　163
    Rowan
19. Chapter 19　　　　　　　　　　　　　　171
    Violet

20.	Chapter 20 Rowan	189
21.	Chapter 21 Violet	201
22.	Chapter 22 Rowan	217
23.	Chapter 23 Violet	235
24.	Chapter 24 Rowan	255
25.	Chapter 25 Violet	275
26.	Chapter 26 Rowan	295
27.	Chapter 27 Violet	305
28.	Chapter 28 Rowan	317
29.	Chapter 29 Violet	325
30.	Chapter 30 Rowan	337
31.	Chapter 31 Violet	353

Epilogue	373
Violet	
Thank you	375
Acknowledgements	377
About the author	379

Dedication

If you're looking for a shadow daddy...
Sorry. He's not in here.
But if you want an MMC who lets you stand fully in your power, who listens, supports, and knows how to stand beside you without trying to suppress you...
Then this one's for you.
May the chaos and magic within you bloom.

Prologue

Violet

The hemp rope around Edward Fitzgerald's throat was beautiful, precise, and tight enough to make him understand he was mine now as we stared at each other. He looked older than I remembered, impressively so, even while tied to a chair in the room that would become his coffin.

His split lip leaked crimson down his pepper-gray faded beard, pooling in the hollow of his throat where ebony rope pressed against his carotid. Not tight enough to kill. Just tight enough to make each swallow a conscious effort, each breath a negotiation with the fibers that would decide his fate.

A fate I held in my hands after forcing them to their knees.

Naturally, Edward didn't recognize me. In this life, I'd never been taken. Never been sold. Never spent twenty-four years as his property, learning the precise pitch of his breathing when he was about to hurt me.

But I remembered everything from my previous life. . . the one in which he'd murdered me.

Even now, with fear thickening the air between us, I saw him as I had back then: polished, wealthy, untouchable. A British aristocrat with enough money to fold laws into origami. I remembered those green eyes—narrowed in disgust when I fought back, and glittering with malicious satisfaction when he overpowered me.

Now I held him by his balls, murky eyes wide with confusion behind the bloodied gag from where he had nearly bitten his tongue off.

"Violet." Rowan's voice, low and controlled, reached me from somewhere behind Edward's chair. "The tie is almost complete."

I stiffened, turning just enough to catch the reassuring silhouette of Rowan's profile in the low light. Dark-clad. Broad-shouldered. Well defined and taller than he had any right to be. Rowan was a god's sinful angel in human form—though the proprietor might disagree. In the deepening shadows, his face was partially hidden despite the sharp contrast of achromatic hair, but those eyes—those impossibly pale eyes—remained steady. This was the Rowan I'd fallen for: focused, measured, disciplined. He was neither gentle nor cruel in his methods.

I crouched in front of our guest, studying the way panic made his pupils dilate. "Good," I said before I clenched my teeth and focused on examining the spectrum of bruises on Edward's face. Such a small man, once he was stripped of his Savile Row armor and Swiss bank accounts. "Do you know where you are, Edward?"

He made a sound behind the silk tie gag: part denial, part plea.

"This is the Second Circle," I said. I trailed my fingers along the ebony rope crossing his chest and felt him flinch. "The hidden domain beneath your favorite nightclub, Oubliette. This is where demons make deals and gods ignore prayers. This is where money means *nothing* and blood means *everything*."

His eyes darted around the stone chamber. The obsidian walls reflected my shadow in fractures, making me look legion. Making me look like all the girls he'd ever hurt, converging on him at once.

Behind him, Rowan finished with methodical precision, adjusting knots with the same care he used when binding me. But this wasn't shibari. I'd learned the difference the first time Rowan had shown me how rope could be art or agony depending on intention.

"Shibari celebrates the body," he'd explained during our first session together. I shivered as I remembered how his fingers guided mine along the patterns he'd tied across my ribs. *"Every knot is designed to enhance, to display, to honor what it holds."*

Then he'd shown me the *other* style.

"Hojōjutsu was a precursor to modern-day handcuffs. The knots are designed to dig into pressure points and apply stress to joints. It was meant

to break the body. With Hojōjutsu," he whispered into my ear, "*it is time that becomes the torturer.*"

Edward was learning that lesson now. The taut rope pulled his shoulders back in something that looked similar to what Rowan called a box tie, only far less elegant than any knot he had ever used on me. Edward's wrists twisted in ways that would leave nerve damage if we kept him here long enough.

I smiled, knowing we would.

Originally, I'd wanted something cruder: Edward hogtied, his ass raised and vulnerable to my spiked stiletto pressing against his hole, making him bleed and beg like he'd once made me. I'd fantasized about his tears, his desperate pleas moistening my lacey thong while I defiled him as he'd done to countless others. That image had burned in my mind.

But Rowan, my umbral knight, had said no. He'd suggested something *simpler*. Such artistry, wasted on this swine. I hated that it wasn't my flesh bearing those beautiful bruises and markings.

"He is secure." Rowan's hand settled on my shoulder, his thumb brushing my neck where my pulse hammered against my skin. Even through my fury, my body responded to him, wet with just a brief stroke. "You may take your time."

Time. Such a strange concept when I had two lives' worth of parallel memories bouncing around in my head. Currently, I was a twenty-year-old college freshman who'd never been touched without consent. In my previous life, I was a thirty-three-year-old sex slave whom Edward strung up and bled out like a pig for the crime of aging out.

While other girls my age were studying for finals and learning how to fall in and out of love, I was sitting in lecture halls with my heart pounding like it was trying to claw its way out of my chest. I woke night after night, choking on the same nightmares, soaked in the same terror I tried so hard to pretend I'd escaped–but vengeance had threaded itself into my bones, seeped into my blood and coiled its spiteful hatred into my heart, refusing to loosen its grip.

In the daylight, I was a survivor.

In the dark, I was still trying to crawl out of the room he once locked me in, afraid and calling out to a family who would never know if I was alive or dead. When I had demanded freedom, begged to fly past the walls, Edward had burned my fucking wings to ash.

Both versions of me wanted him dead. The only difference was methodology.

"You don't know me," I said as I stood and circled his chair. "But you know girls *like* me. Young ones. Pretty ones. Ones you have paid a lot of money for."

His breathing quickened. *Good. Let him wonder how I know.*

"How many did you buy this year, Edward? Three? Four?" I stopped behind him, leaning down close enough that my breath stirred the top of his pepper-gray hair. "I know about the auction houses. The private sales. The discrete shipping containers with air holes." After all, I had been with him many times to watch as they unloaded from his private dock. While I had been a simple exchange due to my young age, I knew others were not as fortunate. "You've been a very bad man, Edward." I stroked his hair gently.

He jerked against the ropes, accomplishing nothing except tightening the knots that were designed to constrict with struggle. "Edward." I tsked. "The more you fight, the deeper the hemp will bite. You should know this, though it was never your preferred method of inflicting pain." I moved my hand down to pat his shoulder comfortingly, resisting the urge to sink my nails into his flesh.

"Violet." Rowan's warning came soft, but I heard the edge beneath it. He knew how close I walked to the edge of my control. His earlier words of wisdom echoed in my mind, "R*evenge without patience is just bloodlust. And bloodlust never satisfies.*"

"Yeah, I know." I sighed and moved back into Edward's line of sight and lifted a knife from the table stationed in front of him. His eyes tracked the blade when it came into view: six inches of Damascus steel that could fillet a fish or a pharynx with equal efficiency.

"In another life," I said, testing the edge against my thumb, "You bought me when I was nine and kept me in captivity for twenty-four years. Do you know what that does to a person?" With the lightest press, the knife drew a thin line of my own blood.

Edward squirmed, making inarticulate choking sounds.

"It teaches you patience. Observation. How to read every micro-expression on your owner's face." I smiled as his eyes widened at what he saw, caught off guard by my lack of response to the cut. "It also taught me quite a lot about *you*. I know you're allergic to shellfish. I know you sleep on your left side. I know you cry out your ex-wife's name when you come." That last part made him go rigid.

"Catherine is a lovely name," I said wistfully.

Tears began to streak his face. His cries pulled out ugly memories of how he used to sob her name while raping me more times than I could count. Apparently, even monsters had people they missed.

"But most importantly," I continued, moving closer, "I know you've already bought other girls in this life. Just because I wasn't one of them doesn't mean they don't deserve justice."

Rowan stepped into my peripheral, a statuesque form clad in black and my body responded without thought. My hip canted towards him, shoulders dropping from their defensive position. Even while facing my owner and serial rapist, even while discussing the worst trauma of my existence, Rowan made me feel safe enough to *want*. He had given me back my wings.

"Show him," Rowan suggested, his voice carrying his calm and confident tone that made my thighs clench. "Show him what awaits him."

I set the knife on the stone altar that served as a table. Next to it lay other tools: specialized instruments for organ removal and containment, should I decide to sell them for a little profit.

Edward's gaze ping-ponged between us and the table. I knew what he saw; two people more than half his age claiming to be prepared to inflict a nightmare of unspeakable pain upon his person. In the normal world, we'd be psychiatric patients. But this wasn't the normal world. This was the Second Circle, where the supernatural world gathered to make deals in blood and pleasure.

"The proprietor of this place knows you're here," I said, letting that sink in. "Do not expect him to save you. It would seem that even demons believe in justice, Edward. Or at least in entertainment."

That's when the real panic started, as his muffled screams echoed in the stone chamber. That's when he understood this wasn't a kidnapping for ransom, a sick joke, or a fucked up kink. The sweet taste of his fear came from the indisputable knowledge that this was not something his money could fix.

Rowan's fingers traced patterns on my spine, and I had to fight not to arch into his touch. My traitorous body was getting even wetter while discussing murder. I was a symphony of desire and rage that Rowan had learned to orchestrate like a maestro.

"Would you like for me to tighten the rope across his chest?" Rowan asked. "It will make breathing far more laborious for him." His tone was as professional and calm as his adopted father's. The absence of arrogance in his voice set an ache deep in my core as I exhaled a shaky laugh.

"You're infuriatingly hot when you talk like that, you know?"

Rowan leaned in, his mouth brushing my ear. "And you love me for it."

"I do, but no—not yet." I picked up my knife again, moving towards Edward with deliberate slowness. "I want him coherent for this part."

The blade whispered against his shirt, parting fabric without touching skin. I'd gotten good with blades in this life, having taken up the hobby recently thanks to a friend.

"Twenty-four years," I said, cutting away cloth to reveal pale flesh. "That's 8,760 days. 210,240 hours. Do you know what I'm going to do, Edward?"

He shook his head frantically, sweat running down his temples.

"I'm going to tell you about yourself."

I pressed the flat of the blade against his sternum, letting him feel the chill against his heated skin. "Starting with the day you bought me. You wore a blue suit. Stuart Hughes. Your favorite, I know. The silk tie we stuffed in your mouth is one of your own. Hermès. If memory serves, you'd worn a tie just like that one on the day you bought me. You'd recently come from lunch, and you smelled like oysters and champagne. I never understood why you ordered them when you were allergic."

His eyes widened. Those were details too specific to be fantasy.

"The auctioneer called me Lot Seventeen. Virgin, unbroken, young enough to train properly." The words tasted bitter, but I forced them out. "You paid with cash. I was worth a small fortune. But enough about me," I continued, pulling the blade away, feeling his heartbeat a staccato of fear. "In this life, you bought another girl. Several other girls."

I set the knife down and picked up something worse: a photograph. One of the items the proprietor had provided along with information on Edward himself. A girl, maybe twelve, standing in what looked like a warehouse. The fear in her eyes was as familiar as a mirror.

"Remember her?" I held it where he could see. "Purchased six months ago. "They aren't at either of your properties, so where are they?"'

He made sounds behind the gag. Denial or confession, I couldn't tell. I didn't care. I was struggling to remain calm, impatient for his death, the folder of photos a heavy burden in my quest for vengeance.

"We will find her," Rowan said assuredly. "My *volchok* is very patient when she is properly motivated."

That's generous. Patience was *not* my virtue; it was Rowan's. But rage could substitute for patience when properly channeled.

I straddled Edward's lap, feeling him try to shrink away. Impossible with how Rowan had tied him. Every movement just drove the ropes deeper.

"You're going to tell us everything," I whispered, my lips close to his ear. "Every girl. Every client. Every supplier. And then, when you've confessed it all, when you've given us names and locations and account numbers..." I licked his earlobe. "I'm going to enjoy watching you get dismembered piece by piece."

Behind me, Rowan made a sound of approval.

I climbed off Edward's lap, my body humming with adrenaline and arousal as I turned my heated gaze to Rowan. His slight nod said he was ready. My subtle smile said I was grateful.

"You see, Edward," I began, pulling the only remaining wooden chair in the room from the wall over to him, "Your story doesn't begin with us abducting you. It doesn't begin with those ropes, or this room, or the moment you had to realize that your money means nothing to me or to this place."

Rowan moved behind me, and I leaned back into his strength, drawing power from his presence.

"Your story begins with mine," I continued. "With a nine-year-old girl who disappeared. A girl whose family searched for years, never knowing if she was alive or dead. But that girl grew up," I said, my voice dropping to barely above a whisper, "So you killed her... And when she came back, when she found herself again with all those dark and gristly memories intact, do you know what she did then, Edward?" I knew he could see the madness and purpose in my eyes as I whispered, "That girl decided that some sins transcend death, especially here in the Second Circle, where impossible things breathe in the shadows.

"So, we're going to tell you a story," I said, settling back in my chair with Rowan's hands resting on my shoulders. "A story about two people who shouldn't exist, hunting a man who shouldn't be allowed to live. A story about what happens when the universe makes a clerical error and gives survivors a second chance."

I smiled and Edward flinched as my voice took on the cadence of a bedtime story. "How every choice you made led you here. How every girl you bought, every life you destroyed, every scream you ignored wove the taut rope that now holds you in that chair."

Rowan's thumbs pressed into the knots of tension in my shoulders, and I had to suppress a moan. His reminder that even here, even now, he could make my body sing.

"But most importantly," I said, "We're going to tell you what comes next. After your confession. After the names. After you've given us everything we need to find every girl you've touched in this life."

I reached out and stroked his face gently, feeling him try to jerk away.

"We're going to tell you exactly how you die, Edward. And then we're going to make it happen."

The stone walls of the Second Circle seemed to lean in, listening. Somewhere in the darkness beyond the candlelight, things that weren't quite human stirred with interest.

"Shall we begin?" I asked.

"Once upon a time," I began, my voice sweet as honey, "there was a little girl who trusted the wrong person. But don't worry, Edward. This story has a happy ending."

I smiled wider, showing all my teeth.

"For me, at least."

Chapter 1

Violet

The barbell piercings were heavier in my palm than I expected, cold and full of promise. Atlanta's city life bustled outside the tattoo parlor's frosted windows. The cushioned cherry-red chair I sat in was sticky against my skin, and voices carried through the curtains that separated me and the tattoo artist.

"Take your top off, and I'll mark where they'll go," he said. He'd introduced himself as Adam, which I thought was a rather common name for someone with so much body art and piercings.

Not that I minded. I enjoyed my fair share of bad boys growing up. But despite his tough appearance, Adam did not give off a malicious vibe. Especially with how his rainbow mohawk caught the parlor's fluorescent light like an oil slick.

"Sure thing," I said as I pulled off my oversized light sweater without hesitation, braless underneath. The cold air from the AC hit my skin, raising goosebumps across flesh that still didn't feel like mine. It's been slightly over two weeks since I'd woken up twenty years old again, and filled to bursting with an additional twenty-four years' worth of memories of another life crammed into my skull where I had been bought when I was only nine. Everything before then matched my current life. Nine years of happiness with a family who loved me before the tragedy.

I spent the first few nights sobbing—an appropriate response in my opinion, though a therapist might disagree. Then I distracted myself, getting ready for college life, pretending I was okay. It wasn't until I watched with morbid fascination the doors of my adolescent home quietly close behind me that the truth slowly began to harden in my mind like cement.

Both of my lives were real.

Even though in this life—my *current* life—I hadn't suffered the horrors from my *first* life, that knowledge did nothing to dull the sharpness of my memories. . . memories of a man who had carved his ownership into my flesh for decades. I breathed and lived, both lives together within me, both taking root inside. The universe—in what had to be some cosmic clerical error—had messed up somewhere, given me memories of both lives, and expected me to sort it out.

So, I did what anybody would have done, aside from screaming endlessly at the enormity of Death's fuck up—I found a way to cope. For me, that meant seeking out controlled pain. Anything to remind me that I was *here* in the present and not hanging upside down as my blood dripped down to the floor, staring at a shadowy ghost that seemed to wait patiently.

Adam stepped closer, black marker clicking as he uncapped it. His hands were steady, professional, as he pressed the tip to my skin in careful, precise movements. Four dots perfectly placed as I willed myself not to flinch at his touch. The byproduct of trauma. Who knew?

"That look good to you?" He tilted his head towards the mirror.

I turned to study my reflection. My typical sunkissed complexion was pallid, which made sense. I'd barely slept since I'd been reborn, and I looked like every goth's wet dream with how deep the dark circles were etched under my eyes despite the layer of makeup I used in an attempt to conceal it. My hands were cold as I examined where Adam had marked—perky breasts, smooth skin, and not a scar in sight. My long, dark brown but nearly black hair spilled down to my hips, highlighted by red streaks I'd recently thrown in myself.

This was the body of a girl who'd never been sold, never been broken, never learned that survival meant enduring things that would make monsters look away. My body housed another life's memories—like a cosmic Airbnb neither of us had signed up for.

"Perfect," I said.

The needles went through fast. Deep, burning pain bloomed into a familiar heat that set an ache between my legs as it anchored me to *now* instead of *then*. Adam slid the barbells through one at a time while I sat perfectly still, counting heartbeats the way I used to count lashes. This was nothing. This was chosen. This was mine.

"All done!" He peeled off his black gloves with a snap. "Gotta say, you're the first one I've had sit that still without making a sound."

I gave him a well-practiced smile that didn't reach my eyes. "I have a high pain tolerance."

If only he knew. Twenty-four years of *that* man's particular brand of education had taught me that pain was just another language. Some people spoke it fluently.

The heat of late August slapped me when I stepped out of the parlor. Atlanta roiled with its usual chaos: buses belching exhaust, horns creating their own furious symphony, the humid air thick enough to chew. My new piercings throbbed in time with my pulse, each beat a small victory. Proof that this body was mine to mark, mine to control, mine to own.

I took the blue line back to campus and watched the city blur past as two souls' worth of memories competed for attention in my skull. In most science fiction or fantasy games, there's always this delicate little art to explaining an origin story. The big reveal: *you have been reincarnated with two souls' memories in you now.* Cue the dramatic music. Maybe an ancient prophecy delivered by a wizened crone or aged wizard nodding sagely while mumbling something cryptic about "Balance" or "Destiny."

But in this new reality I found myself in? There was no balance. No neat diagram of Soul A on the left and Soul B on the right, happily cohabitating together. No polite handshake or tidy agreement on who gets the body from nine to five. The truth was murkier. Messier. Like oil and water swirling inside my chest, refusing to either blend or separate.

It was the most surreal experience to think of myself as both an *I* and a *her* simultaneously. Part of me thought of the Violet who had already died as "O*lder her* trapped in *my* body," while another part of me thought of the Violet from this life as "Y*ounger her* tormented by *my* traumatic memories." Both sets of memories were real. Both were mine. The cognitive dissonance should have driven me insane.

Instead, it just pissed me off.

The moment I awoke with both of my lives slamming together inside of me, I wondered if one of us was meant to devour the other. Perhaps that was the point? I would dissolve into her—or her into me—eventually. One of us would fade into the other until nothing remained but whispers. And every time that thought clawed at me, the thought of one of us disappearing into the other? It made my skin crawl.

Could it be done? Probably. In theory, anything could be done if you were cruel enough. But I never volunteered to be some god's social experiment, so I was determined to coexist with myself.

As time passed, the anger simmered into something unrecognizable. Fury at the cards I had been dealt. If I ever found out which divine sadist had scripted the nightmare of my new existence, I swore to every pantheon from Olympus to Asgard, I would shove a dildo so far up their omnipotent ass that even Dracula would rise from his coffin to applaud my craftsmanship.

My mother used to say, "Anger is often the mask of grief." And she knew best, but I was tired of feeling helpless. It was my turn to take control.

The door creaked, revealing an empty dorm room, bed still ruffled from another sleepless night. Books lined the right side of the wall, color-coded and organized with such meticulous attention to detail that it set me on edge. My roommate's bed was the color eau de nil—a pale green that I only knew the name of because of my Aunt Dawn—and damn near pristine.

The antithesis was my side of the room, where books lay haphazardly on shelves, a cluttered desk, and a full laundry hamper at the foot of my bed bearing both clean and dirty clothes.

I face-planted into my own thistle-colored sheets and immediately hissed as my new piercings made contact with the mattress. The burn reminded me why I'd gotten them. Proof that I could still feel things that weren't phantom pains from a life that technically never happened.

I rolled onto my back, staring at the water stain on the ceiling that looked like a moribund butterfly if you squinted. My body ached with exhaustion that two weeks of insomnia had compounded into my skull with something close to delirium. Thanks to that, my appetite had suffered, being unbearably inconsistent thanks to the relentless nightmares. But sleep meant dreams, and dreams meant reliving moments my twenty-year-old body had never experienced, yet remembered with perfect clarity. My skin prickled with the ghost of restraint, and my jaw still clenched from holding myself together in public.

No. Better to stay awake. Better to plan.

I pulled out my phone, thumb hovering over my contact list as I stared at a picture of my family. It was an antiquated photo of us on one of our annual camping trips that my older brother Liam took. My mom—where I got my looks from—stood between two men. One was my raven-haired father, and the other was his counterpart, his angelic-looking best friend Charlie. *Uncle* Charlie to me. In the photo, I looked put out, having been placed between Uncle Charlie's adopted son—the ever-obtuse Rowan—and my diva queen of a little sister, Amber. She was so young in that picture. I couldn't help but smile at seeing her face.

The photo was both a reminder of everything I had lost and all the things I had gained. I loved them all, which was why the thought of someone being ripped away from their own, as I had been, propelled me forward. Pushed me into action. Drove me to track down the monster that had been responsible for the avalanche of suffering from my first life.

The first thing I needed was money. Not the couple thousand in my checking account for textbooks, dining out, and overpriced coffee, but the *real* sum locked away in my trust fund. The kind of *'fuck you money'* that could buy information, silence, or muscle—all of which I assumed I would need.

But accessing that money meant going home, meant asking for my parents' signatures, and meant explaining why I suddenly needed six figures in liquid assets. I wrinkled my nose as I contemplated who to call.

Mom or Daddy?

Mom would ask too many questions. She would dig into the *why* with her soft voice that never missed the tremor in mine. Daddy would cut straight to the point, but that also meant he'd press for details I wasn't ready to spill.

Daddy and Uncle Charlie were the only two people who knew about my rebirth, having experienced the same thing themselves. And while

I had not told them much about my first life, they were aware that it was—to put it mildly—decidedly unpleasant.

Of all people, I knew they would both understand my dilemma, but I wasn't in the mood to deal with my Daddy's insistent nagging. *Overthinking really should burn extra calories. Daddy's my best bet.*

I exhaled, shut my eyes, and pressed his number before I changed my mind. The phone rang a few times before a familiar voice answered.

A familiar voice, but *not* my father's.

"Violet?"

My eyes snapped open as I sat up. *Shit! Rowan?* My heart quickened at the deepened accent that curled in mockery even when he wasn't trying. *Why is he answering Dad's phone?*

The image of him flashed to my mind: an imposing figure, a stern brow with an aquiline nose framed by his pearly white hair curling around his ears down an angular jawline.

Rowan had been orbiting my life since we were kids, and we had butted heads every time our families came together. He'd always been there, always in the periphery, a storm wrapped in human form. I could vividly recall his younger years: rebellious, angry, feral. The kind of boy who set fires just to watch them burn.

But that boy had grown up and transformed into something controlled and disciplined. A different type of dangerous that allured women, myself included. Despite my better judgement, his aggravating personality didn't stop me from stealing the occasional glance at his gorgeously toned body or admiring what I considered his best feature. . . the palest set of blue eyes I'd ever seen, like falling snowflakes.

We'd never gotten along. Oil and water. Fire and ice. Pick your cliché.

My thoughts were derailed as I thought of what to say. "Uh. . . Rowan?"

He must have caught the confusion in my tone, because a chuckle came through the line, warm and irritatingly self-satisfied. "Are you already drunk in the second week at school? It is barely past lunch on a Tuesday."

The lilt of his accent did things to my insides that I absolutely refused to acknowledge. Growing up, I'd thought his accent was charming, the way he rolled his R's in Russian like Mom and Aunt Dawn did when they spoke Spanish.

Now his voice irritated me. Everything about Rowan Monroe irritated me.

I gritted my teeth. Frustration rose sharply in my belly, hot and unrelenting as it battled with arousal. "I'm glad you know your days of the week. I was trying to get in touch with my father."

"Obviously. I assumed that is why you called his cell," he teased. I could imagine his smug smile and perfectly white teeth.

"Are you at the office?" I asked, trying to keep the irritation out of my voice. "Is Daddy nearby?" He'd been working at Daddy's business for years now, carving out his place with methodical patience.

"We are not at the office, and Levi is not nearby, no." Another pause, perfectly timed to annoy the hell out of me. "We decided to take lunch at the house. I was in the kitchen, grabbing myself a beer, when I saw your call."

"So, you took it upon yourself to answer his phone? And a beer, Rowan? You're only twenty." Exasperation laced my words, feeling oddly exposed at my plan gone awry.

"Do not compare me to the boys you hang out with, Violet. I can handle my own. . . unlike you, *princess*." He *tsked* before he continued. "Besides, I thought it was the business phone ringing. Would you like me to get your daddy for you?"

I pinched the bridge of my nose hard enough to hurt, vexed by the mocking nickname he used for me before replying calmly. "No. Just tell him I need to come home this weekend. Ask if he can pick me up."

"I will do this. Is there anything else I can do for you, *ma'am?*" The sarcasm dripped like honey, and he even attempted a Southern accent that sounded absurd with his Russian lilt.

My patience snapped. "Yes. Go fuck yourself."

I hung up before he could respond, tossing the phone onto my nightstand with enough force to send it sliding, then flopped back on the bed. My pulse raced as if I'd just run a marathon instead of having a two-minute conversation with the most insufferable man I knew. Rowan had that effect on me. Simply just talking with him poked at every nerve until I was raw and bristling from only a few words.

The door opened, and my roommate walked in, bringing with her the scent of vanilla and of the library. It had taken me two weeks to remember her name was Alice, having been distracted by my multiple-life crisis. She was everything I wasn't: tall where I was average, soft-spoken where I was sharp, careful where I was reckless, with raven hair and deep chocolate eyes on a perfectly heart-face. She moved through our shared space like an apology, always trying to take up less room.

"Hey," she said, setting down her mahogany leather bookbag with care. She wore a beige oversized trench coat over her tank top, along with tailored navy wool trousers. Given it was August in Atlanta, I had no idea how she wasn't dying from heat exhaustion.

"Hey." I didn't sit up. I couldn't summon the energy for small talk.

"Did you go to the involvement fair?" She was already unlacing her shoes, placing them perfectly parallel by the door. She had a few OCD tendencies that I didn't mind compared to my messy nature.

"No." I hadn't gone anywhere near campus activities. Eighteen-year-olds planning fundraisers and themed parties felt like watching children play house.

She nodded, peeling off her tank top to reveal a navy bra underneath. "I signed up for the business club. They meet on Thursdays."

"Cool." The word fell flat between us.

She let the silence hang before she asked, "Did you plan on checking out any sorority houses for next semester?"

"Uh, no. Perks of living nearby. Besides, I like the dorms." The words came out strangled, my fatigue slowly winning the war within me.

She nodded as if understanding. "Ah, that's right. I forgot, you're a local." She gifted me with a bright smile. I recalled our first meeting, when she mentioned she had lived abroad her whole life, and someone in her family chose this school for her business degree.

I'd pitied her then, for being in someone else's control.

I shoved my dark hair back and said, "It's fine. I didn't expect you to remember." *Just like I didn't remember your name when we first met.*

Alice busied herself at her desk, and I caught sight of her name embroidered on her bookbag. Classy and somehow alarming, she would proudly display it for others to see. There was a small part of me that wanted to make the effort to befriend Alice, to suggest we grab coffee, to swap stories about professors, to care about whatever boy she inevitably had a crush on.

But a larger part of me was too tired, too apathetic, and overflowing with a lifetime of trauma that held me back. That same part had learned that caring about people just gave them leverage over you.

I rose from my bed and sat at my own desk, suddenly remembering the mess I'd left there like an idiot. *I hope she didn't notice them.* Pages and pages of my handwriting comparing my two lives, trying to make sense of the impossible. Names, dates, and places, all circled and connected like some detective's murder board.

Which, in a way, it kind of was.

One name dominated the chaos, circled in red so many times the paper had torn: Edward Fitzgerald—*buyer, owner, murderer.*

He didn't know me in this life. He'd never seen my face, never heard my name. In this life, I'd grown up safe in my parents' home, riding horses and winning both archery competitions and Brazilian jiu jitsu tournaments.

But I knew where to find him. Men like Edward were creatures of habit, and his habits had been branded into my memory with the kind of clarity trauma provides. Every Saturday, he went to the posh and invitation-only nightclub named Oubliette.

I'd been there hundreds of times in my first life. Dragged along as decoration, forced to wait in velvet-draped rooms while he conducted 'business' behind doors that muffled sound but not enough to hide the screaming. Made to dance for his colleagues while he ventured below into the belly of Oubliette. I stripped for their amusement, pretended to be grateful for the privilege of being owned by someone so powerful. Even now, I remembered the perfumed air thick with sin, and the bright-eyed woman I had come to admire.

Vengeance would give me the justice and moral code I needed for it to feel right. With vengeance, I could weave a web of lies, focusing on retribution towards a corrupt society that sold and killed women, but deep down I knew... revenge would fuel me.

A pitch-black darkness began to devour me from beneath my ribs and wrap its red-hot thorns like a second heartbeat. I could not ignore the calling, nor withdraw myself from a life simmering with grief and hatred.

"Violet?" Alice's voice pulled me back. "Are you okay? You look pale."

I realized I'd been gripping the edge of my desk hard enough to leave crescents in the wood. "Just tired. Haven't been sleeping well."

"The health center has counselors," she offered carefully, "if you need to talk to someone."

What would I tell a counselor? That I remembered being murdered? That I'd woken up in my younger body with all my trauma intact like some cosmic joke? That the man who'd killed me was out there living his life and still buying other girls? That I was going to hunt him down, string him up, and bleed him dry the same way he'd bled me?

"Thanks," I said instead. "I appreciate your concern. I just need some more time to adjust, I think."

"Of course." And she went about busying herself on her side of the room, switching to her studies as I turned back to my notes. The red circles around Edward's name looked like bloody targets.

I'd need my money first, so I could start buying supplies and information. Then I'd need to find a way to get invited into Oubliette, despite having no connections to that world or their clientele in this life. I prayed that the Oubliette I knew was the same one Edward had taken me to.

I glanced at my phone, wondering if Rowan listened to me for once as the new piercings throbbed against my shirt, little points of pain that reminded me I was here, this was real, and I was in control. Both versions of me agreed on that much.

I put my notes away and lay back on my bed, staring at that butterfly-shaped water stain as I contemplated my next steps. The gods might have given me this second chance by accident, but I'd take their mistake and forge it into something sharp enough to cut.

And then I'd carve Edward's heart out.

Chapter 2

Rowan

I heard Violet's voice waver through Levi's phone, clipped and angry, right before she told me to go fuck myself. The line went dead, but her words still echoed in my ears.

There was a hint of... *something* in her voice that was not normally there. She had been clearly bewildered when I had answered, and then she struggled when I poked at her. It had been so much easier than normal to get under her skin.

My ears picked up the conversation of Levi and Charlie outside despite the walls and glass door separating us.

"Violet's going to be fine, Levi. College is where kids can explore and get life experiences." My adopted father's calming voice threaded through the sounds of wind rustling uncut grass.

"She could have done some of her classes virtually. She had that option." *Ah, yes, Levi's possessive nature in full force,* I thought as I eased down my senses, careful not to eavesdrop unintentionally again.

It had been five years since I'd woken up in this boy's body along with its heightened hearing, and I still caught details I didn't want. The boy had lasted only a few months before he'd killed himself to escape the Godsblood curse of heightened hearing. The constant noise drove him to swallow a bottle of pills that the hospital pumped out of his stomach even as his soul was passing on. The trade-off?

Me. Someone not of this time, who died struggling for his last bit of freedom to escape a rigged deal between a mortal and a demon. A free fucked up ticket of reincarnation through claiming the boy's empty body as my own. Where the boy had failed, I'd made it this long only because I had already survived far worse in my first life. Learning to control my heightened hearing and somewhat enhanced sense of smell had felt like child's play.

I took a sip of beer as I walked from the kitchen out to the patio, taking a moment to stare at Levi's phone. I was unable to stop the chuckle that escaped me. Violet Shaw, all spit and fire wrapped in privilege that she didn't even see she had—a princess. I called her that because she was the kind of girl who could tell me to go fuck myself, yet make it sound aristocratic.

"Or a *volchok*," I said, the word slipping out in thick Russian, a language close enough to the one from my homeland, the Wastelands, that my tongue moved comfortably in without thinking. There were brief moments that her spitfire reminded me of a wolf cub, malicious and lacking in domestication. Not that I minded. I preferred strong women.

"Rowan?" Charlie's voice pulled me back to the patio where he and Levi sat with their barely touched burgers. Both men were a reflection of the other, one light and the other dark. Charlie wore his standard polo shirt and jeans, blonde hair tousled against piercing blue eyes. Levi, like his dark twin, wore a black t-shirt and jeans with shortened raven hair and amber eyes.

From the unique and bizarre experience of each of them being reincarnated over a decade ago, these two men had forged a powerful friendship with one another... and that *fascinated* me. Partly because—unlike how I'd been thrust into a stranger's body in a time very different from my own—they had simply reincarnated as younger versions of themselves. But even more than that, it was just how vastly different they had been from one another in their first lives.

Adversity makes for strange bedfellows. Was that the expression?

I set Levi's phone on the table between them, watching both men tense. Having spent so much of the past five years together, they knew the look that must have been on my face. The one that said their comfortable suburban afternoon was about to crack at the edges.

"Easy there, you two," I said, placing down my beer and settling back into my chair, hoping my tone was calming enough. I looked pointedly at Levi. "Your faux life is still intact. It was Violet. She wants to come home this weekend."

Levi's distrustful eyes locked onto mine, the hardened look of assessment sliding across his youthful features. We had been dancing this dance for years—him treating me like a threat to catalogue, me trying not to give him any reasons to be right. It was only thanks to Charlie's word that Levi tolerated me despite how often our families were together. Like a pod, our two families were ingrained with each other.

"Why were you answering my phone?" His gruff voice carried an edge that meant he was already mapping out exactly how he planned to hit me if this conversation went poorly. *Daddy's little princess needs him to save her,* I wanted to say, but I knew it would start a fight I wasn't ready to give up my burger for.

Levi only ever had a violent streak when it came to something related to his family, which left a sour note... the knowledge that he would never consider me *family*.

Joke's on him, I thought. I actually enjoyed it when we came to blows.

As for Charlie? *"No open wounds,"* he had eventually conceded after one particularly bad argument between Levi and I.

After we fought, I like to think we both felt so much better.

"Thought it was the work phone," I lied. The truth was, I'd seen Violet's name and could not resist the urge to answer. There was something about her voice when she was frustrated that I found alluring. Her irritation was a blanket of solace, reminding me that not *everything* in this soft world was bland comfort and willful ignorance, that not *everybody* was a docile sheep.

Disbelief was plain on Levi's face, but he had no way to prove me wrong. Through the noise of his increasing heart rate—one hundred and twelve beats per minute and climbing—I caught the sound of keys jingling and grocery bags rustling. Violet's mother, Sloane, would be inside in thirty seconds, and she'd notice Levi had left dirty dishes in the sink in about forty-five.

"Your wife is home," I said, taking a deliberate sip of beer. "You may want to tend to the pots and pans."

"You're lying."

"You could wait to find out," I said, my voice carrying a big '*fuck you.*'

Levi's face went through several interesting colors before he pushed back from the table and rushed inside. The man had learned exactly how much his wife's anger could cost him, and he treated her like a queen now because of it. While I appreciated his loyalty, there were a few transgressions I couldn't forgive, so I held Sloane on a higher pedestal for her strength more than I did her asshole husband.

Charlie, ever calm like a quiet sea, waited until the door closed before leaning forward and saying, "You really need to stop antagonizing him, Rowan." While his tone was of stern admonishment, his eyes crinkled. "How did Violet sound?"

"She sounded like herself. Angry. Exhausted." I paused, remembering the atypical sound of her voice. "Possibly stressed about something."

That got his attention. Charlie might play the diplomat between Levi and me, but he had developed a real affection for Violet over the years—the daughter he'd never had, perhaps.

"Did she say something to imply she was stressed?" he asked as he set his own burger down.

I shrugged, though my jaw tightened. "She barely gets full sentences out around me." I shrugged, "It could be the move? Or possibly she is scared—"

Charlie interrupted, "Scared?"

Fuck, these overprotective men.

"I said, *possibly* she is scared. It could be nothing... or it could be she has finally noticed what kind of place that school really is."

"Rowan." The warning in Charlie's voice was familiar. This was heading towards an argument we'd had before.

"I know what I know," I grumbled, running a hand through my hair. "In my world, we had Female Seminaries—a pretty name for breeding programs."

The sound of Levi's desperate apologies drifted through the walls, followed by Sloane's clipped responses. Then silence. Soon after, I tuned them out because some things I didn't need to hear again.

"Gods," I muttered, focusing hard on the label of my beer bottle. "Every fucking time."

Charlie's mouth twitched. "At least they're consistent."

Consistent. That was one word for it. Levi and Sloane had the kind of hunger for each other that should have burned out years ago, but somehow hadn't. Even when he'd cheated, even when she'd thrown him out, they'd circled back to each other like satellites locked in orbit.

The most sorrowful part of their tale was that Charlie also lived in that other shared life alongside Levi. At one point, *he* had been Sloane's husband. I still hadn't heard his entire story, but I imagined it was why he kept so close to both of them.

"About Violet," Charlie said, pulling us back to what mattered. "You really think something's up?"

I sipped my beer as I thought over my words carefully. Charlie would listen. He always did. It was Levi who refused to hear anything that threatened his perfect suburban narrative.

"I do," I said. "It might just be my paranoia, but from what I recall from my previous life? We had stories of society before the veil fell. Many of those stories spoke of how deeply ingrained the supernaturals were in everyday life. How they lived among mortals in secret."

"To what end?"

I shrugged. "There were lots of different stories with lots of different reasons. Some spoke of keeping mortals as sex slaves, pets, breeding stock, or food. It was harder to pinpoint when they made an effort to burn all texts relating to it. However," I said, then paused as I took another drink of beer. "Can you guess one point that nearly all the stories agreed upon?"

Charlie shook his head, though I was certain he knew what I was about to say. His shaking was more out of a refusal to accept the truth I was offering as he fought to understand the difference between my old life and theirs.

"In all of those stories, one of the preferred hunting grounds of the supernaturals were the elite and prestigious schools that parents would send their heirs to."

Levi chose that moment to return, shirt untucked, raven hair messed, looking entirely too pleased with himself. The man had no subtlety. Behind him, Sloane appeared in the doorway, equally disheveled but somehow more dignified about it. I could see the telltale flush of embarrassment against golden skin as she waved to us.

"Boys," she said, her voice only lightly accented compared to her sister Dawn, and there was warmth in it. "I'll be starting dinner in a bit. Charlie and Rowan, you two are staying?"

It wasn't a question. We were staying.

I nodded. Sloane had decided years ago that I was too thin, too sharp around the edges, and needed feeding. It was easier to let her mother me. . . it wasn't as if I could explain to her that in my first life, I had often survived on rations and melted snow for months at a time.

She disappeared back inside, long brown hair trailing behind her, and Levi reclaimed his seat, eyeing me with fresh suspicion. "What were you two talking about?"

"Violet," Charlie said simply. "Rowan thinks she might be in trouble at school."

"Rowan thinks everyone is in trouble everywhere," Levi shot back. "According to him, we are all about to be vampyre food or demon bait or whatever monster he is dreaming up this week."

The dismissal stung more than it should have. Five years of trying to warn them, and Levi still thought I was delusional. Despite the extraordinary circumstances of both his own and Charlie's reincarnations, he was a combination of naive and narcissistic to refuse to believe there were even stranger things in the world.

"Do you want to know what I heard when I was on the phone with Violet?" I asked, looking straight at Levi. "She said that she *needed* to come home this weekend. She did not say that she *wanted* to come home. The difference was subtle, but it was there."

Levi snorted derisively. "Did you hear that subtle difference with your superhuman hearing?"

His mockery forced me to my feet, my chair clattering on the patio. "You were so quick to believe me just now when I said your wife was home." My voice was ice and venom as I continued. "Just because *you* refuse to believe me about the Godsblood does not make it less real."

"*Boy*," Levi snarled, "I've heard enough of your crazy fearmongering. This Godsblood you claim to have, the one by a corrupt pharmaceutical company—"

"Not corrupt," I interrupted. "Owned and operated by vampyres."

"I don't give a damn," he seethed, "about your magical blood fantasy, your silly ghost stories, your world-wide vampyre-led conspiracy, or the post-apocalyptic world you allegedly came from." He pointed a finger at me. "Don't drag Violet into your delusional bullshit."

It took an immeasurable amount of patience not to punch Levi in the face. It would have been so easy to break his nose and fracture his cheek. I was standing. He was seated. By the time Charlie pulled me off of him, I could have done some serious damage.

But as much fun as fighting Levi was, I knew it would upset Sloane. Besides, we had more pressing matters at hand.

Instead, I reminded myself that I was speaking to ignorant children who had no idea what darkness lurked beyond the veil. I took a deep breath and said, "Violet could barely keep her voice steady. There was an uncharacteristic tremble there. Your daughter is possibly scared, Levi. And whether you believe me or not, she might be in trouble." I didn't necessarily want to catastrophize the situation, but I needed the man to understand the urgency.

The silence stretched, broken only by the distant sound of suburban life continuing around us. Somewhere, a dog barked. A lawnmower started up. Normal sounds of a normal world that was not normal at all. I picked up my chair and the three of us sat in that silence for a moment.

Charlie was the first to speak, his voice low enough that it would not carry to the kitchen windows. "Levi, you know Violet has been... *struggling* since she started college."

Levi's jaw tightened. "She is having trouble adjusting for *other* reasons." He gave Charlie a pointed look, a soundless communication between them. "Weren't you just telling me it takes *time*, Charlie?"

"It does, but..." Charlie's voice was gentle but insistent. "But from what you have told me about when you dropped her off, I am worried. And I know you are as well. She was so upset today that she hung up on Rowan."

"She hangs up on Rowan because he annoys her," Levi shot back, but there was less conviction in it now.

"Perhaps," Charlie agreed. "But you said yourself that she seems... *different*. And she may be having a difficult time and might not be able to ask for help. Shouldn't we check in on her more often?"

Whatever secret they shared that they were dancing around was annoying, but I couldn't bring myself to care. I stayed silent, letting Charlie do the work. He understood Levi better than I did, having known him far longer than my measly five years. He knew which buttons to push and which to avoid.

"What are you suggesting?" Levi asked, though from his tone it sounded as if he already knew.

Charlie said, "Maybe someone should be close by. Not hovering, just. . . available. In case she needs family."

"I cannot just leave work and move to Atlanta," Violet's father said.

No Shit, Levi.

"No," Charlie said slowly. "But Rowan could."

What? I thought as Levi's eyes snapped to mine, that familiar hostility flaring.

"Absolutely not," he said.

"Think about it," Charlie pressed. "He is young enough to blend in on a college campus. Smart enough to handle whatever situation might arise, and he cares about Violet—even if he is an ass to her."

"I am sitting right here," I point out.

Levi was staring at Charlie as he shook his head. "She's twenty, and he is," he waved a hand in my direction as he said, "whatever the fuck he is. He's a geriatric psycho stuffed into that boy's body. You want *him* to watch over *her*?"

The implied accusation stung. I could have gotten angry. I could have pointed out that I had never looked at Violet that way regardless of my body's age. Instead, I laughed and then said, "Do not project your inability to keep your dick in your pants onto me, Levi. You think I am interested in your daughter? *T'fu*! She is an infant compared to me."

"Did you just make a disgusted noise about *my* daughter?" Levi's face went crimson, fury flashing in his amber eyes. His stubbled jaw locked, like he was ready to lunge across the table. "Fuck him, Charlie. I don't trust—"

"I grew up in a world," I interrupted, "Where staying alive meant eating rats and avoiding things that hunted humans for food or sport. I did not have time for romance then, and I do not have patience for it now." I met his eyes. "Violet will be. . . my ward."

Plus, caring for someone gets you indebted.

I suddenly recalled the last days of my first life: breaking into The Library, stealing a radiant golden tome, being chased through the Wastelands, and finally the Hunter who had killed me for the transgression. I had never told anybody about The Library or how I'd died. It was an ill-timed and disturbing memory.

Charlie warned quietly, voice low but firm, "Enough, both of you." He glanced over to the doorway, and I knew his anxiety stemmed from our conversation.

So they still haven't told her, I mused. Sloane was one of the few normal things in all of our lives. She did not bear the cursed gift of rebirth, nor the knowledge that such a thing was even possible.

"If Rowan says he'll keep an eye on Violet, then he will," Charlie said, his tone did not invite argument, and Levi's gaze flicked to him, the storm in his expression barely reined in.

Charlie held his stare—he was the one person who could tether Levi's fury before it tore through a room. Whatever bond they shared was before me, and it showed. Levi trusted this man with everything... even with his wife, despite his possessive nature. It was a testament to their friendship.

After a few seconds, something shifted in Levi's expression. "If I agree to this," he said slowly, "you keep your distance, boy. You watch, you report, but you do not interfere unless there is actual danger."

I took a sip of beer. "Define *actual* danger."

Levi's nostrils flared, his chest rising and falling as if each breath was a hidden battle before grinding out, "Life or death."

I asked, "What if there is something between normal and life or death? What if she is being groomed and does not know it?"

Charlie made a sound of disgust. "Christ, Rowan."

"I am not being dramatic. I am being realistic. These things? They do not take by force. They seduce. They make you want it. They make you think it is *your* idea to be indebted to them, to be owned by them." I remembered the stories whispered in the ruins of my world. Women who'd fallen in love with their captors. Men who'd begged to be turned. "By the time you realize what is happening, you are already theirs."

"And you think that's going on? At Shademore, where Violet's attending?" Levi's skepticism was still there, his temper tampered down, but underneath it, I heard something else. Fear. He was starting to believe me, even if he did not want to.

I nodded. "I do."

Levi was quiet for a long moment, staring down at his plate. I could see him weighing his options, his protectiveness of Violet warring with his deep-seated distrust of me.

"You watch her," he said to me finally. "You don't approach her unless she approaches you first. You don't interfere with her life unless she is in danger. And you report back to Charlie weekly."

I didn't bother hiding my smirk, though my chest loosened just a fraction at the concession. "*Da*," I agreed. "Those terms are acceptable."

"And if you cross any lines—"

"You will kill me slowly and creatively," I said. "Yes, Levi. We have established this."

"Rowan," Levi whispered, "I've done it once. For my daughter. I *will* do it again if necessary."

Charlie hissed, "Levi!" His entire body tensed as he glanced at me in a panic.

Well, that's one confession I wasn't expecting. However, hearing that Levi had killed someone before actually made me *more* comfortable in his presence, not less.

"I will not touch her," I said delicately. I respected a man willing to kill to protect his family. "She is my *ward*, Levi."

That seemed to satisfy him, at least enough to stop arguing. We moved inside to help Sloane with dinner, and our conversation shifted to safer topics... but I could not stop thinking about that sound in Violet's voice. That particular frequency of fear I had heard too many times in my first life.

She was in danger. Maybe not the immediate, claws-and-teeth kind. But *something* was causing her stress and forcing her to come home this weekend—and I was determined to find out what it was.

Even if she told me to go fuck myself for trying.

Chapter 3

Violet

Wednesday's Sociology lecture droned on about social stratification while I counted beige ceiling tiles and contemplated whether a lobotomy might finally grant me some peace. My professor's voice blurred into white noise as exhaustion clawed at the edges of my vision. Night after night of broken sleep had left me raw, caffeinated beyond reason, and ready to crawl out of my own skin.

My roommate had tried to cheer me up that morning with her usual sunshine and small talk, bless her heart, but I'd barely managed civility before escaping to class. *You don't have to be everyone's cup of tea*, I reassured myself. *Sometimes you just need to be gasoline and set that shit on fire.* I had to remind myself she was only trying to be kind. Now, even the thought of returning to our shared space made my chest tight.

I'd given up by Thursday when I'd tossed and turned through another failed attempt at sleep. I needed to feel like myself again, even if it meant breaking a few rules. I needed Hyacinth.

The bus carried me across town to the Equestrian Facility as the sun began its descent. Atlanta's August heat still pressed down like a living thing, the kind of suffocating weight that made even breathing feel like work. But as we passed the grove of Virginia Pine before the gate, I felt something in my chest loosen for the first time all week.

The stables greeted me with their familiar symphony: the earthy perfume of hay and manure, the creak of settling wood, the soft whicker of horses preparing for the evening. Students and staff moved through their routines, voices carrying across the barn as shadows lengthened through the slats.

And there he was.

Hyacinth was a Cleveland Bay—sixteen-hands high, with a shiny coat like polished copper and a black mane. His ears flicked forward the moment he spotted me, nostrils flaring as if to scold me for taking so long to visit him. His proud head arched, muscles shifting beneath his burnished coat, and warmth spread through my chest in a way I hadn't felt all week.

"Hey, baby," I whispered, stepping into his stall. His familiar scent wrapped around me like a memory: warm hide, sweat, leather, and hay. My fingers threaded into his thick mane, and for the first time in days, my pulse slowed.

I can finally breathe.

I pressed my forehead against his neck, inhaling the salt and earth that clung to him. My hands worked through his mane, untangling knots in motions we'd performed a thousand times before. He snorted and shifted his weight in that way that dared me to hurry up.

I smiled despite myself. "Impatient, aren't we? Hold on, let me grab at least the bridle."

By the time I led him from the barn, the world felt suspended, time bending just for me. I slipped onto his back without a saddle, feeling the warmth of his hide against my legs as his hooves struck a steady rhythm against the packed dirt.

We started slowly, weaving through trails I'd explored with him in previous weeks. With each breath, with each rise and fall of his gait beneath me, the knot in my chest loosened. For precious minutes, I felt unshackled.

When we reached the open field, I couldn't hold back.

"Go," I whispered.

Hyacinth surged forward like lightning freed from a storm. I leaned into the motion, hands steady on the ebony reins as wind ripped past me, tangling my hair and stealing breath from my lungs. The world blurred: gold streaking along the horizon, shadows reaching like dark fingers, the burn in my muscles as I held tight.

For a moment, it wasn't this life or the last. It wasn't Violet the student or Violet the broken girl who'd been bought and sold. It was just *me*, bare and unbound, freedom pulsing in time with Hyacinth's stride.

We galloped until his breathing turned harsh, and only then did I draw him down, circling slowly until his muscles eased. My legs trembled from the strain, but I laughed: an unguarded, reckless sound that startled even me.

When I finally slid down to walk him back, the sky had shifted to indigo, stars pricking faintly against velvet. Grass cooled under nightfall, cicadas humming somewhere in the distance. Hyacinth lowered his head, nudging my shoulder with a huff that nearly knocked me off balance.

"I missed you too," I murmured, stroking his muzzle.

We were approaching the gate when a voice—thick with an Irish accent—cut through the evening air. "Sure, you know fine rightly, ya shouldn't be goin' out without protection."

Stablemaster Aaron stood by the entrance, his red hair catching the stable lights as he clicked open the gate. Those ice-blue eyes fixed on me with a familiar, stubborn set jaw I'd seen countless times on Rowan. I'd learned quickly after starting school that Aaron was nearly as headstrong as Hyacinth and Rowan combined. *A common theme with the men in my life, it seems.*

I waved in acknowledgment, hearing gravel crunch under my boots as I threw the reins forward. "There are few things I can ride as well as my horse."

Hyacinth snorted in response.

Aaron let us through, mindful of his manure-coated boots and Hyacinth's hooves. The careful dance between them had me fighting back a smile. They *really* didn't get along.

"The school's legal team would have me head on a platter if anythin' happened, so they would," he said, locking the gate and leaning against it. His arms crossed over a charcoal grey shirt tucked into grass-stained jeans, sweat slicking his hair despite the cooling air. His red hair and handsome face clashed with his gruff country boy aesthetic. "Look here, Violet, it's the insurance and the liability—the whole bloody mess. This is your final warning, so it is. Catch me again, and I'll be forced to file a complaint that'll put your scholarship in real jeopardy."

"I'll keep that in mind," I said with a smile, though my face said, *'Not a chance.'*

Aaron huffed, reading between the lines and my look. He pulled away from the gate, hand rubbing the back of his neck and leaving streaks of dirt mixed with sweat. "Listen, Violet. I know you've got the trainin', but you can't break rules without consequences." His words softened, his accent lilting as he spoke. "Even a blind man can see the bond between you and that horse."

It was true. Hyacinth and I had grown up together in the fields that stretched between our home and my father's business: both of us headstrong, both unwilling to yield. I loved him with a fierceness that ached, though it hadn't always been this way. The early years had been blood, sweat, and tears until my father hired the trainer who'd finally gotten through to both of us.

"My trainer refused to coddle either of us," I said, leading Hyacinth towards the grooming area. "Forged together in frustration and discipline." I looked pointedly at my horse, making kissy noises. "He won't ever buck me, right, baby?"

"Ah, sure you can't know that for certain, now. A horse is still an animal, and an animal still has instincts." Aaron's voice carried exhaustion and concern in equal parts. "Besides, there's been somethin' in the woods spooking the horses something awful ever since the semester started."

Guilt crept up from somewhere deep as I began preparing to groom Hyacinth. The last thing I wanted was to get Aaron in trouble for my selfishness.

The joys of having a conscience.

"Aaron, listen. . . I'm sorry." The words felt strained but genuine. "I'll try to be more mindful about riding bareback here. Back home, there wasn't a single day I didn't ride. It's like breathing for me."

I knew I had him then. He studied me as I moved around Hyacinth's flank, then handed me a brush. "A good rider can hear his horse speak. A great rider can hear his horse whisper."

I was intimately familiar with the quote. I went to work removing sweat, stimulating circulation, and promoting relaxation. Silence stretched between us until I heard his sigh of surrender.

"If someone else brings it up, I'll have to back them up, so I will."

I peeked over Hyacinth's withers, careful not to let my grin show. "You got it. I swear to be careful, only ride bare when *no one's looking*, never to endanger you or us." I knew I was admitting to my continuation of breaking school rules, but at least I was honest.

"Don't be comin' late for archery this week. It's me own free time your folks are payin' for, so you should make the most of it." Aaron grumbled and walked off, mumbling about being too soft.

I had the best night of sleep since I'd started college.

The next afternoon, after classes finished for me, Daddy picked me up from the Main Hall. Nerves made me slam my door too hard, which didn't help the tension radiating from him before I'd even stepped in. He was upset, and I hadn't even brought up the money yet.

"Hey, Daddy." I kissed his cheek and settled into the passenger seat. He was in his typical black T-shirt and dark jeans. I ignored the anxiety threatening to crest and asked, "Are you okay?"

He gave me a gruff, "Yeah," before pressing a kiss to my temple. "Better now that I've got you here."

His tone was softer than his body language suggested. His jaw remained tight, his grip on the wheel just shy of white-knuckled. But he relaxed slightly once we both clicked our seatbelts.

"Surprised you wanted me to pick you up for the weekend," he said, backing out of the lot. His voice carried careful weight, testing. "Is everything okay?"

The question held more than concern about school.

Daddy was asking how I was adjusting to being so recently reborn—just like he had been over a decade ago. While I hadn't shared any details with him of how awful my first life had been, he knew I carried the dual memories from two wildly different lives with me.

And because he wasn't an idiot, he knew that one set of those memories was pretty traumatic.

"Violet?"

I remembered he'd asked me a question and was waiting for a response. "Everything is fine. Classes are easy thus far. Nothing exciting to report."

"You sure?" he pressed. Daddy was overly protective and trusted few people, so I knew he was always worried. He was a man who loved hard, clung harder, and feared losing his family to something he couldn't fight.

I pasted on a soft smile, gentle enough to ease him back. "I'm sure. I'm okay, Daddy. Thanks for checking." My throat burned with the lie, so I cleared it and turned to watch trees blur past the window.

We rode mostly in silence away from Shademore, away from Atlanta, back north towards the quiet and rural woodlands of my youth—back towards home.

After a while, I asked, "How's Uncle Charlie and his hellspawn son?"

Daddy snorted as we turned down the road towards the house. "Hellspawn indeed. They're fine. Sorry Rowan answered my phone the other day instead of me."

"It's fine. He's just... *Rowan*."

Daddy laughed. "Yeah, that's a word for him."

Uncle Charlie had been in our family's life since I was nine, and his presence had always been a calm and welcoming one. After he'd adopted Rowan, the two of them spent most of their time at the Shaw household. It didn't take long for us to become a two-family unit, more often together than apart.

I already knew the answer, but I asked the question anyway. "Is Mom working this weekend?"

Daddy chuckled, low and amused. "Not when she heard you wanted to come home. She's invited everyone over for a barbecue." He glanced sideways, catching my reaction. "I hope that's okay?"

I hummed, more to myself than him. *Of course, it isn't okay.* A full house meant no space, no privacy, no easy way to discuss money without every ear perking up. Still, I forced my lips into something resembling pleasure.

"I guess it will have to be. Can we drive by the barn first, please? Check on things?"

He arched his brow, but nodded. "Sure. Most everything's been squared away, but we can check."

We drove in silence after that, filled with things I didn't want to say and questions he wanted to ask but couldn't force out.

Gravel popped under the tires as he turned towards the barn. The building rose against the forest backdrop like something from a postcard: majestic, weathered red wood catching late sunlight. I climbed out, stretching, breathing air that hit sharper here, clean and grounding in a way campus never was.

"I got to ride Hyacinth yesterday," I said, unable to keep the smile off my lips.

"Oh, yeah?" His voice warmed. "How's that hellbeast handling school accommodations?"

I laughed. "It shows in his flanks."

"I've never known a more gluttonous animal," Daddy said. "Make sure you remind that stablemaster to stay mindful of Hyacinth's diet, or else you're going to be waddling instead of galloping."

"Speaking of that stablemaster. . ." I trailed off, unsure how Daddy would react. "I rode Hyacinth bareback and got caught by Aaron again."

He smirked. "Violet, be more careful. Aaron seems like a good man from my few conversations with him, but he can't condone breaking school rules."

I bristled at his words, feeling society's bindings tether me to consequences and expectations. *What I would give to just be free and not controlled for a moment.*

"I know, Daddy. I can't say that I didn't pull at his heartstrings a little, telling him how I'd ridden bareback as a child—"

"Don't remind your mother about that. She nearly *lost her mind* seeing you on the beast's back without a saddle."

That pulled another laugh from me as we walked towards the barn, gravel crunching under our boots. The bright yellow wood groaned as Dad pulled the door open, sunlight streaming into the dim interior.

Dust swirled in the light, catching on rough workbenches lining the barn wall. The faint hay smell that clung to everything wafted around me.

Inside, the place felt familiar and foreign at once. Beehives sat quietly along the far wall opposite the workbenches. Wildflowers that once colored the outside field had withered back into the soil. Even the air seemed to hold its breath.

Daddy walked over to a hive, running his hand along one, his face softening. "You remember how you were the one who wanted these? That presentation you gave us all about how bees help the land and the plants?"

"*The Necessity of Bees Towards the Sustainability and Biodiversity of Their Ecosystems*," I said with a smile. "Yeah, I remember."

He laughed and slapped the beehive. "That's the one. You'd gotten all dressed up and called a family meeting to give us that PowerPoint. God, you couldn't have been more than ten or eleven."

I traced my fingers over the worn table edge, wood scarred from years of tools biting into it. "Yeah. . . I was brilliant even then, wasn't I?"

"Brilliant and fearless. Definitely humble," he said with a grin. "Marching right up to the bees without a suit until I nearly lost my mind yelling."

I smiled and turned towards the greenhouse window overlooking dormant garden beds. Years of memories filled with love, Hyacinth, and family. Then for a heartbeat, I felt that *other* me: nine years old, crying in a warehouse, broken in ways I didn't know how to fix. My chest tightened, and I shoved the thought down before it could choke me.

Daddy's voice pulled me back. "You okay?"

I forced a small nod. "Yeah. Just lost in old memories."

I bit the inside of my cheek, nerves curling low in my stomach. This was why I'd asked him to come here first. To remind myself that I was still me, raised by a family who loved me and that I was here in this present, not trapped in some nightmare from another timeline.

But I wanted to hunt my own monster. I wanted to bring Edward Fitzgerald down and stamp justice on his soul. And for that, I needed the one thing my father had access to: my money.

The word felt dirty, but it pressed against me like a weight. I hated myself because I wasn't asking for books or food or rent. I was asking for something I couldn't explain without dragging him into the shadows of my first life.

I looked at him again, his broad frame bent over the hive, his large hands handling the boxes with care. This was my father, who had fought to hold our family together, who had burned and broken and rebuilt just so I could have a home to run to. I should feel safe with him, but anxiety coiled as I wondered how he'd react to my request.

I drew in a breath, holding it until it ached. I couldn't ask for the money yet. Not here, surrounded by the love he'd built for me. I couldn't ruin this moment of us together in the barn that still smelled like honey and woodsmoke—while I could still pretend I was just his little girl.

"Show me the greenhouse additions," I said softly, forcing a smile. "Before Mom starts wondering where you've misplaced me."

He chuckled, shaking his head, and motioned towards the door. But the tension in my chest stayed, heavy and waiting. The money conversation would have to come later, when the weight of what I needed it for wouldn't shatter the peace between us.

Chapter 4

Rowan

The rope lay across my lap, soft jute coiled in patient lines, as I practiced another variation of a leg tie. I knew my nerves well enough by now that this was a calming technique: my therapy, my meditation. A way to remind myself where I ended and where this new world began.

Remembering ties had come easily to me. The application was a little harder since I could only ever practice on myself or the mannequin in the corner of the room. I reminded myself to be careful, to put no pressure on the peroneal nor compression on the femoral.

Shibari was supposed to be artistic and hurt in the right places, not cripple you.

I heard him before he appeared. Steady footsteps that hesitated right before my open door as Charlie hovered nearby, uncertain whether to intrude. The sound of his elevated heartbeat reached my ears—anxiety wrapped in parental concern, a rhythm I had learned to recognize in this strange second life.

"Hey," Charlie said, voice threading through the low grunge vibrating from my speakers. He had dressed in running gear, white on white, his own cure when he wanted to outrun something gnawing at him. The smell of deodorant clung to him. He probably came straight from stretching before his run.

I did not look up as I greeted him. "Is everything okay?"

He stepped inside, finally committing, and dropped into my oak desk chair with a soft exhale. His blue eyes were dark tonight, storm-tossed.

He said, "I wanted to make sure Levi didn't get to you the other day. You've done nothing but hole yourself in your room practicing."

A snort escaped me before I could stop it. "He is nothing but a scared man afraid his mistakes are finally going to catch up to him... especially when he admits to murder so nonchalantly."

We all knew it. Levi had the most to lose in this fucked-up rebirth: his family, his wife, the stability he'd fought tooth and nail to rebuild. A new life meant nothing if the ghosts of the old one still prowled its edges.

Charlie didn't answer right away. His gaze drifted to the rope on my thigh, then back up, and something in his shoulders shifted. Tension winding tighter than the rope on my leg.

"He had a lot to lose. At the time, we both did what we thought was right."

So my adopted father had some participation in it, I mused. I felt almost ashamed for how badly I wanted to pry into the story of how the calm and collected Charlie was willing to forsake a man's life for... what? What was he willing to kill for? Obviously, something to do with Violet.

"Honestly, Charlie, that reveal was not as surprising as it should have been."

That made him laugh a little, the lines on his face dancing. "You two are very similar in that regard."

I shook my head. "Do not compare me to that man-child."

Another laugh before we fell into a comfortable silence. Finally, he relented and asked the question I knew had been weighing on him these last few days. "Do you really think Violet is in danger?"

I paused mid-knot, considering how to answer. Charlie did not deserve lies, but he needed a truth that would not unravel him.

Over the past five years, since my reincarnation, I'd hoped Charlie would have been less doubtful of the supernatural world hidden all around us. I hadn't enjoyed spending that first year retelling story after story of the apocalyptic Wastelands I'd lived in, much less broadcasting my newly acquired heightened hearing to him and Levi over and over again.

But humanity's burden had always been its disbelief. *Our biggest weakness and our greatest strength—cynical skepticism.*

In my previous life, Godsblood had been given to mortals so long ago that it was considered ancient history, even if the aftereffects of that gift were not. Some folks were born with preternatural speed, or inhuman strength, or nightvision, or a second pair of legs growing out of their ass. Others, like myself in my previous life, didn't get a goddamned thing. A real Russian roulette of birth.

Of course, *everybody* had an opinion about the origin and purpose of the Godsblood. Was it a gift or a curse? Was it truly divine in nature, or was *Godsblood* just a catchy name? Were these abilities the next step in human evolution or mutations from generations of living in an irradiated hellscape?

There had been groups of fanatical zealots who pushed one belief or another. But that's been true since the dawn of humanity, hasn't it?

As for myself? I always focused my time and energy on surviving. . . but even I'd had a few theories about the nature of Godsblood based on some of the oldest stories I'd heard or read about how life was before the veil fell.

First, I did not think that *Godsblood* was just a clever marketing term for the source of humanity's random new abilities. No, I believed that was quite literal. I almost pitied the poor fuck—whatever forgotten god it was—who'd been chained up someplace to be siphoned off like a tree being tapped for syrup.

Second, there was the sheer abundance of supernaturals in the Wastelands. Even in the most ancient of stories that told of the time before the veil fell, there was hardly ever any mention of supernaturals successfully breeding with mortals. I was neither the first nor only person who found it suspiciously coincidental how it *seemed* as if supernaturals had a far higher success rate breeding with mortals who had Godsblood in their veins.

Drain a god dry, pump their blood into as much of the populace as you can, then sit back and wait a century or so for that Godsblood to mingle and spread. It made sense, in an utterly evil and diabolical way.

"Is Violet in danger?" I echoed. "No. Not the kind you are imagining. Nobody is going to snatch her off the street or stab her in a parking lot."

"Technically, that can happen to anyone at anytime. You know what I meant, Rowan."

"She got a fast-tracked scholarship, did she not? A golden ticket." I met his eyes. "I would bet she was not the only one."

His jaw tightened. "Levi mentioned it was the most attractive offer out of all of her other applications." He paused. "So what are you saying?"

I shrugged. "They are going to use that to get her close. And once she is there. . ." I looped the rope into another knot around my leg. "They will want her to connect."

"Connect how?"

"Fall in love," I said flatly. "Or at least fall into bed."

His face went rigid. "Christ, Rowan."

"Too much? I can slow down if all this talk of the bees and flowers makes you uncomfortable."

"Rowan. . ."

"Fine. Vampyres are notorious for seduction. They can make obsession feel like devotion." The rope bit into my skin as I pulled it tighter. "Weres? All instinct and hunger. They thrive on bonds, pack, and possession. As for gods. . ." I paused, remembering the burning in my chest, the golden tome that I clutched against myself as the hunter that chased me from The Library. "Gods play on worship. The stories all end the same: they get what they want, and mortals rarely walk away unscathed."

I tried to shake the unease that crept up my spine. I hated talking of the gods because you never knew who was listening, ready to step in and make your life a living hell.

Charlie swallowed hard. "So what do we do? Warn her?"

That made me laugh, a sharp sound with no humor in it as I rapped my knuckles on the floor. "What would you tell her? 'Hey Violet, congratulations on making it into such a prestigious university. It turns out it is also a supernatural breeding program! Surprise, sweetheart, you are now the perfect breeding stock.'"

Charlie winced, burying his face in his hands, and groaned. A rather surprising trait from him I learned he does whenever he feels overwhelmed.

"It is ridiculous," I said, resuming my tie, "But not wrong."

He dragged a palm down his face, letting the mask of calm break slowly. "Levi will not stay still knowing Violet is in that much danger."

He took a deep breath in, "God, I don't think I can face Sloane either, knowing this. . . ."

His voice trailed off, and the agony in his words did little to hide his turmoil. I studied him, seeing the years of lines in his face. The revelation of him being complicit, or perhaps even an accomplice, in Levi's act of murder told me that he was a man who would do anything for his chosen family. Levi, Charlie, and apparently me.

The truth I would never admit—not to Charlie, not to Sloane, and definitely not to Levi—was that this fractured mess we had was the closest thing I had ever known to family. . . if you ignored my first attempt with Faelin. Her name still haunted me. Yes, this current life felt messed-up and broken, sure. But it was still mine. And that meant I would bleed for them if I had to.

"Then we deal with it," I said simply, feeling the rope of responsibility cinch around my throat. "I can move closer. Keep an eye on her. If I have to get a job at the damn place, I will."

Charlie hesitated. "But this veil you mentioned—what happens when it falls?"

I began untying my leg, the rope sliding free with practiced ease, regarding the indentations on my skin with mild interest. "In my life, the veil was gone. I do not know if it was a physical manifestation or simply what they called the hidden nature of it all. Humans and monsters lived side by side—if you could call it living." A hollow chuckle escaped me. "What many thought was a pandemic was really the beginning of the end. Not political or engineered. . . just a god throwing a tantrum because another god fucked him over. Mortals bled for it."

We had spent years poring over religious texts, folklore, myths—anything that would help bring light to my first life in the Wastelands. We had agreed I must have lived some time in the future based on my descriptions, we just didn't know how far ahead. But the common thing we had agreed after our research was what Charlie mumbled, "In every religion, mortals bleed for gods."

I nodded. "Yes, it does seem to be their favorite pastime. . . a morose legacy of fucking with us or killing us."

He flinched at that. "You're sure about all this?"

I let out a long, exhausted breath, growing frustrated at how many times I had rattled off my reasons to only be met by their constant disbelief. "Charlie," I muttered, "Of course, I am not sure. All I have are fragments... stories carved into stone, names whispered in alleys, rumors you do not repeat unless you want your throat slit. Hearsay. That is all I have."

"But you believe it."

I glanced over to him before returning my gaze to the rope hanging slack between my fingers. "I believe in what I saw, what I lived through, what I experienced, and what I learned," I said. "Mostly, I learned how to survive."

Charlie studied me with those storm-blue eyes, brows pinched. He was afraid, I realized, but I could not say if it was for me or for Violet or for the whole of humanity. He was a righteous man, lost on his journey, and always eager to carry the burdens of others.

Finally, he asked, "Think we're overreacting?"

I shrugged. "What is that saying? Hope for the best, prepare for the worst? Allow me to survey the school first. It may not be as I fear. I could be paranoid over nothing." I paused, then added, "Assuming Levi does not bury me in the back yard like he did old Rufus."

Charlie gave a humorless laugh. "No promises. At least you'll be in a good spot. They loved that dog." His tired eyes turned to me. "For now, let us enjoy the barbecue tomorrow and see how things go. I'm looking forward to Sloane's cooking."

I scoffed, throwing a teasing jab at the woman Charlie pinned for, "*You* may want Sloane's, but it is Dawn's cooking I salivate for."

Sloane's sister Dawn moved through the kitchen like fire given form, like a spirit of the hearth if ever there was one. Each dish she prepared was infused with something I could not put into words. South American heritage ran through her blood like molten gold, and she wielded it like the weapon it was. Every dish paraded spices across my tongue in a myriad of wondrous flavors. It was as if she conjured magic from rice and beans, and from banana leaves tied tight around mysteries that made my mouth water.

I especially enjoyed it when she made tamales. Watching her tie those leaves with practiced ease, binding something precious so it could transform. Just like my rope work, just like the knots that kept my sanity tethered.

Charlie stood as he said, "Her tamales really are the best, but I will always prefer Sloane's." He reached out and—in a fatherly gesture—put his hand on my shoulder. "I'm going for my run. Want to join?"

No, I do not. I always did my run in the morning, compared to Charlie, who preferred the evening. *Getting in shape is a psychological process disguised as a physical one,* he'd often say. I did not share the same sentiment of enjoying running in darkened woods.

"*Nyet,*" I said.

"No?" Charlie asked in confirmation. He had started studying Russian once he realized how much the language meant to me—a way for him to get closer to me, for us to share something in common—but he was still unsure of himself. He constantly asked for validation and clarification, even over the simplest words and terms.

"Not tonight. But thank you for asking."

As Charlie left, I relooped my rope and shaped the pattern again beneath my hands. The rhythm steadied my pulse, a metronome against the uncertainty clawing at my throat. It was a long time before I fell into a fitful sleep that night.

The Shaws sure do enjoy their family barbecues, I thought as Charlie and I arrived at their house. Though I suppose it made sense, as they had to cook for a family with dietary restraints. Both Sloane and Violet had Celiac disease, so whenever food was made, it was done in large quantities. *Such as this barbecue ritual of excess.*

The very concept of a barbecue always felt strange to me. In my first life, celebrations had been scarce. American barbecues, I'd come to find, were about abundance spread out over red checkered cloth. Food was piled high enough to feed a small army, and there was a level of waste that would have gotten you killed in the Wasteland.

And I had fallen *in love* with it all.

When the family gathered—plates groaning under the weight of plenty, voices weaving through the evening air—I sat alone and absorbed it all. For them, this was a mundane occurrence. For me, it was proof that beauty could exist without blood payment.

Levi's oldest friend José had come with his family. Both men stood by the grill that sizzled with carne asada and chicken, lazy grey smoke rising to greet the blue unbroken sky. They sipped their beers as they watched José's eight-year-old twins chase Amber, who is Levi and Sloane's youngest. The three kids ran through the yard, kicking a half-deflated soccer ball between them with their boundless energy on full display. Her sunhat bounced on her honey-brown hair as she darted away, shrieking when they gained on her.

Sloane was trying to speak Spanish with José's wife, Isabella—a short and stout woman with a round face, dark eyes, and darker hair. From the few interactions we'd had, I knew her to be a kind woman. Whenever she spoke Spanish to the Shaw family, especially with Amber and Violet, she would take her time to speak slowly in an attempt to get them to reciprocate. The few phrases I'd heard Violet struggle with reminded me of my own time adopting Russian. Over at the picnic table, Sloane's words were halting, and she gestured with her hands when her Spanish failed her.

Then, Sloan's sister Dawn swooped in to translate. With bombastic hand gestures accompanying a rapid-fire staccato of Spanish, Dawn had Isabella doubled over with laughter. Dawn winked at her younger sister, then darted off to harangue Levi at the grill.

Sloane wears her heritage like a coat that is two sizes too big. I knew it was a sore spot for her, given she was Latina in blood, but not in upbringing. She'd had her sister Dawn help her learn Spanish, but I could tell she was frustrated that it didn't come naturally to her. . . the small pinch between her brows when she struggled for a word.

Dawn, on the other hand, had been raised by her mother's side, and it showed. The way she laughed at Spanish and English jokes alike, how she transitioned between the two seamlessly, how she turned what could have been awkward silence into shared warmth. She was a bridge where Sloane felt like a gap.

And yet, she carries it like a burden. I'd heard comments once or twice about their parents and their upbringing. I'd heard enough to decide it had not been good for either of them.

I nursed my beer from a lawn chair, the bottle cold against my palm. Despite Sloane's reluctance, Charlie and Levi had vouched for my drinking privileges despite my apparent age. They both understood the arithmetic of my actual age, and I would be damned if I would be denied a beer. The taste still surprised me—bitter and bright. I savored it as if it were my first.

Levi handed his tongs to José, stepped away from the grill, and headed into the house. Violet's attention snapped to him, and she followed inside. *Curious*, I thought as I closed my eyes and focused my hearing towards the house. I managed to tune out most of the noise around me to catch the edge of their conversation.

"What do you mean you want access to your trust?" Levi asked. His voice resonated with paternal authority.

Money? Violet rarely asked for anything. She didn't need to, since Levi already lavished her with endless indulgences. I had called her princess for good reason—she lived like one, comfortable in the knowledge that her father's wealth would catch her if she fell.

"Daddy, I want to invest in some businesses, and I would like the flexibility to spend without needing your consent."

Invest in some businesses? That didn't sound anything like the Violet I knew. They said that college could change you, but I doubted that three weeks were enough to spark a sudden interest in her personal finances.

I heard Levi's heartbeat quicken. He must have thought the request was just as odd as I did. He said, "If you want to send me the specifics on those investments, I would be happy to look them over together with you or—"

"But Daddy, I want to make the choices myself. Even if I lose money, I want it to be because I made a mistake."

Water running. Glass clinking. Stalling tactics. My enhanced hearing painted the scene in sound: nervous father, determined daughter, money hanging between them.

"Violet, I cannot in good conscience give you access to that much money without hearing more detailed reasoning." There was a pause.

I nearly missed what Levi asked next because he had lowered his voice. "Baby girl, did someone approach you at the school?"

There it is. Good on you, Levi. That was the question that mattered. I had to admit, I was surprised he thought to ask her.

"What? No... not exactly."

Another quickening of Levi's pulse. "What does that mean? Not exactly?"

Her frustrated sigh was followed by receding footsteps. "Just forget it, Daddy."

Running away when the questions get too pointed, princess? That's very telling.

Levi called after her, but I assumed she had retreated to her room. Levi cursed under his breath before heading back outside. He slammed the patio door behind him, and the sound nearly shattered my eardrums.

Fuck, that hurt. I dialed down the volume and watched Levi return to grilling meat with aggressive precision.

Why money? Why now? And why the deflection? The questions circled like vultures. When Violet failed to emerge from whatever hole she had crawled into, curiosity won the war against common sense, and I went to look for her as I abandoned my beer and slipped inside.

If I am going to protect her, I need to understand her patterns. Her hiding places. Her weaknesses.

The house swallowed me in cool dimness, a sharp contrast to the blazing warmth outside. My hearing still throbbed from Levi's door-slam, but I pushed through the discomfort and stretched my senses. Past the kitchen. Past the living room. Up the stairs where the bedrooms were.

There. A thread of sound, thin as spider silk. Violet's voice was low and urgent. I positioned myself at the bottom of the stairwell, close enough to listen but far enough to flee if she started heading back downstairs.

When I got a good feel for it, her voice cracked like a whip, frustration bleeding through the syllables. "Liam!" There was an urgency, a raw edge I had never heard before. "I don't know what to do."

Liam. Her older brother.

"I asked him for access to my trust, and he wanted to know what I was investing in. How did you ask him for your trust money for your coffee shop?"

Her voice was sharp and restless before she went silent, listening. I knew I could reach for it, dial my hearing up until Liam's voice became clear. . . but it would cost me. The strain of increasing my hearing that much always left me half-blind with headaches later. Instead, I stayed where I was at the bottom of the stairs and continued to listen to her side of the conversation.

Not that I needed to hear what Liam told her. I already had a good sense of how he would have asked for his trust money, and it involved a mission statement, financial projections, marketing research, and proposed risks. . . paperwork, projections, and adult responsibility.

None of which, I knew, were Violet's strong suits.

"You wrote a *business plan*? Are you serious?" Her words tumbled down the staircase like broken glass. "That would take me weeks or even months to draft. I almost would rather strip."

Heat coiled low in my belly. An inexplicable spike of anger and fear that snapped me to stand straight. For a pampered princess to go straight to stripping? She seemed desperate. Why did she need money so urgently?

My hands found the stair rail and gripped until my knuckles went white. A thousand scenarios flooded my mind, each one darker than the last. Debt collectors. Blackmail. Supernatural entities who had sold her irresistible temptations, and now the bill was due.

Had some supernatural already found her? Had I overheard the beginning of whatever web they planned to spin and trap her in?

Her voice cut through my spiraling thoughts. "Oh, don't act so high and mighty, Liam. How many times did I catch you with your dick in a groupie's mouth after one of your shows? Not to mention your little run-in with drugs?"

Her words burned, full of fire. I had to bite back a chuckle despite my rising anxiety. She was fearless, or recklessly bold, and despite the fact that we didn't like each other very much, I had to respect her tactical thinking. Violet might be spoiled, but she was not stupid.

Silence followed before her voice, harder now, said, "I will figure out the money. Even if I do end up stripping, you'd better keep that a secret between us."

She ended the call with a curse, then there were footsteps announcing her descent. I moved fast, slipping into the kitchen to grab a water bottle from the fridge like I had just come in from outside.

When she appeared in the doorway, I let my eyes take inventory the way they always did. Black jeans torn just enough to suggest rebellion, a cropped top revealing a strip of pale skin, hair twisted into a high knot that emphasized the sharp line of her jaw. Minimal makeup except for her lips—stained a deep red, as if she had just been eating berries.

College suits her, I admitted begrudgingly to myself. I had been so adamant to Levi that she was simply my ward that I had failed to acknowledge much less respect her growth. The woman in front of me proved otherwise.

"*Princess*. I must say. . . you look ruffled." I set my water down and leaned against the counter, projecting casual indifference while every nerve screamed alert.

She huffed and moved towards the fridge, close enough that I caught her scent—roses and rosemary, innocence and rebellion tangled together like warring perfumes.

When she opened the fridge door, her eyes found the empty space where my water bottle had been. The last one. I could not help the dark chuckle that escaped me.

"Are you looking for something?" I asked.

Her eyes narrowed as she closed the fridge, then fixed on my unopened water with the intensity of a predator spotting prey. Hip cocked, arms crossed, every inch of her radiating controlled frustration.

"You going to drink that, Rowan?"

So polite. So careful. But I could see the storm building behind her hazel eyes, the same fire that had burned through her phone conversation. She wanted something—needed something—and I was in her way. *Time to see what the princess is made of.*

"I would not have pulled it out if I was not," I replied, settling deeper against the opal quartz countertops.

She rolled her eyes and muttered something under her breath—something about me not pulling out much of anything—then stepped closer to reach the cabinet behind me.

I did not move.

She paused, teeth catching her plump lower lip as she calculated her options. She could ask nicely and hope I played gentleman. She could try to squeeze past, which would put us close enough to count heartbeats. Or she could find her backbone and make demands.

Pride versus necessity. Always an interesting battle to watch.

The scent of her shampoo drifted again between us as she hesitated, overwhelmingly sweet as I watched her body fight with the struggle of being cornered and not quite ready to surrender.

"Is there a problem, Violet?"

The question hung loaded between us like a cocked weapon, our turbulent history ever so clear as we eyed each other. In that moment, I was offering her a choice: back down or step up. Walk away or push back. And as always, she was ready to show me who she really was beneath all that privilege and polish.

"You're insufferable, Rowan."

"That is a big word for you, *princess*. I am overjoyed to see that college is paying off for you." I glanced down at the small space between us. "Do you mind? You are standing uncomfortably close." I shifted slightly towards her, letting her torn denim brush against mine.

She did not disappoint, meeting me with fire. "Yeah? You plan on moving your ass out of the way then?"

"Not when you ask so nicely."

"You know, Rowan, sometimes I cannot stand you." She spoke my name with a hint of dissatisfaction, those pearly teeth biting down on her lip to the point I thought she would bleed. Her heart jumped.

Such a feisty little thing. "That feeling is mutual. Although I believe common courtesy is not too much to expect from you. You simply have to ask nicely, Violet. Say, 'Will you step to the side, please?'"

I was pushing her, waiting for her to snap, but she held steady—iron against stone, cold and reserved. Our game of chicken stretched between us, neither willing to yield.

"If you will not move, Rowan, then I will just get it my own way."

"Suit yourself, *princess*."

She drew a breath that lifted her chest, then stepped closer until her body pressed against mine in ways that sent heat spiraling through me. Both arms reached around me, putting her dangerously close as she opened the cabinet door. It swung wide and cracked me hard across the back of my skull, forcing me to duck with a sharp curse.

Our faces ended up inches apart.

Time slowed to an asphyxiated silence. Her eyes were not the simple hazel hue I had always thought—they were flecked with amber and gold, like honey-dewed grass caught in the light of sunrise. With her eyes so close, I realized how pale she was. Dark circles carved shadows beneath her lashes. *She hasn't been sleeping well, either.*

My gaze drifted down, noting how her lips gleamed wet and full as her tongue darted out to trace her perfect cupid's bow.

My jeans grew uncomfortably tight.

"You're staring," she said, her voice oddly hoarse.

I was not one to back down. By all the gods, I let my mouth curve into an inviting smirk and watched heat creep up her throat to stain her cheeks. In my other life, I had been a rugged and scarred man with weathered lines. In this life, I used my attractive youth when necessary to play a little dirty.

Why waste something gifted by the gods?

"So are you, *princess*." I kept my voice low, deliberately rough.

I watched her struggle to form words, pupils dilating as she grabbed a glass and stepped away, clutching it to her chest like armor. I crossed my arms, trying to put distance between us and the heat radiating off her skin.

Just biology, I told myself. Just two bodies responding to proximity and adrenaline. I ignored the fact that I wanted to put that smart mouth of hers to better use.

Violet kept her eyes locked on mine as she filled the glass. She took several gulps, then pressed the glass back to her chest and began backing towards the door, refusing to give me her back.

What a fucking brat. I arched a brow. "You do not have eyes in the back of your head. Turn around and watch where you are going before you hurt yourself, *princess*." Her heart fluttered like a caged bird, panic threading through the rhythm.

Eyes narrowing, she struck out once more. "You are going to regret taunting me."

I shrugged. "And one day you will regret challenging me." I nodded towards the door leading back to her family. "But today is not that day, Violet. Walk like a normal person and get back outside. I will see you in a bit."

She glared at me with enough heat to melt steel, then turned and walked briskly towards the patio. When the last shadow of her disappeared, I let out a held breath.

A spoiled little princess indeed.

Chapter 5

Violet

My grand plans for the weekend had crashed and burned.

Daddy had gotten short with me, Liam proved to be useless, and Rowan's taunts left my mouth tasting like ash. Sunlight filtered through cream gossamer curtains in my dorm room, the sheets twisted around my legs and my laptop balanced on my knees, while I tried to figure out what to do next. I took a long sip of my water, wanting to wash away my failures and focus on the next task at hand.

Might as well grab the bull by its horns.

The screen glowed with search results for Oubliette locations. Their website offering nothing but tasteful black backgrounds and gold script addresses. No photos of interiors. No contact information. Just locations, like breadcrumbs for those who already knew the path.

I clicked through anyway, studying the exteriors. Nondescript buildings in expensive neighborhoods. The kind of places you walked past a thousand times without noticing, unless you knew what hid behind those unmarked doors.

In my first life, Edward had taken me to Oubliettes in multiple cities. Each one was similar in layout, in atmosphere, in the careful way they separated the social floor from the private rooms below. The dancers who worked the main floor were beautiful and untouchable in their confident smiles.

And yet I had been one of the hidden secrets... the merchandise that bled.

My fingers cramped around the laptop edge. The websites revealed nothing useful. No application process, no audition schedules, no hint of how someone gained entry to that world. Edward had simply walked through the doors, and the staff knew his name before he spoke it. I had only assumed it was his money that opened those doors. A reputation he threatened to defile. The right introduction.

I had none of those things.

But I knew how they operated, or at least, assumed how it worked. For as often as Edward took me, I had noticed that new dancers rotated through regularly, providing fresh faces to keep the floor interesting. His favorite had been Monday nights *"because they ran slower,"* he mentioned. Knowing this gave me the confidence that management might be more willing to consider walk-ins. I'd need the right clothes. The right makeup.

I needed money. But more than that, I needed proximity to Edward's world. From what I recalled, he'd disappeared into Oubliette's depths regularly, leaving me topside to wait like a good pet. If I could get inside and work the floor, maybe someone would remember him. Maybe someone would know where to find him now.

I clicked once more on the image of Oubliette in Atlanta and realized it was not too far from me. My stomach turned over, slick and cold. I wasn't afraid of Edward anymore. I wasn't the scared, ignorant child he had once bought. However, there was still a seed of fear planted deep within me from that time long ago. I knew I needed to dig it out before it could take root and blossom. I had to in order to take back my autonomy, especially if I went ahead with this plan.

Vengeance required patience… and the grit to walk back into the same kind of hell I'd died trying to escape before I was hung up to die. It had been my own naivety to assume that going home to ask Daddy for money would work out. While that had proven to be a bad idea, the thought of stepping through Oubliette's doors was even more ominous. Hence why it was my last resort.

The difference? I was choosing my own path forward this time. This body had never been touched by those hands. My memories of love, safety, and trust warred with blurred recollections that flinched at the sound of expensive shoes on marble.

I closed the laptop and shoved it aside. Philosophy class started in thirty minutes. I needed to move, needed to stop thinking about what tonight might require. I grabbed clothes without looking, my bag, my phone, and turned towards the door just as it opened.

Alice stepped through, coffee in one hand, her other reaching for her keys. We collided.

Brown liquid arced through the air, splashed across her cream silk blouse, and down her brown pants. The cup hit the floor, bounced, and rolled under her desk.

"Oh, my god! I'm so sorry." The words tumbled out in the genuine panic I felt. My hands moved on instinct, reaching for the spreading stain, trying to somehow undo what I'd done. My palms pressed against wet fabric, against the swell of her breast beneath.

She smiled, honey-colored eyes crinkling. "I was planning on drinking that instead of wearing it."

I looked down. My hands splayed across her chest, coffee soaking through to my skin. Heat crawled up my neck, into my face.

"Shit, I'm sorry." I jerked back, hands now wet, and reached for a dirty towel in my hamper. "Do you want a towel?" I offered, then felt foolish when she declined. I wrapped my arm around my middle self-consciously.

"It's fine, Violet. I should've been paying attention." Her voice carried that easy grace I'd never possess, the kind of calm that came naturally to women like her.

"No, this is my fault. Let me buy you a new top. I'm going shopping after class anyway."

She started to protest when another voice cut through.

"Your guilt is apology enough."

I turned. The woman standing behind Alice stole the air from my lungs.

Dark skin that caught the light and transformed it into something precious as she stood there in an ivory one piece. White hair falling past her waist in waves that belonged in fantasies, not freshman dorms. Bone structure that suggested aristocracy, divinity, something beyond simple genetics.

Beautiful didn't cover it. This woman looked sculpted by hands that understood raw, primitive desire.

"Did any get on you?" My voice pitched higher than intended. Her clothes screamed money, the kind that made my trust fund look like pocket change.

She laughed, low and alluring. "No. I dodged." She said, her accent bearing subtle shifts in vowels that made English sound like a second language worn comfortably. Similar to Rowan's Russian inflections, but different. Older somehow.

"Holy shit, those are some great reflexes," I gasped, then realized how uncouth I must have sounded to her.

"So I've been told." A hint of amusement glinted in her dark eyes, like I'd missed the punchline. She inhaled, slow and deliberate. "You smell. . ." She paused, tasting the air. "interesting."

My thighs clenched involuntarily. Why did accents do this to me?

"Um. . . thank you?"

Alice nudged her friend, and even that seemed like an elegant gesture as she shot me an apologetic smile. "Sorry. Natalia can be blunt, but she means well."

Natalia. The name rolled through my head like smoke, hard to catch and harder to forget.

I moved to the door, held it open for them both. "I'm serious about replacing your blouse, Alice. I feel terrible."

"Again. . . don't worry about it." She waved me off, already moving towards her dresser. "Someone should have warned me." She gave a pointed look to Natalia, who was examining her manicured nails, clearly ignoring her friend.

"Right. . . listen, I'm heading to class, but I'll probably be out late tonight. Don't wait up."

Alice pulled the ruined blouse over her head, revealing creamy skin against a lace bralette underneath in the same fashion as her friend's. Delicate. Expensive. Elegant.

I felt like a dumpster fire in my oversized hoodie and sweatpants.

"Perfect timing. Natalia and I are going out anyway." She smiled, easy and unbothered by her half-dressed state. "Don't wait on me." She was being polite. We had never waited on each other, but the gesture was still kind.

"Thanks. I'll see you two later," I said, then managed something between a nod and a bow as I turned towards Natalia. Her smile curved, demure and knowing at once.

Total opposite of me. God, why am I so embarrassing?

I fled into the hallway and pulled air back into my lungs as I headed to class. I made a mental note to watch where I was going and stop crashing through this life like an anxious wrecking ball.

The auditorium filled slowly, students trickling in with the desperate energy of people who'd rather be anywhere else. I found a seat mid-section as Professor Wright strolled through the door.

Five-foot-two of controlled chaos wrapped in a sweater that assaulted the concept of color coordination. Striking gray hair caught the overhead lights while his rainbow plaid pants clashed beautifully with the geometric nightmare covering his torso and round wire-frame glasses. Somehow, he made it work.

I typically avoided older men on principle, but his audacity bordered on attractive.

"Students!" His voice boomed, far too large for his frame. "Welcome back to another week of Philosophy 101. I see none of you have fled screaming, which speaks either to your dedication or your masochism."

He dropped his bag on the desk. Pens clattered out, skittered across the floor in six different directions. He kept talking while crouching to collect them, unbothered by the chaos.

"Today we're dividing the room. Males on the left, females on the right. Yes, I know! How very *binary* of me, but bear with it for the exercise."

Murmurs rippled through the auditorium as we shuffled, relocated, and created a physical divide down the center aisle.

"Excellent!" Professor Wright straightened, pens clutched in one fist. "Today's topic: gendered identity, social behavior, and the structures we build without realizing we're trapped inside them." His smile sharpened. "This won't be a battle. Just an exploration of the walls we can't see because we're standing too close."

The discussion started with basic observations and spiraled quickly. A male student near the front leaned back in his seat, dimples flashing. "Biologically speaking, men are built for providing and protecting. Women for childbearing. There's a natural order to these things."

My jaw clenched. *Natural order*. That had been the same justification Edward used when explaining why some people were born to serve, while others were born to *be* served.

A girl raised her hand, chocolate hair falling across her face. "That assumes biology determines destiny. What about the barriers we've constructed? The ones that punish anyone who doesn't fit the prescribed roles?"

The room shifted. Other students leaned forward, arguments forming.

Professor Wright watched like a conductor before an orchestra, waiting for the right moment to let the music swell.

"But if everyone rejects structure, society falls apart," a tall boy by the window argued. "Individual freedom is great in theory, but what happens when seven billion people all want different things? Chaos. Collapse."

The chocolate-haired girl found her spine and sat straighter. "Take, for example, every major plague in history that was met first with fear. Fear of the unknown, of contamination, of each other. But fear never cured anything." She paused, letting the silence build. "Progress came from science, hygiene, and shifts in how we treat each other. If we reverse that progress, if we strip away rights and enforce conformity through fear, are we actually civilized? Or just well-dressed animals?"

My chest tightened. Choice and control. Freedom and survival. The same questions that had circled my skull since waking up in this younger body with older nightmares. . . and Edward's voice ringing in my ears.

"You belong to me, pet. Your words mean nothing here. Your body answers to me."

I dug my nails into my palms, using the sharp bite to drag myself back to the present. After ten more minutes of discussion, Professor Wright finally raised his hands, conducting the chaos towards resolution. "Beautiful. Contradictory. Do you see it?" His eyes gleamed behind wire-rimmed glasses. "This is philosophy meeting psychology. One asks what we are, the other asks why we act the way we do. Neither has clean answers because humanity refuses to be cleanly categorized."

He paced the front of the room, hands gesturing like he was pulling thoughts from the air. "We study the mind, behavior, and the ways we interact and interpret our world. And in that study, we find ourselves staring into mirrors that show us things we'd rather not see."

Kind of like me.

I was uncomfortable in my own skin, in my own grief, feeling my life operated with an expiration date for the unknown. I did not want to come face to face with myself, much less question why I had been resurrected in this life. The concept of 'magic' was something foreign and uncomfortable that society would struggle to make sense of. And honestly? I didn't know if there was anything magical about my rebirth—or Daddy's or Uncle Charlie's, for that matter. Nor did I want to endanger my family by revealing our circumstances. Mankind was not kind, and the thought of becoming a test subject felt like the same chains Edward had placed on me.

Yet I was planning on entering a world I had begged myself to forget.

The discussion continued, voices overlapping, arguments building and collapsing. Professor Wright orchestrated it all with visible satisfaction, thriving in the controlled chaos.

By the time he called for attention, my brain felt scraped raw.

"Your self-reflection journals are due next Monday," he announced. "Make them honest. I want brutal, ugly honesty, not the sanitized version you think I want to read."

Students began packing up, the discussion dissolving into the shuffle of bags and footsteps.

"Oh, before you go." Professor Wright's voice cut through the noise. "Next month, we have a guest lecturer joining us. Professor James Thornwood will be discussing his research into occult studies and their philosophical implications."

The occult? As if real darkness required pentagrams and candlelight rituals.

I left with the crowd, my decision solidifying with each step. Edward's world thought it had broken me once. Tonight, I'd step into Oubliette ready to take back what had never been theirs to begin with.

Chapter 6

Rowan

The bus doors hissed shut behind me, and the noise hit first. Laughter spilling from courtyards, hearts buzzing with life, perfume thick enough to choke on. I'd survived fifty years in a wasteland where silence meant safety, where every sound could mean death screaming your name.

This? This was sensory warfare.

Charlie's scribbled note crumpled in my fist. East Campus Dorm. Simple reconnaissance. Map Violet's territory, catalogue her routines, and get out.

I had told myself the same thing before breaking into The Library. A knife through the ribs taught me how well that plan had worked.

One step onto the manicured lawn and the whispers started. Eyes tracked me like I was prey that had wandered into the wrong hunting ground. My height drew them first, then the rest: build, posture, the way I moved like something that belonged in the wilderness instead of classrooms.

I stand out like blood on snow.

A cluster of girls near the library doors giggled as I passed. Their hearts beat faster, perfume blooming sharper as I got close. I kept walking, jaw tight, cataloguing exits out of habit. The north path led to parking. South curved towards what looked like dormitories. East disappeared between academic buildings.

Violet was somewhere in this maze of youth and hormones and careless laughter. Find her patterns, map her territory, don't engage. My objective was simple.

Until the presence of the vampyre hit me.

If I could have called Levi to gloat, I would have. But the cadence of the vampyre's footsteps—which now trailed me—was a reminder of their predatory nature. Those steps lacked the awkward shuffle or hurried pace of students rushing between classes. Too steady. Too certain. I slowed instinctively, every sense sharpening.

"Why, hello there," her voice cut through the noise, smooth and deliberate. The kind of voice that made men forget to watch their backs.

I kept moving, neither slowing nor quickening my pace. *Predators chase prey that runs*, I reminded myself. I needed to get away quickly, but calmly. I already had proof of the first item I had been concerned about—the presence of the supernatural.

Cold fingers brushed my arm as perfectly manicured nails ghosted over my skin. Again, her voice, deep and lush, rang in my ears. "I'm *talking* to you."

"Not interested," I said without looking.

A brief pause as confusion flavored the air between us. She asked, "Oh? Why such a rush?"

I laughed despite myself. *Not accustomed to food that doesn't acknowledge you?* I turned to tell her off, then sucked in a breath.

Her hair was as colorless as mine, shimmering in the fading sun, strands so fine they drank light and refracted it back like spider silk. Skin as dark as polished obsidian, dark blue eyes fringed with white lashes long enough to cast shadows across sharp cheekbones. She wore a sleeveless white one-piece with matching slacks and heels. Every line of her face was symmetrical, perfected, *practiced*.

Her lack of heartbeat and abundance of onlookers confirmed what I'd already known. A woman that gorgeous wouldn't be able to walk without a gaggle of those enthralled by her beauty, those who would be desperate just to stand near her. She wore a nimbus of hypnotic power that tugged and pulled any who saw her.

Vampyre.

That woman was dangerous in the same way a calm sea or murky river was dangerous. It may appear serene on the surface, but death lurked within those unseen depths.

Her cold grip tightened on my arm, and the air around us pulsed faintly. *Allure.* I'd felt it before, in a wasteland brothel right before a dazed girl's throat had been opened like a second smile.

She gave my arm a slight squeeze as she asked, "Do you want to have some fun with me?" Her voice scratched beneath my skin, trying to hook into my will and drag it to some dark place I would never return from.

Disbelief furrowed my brow as I pried her freezing fingers free from my arm with calm precision. I held her hand—a hand so cold it was nearly painful—and said, "I regret to inform you, but I have no wish to participate... vampyress."

The words slipped out like muscle memory. Too old a habit and too deeply ingrained, burned into my mind from my first life.

Her eyes widened, her perfect composure shattering. "C*e surpriză plăcută*," she murmured. Once she saw my confusion, she translated, "What a pleasant surprise."

That accent... is that Eastern European? Or Romanian? I knew it had to be an old bloodline, for sure.

She tilted her head with a look of curiosity on her face as she stepped closer. "How could you tell? I thought I had my mannerisms perfected."

I let our hands fall, pulling them free in the process. "I have no interest in answering."

"But you are *muritor*," she said as she studied me with blue eyes as dark as an abyssal sea. Her perfume clashed with the raw scent of the summer honeysuckle growing on the school's stone walls.

She'd called me *muritor*. Mortal. A respectful term, as far as most supernaturals were concerned. That helped me narrow her origins down to Romania. Yet despite her beauty, she was a monster all the same. It would be best to tread carefully.

She was near enough that I felt the coolness of her body as we stood in the humid heat of the city. My guess was that she hadn't fed in days. Her next meal would bring back the warmth she needed to stay hidden amongst the living.

In that sultry voice, she asked, "Have I turned you mute, perhaps? Has my glamour stupefied you?"

I arched a brow and crossed my arms. "Hardly. I was waiting for you to slip and give me something to work with." So much for treading carefully.

Vampyre clans were insufferably proud of their heritage, and often boasted their lineage like banners into battle. I had assumed she would have immediately sneered, looking down on me as she recited her great-great-great-grandfather's connection to Dracula, or whatever bloodsucker they had claim to.

"Is that so?" She assessed me, her ravenous gaze narrowing. A low chuckle escaped her, musical and amiable.

I knew the tricks the undead played. . . practiced seduction wrapped in false warmth. Yet, from how she stared at me, I felt her interest was genuine. She seemed more amused than angry that I'd seen her for what she was. I realized she was enjoying this private bit of exhibitionism as her eyes flashed once more, swirling colors of navy and violet.

"*T'fu*," I said and waved my hand dismissively. "I told you once already that I am not interested."

Despite my disgusted gesture, she seemed even more intrigued. "You have a strong will, *muritor*." She stepped closer and placed her hand back on my arm, giving it a gentle squeeze. "*And* a strong body it seems."

What part of no did she misunderstand?

I weighed my next words carefully, tongue pressing against teeth. Depending on how the next few minutes played out, I could be dead before nightfall. However, I knew that if things went well enough, she might not kill me and instead move on to her next quarry.

"To answer your earlier question, you hide it well," I said at last, nodding my head. "If it were not for my ears, I would not have noticed."

She brightened, realization dawning. "Oh, you were gifted by the Godsblood?" She stepped closer, her chest brushing against mine as she gripped my chin between her cold fingers. I watched her teeth extend slightly in morbid fascination. "That explains so much," she murmured.

Does it?

Her mention of Godsblood made me wonder if it was already known to the supernatural world at large, or if she was tied to the family that distributed it.

She took my moment of distraction to lean towards my neck. "*Nyet.*" Firm in my denial, I placed my hands on her shoulders in warning. "That's enough," I commanded.

She surprised me by relenting and pulling back. "I love a good hunt." Her voice was wistful. "I bet you taste divine, but Father asked me not to drink those who are gifted." A once-over, slow and deliberate. "Though he never said anything about *touching*."

I cleared my throat and stepped back until my shoulders pressed against the slate stone building behind me. Students continued passing by, oblivious. The way we spoke felt isolated, like we stood in a pocket of space separated from the world.

"My earlier statement still stands." I studied her. "Why would you come here? This campus reeks of the young and foolish. You seem like a lady who would seek more sophisticated quarry."

Her lips curved, sharp as a blade's edge. "Who says anything about hunting?" She leaned in just enough that I could see faint veins threading at her temples beneath flawless skin. "Maybe I wanted to visit a friend and take a moment to see what it felt like to be a student."

Dangerous answer. Clever enough to disguise her true intentions.

I folded my arms across my chest, anchoring myself against the pull radiating off her. "The dead do not need nostalgia. They need blood. And if you are looking for mine, you will leave here disappointed."

Her eyes flared, amusement sparking. "So certain!" She stepped back then, unhurried, like a carnivore deciding how to test its claws. "You don't smell like the others. Not quite human, not quite... like anything else I've known. Even for one gifted by the Godsblood." A pause, as if remembering something pleasant. "But that other girl also smelled like you..."

My muscles went taut. *Another?* I tracked her with my gaze, every instinct screaming. How common was the gift of Godsblood for her to already reference another?

Regardless, I needed her to be bored with me so I could find Violet. I racked my brain for memories from my first life that could help, and recalled how selective the Clans were when it came to breeding and compatibility.

I gambled on that knowledge and said, "If you seek a partner for your bloodline, the elders will not approve of an unsanctioned breeding."

It caught her off guard. "Unsanctioned?" She scoffed, the sound rather peculiar for someone who held herself so polished. "Yes, it would be unsanctioned, and Father would simply throw a fit. But that's not why I'm here."

Not here to either feed or breed? Interesting.

I played the part of the apathetic mortal. "It is good to know you Dark Bloods are still selective."

She laughed even harder, genuine amusement lighting her features, warm and rich in a way that set warning bells ringing. "Oh, how old-fashioned. I haven't heard that name in nearly a century." She wiped a tear from the corner of her eye. "You really *do* belong to another time."

I clenched my jaw, feeling my heart jump. "You have no idea how true that is."

For a heartbeat, her expression shifted. Amusement faltered, replaced with something sharper. Recognition? Curiosity?

"Your scent changed," she whispered, more to herself than me. "You're hiding something."

My stomach dropped, but I kept my voice even. "You should be careful with your guesses. Curiosity can kill more than just cats." And even more curious was knowing she could smell shifts in emotion.

"Oh, *muritor...* some secrets are worth dying for, don't you agree?"

She leaned close again, close enough I saw hunger flash behind her irises, a hunter rising to the surface.

She won't feed in broad daylight, I reminded myself. *Not with so many witnesses.*

My instincts didn't care about logic. They screamed for me to run as a memory from the Wastelands flashed in my mind: a brothel girl torn to shreds, blood painting walls, her screams cutting off mid-breath.

The vampyre smiled, soft and beautiful, and for the first time, I felt her allure slip past my defenses. If I hadn't been gifted, maybe I would've fallen into her glamour and been enthralled completely. As it was, the pull tugged at something deep.

She truly was a gorgeous monster.

She noted my lack of reaction and didn't seem disturbed. "Ah, lucky you." A pause, then softer, "We are merely tools for those that own us, are we not?"

The question felt rhetorical as she looked away.

Pity, I thought. Because I knew exactly how it felt to be at the mercy of others.

She glanced back. "I hope to see you again, stranger." Her perfume clung to the air like a spell as she brushed past me.

I stood rooted, fists tight, every sense alive with the urge to chase or run.

The threat was gone. But it didn't prove anything. One supernatural on campus didn't mean a conspiracy. It could have been a coincidence. There could have been a dozen other reasons she was here.

I exhaled slowly, forcing tension from my body.

Violet is somewhere in this maze. Find her, map her patterns, and get out.

I extended my senses, filtering through the noise. Hearts pounding in lecture halls, laughter from courtyards, footsteps crisscrossing paths. Too much sound, too many bodies. Like searching for a specific horse's hoofbeat in a stampede.

There.

Violet's voice cut through the chaos. Sharp edges wrapped in false confidence.

My heart clenched as I heard her say, "I am *not* weak. Oubliette is just a place. It does *not* own me."

Every muscle in my body went rigid. *Oubliette.* The name of a place I'd hoped didn't exist in this world, yet. A place that should have stayed buried with my first life. But there it was. Spoken in Violet's voice, casual as breathing, like she had no idea what kind of darkness that name carried.

I stood frozen on the campus lawn, students streaming past me like water around a stone. My mission had been simple: observe, map, leave.

Instead, I'd confirmed the one thing I'd been dreading.

Violet wasn't just connected to something dangerous. She was already inside it.

Well, fuck.

Chapter 7

Violet

The remainder of the day passed in a blur. My academic assignments were completed with a distracted inefficiency. I shot poorly and at one point lost an arrow to the woods behind the pasture. It was a shot I should have made with my eyes closed. My post-lesson evening ride with Hyacinth felt diminished; his powerful—and much to my dismay, *saddled*—gait beneath me barely registered.

If Aaron noticed my sour mood, he didn't comment on it, and instead he helped me clean up after our archery lesson. Although he spent the whole time grumbling about cleaning up the carcasses left behind by some *thing* hunting in the woods on the school grounds. I thanked him for his help before I took a quick shopping trip for the outfits I knew I would need.

Throughout the day and regardless of the activity, my nerves were alight with the fire of frustrated anxiety. Knowing that I was auditioning at Oubliette that night forced repeated panic attacks to continuously rise from the deep pit within me.

I had concocted a half-assed plan that relied far too much on other people letting me get my way. Every time I felt suffocated, I closed my eyes tight and recited: *Count to ten, Violet. You've danced thousands of times at one Oubliette or another for the asshole who bought you. You will be okay.*

Having the dorm to myself was serendipitous. After what felt like the millionth time, I tried to finish my makeup, and my shaking hands dropped the eyeliner. I had to pause again. *Violet Shaw, breathe! I am not defined by what happened to me. I am a survivor.*

The words, though truthful, did little despite how much I wished to believe them. Two lives battled inside me as I prepared for the night. The present me whispered caution and reminded me of everything I stood to lose. Old Violet laughed, bitter and knowing that I was going to possibly die tonight if my plan went awry.

You've died and come back once. What's to think it won't happen again?

Memories from my first life kept assaulting me as I struggled to get ready. Edward's mandatory humiliation of naked bodies while wealthy men sipped scotch and placed bets on which girl would falter first led to the pole becoming an instrument of both torture and freedom.

One mistake had meant the cane: blood running down thighs, welts rising on skin, then back up that cold metal. No excuses. No rest. Just climb and spin and pray you didn't slip in your own blood. Once mastered, the pole meant a night without groping hands or forced sexual favors.

Now, that skill would open doors I needed to walk through, though this body lacked the brutal strength I'd once earned through suffering. There were a handful of moves that I wasn't sure my softer muscles could perform. I didn't know if I had the core strength required.

There was only one way to find out.

This time, my fingers trembled as I applied my eyeliner, but I didn't drop it. When I'd finished my makeup, the mirror reflected back a stranger wearing my face. Someone beautiful and deadly. Someone with purpose.

I am whole. I stand in my power. He does not own me. I own myself.

Final touches were a classy black cocktail dress as I fussed over my sleek hair one last time before I grabbed my bag, stuffed my glittery stage outfit inside, and looked hard at myself in the mirror.

"I can do this," I said aloud like a prayer. "I am *strong*. I am *not* weak. Oubliette is just a place. It *does not* own me."

I didn't want to risk either ruining the new seven-inch heels I'd bought or spraining my ankle, so fifteen minutes later a rideshare carried me to my destination. The drive from the college to the shopping district near

Oubliette was barely a blink, carved through the nicest parts of the city along streets that dripped with wealth.

As I exited the car at the closest stop the driver could get me to, my heels clicked against pristine sidewalks where even the cracks seemed deliberately placed for aesthetic appeal. From a nearby designer boutique—the one where I'd bought the dress I was wearing, along with a replacement top for Alice—perfumed air wafted past me to mingle with the scent of expensive cigars and the subtle tang of new money.

Around me, the buildings rose as monuments to excess; gleaming glass and polished stone that caught the glow of the streetlights and magnified it. The whisper of fabric against skin surrounded me as people brushed past, their jewelry catching the light and sending prisms dancing across the pavement. I practically tasted the privilege in the air, and it was cloyingly sweet.

Only a block away, I saw the monumental building. The club devoured the night, black walls drinking every drop of streetlight, except for the gleaming sign that announced its name. Unlike most nightclubs, which would have had a line snaking around the city block filled with anxious wannabe patrons waiting for entrance, nobody stood outside of Oubliette. That was part of what made it so alluring, so sought after, so upscale—it was invitation only.

I stood at the corner and stared at Oubliette. I took deep breaths as I spent the better part of ten minutes trying in vain to think of an alternate path to Edward. When none came, I walked up the stone stairs and hesitated for a brief moment before I knocked. The weight of what I was about to do sank into my bones, and my heart slammed against my ribs.

"You can do this, Violet," I said to myself. "It's just a club... you're just dancing in a club."

After a few moments, the door opened.

No fucking way, I thought as I tried to breathe. A wall of a man whom I hadn't seen in years filled the doorway. Romeo towered before me, unchanged from my memories from my first life. He was immovable, expressionless, and massive. His black hair was slicked back, his suit cut to hide the weapon I knew rested against his ribs, the blood-red tie knotted at his throat... he was untouched by time and appeared exactly as I remembered him. My lungs seized, refusing air at the sight of him, at seeing this ghost from my stolen years standing solid and real.

Well, that answered my question on how close I'd been to my childhood home. I should not have been surprised at Edward's audacity to parade me around at a nightclub only an hour's drive from where I'd been kidnapped.

Even in my heels, Romeo towered over me. Snake tattoos coiled up his neck, black scales catching what little light touched them. Seeing them again reminded me with clarity of how well I knew their path, how they twisted down his torso to his navel. Being more than just a bouncer for Oubliette, I'd watched him strip and dance before. Now those inked serpents writhed with his pulse, with his breath. I almost took a step back, caught between the instinct to run and the need to do what I came to do.

His dark eyes bore into me, one brow lifting a fraction when he said, "Name?"

My voice trembled a little when I spoke. "Alexis," I lied. I had already decided on my stage name in the event that I secured the job.

"Were you given an invitation?"

"Um, no. I'd heard that a girl named Jules said you were looking for more dancers?" Another truth mixed with a lie slid between my lips.

Breathe. Stay steady and breathe. I feared the quiver in my legs and trembles shuttering through my body would betray me. Standing at the door to the club where Edward tortured me would do that, I suppose.

"Jules asked you to audition?" Romeo scanned my outfit, a doubtful look on his face as he noted the luxury brand cocktail dress that clung to me like a second skin.

Just because I came classy doesn't mean I can't dance, I wanted to blurt out. Instead, I said, "Not directly. As I said, a girl mentioned the work. I figured Monday was a slow enough night for me to swing by to see Jules."

With Romeo being here, the probability of Jules also being here was high. I was gambling on that.

Jules had been one of the girls who danced at Oubliette and one of the few bright spots I could recall from my previous life. Whenever Edward sent us to Oubliette to bleed for him, Jules did what she could to help. . . which, granted, was not much. But she was kind to me in a world where nobody else was. I had loved her for that despite never really understanding why she didn't report what she'd seen. Having her here meant I could unearth those questions.

I guess everyone is tied to one devil or another.

Romeo said, "Jules would know best. Will you be attending alone?"

Relief flooded my veins as I opened my mouth to confirm when a voice sliced through the night behind me. "No, she will be with me."

My head whipped towards the sound, a small gasp escaping my lips.

Rowan?

Dark clad and far too attractive than he had any right to be, Rowan stalked towards me, each step radiating the confidence of a predator who had cornered his prey. I caught the subtle tells of irritation bleeding through his mask—the tightness around his eyes, the barely controlled tension in his shoulders. No one else would notice. But I'd grown up with him. I knew.

Oh, he is pissed.

With my back to Romeo, I glared at Rowan and gave him a look that screamed, '*What are you doing here?*' The asshole just smiled at me, his usually insufferable half-smirk growing into a downright infuriating grin. Heat blossomed in my chest, a bouquet of consternation.

Rowan nodded to Romeo, then looked at me. "Sorry for being late, *princess*. Shall we?"

Impulse and juvenile habits took over. I reached out and pinched his thigh; hard, vicious, and with enough pressure I knew it would leave a hell of a mark—just like I used to do to him on our family camping trips when he *really* pissed me off. It was the *'fuck off, Rowan'* pinch.

The bastard captured my hand in his grip and his mouth pressed against my wrist, his lips against my pulse, hot breath ghosting across my skin. There was a twist low in my belly, a foreign heat that had no business existing from Rowan touching me.

"Patience," Rowan murmured against my wrist, his voice suddenly changing to a honey-sweet tone I've never heard from him. Like he was saying, "*Keep pushing and see what happens.*"

I struggled with how to respond, being unfamiliar with hearing such a tender tone from him.

Then Rowan had to open his mouth and say, "We should save the foreplay for when we are inside, *volchok*."

It was like he knew we were about to step into a sex club filled with potential predators. My patience was shot.

Also, *volchok?* What did that even mean?

"I simply couldn't wait," I replied sweetly. "Don't you want to wait back home for me?"

I snatched my hand away and immediately regretted it. Rowan's eyes glanced down at my fingers fidgeting with my purse—a terrible habit when I felt overwhelmed that I had picked up from my mother.

"Not a chance," he said in a doting tone.

But his eyes told a different story. They were brimming with a cold, glacier-blue fury. Anger lurked beneath his manufactured tenderness. Rowan simmered with the kind of quiet rage that promised retribution. I'd grown familiar with his different levels of animosity over years of pushing his buttons, testing boundaries, and finding the exact pressure points that made him crack.

Shit, he's really mad. Outraged, even.

Romeo's assessing gaze never left us. "You are allowed one guest to accompany you. Is he your partner?"

"No," I said, over Rowan's, "Yes."

Romeo merely raised a brow and waited.

I raised a finger, "Can you just. . . give us one moment, please?" I asked before turning to face Rowan. We took a few steps away from the bouncer in the doorway before I hissed, "Are you *serious* right now?"

"*Da.*" He confirmed as he took one assessing look at my hair, my face, and my outfit. I swear I saw his pupils dilate before he said, "You will take me inside of this place with you, else I will spank your ass all the way back home to your daddy."

Don't tempt me, I nearly said, but refrained. Probably not the best time, especially since all I wanted to do was strangle him. I massaged the bridge of my nose before I whispered, "Fine. But let me be clear that you are *not* welcome here."

Rowan's shit-eating grin did little to stop the anxiety pooling in my stomach as he took my arm into his.

Perfect. Fucking perfect. My plan's going great.

We both looked at Romeo. Knowing my first impression had been shot to hell, I sighed and said, "Yeah. He's my plus one."

Romeo frowned, but turned to grip the iron handle as he said, "Very well." The click of the sleek doorknob resonated in the night. "In that case... welcome to Oubliette."

The door swung open, welcoming us in, and my nostrils flared at the potent cocktail that assaulted them; rich dark leather mingling with notes of sandalwood. Beneath it all lurked a scent both primal and dangerous, a musk that whispered sin against my skin. The interior of Oubliette gleamed in obsidian perfection, every polished black surface catching fragments of the subdued lighting, scattering it across the room like leaves in the wind.

We followed Romeo through the press of bodies. Shadows danced along the walls, alive with purpose as they cloaked figures who lingered in corners. The bass vibrated through the soles of my feet, a heartbeat pulsing through the floor and into my bones. On stage, dancers twisted around poles, occasionally tossing their scraps of clothing into the crowd like confetti. Their diamond-studded clothing caught the spotlight, flesh on display for the hungry stares that followed every calculated movement.

I swallowed and tried to still my thundering heart. This place—and Oubliettes like it—haunted my nightmares, filled my thoughts with terror, and now I stood inside its gleaming black walls... with Rowan.

Deep breaths. Deep breaths, I chanted to myself. *As soon as we get to the bar and manage a sliver of privacy, I'm going to force him to tell me why he is here.*

Rowan followed close behind me, his body radiating heat like a furnace. His hand found mine and he squeezed. I looked down, a frown creasing my face and asked, "What are you doing?"

"I am claiming ownership," he stated. He said it simply, as if his mere presence was enough to send a silent warning to every potential predator in the room.

I whispered, "I don't need your help." I tried to pull my hand away, but he held on. "And I'm *not* yours to claim ownership of." I didn't need his alpha male bullshit in that moment.

A well-dressed drunken man laughed as he nearly stumbled into me. The idiot would have bowled me over had Rowan not pulled me out of the way and held me against his chest. The contact electrified my skin as the scent of pine and smoke wrapped around me. *Oh my god, why does he smell so good?*

Romeo's apology was muffled behind me. The sounds of his receding steps led me to believe he went to assist the drunken patron. I tried to steady my racing heart. "Rowan? You can let me go now."

He made a sound of disgust and released me, his hand still clutched in mine. "Stupid drunk." He assessed me. "Are you alright?"

"Am I—what?" Between the stress from lack of sleep, his foiling my plans, and trying to mentally prepare to be in this nightmarish prison where I had endured so much pain, the question was enough to trigger me.

Whatever air I had in that moment dissipated as my anxiety skyrocketed, forcing my breathing to wheeze in and out in shallow rasps. Rowan's eyes widened, and he immediately folded me back into him.

"Violet, talk to me. Your heart is going crazy."

I laughed, caught off guard by the absurdity of it. "My what? What does that even mean?"

"It means we can turn away and go if needed. Whatever this is, whatever reason brought you here? We can find another way."

Hope bloomed like an unfurling flower greeting spring's promise. He had said 'we' and the words slipped deep inside my chest, nestling in a place I had kept locked away in preparation for this vengeance plot. I hadn't realized how badly I had wanted to hear those words from someone in my other life—that whatever monsters lurked in this beautiful hell, I wouldn't face them alone.

He doesn't know what he's getting into. There shouldn't be a 'we'. He doesn't deserve to get into this mess. The grim realization that I couldn't drag him into this was like cold water being poured on me.

"I can't," I said and pushed away from Rowan. I glanced over to see Romeo finishing up tending to the drunk. I plastered a practiced smile on my face. "I'm fine," I lied.

He arched his brow, giving me a skeptical look, but he said nothing. Romeo's familiar baritone voice cut in, "Everything alright?"

"Yes," I breathed, making every effort to appear composed as I looked back at him. "I simply needed a moment. We're ready."

We all made our way to the obsidian bar. Romeo signaled the bartender, who was fulfilling a drink order for a waitress dressed like a flight attendant. After a silent exchange, the bartender came closer with a phone in his hand. The morbid realization crashed into me that, throughout all the years of captivity in my first life, I'd never thought to steal someone's phone to get away. *How pathetic was I?*

Romeo turned to look at me, his gaze dark and penetrating, as he sized me up. I kept my eyes downcast, hoping to appear as demure as Alice's friend. He still looked stunning. His dark hair framed a face highlighted by his bronze complexion.

He said to the bartender, "Andy, she's here to audition. Ring Jules for her." Then he pointed to a stool at the bar. "Stay put," he said before he headed back towards the front door.

I took in an eyeful of his broad back and tight ass—perfectly hugged by the dark jeans he wore—and couldn't help but wonder if he still danced.

Rowan leaned close, his breath hot against my ear, his voice a low rumble only I could catch. "Violet, do you enjoy ogling men like him?"

I jumped, covering my ear from his invasion as my pulse raced with an electric mix of trepidation and anticipation. "Ogling? Is that why you're here?" I whispered back. "Giddy to see a naked woman for the first time, Rowan? I'm surprised your dad isn't here for your first big boy night out." My words cracked at the edges, betraying my uneasiness at the situation.

Rowan sensed my discomfort. "This is not a place for Charlie, *princess*. Besides," he said with that same insufferable smirk, "We both know that he has eyes for only one woman."

"Ugh, *gross*! Don't bring my mom into this." Being intentionally crude while also pointing out the polygamist elephant in the room regarding our parents was enough to pull a soft laugh from me. "I don't know what those three have going on, but they really need to figure it out and just tell us like we're adults."

Rowan lowered his chin as he sighed dramatically. "I do believe that hell may have frozen over. For once, we agree on something."

I was still pissed that Rowan was there, but I had to admit that his small talk helped settle my nerves... at least a little.

"Good evening," the bartender said, cutting through our private moment. "And what may I have the pleasure of serving you two on this fine summer evening?" He asked in a lilting, sing-song way that forced a smile to my face. The man's voice was like soft butter spread on warm brown bread.

He definitely sings, I thought.

"Water," I said quickly. Years of listening to Jules had taught me the unwritten rules of this place. Girls who drank before dancing became liabilities; clumsy, unfocused, vulnerable. I needed every sense to be razor-sharp. That was usually the first test.

The bartender smiled, genuine warmth lighting his features. His dark braids swung with tiny bells that sang soft music with each movement. His chest gleamed, naked under the dim lights, and I saw circular barbell rings piercing his nipples, catching the light like twinkling stars.

I thought about my own nipple piercings. I still felt like a newborn fawn struggling to take its first steps anytime I had to dress or undress. Unable to help myself, my mouth spoke before my brain stopped it. "Aren't you ever afraid of catching those?" I asked as I gestured to his pierced nipples. I immediately flushed, realizing how personal the question was.

Screw being coy. These bad boys on me are an accident waiting to happen.

He chuckled softly, the sound like velvet against raw nerves, unwinding the tightness inside my chest. "You mean how do you not catch them on things?"

I nodded. "I just got mine, and it's been... an adjustment," I confided. Behind me, I heard Rowan curse, and from my peripheral vision, I saw he had his head tipped back. His eyes were pinched as if in pain.

He's going to have to get comfortable real soon if I'm going to be dancing nude in front of him. The thought sent butterflies of nerves throughout me.

"A little pain is fine with me," the bartender admitted, his melodic voice now as rich as bourbon. A playful spark lit his eyes, transforming his face from beautiful to dangerous. "Though I sometimes tie my hair up, to keep the bells from ringing." He flicked one of the silver bells in his hair, the tiny sound punctuating his words. "I'm Andy. I'll grab your water. And for you, sir?"

"*Kompot*," Rowan said without hesitation.

The word hit me like a jolt, and I snapped my head to him. What the hell had he ordered?

"Ah, a man of culture," Andy chuckled as if Rowan had told him a particularly funny joke. His knowing smile lingered as he turned and disappeared into the press of bartenders and busboys behind the bar.

My eyes shot to Rowan. "What in the world is a *Kompot*?" The word scraped against my ears.

Rowan's laugh caught me off guard; a deep, rich sound I'd only ever heard from him once or twice when he was with Charlie. It was like finding warmth in winter and made my toes involuntarily curl.

He pulled his bar stool closer, sinking into it with that relaxed predatory ease he possessed that prickled my skin. "*Kompot*. It is a drink made from cooked fruits and berries," he said playfully. "You should try it. It is popular with children, so you would enjoy it."

I rolled my eyes. Screw him and his little jabs. "I can't drink alcohol before I dance." I kept my voice flat, practical. Survival mode. Focus on the job, not the man watching me with those frozen lake eyes.

"It is not alcoholic. But nevermind," he said as he shook his head. "You bring me to my first question..." His voice dropped to an intimate register, each word a stone dropping into still water.

I got the impression I was not going to like the conversation as his eyes pierced me, stripping away my carefully haphazard mix of armor.

"What are you doing here, *princess*? Do you realize Levi would burn this place to the fucking ground if he knew you were here?"

I parted my lips to answer, but the words stuck in my throat. I almost slipped and said, "*I'm here to hunt the man who killed me,*" but I knew the absurdity of how that would sound. What could I have said that he would believe?

"*Nothing,*" Edward's twisted voice snaked through my thoughts. "*This man will never understand you, Violet. You aren't special. You are nothing.*"

My fingers curled against the bar top's edge, nails biting into wood, trying to focus on the moment. It was solid. Real. I was grateful when the performance ended, and the club's darkness swallowed me whole; the seductive bass pounding like a second heartbeat, before lights flashed and bodies began writhing once more in shadows around us.

"I. . ." I stumbled. Rowan watched me with those winter-pale eyes, and within that gaze lived worry tangled with something else I couldn't place.

I sucked in air, let it fuel the steel in my voice. "I'm here to dance," I said finally. "To earn some money. Nothing more, nothing less." Part lie, part truth. Daddy *had* denied me money.

"Money?" He said incredulously, as if I had told him Santa was real. I nodded a little too hard, feeling like my jaw would dislocate.

Please buy it, Rowan. Please.

"Daddy wouldn't let me access my trust and I. . ." I couldn't finish. "Money, Rowan. That's all."

He leaned back, that almost-smile playing at the corner of his mouth. "Nothing more?"

"Nothing more." The lie felt acidic on my tongue.

The music swelled from the stage, filling me with a desperation to get up there and take ownership of myself. I needed to banish the ghosts from my past. My stomach knotted. This had been my world once. In another life. In another body.

When I finally get to dance, I thought, *it will be a declaration that my body belongs to me. Only me.*

Rowan shifted closer, becoming a barrier between me and the rest of the club, as if he were trying to remind me where my focus should lie. On him. . .

I said, "You'd better leave unless you *want* to see me naked."

Rowan scoffed. "The shame of nudity is self-imposed. You are like a sister to me, Violet. I do not care if you are nude or not." He nodded towards the stage. "Besides, I respect all women and do not judge their careers. I would not treat you any differently."

He spoke as if nothing else would factor into his outlook. Against my better judgement, I found it oddly endearing.

The bartender took that moment to slide our drinks across the bar. I wrapped my fingers around the cool glass and brought it to my lips.

The water slid down my throat, soothing the burn there, steadying the tremble in my hands.

"Well, that's unexpectedly mature of you." I cleared my throat.

He shrugged as he sipped his drink. "It is not hard to be a decent human being."

I closed my eyes as flashbacks of my other life brushed behind my lids. The overwhelming *absence* of decent human beings in that life forced a sardonic laugh from me. "It's hard for most people." The words were so heavy on my lips.

Rowan's eyes narrowed as he studied me. He reached over, his hand finding mine and squeezed it. "Violet. . ." He paused. "I am only going to ask this because your heart—" He stopped then tried again. "You do not seem yourself. Did someone hurt you? Are you in trouble?"

Despite the deafening pounding of the music, I heard every word he said as my heart clenched.

No, not here. Not now. I can't tell him. I can't tell anyone.

Tears pricked my eyes as I placed my drink down. "No, Rowan. No one hurt me." The lie stung so much I could barely contain the fresh tears that wanted to spill. I felt oddly vulnerable sitting in the city's most prestigious gentlemen's club, knowing I would not be able to escape the path I had taken, surrounded by the very place that tried to break me.

The red string of fate would never let me go.

Rowan took that moment to pull me to him, head resting on top of my head, and I didn't have the strength to fight him. "You can lie all you want with that mouth of yours, but your body betrays you."

My breath caught, and it took every effort to not break.

No, I will not waiver. I pulled away, watching his hands fall to his sides, and shook my head. "I'm not lying, Rowan. Even if I was, it would be for the greater good."

"For the greater good? How noble of you. Are you a superhero now?" He clicked his tongue, but didn't push me any further.

A flash of movement caught my eye, breaking whatever intimate moment there was between us. Jules rounded the corner, her face glowing under the club's lighting. Platinum hair cascaded past her barely covered breasts, held by nothing but wisps of fabric. She commanded the space without trying, her entire being a living fantasy. Men stared. Women measured themselves against her. The unattainable standard of beauty packaged in five-foot-five inches of curves and confidence.

"Hi there, sweetie! I'm sorry to keep you waiting," she said, piercing blue eyes flicking to me with a mix of curiosity and apology. She stepped forward, offering the briefest hug, perfunctory yet warm. "I'm so sorry, but... I don't seem to know your name?"

"Alexis," I replied, voice steady despite my pulse. A small flush warmed my cheeks. "I overheard a girl complaining you needed more bodies here, and your name was dropped."

"Oh! Do you happen to know the girl's name?" she inquired gently.

I shrugged. "No, sorry... I hope that's okay?"

Her eyes lit up, bright and genuine. "Oh, that's alright! We just weren't expecting any girls this week, but as it happens, I can squeeze in an audition now." She pivoted to Andy, speaking with authority. "Let the sound guy know to play one of our entry songs in the next fifteen minutes." She turned back to me. "I'm the one who typically handles the girls, so you can direct any questions to me." Her voice carried a confidence that shrank the room, marking her territory without effort.

"Yes, ma'am."

"Ugh," Jules groaned. "Do *not* call me ma'am. I'm not that old, sweetie. Now, tell me a little about yourself."

My gut twisted as she stared, her eyes dissecting me. Images from my previous life flashed by: Jules placing her hands over my own and guiding me on a pole, her voice gentle but firm as she showed me how to move. "*Arch your back more. Feel the music. Like that, yes!*"

The first hurdle was a fitness test. Was I even in good enough shape to be on the stage?

I cleared my throat. "I have trained in Brazilian Jiu-Jitsu, archery, and equestrianism from a very young age, so... I'm in good shape."

Jules nodded. "Well, the horsemanship will help those legs of yours. I'm not sure about the rest, especially since you didn't mention any dancing."

She stepped around me, eyeing my body. I tried not to fidget with my dress and almost missed Rowan's hand as it brushed against mine, barely there. The whisper of contact anchored me as his fingers slowly grazed mine in a tantalizing spell that made my breath catch. I looked up, flushed, and caught his eyes watching me. My body was on fire, and it wasn't from the club lights.

Jules's voice broke the spell as I yanked my hand away. "Your friend will need to wait here, sweetie. Is that alright?" She glanced between us, curiosity sparkling beneath her long lashes.

"Of course." I cut my eyes to Rowan, noting the hard tick in his jaw, the tension coiling in his shoulders. "My *friend* can wait, right?"

Please say yes, Rowan. I need *this.* I looked at him with pleading eyes.

Which must have gotten through to him, because he replied with a grumbly, "*Da.*"

Jules looked at me, confused, and I clarified. "He means yes. Sorry. He's an idiot who forgets to speak English sometimes."

Jules laughed and clapped her hands together. "Follow me this way, please."

She guided me deeper into the club, her gaze crawling over me like a physical touch. Every instinct in my body screamed caution as she cataloged my walk.

Jules asked, "Did you bring an outfit in your bag, or will you need to borrow one from our wardrobe?"

The next hurdle was a competence test. Was I a professional here to audition for a job, or just a dumb college kid looking to make a quick buck by shaking her ass?

"I brought my own outfit."

"Alrighty, so professional! I love it, sweetie. Now, let's get you dressed for success."

She led me to the changing rooms, which were covered in glitter and smelled of expensive perfume. The other dancers, all lovely ranges of body types, were busying themselves with their own wardrobes. None of them even looked at me.

I felt Jules's gaze, however, as I stripped out of my street clothes and shimmied into the silver mesh of my barely there outfit. Part of me knew that I should have hated the invasiveness. . . but I didn't. If anything, it offered me an odd comfort. A ghost of familiarity.

"You think you have skill on the pole, sweetie?" Jules asked, her tone as warm as homemade cookies.

I straightened my spine, letting a whisper of confidence slide through the cracks in my facade. "I do. I've... danced before. Very well, I've been told." *Told by you once, in another life.*

Jules's smile grew even larger. "I love to hear that note of confidence in you!" She offered me her hand and led me to the side of the stage behind heavy curtains. "A tiny bit of advice? Don't look at the patrons. Just watch the lights and let the music move you. First time's the hardest." She patted my back in a motherly gesture that brought almost tears to my eyes. "Let's see what you bring to Oubliette," Jules said, oblivious to my nostalgia.

I inhaled sharply, pulling in the scent of leather, metal, and sweat. I stepped forward, brushing heavy velvet curtains into the darkness of the stage, there within the dark heart of the club.

Here's to reclaiming myself, I thought, and the lights turned on.

Chapter 8

Rowan

*I*f Violet knew how dangerous this place was, she never would have come. Harsh thoughts that competed with the lighting of the club between sets. It was taking immeasurable willpower to not storm back there and drag her ass home.

As if that would deter her.

Violet had a nasty habit of surprising me lately, and she was beginning to be a sore subject for all of the shit I was having to deal with between her dad and the wild fucking goose chase she led me on. Her existence was chaos, muddled by the choices she made that affected so many around her that she refused to accept the consequences of her actions. It was infuriating. Not to mention, I was back in an Oubliette when I had sworn to myself I would never step foot inside one after my last bout. Oh, how the fates laugh at me.

I could do a horse gag tie to keep her in check, or throw her over my shoulder and spank her like I threatened earlier.

No, that wouldn't work. Violet was a raging storm, leaving trails of terror in her wake, and I could no longer ignore how much space she was taking up in my head, defying my neat, orderly, mapped-out logic with each breath she took. My ward and burden.

Yet when she nearly cried to me... I felt my hardened resolve dissipate like the smoke curling from the nearby patrons' cigars. I could handle bratty and unhinged Violet, but the broken girl who looked at me the same way Faelin had? It almost undid me.

Faelin...

A name from my first life that I had nearly forgotten. Memories of her wet cough and ferocious fever, followed by a failed deal that had led to my endless servitude. All of which had culminated in my failed attempt to steal that cursed book from The Library.

What a life I had lived indeed.

I pushed the thought away and focused on the issue at hand, setting my hand against the cool marble of the bar, and feeling the synergy of supernaturals resonate all around me. It was suffocating and deafening being here, knowing the monsters that lurked in the corners. I may not have the same olfactory sensors as the vampyre I met earlier, but I could *feel* and *hear* the subtle differences of *them*.

In a nearby booth, two identical twins—both of them vampyres—were entwined with a woman. They spared me a glance and their matching heterochromia, one eye so brown it was nearly black and the other bright blue, was striking. Their pale bodies wrapped around the light skinned woman with a practiced grace before one twin buried his face between her thighs. He dove down with the casual possession that comes from centuries of thoughtless indulgence.

I felt the pull of their allure as it touched on those around them, oblivious or simply uncaring, as it fed their delirium that was this hell. No heartbeats, no breathing, just the wet slide of feeding. I only prayed it was consensual.

It wasn't my fight, so I turned to survey the room more.

My sense of smell wasn't nearly as enhanced as my hearing. However, it was still far better than a normal mortal's, and that was how I smelled the wild musk of a *shifter* on the bodyguard. It made sense for the club to have a wolf as a guard dog, but it did give me pause.

He will be difficult to kill, if it ever comes to that.

My ears picked through the club's noise, hunting truth beneath the chaos. Behind the bar, the bartender's breathing came with that distinctive wet gurgle of what I presumed was a siren, like lungs half-filled with water that never quite drowns them. It fit with how his voice had been.

There was one demon—an incubus, possibly—who looked just as human as me and Violet laughing at the other end of the bar; I heard the pulse of his heart thrumming in an impossible rhythm in his belly. A fitting spot for a demon that fed on human lust.

The girl Jules had seemed human enough, either ignorant or simply accepting of those who walked these rooms. The girl whom Violet overheard whispering about needing more bodies was most likely laying bait. Setting lures for unsuspecting girls who were ripe for feeding. I was curious to know how far depravity fell in these walls, *or* how those that are supposed to remain hidden seemed to refuse the natural cycle of things.

And I'm in the fucking middle of this mess, I thought.

When it comes to Violet, nothing seemed to go according to plan. She was obviously in something that was more complicated than what she could handle, and here I was, ready to accept whatever came this way as her fucked up nanny. I was beginning to think that the Fates hadn't glitched when they allowed me to resurrect here, but instead, placed the burden of Violet upon my shoulders, dragging me so deep into the pit of the damned that even Hades would laugh.

I shivered at the thought. Every muscle in my body burned with the need to intervene, to yank her from this place before she stepped onto that stage. The urge crawled beneath my skin like frost spreading across a winter lake.

But that isn't an option.

If it were any other person, I would have left them to deal with digging their own grave, but this is Violet—and Charlie would never forgive me. If I stormed back there now, made a scene, searched for Violet. . . there would be trouble. The problem was that Violet was too damn stubborn. I could have tried to throw her over my shoulder like a sack of potatoes, and she would have responded with violence.

And she would have every right to do so. You would do the same. I ran my hand down my face.

I had spent so many years in the Wastelands protecting myself that when I tried to protect another, it had gotten me a life sentence. Now, I was repeating the same mistake. I hated not sticking to my original plan. Subterfuge and simply reporting back home.

So, I sat imprisoned by circumstance, a wolf forced to watch a member of its pack walk into a trap, maintaining the fiction of indifference while terror for her clawed at my insides. My hands gripped the edge of the bar, knuckles white with restraint, as I battled the raw, primal fear of losing someone again. I'd vowed to protect her.

If I didn't have this fucking bleeding heart.

The music slammed into my chest, matching my heartbeat beat for beat, vicious and unrelenting. Bass crawled up through the floor and into my marrow while synthesizers screamed across the packed room like souls trapped between worlds, sounds reaching for me from every direction. Yet, try as I could, I could not hear past the stage. It was almost as if there was a ward or wall prohibiting my hearing, which only heightened my paranoia.

Fuck, what was I thinking? I should not have let her go back there. She could be getting coerced or kidnapped for all I know. I know what resides in these shitholes. It's always the same—supernaturals indulging in controlled chaos, always at the expense of another. This was no exception.

I couldn't even imagine what they'd have her doing back there and with whom. Something harsh dug into my ribs at the thought of her grinding her hips on some siren scum's cock. I'd be damned if I'd let these fucking dipshits see an ounce of what wasn't theirs.

I told myself five minutes, and then I would go back there, damned or not.

I sipped my *kompot*, letting sweet berry notes flood my tongue. Bits of strawberry and blackberry swam in the blood-red liquid, their bite slicing through the sugar syrup. I didn't ask for it to be made alcoholic, but I wasn't surprised to taste a splash of vodka.

Underage serving is the least of their concerns given the type of clientele they serve, I mused.

I took another sip as it burned a path down my throat. The icy glass against my palm was cool and distracting from my guts tying themselves into knots.

Andy arrived with a water to accompany my drink and asked, "So, my dashing young gentleman, do you think your friend will dance well for us this evening?" He nodded his head towards the stage, and the bells in his hair tinkled with the movement. The noise—his siren voice mingled with his jangling bells—scraped against my eardrums like nails on frozen glass.

I shot him a dismissive look, though I could not quite hide the pride threading through my words as I said, "She is as stubborn as a stone mule. When she decides to do a thing, the thing will be done."

But in truth, I was not sure if Violet had the first clue how to dance on a stage, on a pole, in front of a crowd. Why would she? Where would she have learned anything of the sort? I prepared for this to devolve into a disaster.

"And to see her nude must be exciting for you." A smile broke across Andy's face, genuine and wide, exposing those sharp canines that caught the light like polished knives. That simple change in his expression froze my blood: partly from the predator sitting inches from me, but more from realizing what Violet was indeed about to do.

Shit, shit. Levi would skin me and hang me like a pelt if he knew I saw his daughter...

The music transformed, its rhythm slowing to a seductive crawl that hooked every patron's attention like fish on a line, including mine. *Fuck, too late now.* With grim realization, I accepted my fate. The club's atmosphere thickened as conversations died mid-sentence, glasses froze halfway to lips, and breathing synchronized with the vibrating bass.

Violet emerged into the spotlight, her silhouette cutting against the bleeding crimson and royal purple lights that painted her edges in fire. Her dark tresses trailed down her athletic frame, shiny and thick, before ending above her perfectly heart-shaped ass. Her profile took my breath away. *She looks fucking sinful.* The scent of expensive perfume and anticipation hung in the air, mingling with the sharp tang of alcohol and sweat. My fingers tightened around the cold glass.

Do not fall off the pole.

She did not. By the eyes of every one of the gods, she did not.

Violet transformed on that pole. She wrapped her thighs around the cold metal, muscles tensing with the perfect control of someone who'd done it a thousand times. The arch of her spine and sway of her body told stories her mouth never had. Her chocolate hair whipped across her face as she inverted, the red streaks catching fire under the lights.

For each twist during her dance, the angles and distances and required leverages were executed with the fineness of someone who owned the stage with her presence. Her fingers gripped and released with deliberate rhythm, her body suspended in defiance of gravity. When she slid slowly and sensually down the pole, my cock hardened painfully against my jeans.

Andy made a noncommittal sound, "She does indeed do it well."

I wanted to reply, but my mouth was arid as I struggled to breathe. Her skin gleamed with sweat, highlighting the contrast between fragility and power, and I felt the undeniable urge to lick the sweat off her body. The silver mesh of her outfit clung to curves, cutting through the oxygen in the room until breathing felt like theft. Her legs, strong from years of training, scissored around the pole with a grace that belied their lethal potential, and my hips flexed involuntarily against the chair, wishing they were wrapped around mine.

I knew desire, had even rolled in its grasp when I allowed myself to. But this was a visceral need, a craving for a woman I had only seen as a brat until now. *Violet, you are becoming less volchok and more volk.*

When she hung suspended by just her thighs, her hands reaching towards the floor, the room collapsed into a singularity of want. I watched her, my balls tight while I gripped the glass so hard I felt like it would shatter. Every twist, every curve, every sharp inhale she made pulled me deeper. And against my better judgement, I couldn't look away. I struggled against the bone-deep desire to touch her— an urge both beautiful and savage.

The crowd shifted, whispers slithering through shadows as Violet danced. I caught the flash of sharp teeth, the low rumble of hungry voices, the subtle pulse of power from creatures I'd learned to fear long ago. The vampyre twins nearby leaned closer, fingers brushing against each other while their eyes never left her. A wolf's growl vibrated from another in the corner, too dark to see except for his profile. Even Andy, that siren bastard, watched with a face split between awe and hunger. Danger saturated the air, but Violet moved as if she were the most dangerous thing in the room.

Don't you fucking look at her, I wanted to snarl. Bare my teeth in a possessive instinct as every safeguard screamed at me to snatch her off that stage and vanish into the night.

Instead, I smiled, because for as much as they craved her, they would not break the safety that is their hidden world, and as much as I hated to admit it, there was a perverse pleasure in knowing she would walk out with me and not another. She had chosen this path and—as reckless as it was—the fire in her had always burned beyond my control. *Beyond anyone's control, really.* Hers was a fire I had no right to extinguish. I would walk out with her in my arms, burning just as Icarus had done.

I loosened my grip on my drink; every cell in my body wanted to break anyone who dared breathe in her direction. Instead, I focused on her, burning into memory every flick of her wrist, every stretch of muscle, every subtle arch of her spine. As the thin scraps of fabric fell away, my heart quickened just like everyone else's.

Her body curved around the pole, sliding down with a controlled precision that I knew had to require a rock-hard core and steel-trap willpower. Her nipple piercings caught the light, tiny glints of metal against flesh as her fingers reached for that last piece of her outfit. And then... she smiled.

Ah, gods above and below, she was desire made manifest.

When she completed that final spin, her body flowing down the pole in one liquid motion, an uncomfortable truth I'd buried beneath survival and cynicism began to take root. I wondered what it would feel like to have her cunt wrapped around me—would she ride me with that same wild abandonment? Would she smile the same way as her legs wrapped around my shoulders, forcing me to taste her? I shifted uncomfortably in my chair and groaned into my glass.

There in Oubliette, surrounded by immortal predators with appetites both ancient and depraved, I knew with a bone-deep certainty I would sacrifice anything to shield her and to keep her safe. Dangerous thoughts lingered in my mind, like a wound slowly beginning to fester, daring me to wish for something beyond what I had told myself was possible with my childhood friend.

Fuck.

Chapter 9

Violet

Jules practically danced beside me as I stepped down from the stage, fabric clutched to my chest. My lungs burned, heartbeat rattling against ribs, realizing I'd overestimated my stamina. Pole dancing for an audience is nothing like riding Hyacinth across open fields, the footwork of fencing, or the movements of jiu-jitsu. My body ached in ways I had forgotten.

"Oh my God, Alexis! That was magnificent!" Jules squealed, grabbing my hands, her garnet nails glinting as she bounced on her heels. "I haven't seen anyone dance that well since, well, me, of course."

The irony tasted bittersweet. "Thanks," I managed, the word scraping my throat raw.

"Come on," she urged, tugging me towards the back. "Let's get you changed before you freeze."

But I feel too hot, I almost wanted to whine. I was sweating, dizzy from the high of endorphins.

To think I hadn't performed in. . . well, since before I was killed. The dark thought slithered forth as I fought to push it back down.

Back in the changing room, I wiped the sweat off my body and slipped back into my street clothes. The only item that stayed the same were my heels and I regretted not bringing a pair of flats when my feet screamed against the cold floor, blisters forming where the heels had rubbed my skin raw.

It would take a few months for calluses to form, I thought then realized, I was already planning on doing this for a long time. *Or however long it takes*, I chided myself. I didn't care what demon I was trading with, I wanted Edward served on a meathook.

I finished, and was startled when I caught my reflection. There stood a woman I almost didn't recognize: dark brown nearly black hair streaked with red and clinging to temples, eyes bright with adrenaline and the deepest flush. I looked tired but... like I just had finished the best fuck session of my life. I laughed to myself. I tried to fix my tousled hair and failed.

Stepping back out, I met with Jules who was speaking with another dancer, the lovely redhead I had watched earlier.

Jules was nodding excitedly. "Yes, it's a lovely fit. You'll be able to take a break for a bit."

The girl squealed and gave Jules a big hug and I watched in fascinated mortification as their well endowed breasts squished comically together.

"Oh, thank you Jules!" The redhead said and then saw me. "And you! What a killer set. You were so amazing." Her praise brought another flush to my face and I mumbled a thank you.

"You were so lovely on stage." I provided, motioning to her gorgeous emerald green piece she wore. "And you look so cute. I really adore that color."

"Thanks. It's cliche but green looks good on our pale skin and red hair." She pointed to her red curls that I was immediately jealous of when I saw how tight and glossy they were. "I'm Brianna by the way. My friends call me Bri. Stage name is Red which seems silly but my patrons love it."

She gave me her hand and I felt self conscious shaking it. "Are you Irish by any chance?"

She nodded. "Don't have much of the accent. How could you tell?"

I smiled. "Oh, the Stablemaster at the school has a similar lilt."

Brianna clasped my hand with a warm smile. "You've met Aaron? He's my little brother!"

Small world I suppose. "He's a good guy," I said, falling back on the words Daddy used.

She beamed. "Aw, thank you. I adore him though he can be a stick in the mud." She whispered the last bit, "Doesn't agree with my work, but he's respectful of my choices."

"Then he really is a good guy. I'll try not to give him a hard time next time I see him."

That caused her to giggle before she started off. "He can take a beating. Can't wait to work with you more after my break!" She waved as she left.

"So?" I asked, pulling my hair back with trembling fingers. "Am I hired?"

"Yes. Bri needed to take a break for this semester. She's a junior studying at the nearby school so she's been stressed. This works out well."

I nodded in understanding. "I actually just started there, so I'm happy to hear I might see her on campus. So," I paused before asking the obvious question, "when do I start?"

Jules cocked her head like she was listening to something out of earshot. Her eyes unfocused for a second, then snapped back to me with that familiar, unnerving clarity.

"Four days," she said, holding up four red-tipped fingers. "Come back in four days. I'll speak with the proprietor tomorrow and I know that he'll take a day or two to mull it over." She beamed like a proud mother, and something in my chest cracked.

Don't you remember me? I wanted to scream. *Don't you remember it was you who taught me to dance like that?*

But this Jules had never met me. Less than an hour ago, I was a stranger to her.

I swallowed the words and nodded instead.

"Thanks. I should probably be honest and tell you my real name is Violet, but I'd like to go by Alexis. . . if that's alright?"

"Absolutely. Paperwork needs the legal name anyways." After a moment of silence, she mistook it for nerves. "You were born for this," she continued, oblivious to the war in my head. "The way you move. . . it's like you've been doing it your whole life."

Half my life, I thought. *The worst half.*

I forced a smile. "Thanks for the opportunity."

"Are you kidding? Thank *you* for the audition. The crowd loved you. I'll go over more when you meet with me Friday. Leave your number with Andy. By the way, your boyfriend's still at the bar," Jules said, taking a moment to borrow some lotion from one of the other girls with a quick thank you. "The hot one who looks like he wants to murder everyone."

Rowan. I'd almost forgotten he was there, watching. Watching *me* dance. My stomach clenched.

"He's *not* my boyfriend," I replied automatically.

Jules laughed, the sound pure and bright. "Honey, the way he watched you? You are at least *something* to him."

No, he's just pissed at me right now.

"I really don't think he sees me that way." I stumbled with my words, wondering why I felt so upset at them. *He calls you princess and often mentions how much of a child you are. Not exactly boyfriend material.*

Jules patted me affectionately. "Sometimes it takes a while to admit our feelings."

I didn't answer, just shouldered my bag and followed her back through the labyrinth of Oubliette's backstage area. The walls pressed close, velvet and shadow as my shoulders drew tight with coiled nerves. I wondered what Rowan thought, then felt annoyed at myself for caring.

You didn't perform for him though, I chided myself. While I had never willingly performed for anyone in my previous life and Jules' words of affirmation did not hit the way I thought they would, I had wanted to impress Rowan. Pride is a funny thing. It blooms in the strangest soil, grows thorns when you least expect them.

A few hundred feet ahead, I could see over Jules' head that Rowan was still hunched at the bar, his drink barely touched. Despite the taut line in his shoulders, I was relieved. Coming to Oubliette had been a gamble, and with how unsure I felt of how things would go, he had been my inadvertent anchor despite how annoyed I had been with his presence. Now with his profile sharp in the low light, I steeled myself for the lecture I knew was coming.

As we passed a table, he stiffened. Instinctively, I followed his gaze to where two men and a woman were entangled in shadows, shameless in their public display. One man's face was buried between her thighs, the other stroking her neck. But the light caught enough that I could see the second man's mismatched and unblinking eyes. Goosebumps erupted on my skin. His gaze was locked onto me, drinking in every movement.

I don't like that look. I'd seen it before, in my previous life. The look of an aggressor marking prey.

Jules didn't seem to notice, still chattering ahead of me about how impressed she was, long blonde tresses swaying as she walked, explaining how I was going to be a tough act to follow. As we neared the bar, Rowan pushed off his stool, moving towards us with purpose and against my better judgement, my heart sped up. Even with my heels, we were almost the same height which did little to diminish his suffocating presence. Despite his white hair and icy eyes, Rowan had always held this dark demeanor of *"don't fuck with me."* It had been infuriating growing up with him, but in that moment? I was trying to ignore the mess between my legs.

Jules broke off to speak with Andy as Rowan's hand found the small of my back, firm and possessive. "Time we go," he said, voice clipped as he guided me towards the door.

I opened my mouth to argue, caught in the battle of fading adrenaline and arousal. "Rowan, I—"

"I have been patient enough, Violet." He interrupted, his expression shifting to me. "We leave and if you put up a fight... you do not want things to go my way."

I knew what lust looked like on a man. I'd seen it countless times on Edward and his clients but when Rowan's eyes darkened, a lapse of judgement prompted me to say, "What if I want things to go your way?"

He stilled. I watched with rapt attention his adam's apple move before he leaned down, his lips brushing against my ear lobe with delicate care. "Careful," he warned. "I will not stop regardless of who is watching."

And there go my knees. My body could not feel any hotter than it does right now.

Rowan pulled back and must have enjoyed the look on my face because he gave me that infuriating, knowing grin as his hand on my back reminded me to move as he pressed us forward. "Come on, princess."

From behind, Jules shouted over the club music as we walked away, "See you on Friday, sweetie!"

Without slowing, Rowan asked, "What is Friday?"

I didn't miss a beat. "The day after Thursday," I replied as we squeezed between patrons.

"Not what I meant," he huffed.

"The day before Saturday?"

"If you were anyone else, I would have choked you by now. Why will you see her on Friday?" Rowan shoved open the door to the outside, ignoring Romeo's passing stare as we both walked by.

"Don't threaten me with a good time." I snapped as the night air slapped my overheated skin and I shivered. "But to answer your vague ass question, I'll be back here on Friday to find out if I'm hired."

"So, you insist on this reckless insanity?"

Oh, the nerve of him! Anger rose, hot and furious, pushing down any residual lust I had felt. "I'm twenty years old and plenty confident I can hold a job without someone else's blessing." I seethed at him.

The walk was silent and despite the cool night, the air was thick between us. Rowan was pissed, but he shouldn't have been there in the first place. He had no right. I was a grown woman—technically over thirty years old if you counted my first life. I had no need for a keeper.

Two blocks away, his control snapped.

"What were you thinking?" The words came out low and dangerous, his patronizing tone fanning the inferno inside me.

Obviously he was not hearing me. My stomach still churned with adrenaline and my temper was quicksilver. "I was thinking I'm an adult who's allowed to do what she wants," I snapped back.

"Do you know what that place is?"

"A gentlemen's club with a job opening?"

He made a sound of pure frustration. "It is dangerous."

"What, the pole? Maybe if I shoved it up your misogynistic ass. I've got good upper body and core strength." I retorted, clearly done biting my tongue around him now that we were safely away from prying eyes and ears.

"Not the pole," he growled. "The club. The people *in* the club."

I raised an eyebrow in mock confusion. "Are you scandalized and shocked by what you saw, poor Rowan? Don't worry, I won't tell Charlie that his little boy went to his first strip club."

"This is no joke, Violet."

"Am I laughing?"

My blistered feet ached, each step a new agony. *Probably should have danced barefoot instead of showing off in these ridiculous high heels, idiot.* When we got to a crosswalk and waited for the light to turn, I bent over to rub at my feet through my shoes. There was a cool breeze on my ass, followed by a honking horn and a wolf whistle.

I knew what they saw, my ass in a bright red thong, possibly still soaked from earlier. Above, Rowan let out a few curses and I smiled despite myself. Let the man child deal with his own issues. It's my body and how I display it is none of his concern.

Before I could react, Rowan's arms were around me. I squealed and beat at his chest, but he hauled me against him like I weighed nothing. Flashbacks of unsolicited—or coerced—intimacy hit me. My body straightened in terror and I reacted without meaning to. I threw my palm up, nearly connecting with his nose and he surprisingly dodged.

"Fuck, Violet. I'm trying to help."

"Put me down!" I demanded, squirming in his grip.

Logically, I knew I shouldn't be afraid—it was just Rowan. Despite how much I loathed him, I still trusted him. Yet, knowing that did not stop my body's visceral reaction.

He said, "*Nyet*. I will not."

My BJJ training kicked in. I recalled a dozen different ways to break out of his grasp and two dozen ways to hurt him. I knew how to create an imbalance, disrupt his posture, throw my weight to his unstable side, trap one of his arms as I guided my fall, hook a leg behind his knee, drag both with me as we dropped...

Then what? We roll around on the dirty sidewalk until you can lock a limb? To what end? I knew he was too stubborn to tap out and I didn't want to seriously hurt him... much.

"And why not?" I screeched, trying not to let my fear leak into the words. "If this is about my ass being out, then you can shove your mysog—"

"You are injured and limping and I do not like seeing you in pain this way."

And there he goes again. It was infuriating how easily he got under my skin with his swapping between hot and cold, between kind and cruel. He didn't care that my ass was hanging out. No, he cared about my feet. *He's always surprising me.*

"I can walk," I grumbled. I was uncomfortable with being carried through the streets, but I felt my anger and fear slowly dissipating, trusting in the way he held me.

"On bleeding feet? I do not think that would be best."

I closed my eyes and focused on the pain of my feet—a reminder that this was the present. *He is not Edward. I am safe*, I told myself as my racing heart calmed.

He continued our trek, and I was *very* aware of how my body pressed against his, the heat of him seeping through my thin clothes. My mouth went dry and I tried for humor. "Being carried like a princess isn't as comfortable as the movies make it to be."

I heard him snort, and I was careful to ignore how I was tucked under his chin like precious cargo. His hands were gentle on me, easing away tension as I melted into his arms. His touch did not seem to bother me as much as others did.

Fuck, Violet. You are tired. You are stressed. You are definitely not *sexually attracted to your asshole childhood friend who has a delicious accent that could melt panties.*

I scowled, my brows drawn tight as he carried me all the way to my dorm—a miraculous trek given we were at least over a mile from the dorm. I reached for my keys in my purse and there was an awkward moment of him holding me while I searched for it. He managed to squat so I could put the key in and mercifully my roommate was still gone with her friend, Natalia.

He set me down with deliberate care, hands lingering on my waist before retreating. The outside school grounds streetlamp cast gold bars across worn wooden floors, painting Rowan in stripes of light and shadow. Somehow he had barely broken a sweat. Probably a by-product of his extensive runs with his adopted father, Charlie.

He asked, "Do you need help taking off your heels?"

My gaze lingered on his tantalizing mouth as he said those words. *You need a cold shower and to get away from him*, I reminded myself as I shook my head. "No, I've got it. You should go home."

Folding himself onto my bed's edge, he looked haggard. The mattress dipped under his weight. He sat there, elbows on his knees, eyes tracking me as I chucked heels off, and stumbled around my cluttered side of the dorm. I busied myself pulling off clothes, gathering my bath caddy, grabbing my pajamas.

"Why," he asked with a weary curiosity.

I sat my toiletries down on my desk and sank into the chair, examining my battered feet, noting the pink nail polish had chipped. I made a note to get them fixed and tried not to fidget. "Why what?"

"Why dance at Oubliette?"

I shrugged, aiming for nonchalance. "Money."

"*Ne nesi chush!*" he said with that hint of Russian accent I was getting too comfortable hearing. "Stop lying to me. Your family has money."

"Did you call out *bullshit* in Russian? Rowan, my funds are locked in a *trust*," I explained. "Daddy could release them early, but I'd need a business proposal. Do I look like I'm running a business while finishing my degree?" I gestured to the chaos of my half of the dorm: textbooks stacked on the floor, archery gear in the corner, clothes draped over every available surface. "Besides, there's something in that club I want."

His eyes narrowed. "What?"

"A pony."

"Violet—"

"It's none of your goddamn business, Rowan. Go home. I'm going to that club."

He exhaled slowly before he said, "Fine. But I go with you now."

"What?"

"To the club. When you go, I go."

I couldn't have stared harder at him if he had grown a third eye. "That's the *opposite* of going home! Why... would you go with me?"

"To protect you."

Okay, screw this. I took a deep breath before I spit out, "Why do you even care, Rowan? It's none of your goddamn business where I go, or who I see, or what I do. You're not Daddy, you're not my brother, you. . ." I trailed off, because I honestly couldn't think of what to even call Rowan. Godbrother? Friend? Constant and irritating pain in the ass? None of those were a perfect fit.

We stared at each other for a moment in silence. Once I'd collected myself, I continued in as calm and disdainful of a tone as I could manage. "While I can acknowledge the sentiment behind your desire to protect me, I must point out that such an impulse appears to be rooted in a deeply ingrained and antiquated assumption that by virtue of you being a man, you are inherently more capable, and that I, as a woman, am somehow in need of safeguarding. I find that presumption both reductive and profoundly patronizing. In short," I paused to catch my breath, "Go fuck yourself and leave me alone." Philosophy class really was rubbing off on me.

"You need a bodyguard," was all he said.

I rolled my eyes. "I don't need a bodyguard!"

"And yet, now you have one."

Just let it go, I tried to tell myself even as I stepped closer. I jabbed my finger into that well defined chest hidden under his black shirt, biting out each word. "Listen here, you stubborn shit for brains—"

The door handle jiggled, and Alice appeared mid-knock, catching us in what must have looked like an intimate moment.

"Oh," she said. "Sorry, I didn't—"

"It's fine," I said quickly. "Rowan, meet Alice. Alice, meet Rowan."

She looked uncomfortable, "I can come back later if—"

"No," I interrupted her, "I'm going to grab a shower and Rowan was just leaving."

"Are you sure? If you two were about to—"

"*T'fu,*" Rowan spat out the sound he makes when he finds something disgusting.

Well, good to know you find me repulsive Rowan Monroe. And a big fat fuck you, too.

"It's nothing like that," I said as I walked to the door, slipping on my shower kitty sandals. "He is a childhood friend of mine who has chlamydia. I will never touch him."

Rowan followed, his expression unbothered. "I am on the antibiotics, Violet. I already told you this. It is fine," he said with an infuriating calm.

My eye twitched. "Well, remember to take the full course this time, even if your symptoms clear up. You don't want it coming back even worse like it did last time, right?"

As we walked past Alice, Rowan gestured to me and said, "She is such a good friend, to worry for my health." He flashed her a grin and I swear I saw her panties combust.

I stormed out and once we were in the hall and my dorm's door closed behind us, I shot him a look that could boil blood. "I hate you," I seethed.

He smirked, leaning close enough I caught his scent, pine and sharp and clean. It made my stomach flip and butterflies dance, reminding me how much I hated my body sometimes.

"So you've told me for years. Now, where is your shower?" he muttered.

I pivoted on my heel. "Go. Away. You are *not* following me." I sounded juvenile even to my own ears. I marched towards the showers with Rowan lagging behind me.

"And yet... I will follow you."

I wanted to scream. This man was beyond infuriating. I felt the heat of his glare as I walked away, my sandaled feet slapping against the weathered floors of the school. *Who does he think he is? My keeper? My warden?*

Rowan Monroe was becoming the bane of my existence. How had he even found me at Oubliette? I'd been careful, meticulously so, making sure no one from school knew where I was going. The timing was too precise to be a coincidence. *Is he following me?* The thought coiled in my stomach and—much to my dismay—I felt flattered.

Nope. No way. I am not into stalkers.

What was his game? Why did he care? I struggled to understand his sudden protectiveness. He'd never shown interest in my welfare before. We'd spent years circling each other with barbed words from a prickly distance.

And something about Oubliette had rattled him. Something he'd seen there. Perhaps he'd noticed evidence of what I'd always suspected—that Oubliette served as a hub of illegal activity. But if that were true, then why did all of the girls I'd met there seem so happy? Bri didn't act like she was trapped. Jules was one of the most upbeat people I'd ever met. Is the illegal side of Oubliette confined to those lower floors I had never been taken to?

It doesn't matter what Rowan thinks about me, Oubliette, or the clientele there. I just needed him gone before he destroyed my only opportunity for vengeance. Oubliette was my gateway. My path to Edward. My chance to find that monster.

And Rowan was going to ruin everything if he interfered.

"Violet," Rowan called to me. "Stop. Just... stop for a moment."

I didn't stop. "Walk and talk, Rowan. I'm going to be at the showers in a second, so you should talk fast."

He caught up to me, and lightly touched my elbow. "Violet," he said, voice low, "you have no idea what you are walking into."

His eyes flicked to my blistered feet, then back up to my face. For a heartbeat, his expression was soft, with something like worry swimming in the depths of his eyes. But then it was gone, replaced with the same stoicism he always wore.

"I know exactly what I'm walking into," I said with a smirk as I pulled away from him. "I'm walking into the showers."

I heard him groan from behind me.

I stifled a laugh at that, and left him standing there as I walked into the communal showers, giving him the finger without looking back at him.

Chapter 10

Rowan

"I hate you," Violet said to me.

Unkind. Untrue, but also unkind.

I leaned close to her and said, "So you've told me for years. Now, where is your shower?"

My words grated my own ears. I was exhausted, tapped out from the earlier encounter with that vampyre followed by the strain of searching for Violet with my heightened hearing all evening. Every laugh, every whisper, every heartbeat had crashed into my skull like a jack hammer until I had nearly lost my mind tracking her. Combined with my current hard-on that seemed to refuse to go down, I was surprised I hadn't passed out.

I felt like a dirty grey rag, frayed and rung dry.

But exhaustion was not an excuse to be an asshole or a spoiled princess like the woman in front of me.

She turned and marched off. "Go. Away. You are *not* following me," she said over her shoulder.

So, obviously, I followed her.

She stormed down the narrow hall as best as she could with painfully blistered feet. Each of her steps was deliberate and slow. The blisters bloomed red across her skin, and I saw the small streaks of crimson against her black cat sandals.

Blood. Fresh blood. She had no idea how thin that line was between daring and suicidal tonight. If she'd bled on that dance floor, not even I could've defended her from the speed of those monsters.

Part of me wanted to grab her, spin her around, and lecture until she let me handle this. The quieter, darker part knew she wouldn't listen, leaving me torn between harsh punishment and abandonment. If she only knew how I teetered between humanity and self-preservation every goddamn second. How my old instincts whispered to take what I wanted, consequences be damned. Filled with nothing but her scent and heartbeat surrounding me as I filled her to the—

Fuck, I needed to leave.

I almost stalked the opposite direction as the hallway stretched too long, institutional lighting casting harsh shadows that made her look fragile despite her fury. I could see a crack in her icy demeanor and yet I couldn't seem to get her to agree with anything I was saying. She was a goddamn enigma.

Running water hummed from the communal shower at the far end, reminding me how exposed she'd be. Not just physically. Every glance from the club's shadows earlier had reminded me this world wasn't safe. Vampyres tracking her pulse with their eyes. Werewolves noting her scent. Other supernaturals cataloging her as prey. Fuck, she wasn't even safe around me right now.

I closed the distance and called out to her. "Violet. Stop. Just... stop for a moment."

"Walk and talk, Rowan. I'm going to be at the showers in a second, so you should talk fast."

I reached out and held her elbow; a light touch, barely more than a brush of my fingertips against her skin, sending a jolt through my chest. I spoke with an urgency that forced my voice low as I said, "Violet, you have no idea what you are walking into."

I thought about all the different ways I could explain to her the dangers of Oubliette, of the supernaturals that lurked there, of the supposed proprietor who ran the clubs. I knew there was no way to tell her without sounding like a raving lunatic, that as much as I may have wanted to be honest with her... I could not.

A devilish smirk teased her lips, causing even more of my blood to go south. "I know exactly what I'm walking into. I'm walking into the showers," she said as she pulled away and marched off.

This fucking brat.

I watched her disappear around the corner, her middle finger raised as she went.

The smart thing would have been to leave, to trust she would be fine until she was set to return to Oubliette in four days' time. But smart and right rarely traveled together in my world. My unease over the evening's events anchored me to the spot like I'd grown roots through the floor.

I waited, palms pressed against the wall's chill, head tilted back to keep myself from stalking into the showers with her. The hallway stretched narrow, a tunnel of closed doors hiding whispered lives. It was nearly midnight and hushed voices floated past in currents of gossip, broken phrases about professors and hookups and weekend plans. Each time a door cracked open, I felt curious eyes on me before the darkness swallowed them once more.

Fuck, I didn't know what the hell came over me when I followed her here. I craved my rope, the meditation of knots against flesh. The ritual. The certainty. My rented apartment had the mannequin I practiced on, a warm bed where I could pretend to sleep or spend the next few hours working through this restless electricity crackling under my skin since I watched her dance. Since witnessing what lived beneath her careful mask.

Cause that's fucking normal, wanting to go home and masturbate while thinking of your childhood friend. Treacherous ground, that.

My enhanced hearing picked up the rush of water through pipes, and the distant sound of her humming that same haunting melody she'd danced to. The sound burrowed into my chest, twisted hard. Pulled up the memory in painful clarity: light kissing her skin, her spine's perfect curve, the calculated savagery in her limbs. She'd moved like brutality wrapped in beauty, like she'd been born to capture attention and bend it until it broke.

I shut my eyes against the memory. Gods, if only she had fallen off the pole. So much heartache would have been saved for the both of us.

Gone was any sense of normalcy as invasive thoughts wondered how her skin would look when rope bit into her flesh. I shifted my cock in my pants, wanting nothing more than to venture home, relieve myself, and sleep. It felt wrong in many ways to crave her, yet I could not help the desperate hunger to bite into the forbidden fruit.

She was a brat. She was foul-tempered. Stubborn. I was not reacting to her... I was reacting to the house of monsters we had somehow managed to walk out of. That's all it was. Residual adrenaline.

I slid down the wall until I was crouched, forearms on my knees and head leaned back. The corridor felt narrower with each passing minute, the weight of the building pressing in around me.

In the Wastelands, I'd spent years learning which battles to pick, which threats to neutralize, which dangers to respect from a distance. Oubliette collected them all under one roof, invited them in, served them drinks, and called it entertainment. The thought of Violet swimming through those waters, even with her sharp wits and claws, turned my insides to ice. The way those scum lords watched her, the hunger in their eyes. Violet was prey among predators and while I knew she'd commanded the room and could hold her own to some extent, I'd seen the brutality of those creatures. I'd experienced it firsthand, and the idea of their dirty claws digging into her unmarred skin lit a fire in my chest. I needed to protect her and the only way I could do that was convincing her there was a better way.

But how do you convince a brat to listen? *I could spank her firm ass into pretty shades of red and purple*, I mused. I allowed myself a moment of that image—Violet bent over my knee, her bare ass in the air, the resounding sound of my palm clapping against her skin, her cheeks reddening.

No. She's young. She's my adopted father's niece. Charlie's blood. The family I swore to protect. I had already crossed a line by watching her strip after I promised she meant nothing to me. Although those words were a pure contradiction to the raging boner threatening to burst my zipper. It felt so fucking wrong.

Then why does she feel perfect when I hold her in my arms?

I groaned and hugged my knees to my chest. I would not break the family's trust. I promised Charlie I would watch her, yet I couldn't get her out of my head. Those full pink lips that spit fire and would look gorgeous wrapped around my length. She brought out a side of me I hated when all I wanted to do was bury myself in her.

My muscles burned from holding still in my crouched position. I tried to focus on the issue at hand. I had fought supernaturals before. Back in my previous life, when my face matched my soul—old, ugly, scarred, and cruel. But I had always fought on my own terms. *Nothing like this, though. Never a whole fucking nightclub of them.* Not in a place where they easily outnumbered me twenty to one. Not with Violet's pulse singing beside mine, a beacon to every predator with ears to hear.

I cursed the thinness of my luck.

Violet had stepped into a world I knew spelled death, and my gut knotted with an arctic fear I hadn't felt since being chased through the Wastelands by The Library's Hunter, a fear more visceral than any I'd felt in this new life.

This fear is not for you.

This fear came from more than failing my obligations. No, this fear held a wave of something raw and unspoken that crashed into soft places I had thought fossilized long, long ago.

Chapter 11

Violet

I found Rowan half-asleep on the floor, his arms hooked over his head, chest rising and falling in a steady rhythm that contradicted the coiled restraint I'd seen at Oubliette. He looked... vulnerable. The warrior, the shadow, the walking storm who'd stalked me all evening was sprawled like some fallen angel, all that lethal intention suspended in sleep.

Water trickled down my shirt, the damp fabric clinging to my skin in cold patches that should have sent me scurrying back to my room and leaving him behind. But I couldn't tear myself away from staring at him. I devoured him with my eyes, if I was being brutally honest with myself. His body was sculpted into perfection, all hard lines and symmetry that artists would murder to capture.

After I'd showered, I'd overheard two other girls in the bathroom whispering about him; about the "snowy white god" who'd taken up post outside the showers. They'd giggled behind their hands, eyes bright with interest. One of them had said he looked like a statue, carved and waiting for his lover to wake him with a kiss.

Fairy tale bullshit.

I scoffed, though the sound stuck in my throat. *Lover, my ass.* Rowan was stubborn, infuriating, and absurdly overprotective; a new attitude I hadn't witnessed before tonight.

Honestly? It reeked of obsession.

He'd hovered over me like I was some delicate virgin walking to a sacrificial altar, his eyes hunting every shadow, his body positioning itself between me and anything that breathed. As if he had any clue what I already knew about Oubliette. What I'd already seen. What had been done to me in my previous life, what had been done to that other body... the body that sometimes felt more real than the privileged skin I'd been reborn in.

My shower had been long and deliberate as I scrubbed until my skin felt flayed, shaved until nothing remained to fuss over. The hot water had turned my flesh pink and tender, steam filling my lungs until I felt purged inside and out. I hadn't thought for a second he'd wait for me. But there he was.

I crouched down next to him. His brow pinched, a small line creasing between his eyes, and for a split second he looked like he was scowling even in his sleep. *That face*. Gods, I knew it better than my own reflection at this point.

"Why can't you just be nicer to me?" I whispered, a question I hadn't meant to voice aloud. My fingers turned traitor, reaching forward before I could stop them, brushing a strand of hair off his forehead. The contact barely existed, almost reverent, and I hated the way my chest constricted with the act. Like my body remembered what it felt like to touch someone who mattered.

The moment was shattered by noise, a slammed door followed by loud laughter in the hallway, and I yanked back as if I'd touched a live wire. Rowan's eyes snapped open in that exact moment, a predator roused from hibernation, pupils blown wide and searching. His gaze locked on my face, then dropped, lower, lingering between my legs with an intensity that scorched.

Heat rushed to my skin as his eyes widened, consuming more of me than I should have permitted. Loose shorts. No underwear. The cool air whispered against places I knew he could see. I didn't flinch or try to cover myself. I should have been mortified, an echo of modesty railing somewhere within me, yet the other side of me wished for more.

Don't be an idiot, I told myself. *He's already watched us strip with those murdery eyes of his.*

Still, the way his breath caught—for a fraction of a second—sent a jolt coursing through my veins before pooling hot and wet between my legs. Then just as quickly, the fortress walls slammed back into place. His face turned to stone, unreadable as an ancient text.

The mask of Rowan was firmly back in position.

"You took awhile," he said flatly.

"I masturbated and thought of everything except you while you slept."

He cursed, the word sharp as a blade. "Fuck, Violet. Can you ever *not* be a brat?"

I laughed, bitter and sweet all at once. My thighs burned from crouching, already sore from the night's performance, but I didn't move. The cold tile of the hallway bit into my feet, sending jagged pulses of discomfort up my legs. I should have put my sandals back on. "If I wasn't, you wouldn't know what to do with me."

"But why, Violet?" Exasperation bled through his voice. I had half a mind to argue, to frustrate him more just because I could. But he'd waited for me. That counted for something. So I told him the truth.

"Because I know exactly what I want, Rowan." *And it's you.* The words nearly escaped before I caught them. "It's a game to me."

"A game?" He seemed genuinely confused.

"Wrong word." I shifted, spread my legs wider, daring him to see exactly what I wasn't wearing beneath these shorts. "This is my ritual, Rowan. A game of cat and mouse for my affections."

His breath caught as his gaze slowly moved down my body. I saw it then, briefly, his pupils darkening. His whole body went still, the way a snake freezes before it strikes.

So even he can break, I thought triumphantly.

He didn't move, eyes once again staring at me with a burning intensity. Then, slowly, he turned away. His jaw was tight, a muscle jumping beneath his skin. "The one who earns the most sacred parts of you is a lucky man."

The unspoken words hung between us, heavy as stone: *It will never be me.*

He stretched then, long legs extending until his back gave a satisfying pop. The sound cracked through the quiet hallway like a gunshot. It slapped me with awareness of how solid he was, how much space he claimed without trying. The scent of him—pine and something darker, earthier—invaded my nostrils with each breath.

"Don't have a place to stay?" I taunted, arms crossing over my damp shirt, chin tilting high. The fabric stuck to my skin, cold and clammy, and my nipples ached underneath them. I kept myself haughty. Anything to mask how rattled I still felt from the way his eyes had roamed over me.

"I have an apartment nearby," he replied, voice low and even, like my jab bounced off titanium. His words vibrated through the air between us, deep enough that I could almost feel them against my skin.

I let out a low whistle, mock-impressed. The sound pinballed off the narrow walls of the hallway. "Damn, Rowan. Charlie's really splurging on his adoptee."

That got me what I *thought* I wanted: pain. His gaze bore into me and I felt it then, a heat in my chest that assured me I had struck something deep in his soul and the fire that raged behind his eyes flickered out until only an ember remained. My mouth itched to keep pushing, to smother it until no light existed, a cruel instinct from a past life. I hesitated, a pang reverberating in my heart, unwanted, but existing nonetheless. It surprised me when my mouth snapped shut. *I guess an old dog can learn new tricks.*

The silence stretched between us until the creak of a door broke it. The sound grated against my ears like nails on a chalkboard. A bleary-eyed girl poked her head out into the hall, her room reeking of stale coffee and all-nighter desperation. "Hey, you two. It's nearly one a.m. Can you keep it down, please? Also, no visitors after ten p.m." She eyed Rowan, as if assuming he had been someone's booty call and not a student.

"Sorry," I said while still looking at Rowan. Heat rushed to my cheeks. I stood quickly, my bathroom caddy clattering against the wall, plastic bottles knocking together. Embarrassment burned across my face.

Rowan rose more slowly, unhurried, unfolding from the floor with the kind of effortless grace that made him look even more out of place in the dormitory hallway. The fluorescent lights cast harsh shadows across the planes of his face. "Ready?" His gaze lingered on me a fraction longer than it should have, unreadable, before he turned towards my room.

The walk back was quiet, heavy with everything unsaid. His footsteps matched mine, steady, a shadow by my side. At my door, he paused with his hand braced on the frame. The wood creaked under his touch and I craved—in a momentary lapse of judgement—that it was me instead. He looked as if debating whether to speak.

His voice, when it came, was soft but it cut clean. "You act like claws make you a *volchok*, Violet. But all I see is a kitten hissing at shadows."

My breath stuttered, words failing me for once. The air tasted bitter in my mouth.

He dipped his head, something close to a smirk tugging his mouth, then turned and walked away, leaving me seething in his wake.

I shut the door behind me, leaning against it with my pulse still hammering against my ribs, the metal handle cold against my palm. Rowan didn't fight fair. He never had, which is why I was loath to accept he might be right when the next morning, the school had sent the entire campus an urgent email.

Student found dead in common area. Starting immediately, a curfew will be in effect.

Chapter 12

Rowan

By the time I made it to my apartment, I felt like the physical manifestation of blue balls. Violet's spitfire defiance should have killed my desire. Should have reminded me she was off-limits, dangerous, Levi's blood. Instead, it stoked the fire hotter.

I'd tucked my erection under my waistband, hoping the walk would kill my hard-on, but it didn't work. If anything, my cock throbbed harder, pissed off at being ignored.

The apartment was far nicer than anything I had lived in during my first life. Polished hardwood throughout, stonework walls, and heated tile for the bathroom floor. The kind of place Charlie would pick: expensive, minimal, functional. Floor-to-ceiling windows overlooked Atlanta's shopping district, all glass towers and money. Too much glass for my taste. I had not trained much with guns before, but even I knew anyone with a scope could see straight in.

But the bed looked soft, the leather chair in the corner was worn in just right, and the locks were solid.

Good enough.

Charlie had found it fast. It had probably cost a fortune, but I didn't dwell on that. I couldn't afford my pride taking another hit after Violet's jab about him "S*plurging on his adoptee.*" She had poked that wound without even trying. She was already under my skin, no matter how hard I had fought to keep her out.

I checked the time and saw 1:30 a.m. So much for sleeping. I walked into the bathroom, stripped, and dropped my clothes on the floor. My cock sprang free, still hard as steel.

Her scent—rose, something dark and floral, something *her*—clung to my clothes from carrying her. My cock throbbed harder when I remembered her soft frame against my chest, her hair tickling my chin, her breath hot against my throat, right where my jugular pulsed. Dangerous, letting her that close. Letting her *mouth* that close.

The image of her freshly shaved cunt burned in my mind. I could still smell her, that faint musk when she had spread her legs wider in the hallway. How sweet would she taste? My mouth watered.

Fuck, I needed to stop. Violet was young and furious. . . chaos in human form.

Deep down I knew if I wrapped my hands around her throat, she would hiss and spit while smiling, daring me to squeeze harder. The contradiction was driving me insane. Infuriating and irresistible. Fucking perfect in the worst possible way.

Cold water shower. Now, I commanded myself. I set the knob to the coldest setting, stepped in, and hissed as the icy water sliced into my back.

I waited for the cold to kick in and tame my raging hard-on. I waited. . . then waited some more. Looking down at my still-hard cock, I realized cold water would not be enough. Nothing would ever be enough. I could argue all I wanted that desiring Violet was wrong, but my body didn't care. Neither, apparently, did the part of my brain that kept replaying her spread legs, her smirk, the way she had looked at me. She knew exactly what she was doing.

I palmed the wall and gripped my cock, groaning as I stroked myself. My cock was heavy, aching from being hard for so long. The weight of it in my palm was thick and demanding. I stroked slowly at first, base to tip, letting the cold water beat against my back while heat coiled low in my gut.

I thought back to her dance. The curve of her spine. The flex of her thighs around the pole. The way her body had moved like sex given form, all controlled violence wrapped in silk.

I wanted to run my hands along those curves, trace my fingers to her pierced nipples, watch her squirm beneath me when I twisted the barbells, then hear her sharp intake of breath as pleasure crossed the line into pain.

For someone filled with so much rage, I suspected she would respond to patience as punishment. Slow build. I would watch her, listen for her breath to hitch, map every response her body gave me. And when I wrapped my hand around her throat, she would lean into it like a dare.

My stroke quickened, palm slick now, cock pulsing in my grip. I imagined it: my *volchok* on her knees, those soft pink lips stretched around my cock. I would hold her there, hand fisted in her hair, watching her eyes water as she struggled for air. Then I would pull out just enough to let her breathe before sliding back in, fucking her mouth while my cum dripped down her chin.

"Fuck," I groaned, the word echoing off tile.

My balls tightened, drew up hard against my body. The orgasm built at the base of my spine, white-hot and inevitable. I stroked faster, rougher, chasing it until I came with a guttural sound that was half her name, thick ropes hitting the shower wall. My cock pulsed again and again, emptying itself while the cold water washed the evidence down the drain.

I stood there, forehead pressed against my forearm, breathing hard as the climax faded. My cock gave one last weak pulse, still half-hard even after release.

Why Violet? And why now? She was such an infuriating, insolent, bratty princess whom I grew up with for years. Foul mouthed, quick tempered... and I wouldn't want her any other way.

No. I needed to stay away unless her life was in danger. I would stay hidden. Let her live her college life, fuck whoever she wanted, earn her grades. I would make sure nothing supernatural touched her and that was it—nothing else.

I turned off the shower and dried off. Teeth brushed, I turned off all the lights and set my alarms. Tomorrow was an early day. I slid into the crisp white sheets of my bed and tried not to think about her.

Then another image surfaced: Violet naked, legs spread. My cock stirred.

I sighed and cupped my balls. "Fuck. It is going to be a long night."

To say I was happy to be right is an understatement. I didn't necessarily want to be right, but I sure as hell enjoyed it when I was. So when she called the next morning, sounding reluctant as hell, I couldn't help feeling smug.

"Rowan, I need your help." Her voice was surprisingly demure. I would have killed to read her mind right then and see her face.

"Oh, so *now* you have need of me?" I had been up for hours. Having just finished a run in a vain attempt to escape the guilt of jerking off to her two more times, I'd been working on a new set of ties for suspension when Violet called.

My mannequin—whom I'd named Marie Antoinette—was twisted in a position no human could hold for long. She was the perfect partner for the Shinju suspension I wanted to master.

"Rowan!" She hissed. "Listen, the school has implemented a curfew."

That got my attention. The cerulean rope stilled in my hands. "A curfew? What for?"

There was silence on the line for a moment before she said, "That's not important right now. I need to dance at Oubliette on Friday, and that is obviously going to have to be after curfew." She exhaled a heavy breath. "You, uh. . . you mentioned an apartment?"

More silence as her implied question hung between us.

"You want to stay with me?" I drawled the words out, savoring them. My cock stirred at the thought. What the fuck was I doing? This was the exact opposite of staying away from her.

"Please? If it's not too much trouble?"

I laughed. "Trouble? No trouble at all. . . but this place is only a one-bedroom bachelor pad filled from floor to ceiling with BDSM toys and porn—"

"Oh, for fuck's sake," she nearly shouted. "Just say no, Rowan." The line went dead.

The entire situation was almost *too* good. I waited a few minutes, then called her back. She answered on the first ring, broadcasting her desperation much to my delight. "What is it?"

"Oh, I thought you had wanted my help, but then the line disconnected. I did not get to hear you beg."

She swore a string of expletives. I could picture her: one hand beating her mattress, the other gripping her phone while she snarled.

Her asking for help meant she had to trust me. Meant surrendering some of that fierce independence. My cock pressed against my slacks. The thought of her shame, hot and bitter, made me even harder.

Once her cursing had subsided she said, "I cannot believe I picked up the phone for you."

"I am waiting."

Her words were clipped, her voice terse, as she asked, "Can I stay over at your place on the nights I work?"

"Hmm, I do not think I like that tone. Try again."

Silence. Then she humbly asked, "Please, Rowan. I will be a good girl if you let me stay over Friday night."

I scoffed. *Good girl? Highly doubtful.* But the way she'd asked drew my balls tight and flooded my mind with images: Violet on her hands and knees in my apartment listening to my instructions. Following them. Learning what happened when she didn't.

I cleared my throat. "I do have a few rules—"

Her demeanor changed instantly. "Great. Thanks for accepting. I will text you when I finish with class!" The line went dead again.

I laughed, finished the knot I was tying, and placed Marie Antoinette in her corner. I stood back to admire my work. The Shinju looked clean. Professional.

Then my brain betrayed me as I envisioned Violet's body in the ropes, her hazel eyes staring back at me.

Nope. Fuck no.

I walked into my room and changed out of my sweats and into dark jeans with a pressed white T-shirt. My phone vibrated with an alert. I glanced at it. My heart stopped when I saw the headline.

Student killed last night at Shademore University. Investigation still underway.

I clicked it open and there it was: Violet's school. The headline had a picture of the same courtyard I had been in last night.

Flashbacks hit. The vampyre I had run into, all casual menace and barely concealed hunger. Violet dancing on that stage, bleeding into her sandals, every supernatural in the room cataloging her scent. And now a body. A fucking body, hours after we left.

That fucking brat is trying to hide this from me?

I threw my phone onto the bed and finished getting ready, my mind already made up.

Violet had never seen the hunter in me. She had never seen what I was capable of when something I protected was threatened. She thought her jiu jitsu and archery gave her claws, made her a predator.

She had no idea.

But she was about to learn. Because I was done playing the patient guardian, the concerned friend who kept his distance. If she wanted to dance at Oubliette, if she wanted to play with monsters, then she was going to do it under *my* rules and within my sight.

She was going to regret igniting this. Regret making me care. Regret turning me from an observer into a participant.

Because the thing about hunters? We don't stop until the threat is eliminated and we sink our teeth into our prey.

Chapter 13

Violet

"Shit." I slammed my phone down on the nightstand, the plastic case clattering against cheap laminate. I rubbed my eyes, pressing hard enough to see stars burst behind my eyelids. Things were getting complicated. Rowan had somehow become my inadvertent savior *again*, and I hated the growing list of favors I owed him. He might not keep score, but I did. A running tally in my head that never stopped climbing, each debt carved into my pride like notches on a blade.

This isn't good.

Alice had stumbled in during the early morning hours, her key scratching against the lock before the door swung open. She'd given me a sheepish look when she found me awake, curled in my desk chair with cold coffee and burning eyes.

"Hey..." She mumbled the word through lips stained dark with wine or lipstick, I couldn't tell which, in the dim glow of my desk lamp.

She collapsed onto her bed without bothering to remove her shoes—black stilettos with silver buckles that caught the light. The mattress springs groaned under her weight.

"Long night?" I asked, noting how abnormal it was for her OCD tendencies to let that slide. Alice was the type who color-coded her closet and kept her textbooks arranged by height.

She giggled into her pillow, the sound muffled and girlish. "You could say that."

Rolling over to face me, she somehow made smudged charcoal eyeliner and mascara look elegant, like a magazine spread titled "Morning After

Chic." Her black hair was a tangled mess of waves, and her dress—a sleek emerald number—was wrinkled across the bodice.

"Did you see the news?" she asked, her voice losing its playful edge.

I nodded, my throat tight. "Grateful it wasn't you."

"I carry a knife for emergencies. Though I'm not sure that would matter much based on what I heard about the body."

I grimaced. "Was it bad?"

She sighed, a heavy exhale that seemed to deflate her as she nodded. Sitting up slowly, she pulled off her jewelry with deliberate movements: dangly earrings first, then a delicate silver bracelet, then three rings that clinked together as she dropped them into the ceramic dish on her nightstand. Her shoes came next, kicked off with small thuds against the dark wooden floors.

"Poor kid. He was a senior. Almost done with school." Her voice went quiet as she reached for her makeup remover, the bottle squat and pink on her cluttered dresser. Pensive in a way I hadn't seen before, like she was contemplating mortality for the first time.

"Do you think the school's overreacting?" I asked.

She shook her head, cotton pad sliding over her eyelids in smooth strokes. Black smudges transferred to white cotton, erasing liner and mascara in practiced efficiency. "No, it's their responsibility to work with authorities." She paused, studying her reflection in the small mirror propped against her wall. Her face, half-clean now, looked younger. Vulnerable. "Though I think the curfew is an overreaction. It'll cause more fear than safety."

"Agreed." I rummaged through my desk, pulling out the texts I needed for today's studying. The weight of them in my hands felt grounding, normal—*The Problems of Philosophy* and *Think: A Compelling Introduction to Philosophy*, their spines stiff from being so new. My studies, at least, were something I could control in a world spinning faster than I could track.

"Do you have class today?" I asked.

Alice yawned, her jaw cracking audibly, and nodded. She stood and began peeling off her dress, the emerald fabric pooling at her feet like liquid. Beneath it, she wore black lace lingerie that looked expensive. I noticed her skin looked flushed, almost fevered—a pink heat spreading across her collarbones and up her throat.

"Are you getting sick?" The question came out before I could stop it. Too personal. I had a bad habit of crossing lines without permission. Instincts from my life of servitude: catalog everyone's weaknesses, find the cracks in their armor.

Thankfully, Alice didn't seem to mind.

"No, just a little fatigued." She pulled on an oversized T-shirt—gray and worn soft—that swallowed her frame. "I'll feel better after a nap. I don't have classes until later."

"Today is my training day, so I'll have spare time between riding and rolling to study. Before any of that, though, I'm getting a couple of small tattoos done. But feel free to text me if you feel worse. . ." I stopped, realizing I'd never given her my number.

I scrawled it quickly on a scrap of paper torn from my notebook, the pen—blue ink, nearly out—scratching across the page. I handed it to her before grabbing my bag, the canvas strap settling against my shoulder.

She gave me a smile, genuine warmth crinkling the corners of her eyes. "Thank you, Violet."

Her words settled strangely in my chest, a flutter of something unfamiliar. Gratitude from others still felt foreign sometimes, like a language I'd forgotten.

Rowan stayed behind the fence while Aaron and I geared up. The fence around the pasture was white-painted wood, weathered and peeling in places, separating the practice field from the observation area. I felt the weight of Rowan's curiosity as he watched me carry my bow—a recurve with a rich mahogany riser, the limbs midnight black—in my right hand, the quiver slung over my shoulder. The leather was worn soft from use, smelling of oil and age.

Aaron had already set the field: twenty large targets arranged in a serpentine pattern across trampled grass that was more dust than green. Each target was a hay bale wrapped in canvas, painted with concentric circles in fading red and white. The track he'd carved with his mare earlier created a clear path, hoofprints pressed into hard-packed earth.

My heart raced, anticipation singing through my veins like electricity. I turned to Aaron with a smile that stretched across my face, genuine and unguarded.

"Can I start?"

His mare danced beneath him, her hooves striking the ground in nervous rhythm. She was always more anxious during mounted archery sessions, feeding off the energy. He nodded, careful to stay near the fence where Rowan watched with those pale, unreadable eyes.

I mounted Hyacinth in one smooth motion, muscle memory from years of practice. His body was warm and solid beneath me, muscles coiled and ready with power and magic I relished in. I pressed my thighs against his sides, trusting him completely.

Within seconds, he began to canter, his gait as smooth as running water. He was already anticipating my intent from the tilt of my hips and shift of my weight, the way I breathed, the tension in my calves. We'd done this dance a thousand times.

The first arrow notched smoothly, the shaft cool against my fingers. I barely took aim before releasing, letting instinct guide me. The string sang against my leather bracer—a sharp, clean sound—and the arrow hissed through humid air thick with the smell of grass and horse. It struck the center of the target twenty paces away with a satisfying thunk.

Joy radiated through me, pure and uncomplicated. Hyacinth felt it through my body, the way my seat relaxed, my posture opened. He showed off with a playful kick, his back hooves flashing in the golden sunlight. I easily stayed mounted, as I was expecting his display.

"Hooves down!" Aaron's voice cracked like a whip across the field.

Hyacinth snorted but complied, settling back into his canter. His ears flicked back towards me, listening.

I notched another arrow and let it fly without conscious thought. The world narrowed to movement and breath and the perfect release of tension. The arrow landed just shy of center, close enough. The target seemed to shimmer in the heat, edges wavering.

Eighteen more to go.

Aaron's voice carried across the field, cutting through the drum of hoofbeats. "If canterin' is too easy, do it at a gallop!"

I pressed my heels into Hyacinth's sides, and he responded immediately, lengthening his stride. The world blurred into speed and wind and the rhythmic thunder of hooves against earth. My braid whipped behind me, red ribbon flashing. The air rushed past my face, carrying the scent of crushed grass and Hyacinth's sweat—earthy and warm.

Within thirty minutes, both Hyacinth and I were drenched. Sweat darkened his coat to deep mahogany along his neck and shoulders, foam gathering around his bit. My tank top clung to my back, soaked through. My thighs were trembling from gripping his barrel, my core burning from maintaining balance at speed.

I'd hit fifteen centers out of twenty. Not perfect, but solid.

We circled back to Aaron, Hyacinth's sides heaving, his breath coming in great gusts beneath my legs. Aaron dismounted his mare with practiced ease and helped me gather arrows for a second round. The shafts were warm from the sun, some buried deep in hay that smelled sweet and dusty.

By the end of the second round, my thighs were quivering, muscles singing with familiar exhaustion. My hands ached from drawing the bowstring, the calluses on my fingers burning. But I'd improved my score: seventeen out of twenty.

Rowan remained stoic throughout, watching from his position by the fence. His arms were crossed, his expression unreadable, but something in his posture—the slight forward lean, the way his eyes never left me—suggested complete focus. I was too caught up in the work to care what he thought, lost in the meditation of repetition and skill.

This was ground I could confidently tread. I'd grown up on horseback. Daddy started me on lessons even before Brazilian jiu-jitsu. I trusted Hyacinth with my entire being. We were extensions of each other, moving as one body with two heartbeats.

Aaron found fault with a few of my shots—my elbow dropping on the fifteenth target, my release jerky on the eighth. His critique was sharp but fair, delivered in that matter-of-fact tone that made you want to improve just to prove you could. I made an extra effort cleaning and storing my bow in his office, a small room that smelled of leather oil and old coffee. Saddles lined one wall, bridles hung on hooks, and everything was organized in a way I appreciated.

Hyacinth received his usual rubdown in his stall—fresh pine shavings on the floor, water bucket filled to the brim. I ran the curry comb over his coat in circular motions, loosening dried sweat and dirt. He lowered his head, eyes half-closing in pleasure. His forelock was tangled with bits of hay, his whiskers soft as velvet when I brushed them clean.

"You're such a sweet boy," I cooed to Hyacinth as he let out a happy huff. "Unlike *someone* I know."

Aaron handed me a stack of reference materials as I finished—photocopied articles, their edges crisp and white. "Write me a report on why historically horse archers wore belted-on gorytos and quivers," he commanded, his arms crossed over a faded blue T-shirt with the university logo across the chest. "It's due at our next lesson."

"Standard essay length?" I asked, tucking the papers into my bag.

He considered, rubbing his jaw. The rasp of stubble was audible in the quiet barn. "Fifteen pages."

I grimaced. Fifteen pages on medieval equipment design were going to require serious research time, which I didn't have. "Ten pages, and I'll tell you how I recently came to know your sister."

His eyes widened, green going bright with alarm. "Sure; look, I hope it's not the divilment I'm fearing."

It was everything he feared.

Oubliette and the dancing. But Aaron was surprisingly understanding, more like Rowan than I'd expected—cautious but not judgemental. True to his word, though, he didn't back away from the ten-page assignment and reminded me to balance studies with work.

"Bri has only ever said good things about that place takin' care of her. Fair's fair," he said with a slight smile.

I thanked him and jogged back to Rowan, my legs protesting the movement. Everything ached in that good way that came from hard work. He was waiting patiently by the gate, one hand resting on the white-painted wood, the other in his pocket.

"Hey," I said, slightly breathless.

"Hey." He held the gate open for me, the hinges creaking softly. I helped him lock it behind us, the chain rattling as it settled into place. The padlock clicked shut with metallic finality.

"You were incredible," he said, and something in his tone—low and sincere—made heat bloom in my chest like spring flowers opening.

"High praise." I tried to sound casual despite the flutter in my stomach, the way my pulse kicked up at the warmth in his voice. "That is honestly my favorite thing about school."

"I can tell." His pale eyes met mine, holding me captive for a heartbeat too long. The golden light of early evening painted him in amber and shadow, softening the sharp angles of his face. "You deserve whatever scholarship you earned."

My breath hitched, caught somewhere between my lungs and my throat. I stumbled over my next words, my usual eloquence abandoning me. "Oh, um. Yeah. Thanks."

Smooth, Violet. Real smooth.

Trying to recover, I asked, "Same deal? Stalk me to the showers, then leave me wounded at my door?"

He laughed, the sound rich and warm, wrapping around me like silk. "Sure, *volchok*."

The pet name sent a shiver down my spine despite the heat. I wondered what it meant, though anything at this point was better than *princess*.

"Let us go," Rowan said. "I can fill you in on the rules of my house."

"Oh, boy." I fell into step beside him, hyperaware of the space between our bodies—maybe six inches, close enough to feel his body heat in the humid air. "I can't wait."

Sarcasm dripped from my voice, but underneath it, something fluttered. Anticipation, maybe? Or trepidation for the murder, the danger, the complications piling up like debts I couldn't pay. Or the beginning of something I'd refused to admit.

Chapter 14

Rowan

Violet did not seem to mind the rules I gave her. Her roommate was gone before we returned, giving us privacy to discuss the finer details while sitting in her dorm, the dark wood flooring gleaming under lights that cast everything in amber warmth.

First, meals were to be consumed prior to her shift. If she absolutely had to eat or drink at Oubliette, she would only consume items we brought ourselves. Nothing from the club. Nothing touched by the staff or clientele.

Second, she would keep a spare set of clothes at my place. I hadn't made this official yet, but with time, I planned to note her sizes and shop for a few pieces myself. The thought of her wearing something I'd chosen sent an unwelcome heat through my chest.

Third, no one-on-one dances. No private rooms. No circumstances where she'd be alone with a patron. Thankfully, this was something she agreed to immediately, her hazel eyes clear and certain when she'd nodded. She didn't think it would pose a problem for Jules.

Fourth, she would take the bed. I would sleep in the living room. She'd argued this one, but I'd been immovable. The bed was hers. End of discussion.

Fifth, Violet could have freedom from my constant presence, but only if she was strict about traveling from dorm to shower. Direct routes only. No detours. No wandering unless it was in large public places like bus terminals, where there were plenty of people. Otherwise, I would shadow her every step.

She had agreed to the rules initially, but—true to her nature—quickly revolted. After spending a few hours with me, my presence a constant blur at the edges of her vision, she'd begged me to leave her alone for an hour or two before her late evening training. Studying for tests, she'd claimed, her voice carrying that particular edge of desperation that told me she needed space to breathe.

So, I'd given it to her... and I promptly went hunting for answers.

I haunted the university's grounds like a ghost, testing old skills I hadn't used since my first life. The oak trees were ancient, their branches thick enough to bear my weight without creaking. I climbed them with careful rigor, bark rough and solid under my palms, the scent of green leaves and wood filling my nostrils. I scaled a few walls, hiding from students who passed below in clusters, their voices bright with weekend plans and exam stress.

It was exhilarating using a younger and stronger body compared to the one I had died in. I almost lost sight of my quest.

Then, finally, I found her.

In an alcove formed by oak trees near the library, I found my vampyress hidden in the treetops—a fitting location for a creature who'd lived centuries. Her ivory dress was spread around her like an offering to the grove, and the bright fabric caught the dappled light of the setting sun as it filtered through the canopy above. She'd nestled into the crook of a massive branch, her body relaxed in a way that suggested complete comfort. In her pale hands, she held a leather-bound copy of *The Epic of Gilgamesh*, the pages yellowed with age.

She did not look up from her book when I approached, though I knew she'd sensed me the moment I'd entered the grove. She said, "I could have sworn I put up a glamour." Her voice carried that particular musical quality unique to her kind. Like wind chimes made of bone.

I sat down on a lower branch nearby, careful not to brush against her. Even accidental contact with a vampyre could be dangerous if they were hungry or annoyed.

"It seems you can hide from many, but not all, vampyress."

She snapped the book closed with a sound like a gunshot in the quiet grove. In the shadows of the grove, her eyes appeared midnight like the vast sky—pupils blown so wide the irises disappeared—turned to me with an intensity that would have made most mortals flee.

"Indeed. Why have you come?"

Excellent question. . . why have *I come?* This was foolhardy, but I could not seem to steer myself away from danger. Not when Violet was involved.

"Did you do it?" I refused to be subtle. No point dancing around the question when we both knew what I was asking.

Her eyes flashed, literally glowed with offense for a heartbeat before dimming back to passing as human. "No."

"No?" I sounded as incredulous as one could with a one-syllable word.

She met my abrasion with unexpected gentleness, her voice softening. "I did not kill that boy. Not when it could threaten someone close to me."

"Oh?" I tilted my head, studying her. The faintest flutter of her heart pattering—a telltale sign she'd fed recently—sounded nothing like the thunderous pounding of a human heart. The lack of breathing, the utter stillness of her chest, the nearly radiant light of her eyes, and how her skin seemed to absorb sunlight rather than reflect it were just some of the symptoms of vampyrism. The signs were so blatant when you knew how to look for them that it made me wonder how vampyres had remained hidden throughout all of human history.

Then it occurred to me that she had casually mentioned that she cared for someone attending Shademore. Was that why she was hanging around the campus and not feeding to her shriveled heart's content? It had been days since I had seen her, and I knew she must be ravenous. Was there a reason why she was withholding herself?

No matter. I continued my inquiry. "But you know who did."

She shook her head, platinum white hair catching the dappled light like spun webs. "I have an inkling, but nothing solid as of yet." She pressed a finger briefly to her temple, the gesture oddly human. "Without any evidence, there is little I can do."

"But when you find proof of who was responsible? Will you turn them over to the police?"

"No," she answered. "The laws of you *muritors* mean next to nothing to us. The freshly formed *Pax Tacere*, however, carries significant weight."

"Obviously," I said.

Truthfully, though, I knew next to nothing of the *Pax Tacere*—some secret pact formed between the supernaturals before the veil fell—because it was already ancient history by the time I was born in my first life. Of course, *she* didn't know of my ignorance, and I wasn't about to parade it around.

But I made a note to look into it. Knowing it was recent meant there could be information hidden somewhere in the libraries Charlie and I ventured to. It was something.

She shifted on her branch, her ivory dress whispering against bark. "Even if I *did* have evidence that proves who killed that boy, I doubt I would bother to take it to my father. Neither he nor the other kin wish to ruffle the veil, and I do not blame them. Not when gods are roaming."

That got my attention. "The veil is a physical thing? And which gods?" I met her eyes, curious whether she'd answer, knowing I was pushing my luck. She was being oddly forthcoming with information, more than I'd expected from a creature notorious for hoarding secrets.

"I'm surprised you have to ask that question, handsome. You seem so," she bit her lip as she pondered her words, "well informed." Her fingers traced the embossed title on her book's cover, the gesture almost nervous. "All I will say is that no kin nor clan wants the scales tipped either for or against them right now, lest they suffer the attentions of the current reigning gods... gods who are ever so insecure on their thrones."

Classic immortal politics. Everyone is jockeying for position while pretending to maintain the status quo. It's not much different from my first life.

"It sounds as if you are in a tight spot, then. Are there any kin specifically giving you... trouble?" It was no business of mine what went on between supernaturals and gods. However, considering I had cheated Death once after dying to The Library's Hunter, I felt it was in my best interest to understand the current political landscape.

She regarded me with a dissecting stare, her head tilting at an angle wrong enough to remind me she wasn't human. "Why do you ask, *muritor*? Are you offering your aid?" She laughed as she said it, as if the very thought of my help was hilarious to her.

This is a stupid thing to say, I thought as I said, "And if I am?"

She laughed harder, the sound like silver bells mixed with breaking glass. "And if you are what? How could *you* possibly help *me*?"

I knew this was a gamble, but I'd already come this far. I took a deep breath before I said, "You said you have a suspect for the murder, but lack evidence? What would you do if I found that evidence?"

Her laughter died down. "Oh, you were being serious?" She sat straighter, and as she spoke, her voice carried the weight of centuries, coloring each word. "Between the Strega's Nine Sins and Death's ire, *nobody* wishes to have attention drawn to them in this moment. . . lest they desire to join a Grim on their journey to the beyond."

Nine Sins? That was something else I should look into, but her comment on Death is what had me curious.

"So even you immortals fear Death?" That tidbit of information was fascinating. I knew supernaturals could die, having hunted a few myself in my previous life. But immortals? This was gold. And while I had seen depictions of Grims in lore, I had no desire to meet one in person.

She snickered. "Some things are worse than dying, *muritor*. All things end. That is the way of things." Her eyes held mine, ancient and knowing. "Even those who evade a Grim or cheat Death itself come to learn that lesson before the end. The finality of Time greets them. . . eventually."

"Unless you manage to cheat even that," I said quietly.

"An interesting choice of words," she mused. "I only know of two that have escaped Death and Time's grasp." She leaned forward slightly, her voice dropping to barely above a whisper. "I would be careful if that is the information you seek."

I took note of her warning, filing it away with all the other dangerous knowledge I'd accumulated. "Thank you. I will remember that."

Her gaze was steady, scrutinizing, peeling back layers I'd rather keep hidden. "Tell me, what do you plan to do if you find out it is one of our kind? Banter until they confess, or simply offer your neck with your stupidity?"

"Vampyress," I said, my tone grave and sincere. "I would never insult the intelligence of your kind."

"You insult it by seeking me out when it should be the other way around." There was no heat in her words, just observation.

I stood, brushing bits of bark from my dark jeans, and turned my back to her. A clear sign of trust among predators—exposing the throat, the spine, all the vulnerable places. "I merely wished to know if it was you."

"And you trust me?" The question carried genuine curiosity.

I waved as I walked away, my footsteps silent on the grass. "You have given me no reason not to." I looked back at her, still perched in her tree like some ethereal creature from a fairy tale. "If it is one of your kind, I pray they know the old ways and will adhere to them like you do."

"Do not pray, *muritor*. You will only be disappointed." Her voice carried across the distance between us, clear as crystal. "Were I any other of my kin, you would have been dead the moment you stepped near." She hesitated, seeming to consider her next words carefully. "What I heard through my connections was that the boy's body had been ravaged, similar to a wild animal. . . do with that what you will."

That gave me weighted reassurance. Our acquaintance was etched in a thin line of trust, built on hidden stories neither of us wished to disclose.

"You may leave," she commanded in mock authority, a small smile playing at her lips.

As if I would have waited for her permission.

Chapter 15

Violet

Rowan shadowed me later that evening to my second Brazilian Jiu-Jitsu practice, with the same relentless patience he'd shown all day. Aside from the brief reprieve he'd granted me, we'd spent most of the day together. Despite that, he refused to falter in his surveillance.

He positioned himself against the wall near the mats, arms crossed, those pale eyes tracking every movement as I rolled with my training partners. I'd stopped trying to pretend his presence didn't affect my performance. It did. Everything felt sharper, more precise, like I was performing rather than simply training.

When practice ended, and I'd changed back into street clothes, he was waiting exactly where I'd left him.

The walk back to my dorm was quiet, our footsteps falling into synchronized rhythm on the concrete path. Students passed us in clusters, their voices bright with weekend plans and exam stress. Rowan said nothing, but I felt his attention like a physical weight, cataloging every person who came too close, every shadow that lingered too long.

Exhausting. This was exhausting. But it was also, in a way I refused to examine, comforting.

We climbed the stairs to my floor, and I unlocked the door with my key—the metal scraping in the lock, the familiar click of the mechanism releasing. Rowan followed me inside, removed his shoes at my prompting, and sat on my bed. He settled cross-legged against the headboard, pulled a book from the bag he'd been carrying, and opened it with the ease of someone who'd done this a hundred times before.

Go ahead, make yourself right at home in my personal space. I should have resented it. Should have demanded he wait in the hallway or the common area like a normal guest. Instead, I just dropped my gym bag and headed for my desk, pulling out the textbook I needed for that night's studying. It was nearly nine, almost curfew, so I knew I needed to shower, which meant Rowan would be leaving soon after.

We'd barely settled into comfortable silence when the door opened, and Alice stepped in, her arms loaded with textbooks and her laptop bag hanging from one shoulder. She stopped short when she saw Rowan, surprise flickering across her features before transforming into something like amusement.

"Funny seeing you here, Gonorrhea Boy." Her tone was teasing, friendly, completely at ease.

Rowan glanced up from his book, his expression utterly unbothered. "It is chlamydia, but thank you for your concern."

She smiled at that, genuine warmth crinkling the corners of her eyes.

A dark, unwelcome emotion rose in my chest—hot and possessive and absolutely inappropriate. *Jealousy?* I shoved it down before it could show on my face.

"He's helping me study," I said quickly, my voice coming out sharper than intended. "I hope you don't mind?"

Alice moved with her characteristic calm, setting her things on her desk and shrugging off her jacket—a light cardigan in soft gray. "Not at all. Natalia was here earlier but said she had something to do. I don't mind the company, really."

Relief washed through me, unexpected and profound. Most roommates would have objected to a six-foot-five man occupying their shared eight-by-twelve dorm room.

"Thank you," I said, meaning it.

Rowan's curiosity had apparently been piqued. He set his book aside—keeping one finger between the pages to mark his place—and asked, "Is Natalia another dormmate of yours?"

We both shook our heads in unison, and I waited for Alice to explain. I was curious about Natalia myself—the striking woman with flowing white hair and flawless dark skin who'd visited a handful of times, always seeming slightly otherworldly in our mundane space.

Alice hesitated, her hands pausing where they'd been arranging textbooks on her desk. Finally, she said, "She's a very close friend. We grew up together, actually. Her family has known mine for generations, so it only made sense we'd end up at the same university."

Rowan let out a low whistle, his attention fully focused on Alice now. "A strong family tie, then."

She nodded, and I watched something complicated cross her face—affection mixed with pain, loyalty mixed with burden. "My mother was her wet nurse until Natalia outgrew the need. We lived on the family estate, and when my mother died. . ." She paused, swallowing hard. "Natalia refused to let her father force me out. She insisted I stay, that I was family regardless of blood."

Surprise rippled through me. That kind of loyalty, that protection across class lines, spoke to a bond deeper than simple friendship.

"You two must care deeply for each other," I said, trying to imagine growing up in that dynamic—servant's daughter and wealthy heir, boundaries blurred by genuine affection.

"We do. Very much so." Alice's voice softened with unmistakable love.

"Where exactly did you grow up?" Rowan asked, and I noticed his posture had shifted. More alert, focused in that particular way that suggested he was filing information away rather than making idle conversation.

"Romania." Alice pulled her hair tie out, letting her dark tresses fall free around her shoulders as she massaged her scalp.

"Ah, a very lush country. Filled with rich folklore traditions." Rowan's tone remained casual, conversational, but something in his eyes had sharpened.

I watched Alice stiffen—subtle but unmistakable, her spine straightening, her hands going still. "It is, but most of that folklore stems from generational families holding ties to the old ways. Tradition, superstition, that sort of thing. Nothing anyone takes seriously anymore."

"And you came all the way here to the States for university?" Rowan's tone held a genuine curiosity.

"The school was paid for and chosen by Natalia's father." Alice's voice had gone carefully neutral, each word selected with care.

I heard the hidden message beneath her careful phrasing as clearly as if she'd screamed it: *I didn't choose to come here. I was sent.*

"Well, it must be nice having Natalia visit," I offered, trying to ease whatever tension was thickening the air.

Alice seemed to consider this, her expression softening slightly. "It has been, though I'm certain her father isn't pleased about it. She has duties back home she's been avoiding by coming here so often."

"Sounds awful," I muttered, thinking of families who treated their children like obligations rather than people. Like property to be managed rather than individuals to be cherished.

Like Edward treated the girls he owned.

"Some of us are held down by things others cannot understand." Alice's words came out quiet, weighted with meaning that felt both universal and intensely personal.

Rowan's eyes cut to mine immediately—not a glance, but a full, loaded stare that pinned me in place. His wintery gaze held understanding and recognition, and something that made my breath catch.

I turned away, breaking eye contact before the weight of his perception could crack something open inside me. "Well, I'm glad we're dormmates. You're easily lovable, Alice. Unlike someone I know."

I didn't look at Rowan as I said it, but I felt his attention on me like a heat-seeking beacon. He let out a small chuckle and returned to his book, apparently unbothered by my barb.

Alice smiled then, the expression genuine and warm enough to push back the heaviness that had settled over our conversation. "That's sweet of you to say, Violet. I feel the same."

She settled at her desk with her laptop, and the room fell into comfortable quiet—three people coexisting in shared space without needing to perform or explain or justify.

I should have felt trapped with Rowan constantly in my orbit, invading my privacy, occupying my bed like he had every right to be there. Instead, I felt something dangerously close to safe.

And that terrified me more than his surveillance ever could.

Chapter 16

Rowan

Wednesday morning, barely past six, the campus was still quiet except for the dedicated few who rose before dawn. Violet was walking to her morning class, eyes downcast as she rushed through the central courtyard with the single-minded focus of someone trying to remain invisible.

As I waited in a nearby oak tree—my feet dangling from a thick branch roughly fifteen feet above the ground—I pushed down my frustrated annoyance. Violet had left without waiting for me, as a rather disheveled Alice explained when I knocked on their dorm door. I wondered if I should I have installed a GPS tracker on her phone? At least then I would be done with the cat-and-mouse game she seemed determined to play.

The bark pressed rough against my dark jeans, and my hands were sticky from sap that smelled sharp and green—pine resin that would take scrubbing to remove. It had been years since I'd climbed consistently, not since my previous life when trees meant surveillance points and elevated positions meant survival. My muscles burned with the pleasant strain of supporting my weight, my core engaged to maintain balance, my forearms tight from gripping branches.

I miss this. The clarity that comes from physical exertion, from using my body the way it's meant to be used.

A group of three girls dressed in workout gear passed beneath my perch, their voices bright with morning energy despite the early hour. One glanced up, following the line of the trunk, and her eyes widened when she spotted me.

She grabbed her friend's arm, pointing. All three stared for a long moment—taking in the sight of a six-foot-five man casually lounging in a tree like some overgrown cat. I could see the exact moment recognition shifted to appreciation, the way their gazes traveled over my frame, lingering on places that made their intentions clear.

One whispered something to her companions that made them all giggle. They looked back up at me with eyes that held invitation before walking away quickly, glancing over their shoulders twice.

I knew I was drawing attention. Knew I looked absurd perched in a tree on Shademore's campus.

I did not care.

Violet was getting closer, her purple duffel bag slung over one shoulder, dressed in a simple grey tank top and navy shorts with a to-go cup clutched in her other hand. Steam rose from the cup's small opening, carrying the scent of coffee and something sweet. Her hair was pulled into a high ponytail, the red streaks catching early morning sunlight that filtered through the oak's leaves in dappled patterns.

I timed my descent perfectly, releasing my grip and dropping directly into her path.

She startled violently, her drink sloshing in its cup, her free hand flying to her chest. She gave me the most disgusted look I'd seen yet—nose wrinkled, lips curled, hazel eyes flashing with genuine irritation.

"You couldn't wait in the dorms like a normal fuck boy?"

"And miss out on your delightful reaction?" I brushed bark from my jeans, noting the dark stains the sap had left. My white shirt stuck to my skin. "Never."

She pushed past me with her shoulder—a solid hit that would have moved a smaller man—and I followed, falling into step beside her with ease.

"You can go home. I have tests this afternoon, so I'm going to be studying for the next several hours." She didn't look at me as she spoke, her gaze fixed forward like she could will me out of existence through sheer determination.

"Why not study in your dorm, then?"

"Because I wanted a change of scenery, Rowan. Is that okay with you?"

"Of course it is. I, too, would like a change of scenery. This way, I can even help you study," I offered.

She said nothing, but I heard her teeth grind together.

We walked through the halls of the humanities building—old stone and dark wood, the architecture reminiscent of Gothic revival with its pointed arches and heavy timber beams. Eventually, we emerged into an open courtyard where wooden picnic tables were scattered across close-cropped grass bearing the dawn's speckled light. Some tables were occupied by students already deep in study, others sat empty in the shade of ornamental cherry trees.

"Are students normally up this early studying?" I asked.

"Yeah, why wouldn't they be? You'd probably be surprised how early and late some study groups will meet up. It's going to be even more packed when we get close to midterms and finals."

"It is no small wonder that boy was killed, then. If I were a killer, this campus would make for the perfect hunting ground."

"Because?" she inquired as we continued our trek across the courtyard, weaving through old cobbled paths.

Her question reminded me that she did not see the world the same way I did. "Small groups. Some solo. Everyone in their own little world and not paying attention to where they are going, much less who is around them."

Violet stopped at that, glancing my way. "When you put it that way, it sounds kinda obvious what happened, doesn't it?"

I nodded.

Violet found a table isolated from the others, tucked into a corner where stone walls met on two sides, and set down her belongings with more force than necessary. Her bag hit the table with a heavy thud.

"Psychology 101 has a quiz coming up on Friday." She pulled out her textbook, the thick, glossy cover proclaiming Introduction to Psychology in bold letters, and flipped it open with aggressive efficiency. "I need to memorize symptoms and tie them to possible diagnoses."

It sounded interesting enough. Psychology had never been accessible to me in my previous life—survival consumed too much energy to contemplate the mechanics of human behavior when understanding it instinctively meant the difference between living and dying.

But in this life, Charlie had made it a point in my homeschooling to ensure I was well-rounded. Psychology and Philosophy had been some of my favorite topics.

"Well, anything related to dependency disorders, you have locked down." I kept my tone light, teasing.

She threw me a glare that could have melted steel. "And anything possessive or obnoxiously controlling is very clearly you."

"That does not sound particularly scientific when you phrase it like that." I settled onto the bench across from her, stretching my legs out beneath the table.

She mumbled something obscene under her breath—I caught "asshole" and possibly "smug bastard"—before she pulled out notebooks and highlighters with color-coded caps.

"Psychology is the scientific study of the mind and behavior," she recited, her voice taking on the particular cadence of memorized information.

"What is the specific topic for this quiz?"

"Emotion and motivation across cultures." She listed it off while flipping to the relevant chapter, her finger scanning the page.

"Hmm." I leaned back, considering the topic as my foot casually brushed against hers. I could feel the heat of her skin against my dark jeans, sending a jolt of pleasure up my leg. "I am partial to arousal theory myself."

She looked up sharply, and I watched color creep into her cheeks, highlighting her sharp beauty. "Too bad. That's next week's lesson." She paused, her eyes scanning ahead in the textbook. Then an audible, "shit" escaped her lips.

"Sounds as if you are mistaken," I said, fighting back a smile.

She groaned and dropped her forehead into her hands, her voice muffled. "I cannot *believe* I have to study *this* with you being so. . . so insistently annoying."

"I will find motivation to maintain alertness throughout this activity." I let my voice take on a professorial tone, deliberately invoking dry academic language. "As I was growing rather bored waiting on you to finish your futile attempt at escape."

"Don't be an ass." She lifted her head, and despite her scowl, I caught the ghost of a smile. "But that's actually a decent way to describe the Yerkes-Dodson principle."

I smirked. "I know. Shall I continue explaining arousal theory's application to our current situation?"

"Talking about your arousal?" She flushed deeper, the color spreading down her throat into places the darkness in me craved. "I'd rather not, but since you seem well-informed, let's discuss Yerkes-Dodson properly."

"With pleasure." I leaned forward, resting my forearms on the table.

"Please... just don't." But she was smiling now despite herself, her eyes sparking with reluctant amusement.

I laughed, the sound carrying across the quiet courtyard. *This*, I thought. *This is what I've been missing.*

Not the physical proximity, though I craved that too. But the verbal sparring, the intellectual challenge, the way she met me word for word and refused to back down, even when I clearly had more knowledge on the subject.

We spent the next two hours dissecting theories of motivation and emotion, her asking questions and me providing explanations that ranged from textbook accurate to deliberately provocative. By the time we finished, her notebook was covered in notes and diagrams, and the tension in her shoulders had eased into something approaching relaxation.

Small victories I cherished, given the tension in the school.

The school's murder remained unsolved despite the heavy police presence that had transformed the campus into something approaching a surveillance state. Officers patrolled in pairs, their uniforms dark blue and official, their expressions projecting competence they didn't possess. Students felt the weight of their presence—conversations quieting when cruisers rolled past, movements becoming more cautious, more contained.

It was a false sense of safety. *Security theater* designed to comfort rather than protect.

I had been meticulously careful to avoid the police during my evening reconnaissance after dropping Violet at her dorm. I'd spent hours scouring the grounds for clues the authorities might either miss or—more likely—overlook as a clue entirely. After all, the police were looking for a human suspect and wouldn't even notice anything that would have suggested a supernatural explanation.

Since my meeting with the vampyress in her oak tree sanctuary, I had not encountered her again. But the fragment of information she'd provided was enough to confirm my suspicions that something beyond mortal evil had taken that student's life.

Last night's scouting had given me time to learn the campus geography with intimate detail. Every building, every path, every shadowed alcove. Even the stables where Violet rode had become familiar territory after Aaron confirmed my relationship with her through Levi.

I had been genuinely surprised when Levi gave his blessing for me to access the equestrian facilities. Surprised and grateful, two feelings I was unaccustomed to feeling towards him. Little did Levi suspect that those moments watching Violet ride Hyacinth had become something I looked forward to with an intensity that should have concerned me. How her body moved in perfect synchronization with the horse, the way her face transformed by genuine peace and joy—it was the only time she ever seemed to be truly at ease. The sight tightened something in my throat every time.

Despite the short time, somehow we'd fallen into something approaching comfortable silence around each other. Close proximity would do that, I supposed. It was as if we were both studying each other intimately without wanting the other to know. We'd learned each other's rhythms, our tolerances, the precise moments to speak and when to simply exist side by side.

Still, our tempers flared from time to time.

Such as right now, I thought, staring at her plump round ass walking away from me.

"I need you to lay the fuck off, Rowan!" Her voice echoed in the stone corridor as she rushed from the communal showers back towards her dorm, her hair damp and smelling of expensive floral shampoo I unconsciously smelled for, her shower caddy clutched against her chest like a shield. She was dressed in a white t-shirt and shorts that hugged her ass in ways that made my hand twitch.

It was nearly eight p.m., and students were beginning to settle for the night, mindful of the ten o'clock curfew that hung over campus like a guillotine blade. Doors closed. Voices lowered. The building took on that particular quiet of enforced containment.

"Go home, for fuck's sake!"

"I plan to," I said, matching her pace easily despite her attempts to outdistance me. "But I thought you wanted to grab dinner before I left—"

"I can walk one hundred yards to the cafe, Rowan!" She whirled on me, and I saw genuine distress beneath her anger. Her eyes were too bright, her breathing elevated beyond what the short walk warranted.

She was upset, and I could not determine why. We'd had a pleasant enough day—studying together, walking between her classes, sharing a quiet lunch where she'd actually laughed at something I'd said.

"People are going to start thinking things if you keep walking me all the way to my room," she said, her voice dropping lower as two girls passed us in the hallway, their curious eyes taking in our proximity.

Oh. Really?

"What kind of things, Violet?" I kept my voice neutral, genuinely curious what assumptions bothered her enough to trigger this reaction.

She flustered, color flooding her cheeks. "Just—go away."

"I never expected you to be so prudish." The observation slipped out before I could consider whether it was wise.

"I am not prudish!" Her voice pitched higher, and she glanced around to ensure no one was listening before hissing, "But a girl wants to masturbate away from her fuck boy occasionally!"

I laughed. I couldn't help it. The image of her, frustrated and wanting, desperately trying to find privacy for self-pleasure while I hovered outside her door like some Victorian chaperone, was absurdly funny. *And if she thinks being honest or crude will scare me, she is about to learn how quickly I can match her pace.*

"We both know you are severely lacking in fuck boys, Violet."

That raised her hackles beautifully. She stormed closer, jabbing a finger hard into my chest. "I've had my fair share, thank you very much."

Proprietary fury struck through me, hot and immediate and absolutely irrational. My jaw clenched hard enough to ache. "And who the hell did you let touch you?" The words came out sharp, edged with anger, as my fingers ached to leave imprints on her ass.

"Whoever I wanted!" She jabbed my chest again, punctuating each word. "Why does it matter? Because it is *my* choice, Rowan. My body. My decision."

"Your father would never have allowed—" I started, falling back on logic and parental authority.

"Daddy wouldn't know!" She cut me off, her hazel eyes flashing in gold and green. "I snuck out to do it, obviously. What, you think I asked permission?"

I was angry now, genuinely angry in a way I hadn't felt in years. "That was not safe, Violet. What if someone had tried to hurt you, or worse—"

"I can take care of myself!" She shoved me, and I let her move me back a step. "I'm not some delicate princess like you keep calling me."

"You are a *spoiled* princess," I fired back, my patience finally snapping. "Is that why you are so angry with me? Me following you, protecting you, keeping you safe? It prevents you from going out and rutting the night away with some frat boy?"

Her eyes went wide, then narrowed into dangerous slits. "And what if it is? It's none of your business who I decide to *rut* with, Rowan." Her voice turned cold then. "Or is this jealousy? Is that it? Are you jealous that I'd rather sneak away to find a *real* man to fuck me? A man whose face I could use like a god damn throne? Just like the *princess* you claim I am?"

My cock swelled immediately, blood rushing south so fast it made me dizzy. An image slammed into me: Violet straddling my face, her hands tangled in my hair as I struggled to breathe.

Fuck.

"You would not know how to handle me, Violet." My voice had gone rough, barely controlled.

She threw her hands up, nearly dropping the shower caddy as plastic bottles clattered to the floor, rolling across the tile. "Oh, because you absolutely scream *well-experienced*. Go fuck off and find your next girl to stalk. I'm done with you tonight."

"Gladly." I bit the word out, my pride stung, and my cock still painfully hard. "Go kill your toys' batteries thinking about me."

We stormed off in opposite directions—her towards her dorm room, me towards the stairs—both of us acting like petulant children rather than adults.

I did not care.

She was like a splinter embedded deep in my flesh, impossible to extract, the foreign object slowly being absorbed and integrated until it became part of me. Growing with me. Changing me in ways I couldn't map or predict or control.

Maddening. She is absolutely maddening.

After our fight, I left campus entirely for an hour, desperate to burn off the restless energy crackling through my system like electricity seeking ground. I was careful to avoid well-traveled areas, sticking to the paths I'd mapped during previous evening hunts. I made my way back to where I'd first encountered the vampyress, that grove of ancient oaks near the library where the veil between worlds felt thinner.

The trees there were perfect for what I needed—thick branches, dense canopy, enough height to see campus spread below while remaining hidden from casual observation. The stone walls surrounding the older buildings provided handholds and ledges, routes I could navigate in near silence.

I climbed until my muscles screamed, until sweat soaked through my shirt and my hands bled from fresh scrapes. Pushed my body until the image of Violet straddling my face finally faded enough that I could think clearly. I needed my rope. The methodical movement kept my mind busy and prevented me from craving untouchable things.

By the time I returned to her dorm building, I was sweaty but spent, the violent edge of possessive anger finally dulled to something manageable.

Alice met me at the door, either arriving or departing—I couldn't immediately tell which. She wore a light jacket over her summer dress and carried a small purse, suggesting the latter.

"Oh, Rowan." She smiled, stepping aside to let me enter. "I'm meeting my friend, so I won't be back before curfew. Violet's sleeping. I imagine she's exhausted after all those nightmares."

I went still, every muscle locking. "Nightmares?"

Alice's expression shifted to something like guilt, as if she'd revealed a secret she shouldn't have. "Sorry. I thought you knew, given how much time you spend together. She'd been cranky lately, and I connected it with her lack of sleep."

I shook my head, keeping my voice level despite the sudden spike of concern. "Explain. Please."

She glanced down the hallway, confirming we were alone, then lowered her voice. "She gets nightmares regularly. Normally, I sleep through them, but the worst ones..." Alice's face softened with sympathy. "She cries out. Says things. I've gotten up once or twice to soothe her, and it seems to help settle her back into deeper sleep. She doesn't realize it, and I don't plan on telling her."

Gratitude flared through me, unexpected and profound. "Thank you. Truly. For taking care of her."

Alice shook her head, something sad crossing her features as she reached for me. "Natalia gets them sometimes, too, so I knew what to do. What helps." She squeezed my arm gently. "She's lucky to have you watching over her, even if she won't admit it."

Then she was gone, disappearing down the hallway with quick steps, leaving me alone with the knowledge that Violet suffered through horrors even in sleep.

I entered the dorm room quietly, easing the door closed behind me with barely a click. Sure enough, Violet lay in her bed, dressed in a thin white T-shirt and sleep shorts that did almost nothing to preserve modesty. Her breath was steady, the deep rhythm of genuine sleep, but her brow was pinched—a small crease between her eyes that spoke of discomfort even in unconsciousness.

I sat on the floor beside her bed, my back against the wall, and simply waited.

Watching her had become something of a habit over the past few days. Not in a way I could justify or explain, just a bone-deep need to confirm she was safe, breathing, still here.

Thirty minutes passed in quiet observation. I listened to her heartbeat—steady at first, the reliable rhythm I'd memorized without meaning to. I watched the rise and fall of her chest, the way her hair spread across the pillow, the vulnerability of sleep softening features that were always so guarded when awake.

Then she began to toss.

Quick, jerky movements that made me tense. Her head thrashed against the pillow, expression pained, her hands clenching the sheets, her legs kicking out. I was afraid she would hurt herself—slam her hand against the wall, fall out of the narrow bed, wake disoriented and panicked.

My hand reached out instinctively, settling against her forehead. Her skin was warm but not feverish, slightly damp with perspiration.

"No. No. Stop." The words came out slurred, desperate, her voice younger somehow. Smaller.

Her heartbeat jumped—from forty beats per minute to nearly a hundred in seconds, erratic and panicked as if fear itself coiled in her dreams and wrapped around her heart.

I debated waking her, shaking her shoulder until consciousness returned and banished whatever horror played behind her closed eyes. But Alice's method had worked, she'd said. Soothing rather than waking.

"Shh, you are safe, Violet." The words felt oddly familiar on my tongue, and I realized why—I'd said them before, in my previous life, to children who'd lived in the brothels where I'd sometimes worked security. Children born into that world, who'd never known safety, who'd cried from nightmares I couldn't even imagine. "Everything is alright."

Her chest heaved with a sharp intake of breath, and my eyes drifted lower before I could stop them.

No bra beneath that thin tank top. Her nipples were taut, the barbells of her piercings visible through white fabric. I could see the slight swell of her breasts, the curve of her waist, the lean muscle of her stomach.

I forced my gaze away, guilt slamming into me.

She is vulnerable and terrified, and you are noticing her body like some creep.

But my eyes found another detail I'd somehow missed before—a tattoo on her left thigh, partially visible beneath the hem of her shorts. Delicate line work, though I couldn't make out the full design from this angle but it was fresh like the ink on her arm.

When had she gotten that done? How had I not noticed?

Because you are not supposed to be staring at her thighs, you bastard.

"Stop, please." She whimpered, and the sound drove a spike through my chest.

I kept my strokes gentle, my fingers carding through her hair with the same rhythm I'd use to calm a spooked horse. "Shh. It is okay, Violet."

My knuckles ventured farther, stroking down her cheek with feather-light pressure, then lower to the column of her throat. I could feel her pulse beneath my fingertips—still too fast, still panicked, but beginning to slow.

"Rest. No one will hurt you while I am here."

It seemed to be enough. . . she made a small, happy noise and nuzzled against my touch, turning her face towards my hand like a cat seeking warmth.

My cock jerked in immediate response, and I cursed my body's betrayal.

She is asleep. She is having a nightmare. This is not the time.

"Safe. You are safe," I repeated, keeping my voice low and soothing despite the guilt churning in my gut.

She let out a sigh—long and releasing, as if exhaling the nightmare itself. Her heartbeat steadied, dropping back to normal rhythm. Her breathing deepened, her body relaxing by degrees until the tension bled out of her muscles entirely.

Despite our complicated relationship, despite her constant protests against my presence and my frustration with her reckless choices, it pained me to see her this way. What had her fearing so much?

I stayed for hours, unable to leave her side. Every time I considered slipping out, her breath would hitch, or her face would tighten, and I'd freeze. Afraid that moving would trigger another nightmare, that my absence would leave her vulnerable to horrors I couldn't fight.

It was past midnight when I finally forced myself to stand, my body stiff from sitting on the hard floor. I took one last look at Violet—peaceful now, her expression soft, her breathing deep and even. Then I left, closing the door with a quiet click as the sound of rolling thunder promised rain.

The walk back to my apartment felt longer than usual, my mind circling through everything I'd learned. Her nightmares. Her past lovers

that made possessive rage burn through me. The way she'd looked at me during our fight—angry and flushed and so fucking beautiful it had stolen my breath.
I am in trouble. Deep, irrevocable trouble.
And I didn't know how to stop falling.

Chapter 17

Violet

Thursday morning started off weird, thanks to Rowan.

I stood around the corner of Whitestone Hall, my back pressed against the cold stone still damp from last night's rain, as I wondered what the hell I was watching him do. Students streamed past me in both directions, their voices a low hum punctuated by occasional laughter, the scrape of backpack zippers, the hollow thud of a coffee thermos hitting the ground. None of them seemed to notice the tall angelic man crouched in the dirt outside the lecture hall entrance, head tilted, studying the ground like it held the secrets to the universe.

Rowan.

My self-appointed shadow for the past four days. My unwanted bodyguard. *My—I don't even know what to call him anymore.* The boy I'd known growing up had been quiet, observant, careful. This version? This Rowan, who'd inserted himself into my life with the inevitability of a winter freeze?

He was something else entirely.

I wanted to move closer, to see what commanded his attention with such focus, but I didn't want him to know I was there. I wanted to watch him, to study him.

Rowan shifted his weight, the movement fluid and economical. Pale morning sunlight caught in his hair, turning his pearly hair almost translucent against the dark collar of his leather jacket. Pine. Even from here, I caught the scent of him, sharp and clean, cutting through the smell of wet concrete and the cloying perfume of the girl who'd just walked past.

That scent filled every space he occupied, saturated the air until it felt thick, overwhelming, impossible to ignore. Like standing too close to a bonfire—the heat became part of your skin whether you wanted it or not.

"I know you are there, Violet."

His voice cut through the morning noise, smooth and certain. Not loud. He didn't need volume when every word landed with that kind of precision.

My breath caught.

He stood in one fluid motion, turned, and those pale eyes locked onto mine. Ice-blue and ancient, seeing too much, stripping away the comfortable distance I'd tried to maintain. His posture shifted—spine straighter, shoulders broader, chin slightly lowered. A predator's stance. The boy I'd known growing up wouldn't have looked at me like that, wouldn't have held himself like violence wrapped in skin, like he was deciding whether I was a threat or prey or something worth pursuing.

This Rowan was different. This Rowan made my pulse spike, my breathing shallow, and every survival instinct I'd honed scream.

"Will you not come closer?"

I shook my head before I could think better of it, my fingers fidgeting with my bag. My heart slammed against my ribs. "Your presence is overwhelming."

His brow creased, confusion flickering across features that gave away so little. "I do not understand."

Of course you wouldn't.

How could someone like him—someone who filled every available space with that masculine scent, with the sheer force of his attention, with a physicality that made the air feel thinner—possibly understand what it was like to be on the receiving end? He was the storm. He'd never been the thing caught in the storm's path.

"It doesn't matter." I forced the words out and tried to sound dismissive rather than rattled. "What were you looking at?"

"Your footprints."

Matter-of-fact. Like that was a perfectly normal thing to be doing on a Thursday morning outside Whitestone Hall.

I scoffed and said, "There's no way." Between the dozens and dozens of students who'd walked through there that morning, surely any prints I'd left would have faded into the general chaos of disturbed dirt and mud.

Rowan pointed to something near the entrance, a spot where water had pooled and then receded, leaving behind a perfect canvas of damp earth. That gesture, that silent invitation, caused my curiosity to pull me forward.

Students flowed around us like water around stones, oblivious to whatever strange ritual was unfolding. The dirt patch was small, maybe three feet square, trampled by countless feet into a minefield of overlapping impressions.

"You do not walk straight into anything."

I bristled, every defensive instinct flaring hot and immediate. "Excuse me?"

His eyes crinkled at the corners when he smiled, and my traitorous heart stuttered in my chest. Pulse kicking up, breathing coming faster, heat crawling up my neck despite the cool morning air.

Well shit.

"You circle into places before you enter. Look," he pointed. "There." He crouched again, and I followed his movement. My gaze was drawn to the way his jacket pulled tight across his shoulders, the way his long fingers gestured towards a set of faded prints mixed among so many others.

I squinted at the smudges in the mud. "There's no way to tell if those are mine."

But even as I said it, I was looking at the prints he indicated. Since he'd pointed it out, I saw the pattern. It was there if you knew what to look for—a series of wide arcs approaching the entrance to Whitestone Hall, then a tight curve away, before finally straightening out and veering off the path to the door of the lecture hall. Not the direct path most people took. Not the efficient route.

"The stride matches your size shoes, they come from the direction of your dorm, and," he looked down pointedly, "Those are your size and shape of shoe." I felt his analytical gaze as he assessed my feet. "Why don't you step over it?"

The challenge in his voice made my teeth set on edge. I obliged, placed my boot directly over the faded impression, and felt something cold slide down my spine when it fit perfectly. Not just close. *Perfect.*

"How the—"

"Most animals walk in a straight line for energy efficiency." His voice took on an educational tone, patient and clinical, like he was explaining basic arithmetic. "Very rarely do they make the extra effort to deviate from that unless they are being chased or feel threatened."

I stared at the print, then at the hundreds of others nearby. He was right. Most of them cut straight paths—direct lines from point A to point B, the way normal people moved through the world without thinking about it. Mine curved, hesitated, approached from angles.

Exposed. That's what this feels like. Someone peeling back my skin to examine the machinery underneath, cataloguing my tells, my patterns, the unconscious behaviors that gave away more than I'd ever intended to share.

Some primal part of my brain—the part that remembered being watched, catalogued, studied like a specimen in a glass case—screamed at me. Memories of previous life were constantly intertwined and swirling with this one, painting everything with a brush of surveillance and threat.

Edward had studied me like that. He'd watch until he knew which positions made me cry the hardest, which words made me flinch, which friends of his I would do anything to avoid. He'd used that knowledge like a weapon, a currency, a tool of control.

I shoved that memory down and clenched my jaw until my teeth ached.

This man is not Edward. This is not the same.

This was Rowan. Sure, he was strange, and rude, and a gigantic pain in my ass... but he was also my childhood friend. He'd appointed himself my protector without asking, and he'd shadowed me for days with a patient inevitability. He was someone who looked at me like I was worth defending, even when I told him to fuck off.

The invasive feeling shifted, twisted, turned into something else. A feeling closer to being *seen* rather than *watched*—being *known* versus being *studied*.

"You ever think I just don't like walking in a straight line?" The deflection was weak, and we both knew it. My voice lacked conviction, lost somewhere between defensive anger and reluctant fascination.

Rowan shrugged, the movement elegant for someone so large. "Or maybe you do not enjoy people getting close to you." He straightened, and I had to tilt my head back to maintain eye contact. Six-foot-five of muscle, looking down at me with those pale, icy eyes. "Regardless, I am glad to see I can find you even when you attempt in vain to be sneaky."

"It's creepy how you knew I was nearby." I shoved my hands in my jacket pockets and tried to sound annoyed rather than unsettled.

His smile widened, knowing and amused and carrying just enough wickedness to make my stomach flip. He extended his arm in a sweeping gesture—*lead the way*—and cocked his head slightly. "Where to?"

Shit, how can I lose him? Days of trying to slip away between classes, of taking different routes, of varying my schedule, and here he still was. My shadow. My hunter. My—whatever the hell he thought he was.

And now I have him for the rest of the day. Joy.

"There's a café nearby," I said with a sigh. The words came out resigned. I paused, searching for some way to regain the upper hand, to shift the dynamic back towards something I could control. "Can I buy you breakfast?"

"Only if you promise not to expect me to put out afterwards," he taunted.

"You'd make for a poor fuck anyway."

He chuckled, the sound low and rich and doing absolutely nothing to calm my racing pulse. "So you keep saying."

I coughed, feeling oddly guilty about our last big argument, and asked, "Coffee? Or do you need another fruity drink?"

"If you are trying to get to know me," he said, "I actually like Chai tea lattes."

Of course you do.

"So do I," I said. The admission slipped out before I could stop it, before I could pretend we had nothing in common, that this connection was one-sided and unwanted. "You're in luck. The café has some of the best Chai I know of around campus and gluten-free pastries."

"I am looking forward to it," he said with a smile that did things to my belly that I absolutely refused to examine.

Chapter 18

Rowan

Atlanta's Friday afternoon was sweltering, humidity thick enough to chew, the sun beating down on concrete that radiated heat like an oven. Unbearable. Hot. Tourists and students crowded the sidewalks, their voices a cacophony I had to consciously dial down.

Back in my apartment, I was eager to clean in preparation for Violet's stay. The space already looked immaculate—I'd never been able to tolerate mess, not after living in squalor my entire first life—but I needed to be certain. I changed the sheets to fresh white linens that smelled like lavender, fluffed the pillows, and made sure Marie Antoinette was hidden away under the bed where Violet wouldn't stumble across her. Satisfied, I gave Violet a call, hoping to catch her between classes.

She picked up on the third ring, her voice slightly breathless. "Couldn't survive a couple of hours without me?"

Her question hit closer to home than I wanted to admit. I hated how her absence left me restless, stalking my apartment like a wolf without territory. I hated how her smile—rare as sunlight through storm clouds—could thaw parts of me I'd thought frozen in my previous life. Most of all, I hated how much I craved our battles, those moments when we circled each other with words sharper than blades, both of us bleeding but neither willing to yield. So, I deflected my emotions the only way I knew how to.

"I cannot come without hearing your voice," I said, letting the double meaning hang between us.

"Oh, so you must be finished then." I heard the smile in her voice, the teasing lilt. "I've got a class to run to."

A bell chimed in the background—the distinctive sound of the campus cafe's entrance. I filed that information away, mapping her location without conscious thought.

"Finished? *Nyet*, just getting started." I heard her chuckle at that as I continued, "Are you eating before tonight's activities?"

"Well, *someone* gave me a few stupid rules I need to follow, and I am trying to adhere to them." She grumbled, and I could picture her scowl perfectly. "It's hard enough finding celiac-safe food anywhere, much less on campus."

Fuck. I forgot about her celiac disease.

"I am sorry, *volchok*. I forgot how difficult it can be. I can keep a few things here for you." I grabbed the dry-erase marker from the counter, scribbling a note on the whiteboard attached to my fridge: *Gluten-free options—bread, pasta, snacks.* "Will you be long? I can meet you at your dorm."

I hated how desperate I sounded, like some lovesick fool instead of a man who'd survived fifty years in a frozen hell.

She took a few breaths before replying, the sound slightly muffled. "Omp, sorry. Shoving food down the hole. Text me your address, and I will get a ride."

"No." The word came out sharper than I'd intended. "I thought I was clear about being alone with strangers—"

"Fine, Rowan." Her voice carried that edge of exasperation I was becoming familiar with. "Meet me at the campus terminal—which is public by the way— and you can show me how to get to your place."

I willed my heart to slow down, forced my breathing to regulate. "Alright. In an hour?"

"Sure," she conceded.

The blue line was cramped, filled with students ready to start their weekend and out-of-towners eager for Atlanta's upscale restaurants and nightlife. The city seemed to carry that allure, offering endless entertainment for those who could afford it. I stepped off the bus onto the campus, the bus stop's concrete still warm under my soles despite the approaching evening.

There was no shortage of visitors milling around—students in university colors, tourists consulting phone maps, businesspeople in sharp suits rushing towards dinner meetings from nearby office buildings. The campus bus stop was a chaotic convergence of bodies, but it was also public, which meant whoever had killed that student ideally would not be stupid enough to attack someone in a large crowd.

I glanced over passing bodies looking for Violet. In this crowd, it would have been impossible for most.

Not for me.

Despite how frayed my nerves were, my enhanced hearing picked up thousands of conversations at once. I focused, listening for the sound of her stride among the chaos. I filtered out the meaningless noise, searching for that particular cadence I'd memorized without meaning to.

There. The familiar rhythm of her brisk walk.

I turned in her direction and was greeted by her smile—genuine and unguarded. My chest tightened.

"Rowan, finally made it?"

Relief surged through me, cool and sweet. I took her hand in mine without thinking, her palm warm against my skin. The contact sent electricity up my arm. "I can always find you, even in a crowd like this."

She laughed, the sound reverberating in my ears as I consciously turned down my hearing to save my sanity. "Don't remind me. You're like a bat, somehow always knowing what direction I'm coming from."

"How fitting." I kept hold of her hand as we navigated towards the platform, my heart racing to match hers. "Like a bat, I too can be cuddly and clingy."

"Gross," she said as she wrinkled her nose.

I found the expression endearing. The way her whole face scrunched up with her hazel eyes narrowing. "You look like your mother when you do that," I said.

"Ugh, *double* gross!" She pulled her hand free to swat at my arm. "Don't ever let me do that again."

"Noted." I reached for her bag—a massive duffel in dark purple—and nearly dropped it when the weight registered. Easily over sixty pounds. "What is in this?"

"Only my essentials," she said breezily, as if that explained everything.

By essentials, she really meant her entire wardrobe–those killer heels I'd watched her dance in, and probably enough cosmetics to stock a small boutique–I'd come to find out later. The bus ride was relatively quick, the vehicle swaying on its route while Violet chatted about her exams. Her voice washed over me, familiar and grounding. I said little, enjoying the musical quality of her voice. Safe. Comforting. Mine.

Walking up the stairs to the third story of my building—industrial concrete painted gunmetal gray, the stairwell smelling faintly of cleaning solution—I handed Violet the newly made spare key. I'd had it cut that morning at the hardware store, choosing the shape myself from their novelty options.

It was bright hot pink, the end painted with the shape of a prancing horse.

She squealed, the sound high and delighted. "Oh my god, Rowan! It's perfect!"

I laughed despite myself, warmth blooming in my chest at her reaction. "Here, test it out."

She took it with reverent hands and inserted it into the lock. The deadbolt turned smoothly, the door swinging open with a soft click. She hugged the key to her chest like it was precious.

"I love it. I've got to think of a name for him."

"Him?" I raised an eyebrow.

She stepped inside, working on slipping off her sneakers—white canvas, grass-stained and worn. "Don't presume to know his gender, Rowan!"

"Ah, right. Sorry," I said, fighting back a smile.

I showed her around the apartment, pointing out the master bedroom with its platform bed and white linens, the bathroom with its industrial fixtures and rainfall shower, the study I'd converted into a workspace. She oohed at the floor-to-ceiling windows overlooking Atlanta's shopping district, the view a glittering expanse of glass towers and neon signs just beginning to light up as evening approached. For once, I was glad for the space, given how it impressed her.

Then she threw herself onto the freshly made bed, landing with a bounce that made the mattress springs sing. Her hair spread across the white pillows like spilled ink and wine.

"You have a swank place." She stretched like a cat, her spine arching. "Decorated it yourself?"

"No, it came furnished." I leaned against the doorframe, watching her claim the space as her own. "Courtesy of the adopted father."

I threw her earlier barb back at her, my tone dry.

Her face fell, guilt flashing across her features. "Listen, Rowan... that was unkind. I am sorry about that."

"*Only* that?" I pressed, curious how much ground I'd gain.

She refused to look my way, suddenly fascinated by the texture of the duvet. "Yep, only that. You mind if I get water?"

"I will grab it for you."

I was in the kitchen filling a glass with filtered water from the fridge, ice cubes crackling as they settled, when I heard her scream. Instant recognition flooded through me, along with a spike of adrenaline that had my body moving before my brain caught up.

Fuck. She's found Marie Antoinette.

"Rowan!" Violet rushed into the kitchen, her face ashen, hazel eyes wide with shock. "You've got a body under your bed!"

I groaned, setting down the glass with more force than necessary. Water sloshed over the rim. "Violet, why were you looking under the bed?"

"I was looking for your porn stash!" Her voice pitched high with residual fear and indignation. "I didn't realize that's where you kept the corpses!"

She was clearly shaken, her hands trembling slightly, her breathing elevated. I could hear her heart hammering against her ribs, the sound like a drum to my enhanced hearing.

Might as well come clean.

"My porn is on the computer in the study. I can give you the password later." Wide eyes stared back, unable to determine if I was joking or not.

I took her hand in mine, her fingers cold with shock. "Listen. What you saw is not a corpse. Here, let me show you."

"Show me your collection? It's not the one I was expecting, so I'd rather not."

"It is safe. I promise."

"That's what all serial killers say," she whispered.

I chuckled as we walked back to the bedroom together. I knelt beside the bed and reached under, wrapping my fingers around familiar rope and smooth plastic. Pulling out Marie Antoinette took some maneuvering—she was still in her last tie, the Shinju suspension I'd been practicing. Her limbs were positioned at angles that would be difficult for a living person.

Violet eyed the mannequin warily, her body tense like she was ready to bolt. "Why is she headless?"

I pointed to where the neck ended in a smooth post fitting. "Most mannequins are. That is why she is called Marie Antoinette."

"The queen?" Her voice carried skepticism mixed with reluctant amusement.

"Is there another?" I asked.

She bristled, some of her color returning. "God, no. But I just wanted to make sure." She eyed the tie work, her gaze tracking the patterns of rope—cerulean blue against cream-colored plastic, the knots precise and complex. "So. . ."

I mirrored her posture, crossing my arms. "So. . ."

"Shibari? Not dead corpses?" Her eyes glinted with the faintest trace of incredulity, but underneath it, something else. *Interest, maybe? Or curiosity?*

"That is what you focus on after discovering my secret?" I couldn't hide the surprise in my voice. Most people would still be processing the shock. "But yes. . . shibari. I am surprised you recognize it."

She shrugged, kneeling down to admire Marie Antoinette more closely. Her fingers hovered over the rope work, not quite touching but clearly wanting to. "I've always loved the premise."

Is that so? I couldn't help the approving twitch of my cock as she admired my ropework.

"Rowan, the tie is lovely. It's so pretty."

My gaze lingered on her—on the vulnerable curve of her neck as she bent forward, the soft skin where her pulse fluttered visibly. I resisted the urge to stroke my fingers down that exposed expanse, to feel her heartbeat under my palm.

"Gorgeous, actually." And I didn't mean the tie as I cleared my throat. "Thank you," I managed, my voice rough.

I heard her take a deep breath, her lungs expanding, her heartbeat steadying. Tentatively, she touched Marie Antoinette's shoulder, her fingers tracing the rope pattern. "Have you ever thought about tying a real person instead of a doll?"

"It is a mannequin," I corrected softly, my throat tight. I sighed, eyes flicking towards the hallway as if searching for words in the shadows. "And no. I—" I hesitated. *How do I explain this?* "It requires trust."

"Right, trust. Makes sense. I guess we don't share that." I heard the longing in her voice, barely hidden beneath casual agreement. The way her breath caught slightly, her pulse kicking up.

But we do, I want to say. Otherwise, why would she have been in my apartment? Why would she let me go with her to Oubliette?

Instead, I cleared my throat and forced myself to step back before I did something stupid. "It is nearly time for you to head to Oubliette. Do you need help changing, or. . ." I trailed off, leaving the offer hanging between us.

She stood, shaking her head. Her hair swung around her shoulders, catching the light from the windows. "Nope. I should be good. Just give me thirty minutes, and I'll be ready."

"Sure." I turned to leave, then stopped at the threshold. "Should I. . . take Marie out?"

Violet eyed the mannequin once more, her expression thoughtful. "Might be best. Instead of keeping her under the bed, where does she normally reside?"

"The living room. It is where I do my ties."

"Cool." She smiled, genuine and warm. "Maybe just shove her in the corner so she can scare us shitless when we get home tonight."

I laughed, the sound surprising me. Taking Marie Antoinette carefully, I carried her to the living room and positioned her in the corner as requested—still in her suspension tie, her ropes catching the amber light from the pendant fixtures.

For the first time since this fucked-up arrangement had started, I felt something like normalcy settle over the apartment. Maybe this would work out. Perhaps Violet living in my space would not be the disaster I'd feared.

Dark thoughts teetered on the edge of my logic. Or maybe this would be a different kind of disaster entirely. One I was walking into with my eyes wide open.

Chapter 19

Violet

Jules greeted us at the entrance, an ebony-clad Romeo positioned stoically behind her like a shadow given human form. Somehow, she'd anticipated our arrival, her blue eyes bright with welcome beneath the club's crimson and violet lighting that painted everything in shades of sin.

"Violet! So glad you made it. And early, too?" Her platinum hair was tied in two impossibly perfect pigtails adorned with trailing white ribbons that cascaded down her bare back, the silk whispering against her skin with each movement. "So nice to have young ones who understand professionalism."

Her well-endowed breasts were barely contained by a simple white two-piece bikini that left little to the imagination, the triangles of fabric straining against curves that defied physics. Gold glitter covered every inch of exposed flesh—and there was considerable flesh exposed—catching the light with each breath, each shift of weight. She looked like sex personified, wrapped in innocence and dusted in precious metal.

"I thought you could not wear white after Labor Day?" Rowan's voice rumbled behind me, apparently unbothered by Jules's state of undress. His tone carried that particular dryness I was beginning to recognize as his version of humor.

Jules turned those vivid blue eyes on him, one perfectly sculpted brow arching. "Superstitious?"

"Not particularly, but most Southerners are." He stepped closer, his presence a wall of heat at my back. "I am surprised you are not."

Jules pursed glossy pink lips—the color of cotton candy, matching the scent that seemed to follow her everywhere—in contemplation. "This ain't the mountains, honey. Although Appalachian folklore runs deep and rich about luck, death, and protection."

"Folklore such as?" Rowan's curiosity sharpened his voice, transforming casual conversation into interrogation.

"Oh, all kinds." Jules's smile widened, showing perfect white teeth. "Don't whistle at night, don't walk over graves, don't speak of evil lest it come visit."

"When you say *evil*, do you mean supernaturals?"

A strange tension crystallized between them as we continued towards the bar, the air thickening with unspoken challenge. Jules smiled and patted Rowan's arm with familiar ease, her fingers lingering against his forearm. "Don't worry, honey. Those Appalachian superstitions are over a hundred miles away."

His response came dry as bone. "Appalachia is not the only place with folklore."

As we walked past the bar, Andy called out to us and interrupted Jules and Rowan's back and forth. Jules waved us to the bar as she said, "Go on and pay him a visit. He'll be all pouty if you don't go say hi and nobody likes a sad bartender."

Jules headed backstage as we turned towards Andy. The genial bartender waved and shouted out, "Hello, friends! So glad to see you both again." His dark-eyed gaze washed over me with open appreciation, noting I wore the same sleek black dress from my previous visit—simple, elegant, easy to move in, and easier to remove. "Back for more, eh?"

I smiled, genuinely pleased to see him. Something about Andy's easy charm felt safe and unthreatening. "Couldn't stand another day without seeing your face."

He laughed, the sound rich and warm beneath the club's throbbing bass. "Careful. Compliments get you *everywhere* around here."

"I'm counting on it," I said with a smile.

Rowan brushed up behind me, and my spine straightened involuntarily, hyperaware of his proximity. Heat radiated from his body, seeping through the thin fabric of my dress. His scent enveloped me.

"Hello, Andy." Rowan's voice carried an edge I'd come to recognize as possessive—controlling, even. "Do you want to let the lady start her shift?"

He was being overbearing again. I elbowed him playfully, hoping to defuse whatever territorial nonsense was building in his chest. "There's nothing wrong with a little mingling."

He turned to me and gestured towards the hallway where Jules had disappeared. "When the mingling delays your start time and keeps us here longer? I disagree."

His perpetual state of grumpiness was starting to wear on me. "What do you *need* to be happy, Rowan?"

"I could think of a few things that might ease my anxiety about this whole charade you seem so intent on pursuing." His voice dropped lower, intimate despite the pulsing music.

I poked him again, daring him to vocalize whatever pent-up desires seemed desperate to escape the fortress he had constructed around himself. "Whatever could the stoic Rowan want?"

He grabbed my waist then, pulling me into his arms with enough force to steal my breath. With my heels, we stood nearly eye level. I couldn't help but stare at his gorgeously pale irises—blue-gray like winter ice, like frozen lakes that you would drown in if you fell through. They glimmered in the club's strobing lights, reflecting crimson and purple back at me.

"Do you really want to know, Violet?" He pressed me closer, eliminating every centimeter of space between our bodies. His mouth brushed against the shell of my ear, breath hot and relentless against sensitive skin. "I want to gouge out the eyes of every single person in this fucking club for daring to look at you."

"Oh, *fuck*." The words slipped out before I could stop them, helpless and hungry.

Somehow, his admission of violence was unbearably arousing.

He let out a dark laugh that slithered between my legs in an unrelenting pulse, as if he knew exactly what depraved thoughts had crossed my mind. "I do not know what you are really searching for here, *volchok*, but I plan to let every fucker in this room understand you are not theirs to touch."

His thumb stroked my waist, leaving a trail of fire despite the fabric. I have felt threatened or frightened, but with Rowan? There existed only a perplexing surge of *desire* for him and his possessive madness.

"How are you going to do that?" I asked. "You planning on pissing on my leg?" I retorted, clearly enjoying this side of him—raw and unfiltered, the civilized veneer stripped away to reveal something feral underneath.

"No." His voice turned to gravel.

"Then how will they know?"

"Violet..." He seemed torn, waging a war within himself as he looked into my eyes.

"Do you wanna show me, Rowan?" I dared him, tilting my chin up in challenge.

He let out a growl, his restraint finally snapping like overstressed rope. "If you insist."

His lips crashed into mine in a searing kiss that scorched through every ounce of resistance left in me, as if he had mapped the exact shape of my defenses and knew precisely how to demolish them. The kiss tasted like possession and promise, his mouth claiming mine with brutal urgency. Heat exploded through my body, pooling low in my belly, making my thighs clench. Before the kiss could deepen, he pulled away, leaving my mouth swollen and burning.

"This is how," he said, apparently undeterred by whatever had just transpired between us, despite the exhibitionist nature of our public display.

Oh, this absolute asshole.

"You cannot just do *that*." I huffed, my skin pebbled from the ghost of his touches, my nipples hard beneath my dress.

"I clearly just did." He gave me his infuriating grin—all teeth and triumph. "And now everyone will know."

I shoved him hard, gathering my scattered wits like dropped weapons. "Know what? That you are an overbearing ass?" I snapped and took a step back, desperate for distance, in an attempt to rebuild the wall between us. A wall he seemed determined to demolish brick by brick.

He shrugged, his smirk growing even more infuriating. "Overbearing? No. Vigilant? Yes."

"As if. A word of advice? Use your tongue more next time," I snapped. "Now be a good boy and wait here."

Rowan had the gall to offer me a mocking salute. Andy possessed the foresight to appear busy polishing the same glass he had been holding prior to our little display, though I caught the amused quirk of his lips. I complimented Andy on his daring choice of leather pants and crimson crocodile boots before heading backstage, my heels clicking against polished floors.

As I walked, I surveyed the main floor. The crowd had swelled since our last visit. Every table was occupied by men and women of varying ages, all wearing designer clothes, jewelry, and watches. Several gazes tracked our direction. I knew those looks. . . assessing, cataloging, pricing.

I was nearly to Jules when a hand wrapped around my wrist and the cloying smell of cologne filled my nostrils. A voice tinted with an accent said, "I have decided to grace you with the honor of giving me a private dance, *mon amie*."

My body reacted on instinct, snatching my hand away before I'd even looked at the speaker. I turned to see a well-dressed man staring at me with a pair of heterochromic eyes—one blue, the other brown. I recognized him from a few nights ago; the memory of how he'd hungrily studied me from his shadowed booth was still fresh in my mind.

Revolted—partly from how possessive his touch felt, partly from how he looked at me—I said, "I don't do private dances."

He smiled, shrugged, and opened his mouth to say something, but I'd already turned my back to him and kept walking. *Pretentious and presumptuous prick*, I thought as I weaved my way through other patrons.

In my first life, I didn't have the luxury of choosing who could touch me or when. *But I sure as shit do now, and I plan to enjoy that simple privilege.*

Jules greeted me just beyond the velvet curtains that separated the public space from the dancers' domain. She nodded towards the bar and said, "Your friend is very protective of you." Her statement carried hidden meaning, a question wrapped in observation.

She's worried he's going to be a problem. Shit, I'm worried about that myself. "With the school's recent death, he has been somewhat... intense." I hoped she would accept that excuse, that she would not see Rowan as a liability.

My lips still burned from his kiss. I couldn't identify any logical reason *why* I was comfortable with him getting away with a stunt like that.

You know why, a dark voice whispered in my mind.

I shoved it away.

Jules led me down a different corridor than before, this one lined with velvet walls in deep burgundy and doors that looked suspiciously soundproof. We stopped before a door marked with a simple brass plaque: *Office*. It opened at her touch, revealing the most ostentatious room I had ever laid eyes on.

Sleek black furniture dominated the space—glossy finishes and clean lines creating a sharp, contemporary aesthetic that screamed money and power. A wrap-around mahogany desk occupied the far corner, its surface gleaming beneath recessed lighting. The room smelled like expensive leather and something floral I could not quite identify. Jules stepped behind the desk and pulled out a thick stack of papers, the pages crisp and official-looking.

"Here is the employment paperwork. Standard contract, tax forms, the usual bureaucracy." She tapped perfectly manicured nails—white with pink accents—against the documents. "You can have a seat here and fill these out while I make a copy of your license."

My anxiety spiked, sharp and immediate. Panic clawed at my throat before I could suppress it. *Easy, Violet. Standard procedure. They cannot steal your identity with just a driver's license, right?*

I clutched my small purse, realizing how ridiculous my paranoia was, before producing my license for her inspection. "Of course. Here you go."

She walked towards a door I had not noticed—presumably leading to a copy room—leaving a trail of cotton candy perfume in her wake. I sat in one of the low chairs at the desk and began filling out the paperwork, scanning clauses about conduct and compensation, when the sound of the door clicking made me look up.

"That was fast—"

The words died in my throat.

A man filled the doorway, and *filled* was the only appropriate descriptor. His olive skin possessed an almost supernatural polish, gleaming like burnished umber beneath the office's warm lighting despite the ivory white suit he wore. Gold finishes and thread highlighted features that seemed carved rather than born—sharp cheekbones and square jaw, lips that promised either salvation or damnation depending on his mood. His presence expanded to fill every corner of the room, reminding me of a certain someone who left me perpetually breathless.

Why is everyone in Oubliette so devastatingly attractive?

"Oh, hello," I managed. "I am... I'm sorry, but Jules stepped out momentarily."

He smiled then, revealing perfectly white teeth. His canines seemed oddly sharp, catching the light in a way that made my pulse kick up.

"Thank you. I am aware of everything that transpires within this club." His voice was liquid smoke, rich and warm, with an accent I could not quite place yet similar to my family's. Spanish, perhaps, but older somehow. Refined.

That is an oddly specific statement, I thought, uncertain how to respond to such a declaration.

"Oh. Well, then you know she will return soon." I offered weakly.

He crossed the room with predatory grace, each step deliberate and silent despite what looked like expensive dress shoes. Sitting on the desk's edge, he looked down as if studying me. I noted his footwear—the same reptilian leather as Andy's boots, though these were iridescent black that shifted to deep green in certain light. Actual crocodile, I guessed... and obscenely expensive.

He towered over me even while seated, much taller than I was accustomed to—taller it seemed than even Rowan, which seemed impossible. Or perhaps it was simply how low the chairs sat, designed to make visitors feel small and vulnerable. Either way, his presence sent butterflies rioting through my stomach as I fought the flush threatening to stain my cheeks.

He offered me his hand, palm up in invitation. "I am Damien, the proprietor of this establishment."

I really was terrible at first impressions.

"Oh, I am so sorry for not realizing." I placed my hand in his, expecting a handshake.

Instead, he pulled my knuckles to his lips, pressing a kiss against my skin that lingered just long enough to cross from polite to provocative. His lips were warm, soft, and I felt that touch reverberate through my entire body like a struck tuning fork.

"The pleasure is entirely mine... Violet? Or would you prefer Alexis? Though I am rather fond of *gatita.*"

Did he just call me a kitten? I blushed, unable to ignore this man's magnetic pull. Heat crept up my neck, staining my cheeks. "Either is fine." I paused, reconsidering. "Actually, Violet. I would prefer to reserve Alexis exclusively for my clients."

Damien nodded, accepting my boundary without complaint. His amber eyes—and they were genuinely amber, like honey backlit by sunlight—surveyed the desk where my half-completed paperwork lay scattered. He made no comment about the unfinished state.

"You are welcome to use whatever name you wish while within these walls, *gatita.* I offer you my most genuine gratitude for choosing our fine establishment."

I hung onto every word that came from his mouth. His voice had a timbre and lilt that set my core quivering, unable to look away. What was wrong with me?

I realized I *was* staring at him and that he was waiting for me to say something. "Oh, uh... well, it wasn't much of a choice. I simply need supplemental income." The words tumbled out before I could filter them.

"Oh?" He tilted his head, curiosity sharpening his features.

And suddenly I was fumbling, scrambling to recover. "Not to imply this establishment is anything less than exceptional for employment. I'm genuinely excited to work here. Jules is amazing, and—"

As if summoned by her name, Jules swept back into the room and stopped abruptly upon seeing Damien. Her demeanor shifted from casual to deferential as she said, "I did not realize you had returned already. I would have greeted you properly." Despite her precarious heels, her steps quickened as she hurried to stand beside me.

He waved a hand with elegant dismissal, continuing his assessment of my paperwork. "It is of no consequence. So, this Violet. . . she is the one you spoke so highly of?" His eyes found mine again, and I squirmed under that penetrating gaze—as if he could see through flesh and bone straight into my soul.

"Yes," Jules said as she placed a hand on my shoulder. It was a maternal gesture that caught me off guard. "Honestly, her skill on the stage nearly rivals my own."

I knew I was good—you didn't survive years of forced performance without developing exceptional skills—and while the validation felt gratifying, I was stunned by her admission. I recalled from my first life how breathtaking Jules had been on the stage. She *literally* taught me everything I knew about the pole.

He acknowledged what she'd said with a slight nod, then placed my paperwork down with careful precision. "That is good to hear. As long as she is an employee of Oubliette, she will have my protection."

The words settled over me like a weighted blanket—comfort and confinement in equal measure.

Jules squeezed my shoulder as she said, "I will ensure it is known throughout Oubliette." She paused, something flickering across her features. "And the one she arrived with?"

Damien gave the smallest shrug. "Am I expected to be hiring him as well? Is he meant to serve as Romeo's partner at the front door?"

Suddenly, I felt as if I were trapped in the middle of a negotiation—Damien as the boss, Jules as the consigliere, leaving Rowan and I as nothing more than assets being discussed like property. While I appreciated Jules's support, I refused to let Rowan suffer any consequences for my choices.

I cleared my throat. "May I interrupt?"

Both sets of piercing eyes turned to me, amber and cerulean, and I willed myself to remain steady beneath their combined scrutiny.

"Given Shademore's current predicament, Rowan—my friend—will want to accompany me during my shifts here."

When he spoke, Damien's voice carried a polite curiosity undercut with steel. "And this becomes a concern of mine. . . in what way, precisely?"

I pushed forward, knowing full well this could destroy my entire plan. But after Rowan's stubborn display of protectiveness, I couldn't simply discard him. He would march straight to Daddy, and then I would have much larger problems than negotiating with the proprietor of a gentleman's club.

"It isn't a concern. He is merely providing security." I chose my words carefully, building my argument. "It will not interfere with my dancing, and honestly, since I have no intention of offering private dances, I anticipate my evenings will be relatively brief. In and out, efficient and professional."

I was gambling everything on this negotiation. I knew from observing other dancers that one-on-one sessions were optional—an additional revenue stream rather than a requirement. After enduring years of assault in my previous life, I possessed zero interest in having strangers touch me, regardless of compensation.

Except with certain people, noting how neither Jules nor Rowan's contact triggered my usual panic response.

I filed that observation away for later analysis.

Damien contemplated my words, his expression unreadable. Finally, he directed his scrutinizing gaze to Jules. "She is nearly on par with your skills, you said?"

Jules glanced at him and nodded, her fingers squeezing my shoulder once more. "With time and proper training, I believe she will surpass me."

I gaped at her as my words tumbled out unchecked. "There is absolutely no way I could ever match you."

She looked down at me with the ghost of a smile playing at her lips. "How would you know? You've never even seen me dance, girl."

Shit, she was right. My face burned red as I realized my mistake. I *hadn't* seen Jules dance—not in this lifetime. I stammered, "Well, I assumed that... I mean, you *have* to be amazing if you are in charge of scouting the talent for a place as prestigious as Oubliette, right?"

"You ain't wrong about that, sweetie." She laughed, then said, "Listen, you may not recognize it yet, Violet, but you shine on that stage. I don't know *where* you learned to dance like that, but I would never diminish another woman out of jealousy." She patted my shoulder before returning her attention to Damien. "We need her, sir. With Bri on leave, *she* will be our weekend highlight."

"Very well." Damien's acceptance came swift and final. "If you and your guardian truly are inseparable, then I shall have to grant my protection to the boy as well. And given the current happenings at the university, that protection shall extend beyond the walls of Oubliette."

Protection? This guy really does *talk like he's a mob boss. What in the hell do we need protection from?* I started to ask that very question, but Jules's shocked gasp cut me off.

"If you're offering to exert yourself outside Oubliette—"

"Enough." He raised a hand to silence her as his amber eyes drilled into me with an intensity that caught my breath. "I have made my decision." He stood with fluid grace, and I interpreted that as dismissal.

I started to gather my belongings and paperwork when Jules gently took my arm and said, "Sweetie, the paperwork can wait until after your first set. Damien plans to watch."

She pointed to the wall on our right. A small click sounded, and the wall slid into the floor, revealing an immense flat screen displaying multiple camera feeds of the club's interior.

My stomach dropped. "None of those show the private rooms, right?"

Jules shook her head, white ribbons swaying with the movement. "Private rooms are exactly that—*private*. We don't monitor what goes on in there. But everything that happens on the first floor is out in the open and monitored."

I noted she specified only the first floor, which meant the levels below remained unmonitored as well. *Interesting.* She steered me towards the door, and the television screen shifted from multiple displays to a single feed focused entirely on the stage.

Jules practically vibrated with excitement. "Ready to show them your skills again?"

I nodded, and we left Damien alone to observe my performance.

After my first set was done, I sat in the dressing room backstage reflecting on how it went—the crowd's reaction, which parts did I miss, which parts did I hit, was I good enough, did my nervousness ruin my dancing?

First performances never got easier. That fundamental truth remained constant in this life as it had in my previous one. With time, I'd come to realize that regardless of how many people you performed in front of, it was *who* was in the audience that was the real cause of nerves. I should have been worried about Damien's assessment, but for some inexplicable reason, I was more concerned about Rowan's.

It didn't help that I couldn't tell what was going on in his head while I was dancing. His face, his entire demeanor, reflected something I couldn't place—not quite fear, anger, or lust but a cocktail of all three, unique to him alone. His eyes never left me as I moved across the stage, almost like he was rooted to the bar like a sentinel positioned to monitor all entry points while keeping me centered in his sightline.

I hated myself for finding comfort in it.

I wanted to loathe him on principle. He was nothing more than a childhood friend turned arrogant protector, behaving as though I needed rescue when I had spent years mastering ways to break a man's body. My purple belt in Brazilian Jiu-Jitsu was not decorative—I had *earned* that belt through blood, sweat, and countless hours rolling on the mat.

And while it sounded reductive, I didn't trust anyone. Decades of sexual slavery had taught me that lesson with brutal efficiency. Both men and women were searching for transactions—creatures who viewed bodies as commodities with price tags and expiration dates.

However, the last few days had forced me to reconsider my beliefs. Rowan had demonstrated repeatedly how he could respect my autonomy despite his overbearing presence. I understood the *why* behind his protectiveness, even as it chafed against my independence. His constant presence should have felt like surveillance, reminiscent of how Edward and his men once monitored my every movement.

Instead, it felt like security. A fortress standing between my difficult present and my uncertain future.

That didn't prevent my anxiety from rearing its vicious head at unexpected moments. At times, my memories felt like a tangled mess of privilege and trauma, creating a cognitive dissonance I couldn't reconcile.

And yet, thinking back to the way he hugged me sent coils of warmth through me. I wasn't alone.

"Sweetie!" Jules's voice broke me out of my reverie as she enveloped me in an enthusiastic hug. "Your transitions were absolutely on fire out there!" She patted my head maternally. "That has to be the best first set we've ever seen around here. Damien was pleased."

Had Jules been anyone else, I would have dismissed her as a vapid party girl masquerading as a mother hen. But after our earlier conversation with Damien—combined with the memories from my previous life—I'd come to accept Jules as one of those rare and precious things: a genuinely *kind* person. In a world populated by predators and prey, Jules existed outside that brutal equation.

So why does she seem oblivious to what truly transpired at Oubliette?

The question created a rift in my perception of her. Sometimes I wondered if Jules was the only normal person in my increasingly strange existence—a beacon of ordinary kindness in a life fractured by complications. Despite every warning bell clamoring in my head, I found myself accepting her friendship with something dangerously close to gratitude.

"Alexis, did you hear me, sweetie?" Jules asked, using my stage name as her voice penetrated my inner spiral. "I said you're on again in five."

"Yeah. Sorry." I nodded and began preparing to go back on.

The space in the dressing room buzzed with energy and conversation, thick with the scent of hairspray, perfume, and the particular musk of women preparing for performance. I focused inward, settling into the headspace I required for dancing.

Because dancing wasn't about sexuality—not really. It was about *control* for me. Ownership of my body and knowing it was beautiful in all the ways I chose to use it.

On that stage, I dictated the terms of engagement. Men could look but never touch. They could want but not have. For a woman who spent decades being touched without consent, that reversal of power felt like oxygen after drowning. There existed intoxicating freedom in controlling my own body after years of captivity, in choosing exactly how much of myself to reveal and to whom.

I adjusted my costume—black, minimal, designed to showcase strength rather than vulnerability. Someone approached from behind, and I tensed reflexively before recognizing the touch as non-threatening. Turning, I found a petite brunette with generous curves poured into a gorgeous sequined navy ensemble. She offered me a bottle of water, her smile genuine.

"You must be the new girl. I'm Erin." She extended the water. "You made those transitions look absolutely seamless."

Out of courtesy, I accepted the bottle despite having brought my own. Rowan's first rule—don't accept food or drinks from anybody in Oubliette—was one that made sense. "Thanks. It sounds like I'll be helping out while Bri is gone."

"Bri is phenomenal," Erin said, "But you are a natural out there. And we are all just thrilled to have you on the squad!" She waved and departed, leaving me to my preparations.

Jules's voice cut through the dressing room chatter. "One minute, Alexis!"

I threw the water bottle Erin had given me into the trash, rolled my shoulders back, lifted my chin, and stepped into character. The music shifted—something with a slow, hypnotic beat that crawled under skin and settled into my bones. My song. My signal.

Stage lights blinded me momentarily as I emerged from the wings, but I didn't need to see. I knew exactly where to place each foot, each hand, each calculated movement. The pole felt cool against my palm as I made my first circuit, establishing dominance over the space.

As my eyes adjusted to the lights, I began distinguishing individual faces in the crowd. Businessmen with loosened ties and lazy smiles. Even a few college boys spending their fathers' money on fantasies they couldn't afford themselves. A handful of women were watching me with either curious fascination or territorial hostility.

And Rowan. Always Rowan.

He sat in the same spot at the bar as he had the other night during my trial dance. His eyes reflected stage lights like a predator's in the darkness.

I executed my routine, muscle memory carrying me through complex sequences while my mind floated somewhere between present and past. My body knew these movements intimately—the arch of my spine, the flex of my thighs, the controlled fall into gravity-defying holds. Each transition flowed into the next like water, like violence, like sex.

As I completed my final sequence—an inverted split that required core strength most people couldn't fathom—I allowed myself to meet Rowan's gaze directly. A challenge. Something electric and dangerous crackled between us across the crowded room.

His expression revealed nothing, but his posture shifted subtly, weight transferring forward like a fencer preparing to advance.

I smiled at him before dismounting, knowing he witnessed my very deliberate provocation.

Back in the dressing room, I wiped away sweat and changed into my street clothes. My body hummed with residual adrenaline and something else, something that had more to do with Rowan's presence than the dance itself.

I reached into my bag, snagged my water bottle, and took a long swig to quench my parched throat. I was eager to leave, knowing Rowan would be at the bar nursing his sickly sweet fruit juice concoction. *Where he will station himself every night from now on. Every single time I dance.*

The thought should have irritated me. Instead, I smiled.

Reaching the hallway leading from backstage, I stumbled. My legs felt strange—disconnected, like they belonged to someone else. I tried moving forward, and my bag slipped from nerveless fingers, contents scattering across the polished floor.

What the fuck?

"Whoa there, easy now." A feminine voice accompanied strong hands catching me as I pitched forward.

My vision blurred, edges going fuzzy and indistinct. Fear crystallized in my chest, sharp and immediate as a wave of heat blasted through me.

Have I been drugged?

"Please." The word emerged slurred, my tongue thick and uncooperative. Fear threatened to take over, but the drug's effects were quick, forcing me to accept my helplessness once more.

"Jules!" The woman holding me screamed, and suddenly the scent of cotton candy flooded my senses.

Jules. I can trust Jules. Can I trust Jules?

Thinking was becoming difficult. Fire erupted beneath my skin, consuming me from the inside. Too many sounds—the music pounding through walls, conversations bleeding together into incomprehensible noise. Too much light—every bulb felt like staring into the sun. Sensations burned through me as if my clothes had transformed into sandpaper, abrading flesh with every breath.

I squeezed my eyes shut and clamped my hands over my ears, but I still heard and felt the music throbbing through walls. Each bass note shot agony through my skull.

A hand touched my cheek, cool against my burning skin, and I looked to see who it was. Two pairs of eyes, one piercing blue and the other rich brown, stared back at me. The woman beside Jules possessed sharp, angular features that suggested Indigenous heritage, though her pixie-cut hair glowed neon blue beneath kohl-lined eyes that looked ripped from anime. She appeared like a manga character manifested in three dimensions, and the incongruity made my drugged brain stutter.

A glowing haze surrounded them both. Jules was bathed in pink warmth while her companion was haloed in a deep inky purple. What was I given?

"She's been drugged, Jules." The blue-haired woman half-guided me, half-dragged me towards a room.

Jules's voice carried panic I'd never heard from her before. "There's no way. Nobody would *dare* do something that stupid. Certainly not while he's actually *here*, in the building."

"Well, for someone who claims to be omniscient within his domain, I think he could benefit from a little humility." The other woman's voice dripped sarcasm.

"Don't you fucking start, Celine." Jules hissed, and I couldn't stop the laughter that bubbled out of me. It had been a long time since I heard Jules swear.

You sound just like when I failed to transition from a sneaky-v to a cradle spin.

"What did she just say?" The woman named Celine asked.

Jules said, "She's delirious. Poor girl. On her first night, no less."

"It's one hell of a welcome," Celine said as she lowered me onto a reclining chair, the soft and supple leather cool against my burning skin. "Does she have someone here with her? She keeps whispering a name."

Celine is a pretty name too, I wanted to say, but I couldn't form the words with my mouth. My eyelids were too heavy to keep open. My hearing suddenly felt muffled, like I was underwater, but I caught the sound of Jules rustling through something.

"Yeah, her friend or boyfriend is at the bar. Here, let me apply a cool compress. She's burning up."

There was a blessedly cold pressure on my forehead, and I reached up to caress Jules's arm. *Oh my god, that feels so, so good. Don't stop.*

"Well, *that* is interesting," Celine said. "You don't suppose somebody slipped her. . . you know?" Her voice trailed off, but her tone held a terrible implication.

"No, don't be ridiculous. Nobody would—"

"Yeah," Celine interrupted, "You said that already. '*Nobody would dare.*' But Jules, just look at her." She gestured to me before she continued. "The kid's exhibiting all the early symptoms. Disoriented, uncoordinated, flushed, feverish, elevated heart rate, heightened physical sensitivity."

There was silence before Jules said, "Maybe she was just roofied?"

A hand ran down my arm, causing me to shudder, moan, and hiss. It felt like ice against my molten flesh, like a million kisses tickling across my skin. *No. Stop*, I thought even as I leaned into the touch. *Rowan. Please come, Rowan.*

I wanted only *him* to touch me right then. I *needed* his hands on me. I wanted choice in whatever was happening to me, and it was him.

"Convinced?" Celine asked.

As I curled into myself—trying in vain to contain the inferno that raged within me—Jules's voice sounded distant. "What should we do?"

Celine laughed. "Well, *I* am certainly not fucking her. She's not my type. So. . ."

"Right." There was a long pause before I heard Jules's voice. "I'd better go get Rowan."

Chapter 20

Rowan

I knew something was wrong when Violet did not immediately come to me after her final set.

The *kompot* sat in my glass, crimson liquid reduced to little more than dregs and dissolved fruit at the bottom. My fingers drummed against the bartop in a restless rhythm that betrayed my impatience. Even Andy seemed to notice, his dark eyes flicking towards me with something approaching concern as he polished glasses that already gleamed.

"I'm sure she'll be along any minute," he said, his usually melodic voice careful. Measured. As if he sensed the predator coiling tighter in my chest with each passing second.

His commentary did nothing to ease the anxiety gathering like storm clouds in my thoughts. I twirled the glass on its base, the motion sharp and precise, then downed the remainder of my drink. The sweetness coated my tongue—strawberry, blackberry, sugar syrup cut with vodka—but I tasted none of it.

I'd already restrained myself earlier in the night when the piece of shit vampyre had forced his hand on Violet. Before I could even take a single step, she'd already handled the situation—like the spitfire I knew her to be. It made my cock hard seeing her shoot down another man.

But this was different.

"If she is not here by the time I finish this drink, I may pay a visit to the proprietor myself. . ." The words hung between us, a promise and a threat. Andy paused mid-polish, his hands going still.

Hell was about to break loose.

In that moment, Jules burst through the velvet curtains with a panicked energy that confirmed every instinct that had been screaming danger in my skull. I stood so abruptly the barstool nearly clattered to the floor, the legs scraping against polished wood.

"Where is she?" I asked, already moving.

I caught Jules's arm—her skin warm beneath my palm, her pulse hammering against my fingertips like a frightened bird—and steered her back towards the curtains she had just emerged from. Her cotton candy perfume was overpowering this close, sickly sweet and cloying.

"She's fine. No, wait. She's safe, but she's not *fine*." The words tumbled out of her in a rush, tripping over each other. "I need you to come with me. She needs you. Or at least I think you'll be the best person to help her."

In her panicked state, she hadn't realized I was already leading us backstage, my grip firm enough to bruise. Whatever had happened to Violet, I was about to rain Hell's fire down on every soul responsible.

If one hair on her head has been harmed—

The thought cut off as Jules led me through the maze of hallways, heading deeper into Oubliette. The walls there were the same deep burgundy velvet, but the doors were different. Soundproofed, I suspected, given their thickness.

She stopped before a door and pushed it open.

The room beyond was small, intimate, furnished with a leather settee and low lighting that cast everything in amber and shadow. Violet lay curled on the settee, her body trembling, her skin flushed a deep rose that looked wrong against her natural coloring. A woman I didn't recognize sat beside her—petite frame, high cheekbones, hawkish nose, and neon blue pixie-cut hair. Her eyes were lined with orange kohl that made her look like a cartoon character.

Who and what was this? I rounded on Jules, my voice dropping to a dangerous level. "What happened to her?"

"I don't know! I swear, Rowan, I don't—"

"She was fine when I left her with you." I took a step closer, watching Jules's eyes widen. "I left her under your protection. Under *Oubliette's* protection. So, explain to me how she ended up like *that*." I pointed at Violet, my voice calmer than the storm breaking within me.

"Celine found her in the hallway after her last set," Jules said, her words coming faster now. "She could barely stand. Someone must have slipped her something, but I don't know who or when—"

"You do not know?" My hands clenched into fists. "Or you will not tell me?"

"I don't know!" Her voice pitched higher. "Nobody should have done this, not with *His* protection—"

His protection? Whose? Irrelevant in that moment. "Yet someone *did*." I grabbed her by the throat and slammed her against the wall hard enough that her head cracked against velvet-covered stone. Her eyes went wide, mouth opening in a soundless gasp of pain as my fingers tightened. "So, your protection means nothing."

I was not one to harm without reason, but seeing Violet frail like this? Some rational part of me snapped. We were pawns in a game for monsters, and Jules had not given me much reason to trust her.

"Rowan—" she choked out, hands scrabbling at my wrist.

Electricity crackled behind me, the air ionizing with the sharp and pungent smell of ozone. I felt the hair on the back of my neck stand up, my skin prickling with the proximity of power that should not exist in mortal hands. Jules's eyes widened further, reflecting a flash of cerulean over my shoulder. A blue glow haloed her terrified face.

"You should let her go, lover boy."

The voice behind me was unearthly, layered, and echoing. It was as if multiple voices spoke in perfect unison—a female and *something* else. Something ancient and hungry.

Still holding Jules by the throat, I looked over my shoulder to see the hawk-nosed woman standing now. Her hands crackled with electric blue energy that danced between her fingers like living things. Her eyes had gone completely black—no whites, no irises, just two pits of endless void that swallowed any light near her face.

"Warlock," I said. Recognition slammed into me like a fist to the gut as her demonic energy danced between us.

I had only encountered one Warlock in my previous life, and that single meeting had taught me exactly why they were hunted by every supernatural kin or clan that discovered them. Whereas some mortals made pacts with demons or gods—uneven trades that cost them dearly for a scrap of power—Warlocks reached out to forces far more exotic and dangerous. They shared their lifeforce with whatever entity answered their call from the dark spaces between worlds. Chaos incarnate. Forgotten gods. Abyssal horrors that should never touch a mortal mind.

In my previous life, the supernatural community killed Warlocks on sight. Too unpredictable. Too powerful. Too likely to tear holes in reality simply by existing.

And Jules has one as a friend. Interesting. Inconvenient as fuck right now, but interesting.

"Please, Rowan. I'm trying to help." Jules's voice was desperation and pain. Her bright blue eyes were stormy, begging me to believe her. I searched her face for any subtle twitch, looking for the lie that hid beneath her words. I could not find any.

Behind me, Violet let out a moan, and despite the anger simmering, I knew I needed to at least listen to what she was going to say.

I released Jules, shoving her aside hard enough that she stumbled. She collapsed against the wall, coughing and gasping, her hands flying to her throat where my fingers had left red marks. Those were going to bruise purple before breakfast. I should have felt remorse for the marks, but I held little regard when it came to protecting those under my care.

The Warlock's electricity dimmed, but did not disappear entirely. Blue sparks still danced across her knuckles like restless insects as she said, "Great friend you've got here, Jules." Her voice returned to something approaching human, despite each syllable being drenched with sarcasm.

Jules could only glare at her companion, then stood on shaky legs and crossed to where Violet lay shivering. I was beside her in two strides, dropping to my knees and taking Violet's hand in mine.

I drew in a sharp breath when I felt the heat radiating from her skin. She was burning up, fever-hot, sweat beading across her forehead and upper lip. Her eyes were closed, lashes dark crescents against flushed cheeks, and she trembled like she was freezing despite the fire consuming her from within.

"What is happening to her?" My voice came out rough, scraped raw with fear.

Jules knelt beside me, reaching out to brush a crimson streak of hair from Violet's face with surprising gentleness. "Someone must have slipped her something. I'm so sorry, Rowan. This is unprecedented. We've never had a dancer drugged before."

"But how..." I searched the immediate area, looking for Violet's bag. It was missing. I turned to Jules, my eyes hard. "Where are her things?"

"I think her bag is still in the hallway? In our rush to get her somewhere private, I forgot to grab it. Celine, could you—"

"Yeah, yeah, yeah," the Warlock said as she headed for the door.

I checked Violet's features, ensuring nothing else stood out, and knew that if things became worse, I would burn this fucking place to the ground along with everyone in it. The certainty of it was as sure as fire was hot or that the sun would rise tomorrow. I would destroy anyone who hurt Violet. Simple.

Celine returned moments later, clutching Violet's purple duffel. "Here." She thrust the bag into my arms with more force than necessary, the weight of it solid and familiar.

I rifled through the contents with methodical efficiency, cataloging each item. Her stage costume, black fabric and silver mesh. Makeup bag. Wallet. Keys.

And a water bottle I did not recognize.

The brand was wrong. The shape was wrong. Violet and I had gone shopping together *specifically* to ensure that she brought her own food and water into this den of predators. It was my first rule. I knew every item she'd packed, had watched her check and double-check the bag before we left my apartment. I held the bottle up to the light. Clear liquid, seemingly innocuous. But the cap had been opened, and about a third of the contents consumed.

"This is not hers," I said, my voice flat and cold.

I unscrewed the cap and brought it to my nose, inhaling carefully. Nothing. No scent, no discoloration, nothing to suggest tampering. But it was the only variable that made sense. I lifted it to my lips, prepared to take a drink myself—if it was drugged, it would be better to know what I was dealing with.

"No!" Jules screamed and slapped the bottle from my hand with enough force to send it flying.

The bottle hit the floor, plastic cracking, water spilling across polished wood in a spreading pool that caught the amber light.

"You fool!" Jules's voice pitched high with genuine fear, her eyes wide and wild. "You don't know what's in that."

I stared at her, then at the spilled water, then back at her flushed, terrified face. "I was planning to find out."

Celine stepped forward, crouched down, and picked up the bottle. Water dripped from her fingers as she examined it, then—to mine and Jules's surprise—she brought the bottle to her lips and drained the rest of the water.

"What the fuck, Celine?" Jules said. It felt out of place for her to curse in such a way. She'd always seemed so prim and ditzy from our few interactions.

"Mmm." Celine swallowed, then let out a satisfied sigh. "Yep. That's some good ol' succubus blood, right there." She found the cap where it had rolled beneath the settee, screwed it back on despite the crack in the plastic, and held the bottle up like a sommelier examining vintage wine.

I let out a string of curses, causing Jules to turn her eyes to me. "You know what that means?" she asked with fear on her face.

"I know a little." I'd heard of succubus and incubus blood in my previous life, though only in whispered warnings and shreds of stories. I recalled a tale I'd been told once about a vampyre lord who kept a cellar stocked with succubi of various ages, like a demented wine cellar.

Celine must have taken my silence as ignorance, because she explained, "It's an aphrodisiac and invigorator, for those of us who traffic with demons. But for mortals?" She raised an eyebrow at me as she gestured towards Violet, trembling on the settee. "It's rather excruciating unless someone can... y'know."

I glanced back at Violet, watching her chest rise and fall in rapid, shallow breaths. Her hands had clenched into fists, knuckles white, and small sounds escaped her throat—wordless, pained, desperate.

I ran a hand down my face, exhaustion and rage warring for dominance. "What needs to be done?" I forced the words out through clenched teeth.

Jules was still processing, her face pale and drawn. "I didn't think someone would be stupid enough to drug a mortal with—"

"Jules." My patience, already threadbare, snapped entirely. "I need to know what I need to do, and I need to know *now*."

Her face somehow went even paler, color draining until she looked nearly translucent in the low light. "The symptoms need to be relieved, and that can only be done with the proper... stimulation. Exchanging of auras and energy. Male or female, but I assumed you'd want—"

"No." My gut clenched at the worst-case scenario. "Absolutely not."

Jules was shaking almost as hard as Violet, her hands trembling where they clutched her own arms. She looked as if she were about to cry before Celine let out a barking laugh—loud, unhinged, genuinely delighted. Her pupils had blown wide, nearly eclipsing the brown of her irises, and she stumbled sideways like a drunk navigating an invisible obstacle course.

"Oh, fuuuuuuck." She fanned herself with one hand, the other still clutching the cracked water bottle. "That is some grade-A strong shit right there. I haven't felt this fucked up since Admiral Eddie's Cocktail Party."

Then she collapsed onto the floor with all the grace of a felled tree and began making snow angels against the polished wood, her limbs sweeping wide arcs as she giggled like a child.

"I am surrounded by incompetence," I muttered as I moved to gather Violet in my arms.

She felt lighter than the other night, but I knew that was just the adrenaline coursing through my veins. Her body was all lean muscle and delicate bone wrapped in skin that burned against my palms. I cradled her against my chest, one arm beneath her knees and the other supporting her back. Her head lolled against my shoulder, and she let out a small whimper that shot straight to my heart like an arrow.

Jules helped me gather Violet's scattered belongings, shoving them haphazardly into the duffel and pressing the bag into the crook where Violet's body curved against mine.

"Cold water for the fever," Jules said, her voice steadier now that she had a task to focus on. "She'll need fluids. Electrolytes, if you've got 'em. And I'm sorry, Rowan, but she needs... relief."

She emphasized the last word so heavily it might as well have been written in blood. I knew what she meant. I knew, and every cell in my body rejected it.

"No." The word came out flat. Final. "I will not touch someone who cannot give their consent."

Jules shook her head, frustration and sympathy warring across her features. "You don't understand, honey. These next several hours will be excruciating for her unless someone—"

"Woman, I said no." I cut her off, my voice hard and cold as a glacier. "She will come home with me. I will tend to the fever. I will keep her safe. But I will not take advantage of her in this state."

Celine cackled from her position on the floor, still making her snowless snow angels. I threw her a look of pure disgust.

She gave me the middle finger without stopping her floor movements, her grin wide and manic. "God, I forgot how good this feels. It's been *decades* since I've had a taste."

Jules sent me an apologetic look. "I'll help you leave. Are you heading straight to the apartment?"

I nodded, making my displeasure clear in every line of my body. "Do you have a car that could take us? Does Oubliette?"

Something flickered across Jules's face—surprise, maybe, or calculation. She glanced at Celine, who had gone still on the floor, her drug-addled gaze suddenly sharp and focused. Something passed between them that I cared little to know.

"No," Jules started, then seemed to reconsider. She shook her head. "We don't have a car, but I can still help. Come with me."

She led me out of the spare room and down the corridor, but instead of heading back towards the main floor, she turned in the opposite direction. The hallway seemed to stretch longer than I thought possible, the perspective somehow wrong, as if distance itself bent to accommodate more space than the building's exterior could possibly contain.

Magic, I thought. *Of course, this building would be enchanted in some way.* It was certainly not the first magical building I'd been in. I had a brief memory flash through my mind—breaking into The Library. Considering that misadventure had ultimately ended with my death, it was not a memory I wished to dwell on.

We reached a set of stairs descending into darkness. Jules paused at the top, her hand on an ornate iron railing that radiated cold even from a foot away.

"Follow me," she said, and began her descent.

I clutched Violet closer to my chest—her heartbeat rabbiting against my ribs, her breath hot and rapid against my throat—and followed Jules down into whatever lay below Oubliette's main floor.

The stairs spiraled down and down and down. The temperature dropped with each level we descended, the heat of the club dissipating with each step. The air tasted different here—old stone and mineral water, with an underlying current of something I couldn't place. Old Magic, perhaps?

Finally, we reached the bottom. A massive wooden door loomed before us, easily twelve feet tall and half again as wide. The wood was ancient oak, though darker than any oak I'd ever seen. Carved into its surface were symbols I recognized from my previous life—protection wards and binding sigils that made my skin prickle just looking at them.

Above the door, carved into the stone lintel in elegant script, were the words from Dante's inscription over the gates of Hell. *Lasciate ogne speranza, voi ch'intrate.* Abandon all hope, ye who enter here.

How fitting and ominous.

I turned to Jules, my arms tightening protectively around Violet's trembling form. "This is not a trick, is it?"

Her heartbeat remained steady—no spike, no flutter, no telltale signs of deception. She met my eyes directly, her own clear and earnest despite the red marks still visible on her throat.

"No," she said simply. "I swear on my life, Rowan. I mean you and Violet no harm."

I had no better options. Violet needed help, and she needed it now. Whatever lay beyond that door could not be worse than leaving her to suffer. I followed Jules through the massive doorway, and the world changed.

The air shifted first—pressure equalizing with a pop that made my ears ring. Then came the wind, an impossible yet constant wind, carrying scents from a thousand different places. Jasmine and motor oil. Sea salt and woodsmoke. Fresh bread and copper blood. The olfactory chaos gave me a headache.

We stood in a vast corridor that defied every law of architecture and physics I understood. Doors lined both walls as far as I could see in either direction, hundreds of them, maybe thousands, stretching into infinity. Each door was unique, crafted from different materials, in different colors, and of different styles. Some looked ancient, iron-banded and weathered. Others appeared modern, sleek steel and frosted glass. A few seemed to shift as I looked at them, their surfaces rippling like water.

Between each door, jutting up from black iron sconces, were flaming torches of bright blue fire. They gave off neither smoke nor heat, only a clean blue-white light to illuminate the long hallways. The lack of smoke choking the hallways—the lack of even the *scent* of smoke—was unnerving.

With my enhanced hearing, I expected to be assaulted by sounds from behind the doors. Soundproofed or not, my hearing was supernaturally exceptional. I was preparing to be bombarded by muffled voices, laughing, screaming, the unmistakable rhythm of sex. I waited for the cacophony of music to bleed through—jazz and metal and classical and techno, layered atop each other in a discordant fury.

But there was silence. Nearly absolute and utter silence.

I heard the heartbeats of Jules and Violet and the ever constant rustling of the wind as it rushed down the corridors. . . but that was all. *It's as if we're the only three alive in all the world.* It was beyond unnerving. I would have preferred the noise.

Jules moved through the corridor with confidence, navigating the endless doors with the ease of long familiarity. She walked for what felt like several minutes, but could have been seconds or hours. Time felt slippery in that place, unmoored from its usual progression.

Finally, she stopped before a door that stood out among its neighbors.

It was painted hot pink, the color so vibrant it almost hurt to look at. Stars had been painted across its surface in what looked like a child's hand—simple five-pointed shapes in yellow and white and silver, scattered with no discernible pattern. At the center of the door was a portrait of three figures, and despite its crude execution, I recognized one of the figures immediately.

Three women holding hands, with Jules in the center. Her platinum hair was unmistakable, even rendered in simple brushstrokes. To her left and right were two other women I did not know. From their feet, the night sky spilled downward, stars and galaxies bleeding into the world they stood above, as if they were goddesses looking down upon creation itself.

She placed her palm against the door, and I felt power surge through me—not the electric crackle of Celine's Warlock magic, but something even older. Gentler. It was the feeling of the first warm day after a long winter.

"This is my door," she said, glancing back at me over her shoulder. Her blue eyes caught the corridor's impossible light, reflecting colors that should not exist. "If you think of your apartment—visualize it clearly, every detail you can remember—you'll arrive there when you step through."

Realization dawned on me then, but words escaped me. My brain struggled to process what she was offering, what this implied about the nature of reality and the magic woven through it. And about Jules herself. Who was she? What was she?

She must have read the shock on my face because she offered a small, sad smile. "Go, Rowan. You clearly know more about what lies beyond the veil than most mortals. We can ask each other questions another time. Please. Go. Violet needs you now."

Jules opened the door, and I looked through to the other side.

Nothing. An absolute void. A darkness so total and complete it seemed to have weight and texture, pressing against my eyes like a physical force. *Look upon me*, that absence screamed, *look upon me and tremble.*

Under normal circumstances, I would have been more cautious. I would have asked more questions. I would have considered the implications of stepping through a door that bent the very fabric of space.

But these were not normal circumstances.

Violet shivered in my arms, her body wracked with tremors that seemed to originate from her very bones. Her breath came in small, pained gasps. She whispered something I couldn't make out, her lips moving against my neck. I knew that I did not have the luxury of caution.

I thought of my apartment and stepped through the door.

The sensation defied description. It was not walking, not falling, not flying. For a fraction of a second, I existed everywhere and nowhere simultaneously. I felt the weight of infinite space pressing in from all directions, felt myself stretched thin across impossible distances, felt Violet's body in my arms as the only solid thing in a universe of unreality.

I opened my mouth to speak—to tell Violet we would be okay, to apologize to her for not protecting her, to confess a thousand things—but there was no sound in that place.

Then came the pull—a hook behind my navel, yanking me forward with force that should have torn me apart but instead compressed me back into a singular existence.

The space around me suddenly felt alive. Crystalline walls formed, appearing to be made of compressed starlight. They pulsed with colors I had no names for, hues that existed outside normal human perception but which I could somehow see. The floor beneath my feet glowed, but it felt wrong—as if I walked on the surface tension of reality itself.

Sound rushed in. The familiar hum of my apartment's air conditioning, the distant traffic from the street below, the whisper of wind against windows. Then the eldritch light and otherworldly colors dimmed, being replaced by the soft amber glow from my bedroom's recessed lighting. Next came sensation—solid floor beneath my feet and cool air against my face.

I stood in my bedroom.

I turned, half-expecting to see Jules's concerned face, the hot pink door, the impossible corridor beyond. Instead, I saw only my bed with its crisp white linens undisturbed, exactly as I had left it.

The door I'd stepped through did not exist. There was only the familiar wall, exposed brick, and empty space.

The experience reminded me—suddenly and violently—of being reborn, but I didn't have time to dwell on the similarities. Violet shivered in my arms, a violent tremor that ran through her entire body. Her skin burned against mine, fever-hot and getting worse.

Contemplate the impossible, reality-warping teleportation later.

I hugged her closer to my chest, pressing my face into her hair and breathing in her scent—rose and sweat and something underneath that was uniquely *her*. I whispered a brief thank you to whichever god or Fate had gotten us home safely and quickly. Though from what the night promised to bring, it felt as if we'd traded one devil for another.

Chapter 21

Violet

My skin was on fire, stretched too tight over bones that felt like they were trying to escape my body. I forced myself to wake, to claw my way up through layers of fever and delirium that dragged at me like quicksand.

I was sitting on the cold floor of an opulent bathroom—glossy white subway tile against black marble flooring with brushed gold fixtures that gleamed under recessed lighting. A double vanity stretched along one wall, topped with matching mirrors framed in ornate gold. A stack of plush cream towels sat folded beside twin sinks that looked like they'd never been used.

Water rushed somewhere nearby, the sound echoing off hard surfaces. I heard a string of expletives in a rough and frustrated voice that was achingly familiar.

"Rowan?" My voice came out barely above a whisper, my throat raw and parched.

My eyes searched for him, and his frame filled my vision. He crouched to my level, his body outlined in a comforting blue haze reminiscent of the one I had seen around Jules. He placed his hand on my forehead. The coolness of his palm against my burning skin felt glorious, like snow against sunburn.

"Feels good," I managed, leaning into his touch despite myself.

Rowan's concerned voice broke through the haze that had wrapped around my thoughts. "Violet, what hurts?"

Everything. I wanted to say it—to list every sensation tearing through my body—but I could barely force words past my swollen tongue. Sleep beckoned, sweet and dark, but an angry ache pulsed in my core, threatening to split me apart from the inside.

I groaned and wrapped my arms around my stomach, curling into myself. "It hurts."

"Shh, I know. I know it does. I have you." Rowan's arms gently tugged at my clothes as he peeled off my shirt.

I felt my socks disappear next, then my pants, then my underwear sliding down my legs. The marble was mercifully cold against my heated skin, and it was everything I'd ever wanted in that moment. I was covered in sweat, and sticky everywhere—my back, my thighs, between my legs where arousal had slicked my skin.

"Rowan, please." I didn't even know what I was asking for anymore. Relief? Death?

Him.

Strong arms lifted me from the ground, and soon I felt my feet slowly dip into the freezing bathwater. It felt glorious against my burning soles. I started to shake, violent shivers tearing through my body.

"Is it too cold?" Fear colored his voice as Rowan pulled me back out, and I shook my head frantically.

"No. Please. It's perfect."

I felt his body tense, muscles coiling beneath my weight, and then we began our descent. Water sloshed against his white shirt as he lowered us both in, soaking the fabric until it clung to the ridges of his chest and abdomen. I couldn't help but stare at the glorious lines of his body, his nipples taut against the chill, and the urge to bite them was nearly unbearable.

I wanted to taste him. Run my tongue from the hollow of his throat down the planes of his chest to where his navel dipped lower, following the trail of pale hair that disappeared beneath his waistband. It felt like the only thing that could stop how dry and cottony my mouth had become. I needed his skin, the salt of his sweat, the taste of *him.*

Rowan let out a low groan, the sound filling my ears like honey. "You are mumbling your thoughts aloud, Violet."

His voice sounded strained, stretched thin.

I focused, realizing he was right. I'd been speaking without conscious thought. "Sorry. I don't know what's wrong with me."

"Nothing," he said, clearly doing his best to keep me above water with his arms buried deep in the bath. "You are struggling with what someone gave you. Can you sit on your own?"

I nodded, the motion harder than it should have been, but I managed to stay upright when he withdrew his support. The water had already turned from feeling cold to lukewarm, but Rowan's arms were covered in goosebumps.

"Are you okay?" I asked.

He laid his arms over the tub's rim and rested his head on them, his wet shirt dripping onto the bathroom floor. "Fine. How do you feel?"

"Hot? No, like an inferno." I touched my own skin, then reached out to touch his, concerned. "I can't tell what's wrong, but *I* feel wrong. Like my body doesn't fit right." It was the only way I could describe the sensation—as if I'd been shoved into skin two sizes too small.

His eyes closed, worry etching lines into his brow. "Let us stay here for a while, and then I will take you to bed."

I snorted at that, and even that simple gesture left me dizzy, the room tilting. "How very forward of you, Rowan."

His eyes cracked open, and I could tell he was exhausted. Dark circles shadowed the skin beneath his pale eyes, and his jaw was tight with tension. "I hardly think you would forgive me if I tried anything when you have clearly been drugged."

"Have I?" The words came out sharper than intended. "I don't *feel* drugged. I'm just hot, in pain, and I'm—"

Horny.

My mouth snapped shut as that realization slammed into me. *I'm not just horny. I'm on fire.* The thought sent a jolt through my body. Pain and pleasure were often two sides of the same coin—I'd learned that in my previous life, learned it in ways that still made my stomach turn. But there, in that moment with Rowan, I felt the pull of delicious temptation.

We sat together in the tub in silence for a long while. I could tell Rowan was worried by how often he reached over and placed the back of his hand on my forehead. Whenever he touched me, I felt as if I could melt into him; each time felt even more sensual than the last. As my fever eased, the intense pain radiating throughout my core intensified.

"Violet, how are you feeling now?"

Fucking feral, I wanted to moan. Instead, I bit my lip, clenched my thighs together, and said, "I think I'm fine."

But even I didn't sound convinced.

He checked my temperature again. "You are a little cooler now. It seems the cold bath brought your fever down. Let us get you dried off and into bed."

I moved to stand, and he gently pushed against my chest, stopping me. The pressure of his palm so close to my breasts sent a wave of pleasure crashing through me so intense I gasped. The cold water lapping at my nipples only intensified the sensation.

"*Nyet*, wait." He grabbed one of the plush towels hanging on the side of the tub, helped me stand, and wrapped it around me like a cocoon. "I have you."

I whimpered and accepted his help, watching him guide each leg over the tub's rim, his hands steering my hips with care. Everywhere he touched left trails of fire that stoked the inferno raging between my thighs. The urge to touch myself was getting stronger, nearly overwhelming.

"Rowan, what was I given?" I could guess, but I needed to hear him say it.

Rowan hesitated, and I knew I was right before he even spoke. "An aphrodisiac. But a very potent one. Your body is struggling to process it."

I accepted the information as panic prickled up my spine, sharp and cold despite the heat consuming me. "That's... inconvenient."

Rowan chuckled in agreement. "Yes. It is. It is also offensive."

I waited patiently as Rowan emptied the tub, the water swirling down the drain in a miniature whirlpool. He helped me dry off with brisk, efficient movements, then disappeared into the walk-in closet. My vision felt clearer then, noting he was no longer hazed in blue. I felt weak, yes, but no longer dizzy. He emerged moments later in gray sweats and a fresh, crisp white shirt.

After a long moment of silence where he seemed to be gathering courage, he spoke. "Can I trust you to walk, or will you trust me to carry you to the bed?"

My arms reached for him in answer. He gently pulled me against his chest and lifted me off my feet. I decided I could get used to this, feeling like the princess he teased me for being. He carried me to his bedroom and laid me on crisp white sheets. I slid into them with a sigh that was half relief, half frustration.

All of my thoughts were slow and fuzzy, but I wasn't nearly as feverish as before. My horniness, however, had only gotten more ferocious. Unfinished desire coiled taut within me like a hungry snake. Angry. Insistent. Demanding.

I can't masturbate in Rowan's bed. Can I? I flushed at the thought, caught between shame and arousal.

Rowan tucked the sheets around me and checked my forehead one more time, muttering something that sounded close to approval.

"Rowan—" I started, then looked away, unable to meet his eyes. "Do you mind if I. . ."

He went rigid as a statue, and I watched his eyes dart over me, assessing. "If you. . . what?"

"I just need a few minutes alone. *Please.*" The plea escaped before I could stop it.

Realization dawned on him then, his expression shifting from concern to something darker. He nodded and stepped towards the door. "Call me if you need me."

I need you right now, I nearly said. "Okay."

The door closed behind him, casting the room in shadow, broken only by ambient light filtering through the floor-to-ceiling windows. I slid my fingers between my legs immediately, desperate for relief from the ache that threatened to consume me.

I was swollen and wet, my body responding to the drug with a ferocity I'd never experienced. My fingers circled my clit as images rose unbidden: Rowan's face buried between my legs, his steel eyes watching me as he devoured me.

It's just the drug, I told myself even as a moan slipped free. *Totally normal to imagine your childhood friend tongue-fucking you.*

My arousal coated my fingers and dripped onto the pristine white sheets beneath me. I should have been embarrassed, but I couldn't stop. My heart beat faster than it ever had, a frantic rhythm that bordered on painful.

Just imagine whatever you need to get off and move on.

But my brain was unrelenting. In my head, Rowan's eyes watched me as I touched myself. I imagined the slow curve of his smile as he made me beg. I spread my legs wider—both in fantasy and reality—desperate for his touch. For him to slide his fingers inside me and curve them exactly the way that would bring me to orgasm.

My body's heat built again, and within minutes I was sweat-soaked, biting the sheet to muffle the moans threatening to escape. *He's right outside the door.*

I used my other hand to slide fingers inside myself, moving them in a frenzy. *Can he hear me? Does he know what I'm doing?*

Of course he does.

The thought brought another wave of pleasure that left me shaking, but it wasn't enough for release. I could feel myself teetering on the edge, but something was stopping me from falling over. I needed more. So much more.

And I was afraid to admit I knew exactly what that *more* was.

The sheets against my skin began to hurt, fabric abrading hypersensitive flesh. My stomach twisted in painful knots, the orgasm hovering just out of reach but unable to break.

"Goddammit. . ." I let out a pained moan, unable to hold it in anymore.

I didn't know why I couldn't come, but I had a sinking feeling Rowan might. I sat up and ripped the sheet from my body, frustrated beyond reason. The nightstand held a glass of water and my phone. I reached for the water, but in my attempt, I lost my balance and tumbled to the floor.

I cried out in frustration as the door burst open. Rowan filled the doorway, his eyes wild with concern. "Violet, are you okay?"

My heart sank because I knew—instinctively, bone-deep—that I wanted him. Needed him. And if I voiced it, he would feel obligated. Duty-bound.

That was something I would never do to someone. To have the freedom to choose who you shared your body with ripped away, to be forced into something you didn't truly want? I knew that horror intimately.

Tears pricked my eyes as he crouched beside me and helped me up, his hands gentle but firm. "I'm sorry, Rowan. I'm fine. I just fell."

He was quiet, but I watched his nostrils flare as he inhaled deeply. The room reeked of my arousal—musky and obvious and mortifying.

"Rowan, I am so sorry." My voice sounded hoarse even to my own ears.

I needed relief, but not at the cost of his agency. Not at the cost of his choice.

"Shh, it is fine, Violet. Let us get you back to bed." He stopped then and stared at the mattress.

Dead center, there was a large wet spot where I'd been lying—clear evidence of exactly what I'd been doing. Shame burned through me, hot and acidic.

"Rowan, I—"

"I will grab you a towel." He moved to the bathroom, and my fear slithered through my chest, coiling tight. I was suddenly self-conscious about how my body must look to him—desperate, wanton, out of control.

"Rowan," I called after him, but he'd already returned.

He didn't comment on the wet spot. Simply laid the towel over it, then turned to me. "Here. Lie down."

I hugged myself and complied, curling into a ball on my side. He pulled another smaller towel from where he'd tucked it behind his back and began wiping the sweat from my body with careful, methodical strokes.

I began to quiver again. "It's b-better if you don't touch—"

The cloth brushed my nipple, and I let out a strangled cry, pleasure so intense it bordered on pain shooting straight to my core.

Rowan jerked back like he'd been burned. "Fuck, Violet. Are you okay?"

"Please." I was grasping at the last threads of my restraint, ready to beg just to feel him. *But it's not fair to him!* The warning burned through my mind even as my body screamed for his touch. His scent enveloped me, both heightening my desire while also making me feel inexplicably safe.

"I can't... Rowan, I *need* something."

Rowan's eyes were shadowed, but I could sense the tension radiating from his body like heat shimmer off summer pavement. "I have... I have a toy. Would that help?"

My cunt clenched at the thought.

"Yes," I said, my voice rough and hungry. "*Please.*"

He disappeared into his closet, and I heard rustling before he returned. The toy was small, silicone, and purple—my favorite color, though I doubt he knew that. It was a basic cordless massager, something easily purchased online. Discreet. It might be enough.

Or not, I thought, when all I wanted was to feel him deep inside me.

Consent, I chided myself viciously.

He handed it to me, carefully avoiding touching my fingers. "It is new."

"Thank you," the words came out shakier than I intended.

He turned to leave, and my traitorous mouth betrayed me. "Do you want to stay?"

I nearly regretted the words until I saw the way he stared at me. His entire demeanor darkened, his presence suddenly heavier, more dangerous. It was thrilling and terrifying, and so unbearably erotic I nearly came undone from his gaze alone.

But I knew it was only adding fuel to the inferno already consuming me.

He moved closer, clearly hesitant but unable to stay away. "Violet, I do not think you can truly consent right now—"

"I'm clearheaded enough to know what I'm asking, Rowan." I snapped, unable to help the urgency threading through my words. "I don't want to be alone, but I don't want to force you into anything you don't want."

He stood inches from the bed now, and I saw the growing length of him straining against his gray sweats.

Oh my god, he does want me. That realization sent warm curls of pleasure straight to my core. I pushed further, begging him to hear the truth in my words.

"I don't want you to accept out of some messed-up sense of duty. I'll manage if needed." Despite the strength of my words, my body tightened with anticipation, desire flooding through me so intensely I felt dizzy and weak at how delicious his cock looked.

Yes. I want that. You. Everything.

I must have spoken aloud without realizing, because his eyes widened slightly.

"Is that what you really want? Everything?" His voice had gone rough, scraped raw. "This?" His hand reached down, touching himself through his sweats, and I nearly lost control right then.

God, yes. I nodded. "Only if you want to."

He closed his eyes, pain and desire warring across his features. I watched his jaw clench, watched him wage whatever internal battle was tearing him apart. Finally, his restraint cracked. "Of course I want to, Violet. But I will not fuck you. Is that alright with you?"

I scooted farther into the bed, making room for him. "Yes," I whispered.

He climbed in—gray sweats, crisp white shirt, and all—and the mattress dipped beneath his weight. I caught his scent again, and my body reacted immediately, fresh arousal dripping between my legs.

We settled against each other, his chest to my back. I reached out tentatively, touching his forearm where it rested near my hip. He made no move to reciprocate, letting me lead.

"You can touch me," I said softly. "I've been... coerced before. Touch is usually hard for me." The admission cost me, scraping against pride and shame in equal measure. "But I want you to."

Rowan was quiet for a long moment. "Violet—"

I shook my head, a rising tide of shame and guilt masked by the unrelenting desire threatening to shatter me. "Don't, Rowan. I just needed you to understand. I feel safe with you. Only you. I want *you* to touch me." And I meant it, with every scarred shred of my soul. Being held by him was like aloe on a burn, soothing despite the pain I knew would come later. I needed him to understand that this was *my* choice.

He let out a pained groan that vibrated through his chest and into my back. "When you talk like that, Violet, I cannot help but want to give you everything."

His arms wrapped around my ribs, warm and strong, creating a cage that felt like safety rather than confinement. Comforting.

When his hands trailed up to cup my breasts, I couldn't help the way my body arched into him, my ass grinding into his pelvis. The contact pulled moans from both of us, the sound harmonizing in the quiet room.

He kissed my shoulder then, a gentle press of lips against sweat-dampened skin, before his fingers found my nipples. He rolled the piercings between his thumbs and forefingers, the metal barbells shifting and tugging in a way that straddled the line between pain and pleasure.

"If you want to stop at any point, just say it," he murmured against my skin.

"Never," I whispered, reaching down to touch myself.

My fingers slipped between my folds, and I felt how drenched I was. The wetness was excessive, coating my inner thighs. "Shit, this doesn't feel normal."

"How wet you are?" Rowan's voice held no judgement, only warmth. "Everything about you is normal, Violet."

The words settled over me like a blessing, soothing insecurities I hadn't realized I was carrying. I circled my clit with shaking fingers while Rowan peppered kisses along my throat and shoulder, his fingers twisting my nipples until I was a whimpering mess.

"Fuck, don't stop, Rowan. That feels so good."

He made an approving noise, a rumbling purr I'd never heard from him before. "That is it, *volchok*. Bring yourself to pleasure."

He palmed my breasts, pulling my nipples taut as pain and pleasure surged through my core in alternating waves. "Oh my god." I cried out, bucking my hips against his.

"Use the toy, *volchok*," he commanded, and I shuddered in compliance, sinking deeper into his embrace.

His damp shirt rubbed against my overstimulated skin, the fabric too much and not enough simultaneously.

"Can you take off your shirt first?" I begged. "Please?"

Distantly, I registered him pulling away to comply. Fabric rustled, and then he returned—bare chest to my back, skin against skin. It was glorious.

"The toy. . ." he reminded me gently.

"Am I too heavy—" I started to ask, suddenly self-conscious about lying across one of his arms.

He pinched a nipple hard, the sharp bite of pain cutting through my spiraling thoughts.

"Violet..." His voice felt as if it rolled directly over my clit, a physical sensation. His hips pressed into the curve of my ass in delicious torture.

"Yes! Sorry." I fumbled for the toy with trembling fingers and pressed the button.

It vibrated to life, the sensation intense as I brought it between my legs. A deep moan tore from somewhere inside me, primal and desperate. I should have felt embarrassed by how wanton I sounded, but Rowan's calm presence was grounding.

I am free.

"Rowan. I don't think I can stop. I was so close earlier."

He held me tighter, his embrace turning to steel, hands roaming along my body—playing with my nipples, cupping my breasts, tracing the curve of my waist. I was on fire, every inch of skin soaking in the attention he lavished on me.

"So fucking perfect," he whispered against me, nipping and biting at the junction where my neck met my shoulder. The slight sting pulled moans from my lips.

Yes, don't stop. Tell me more. I want to hear you.

The words must have escaped me because Rowan didn't stop. His voice wrapped around me, filthy and sweet in equal measure.

"You are perfect, soaking my sheets like a good princess."

"These perfect breasts deserve to be slapped and bitten."

"I want to eat that pretty pink cunt of yours while you drench my face."

"Spread those legs wider. Yes, good *volchok*. Let me see you play with yourself."

I couldn't breathe. My body was strung tight as a bow, unable to form coherent thoughts as he whispered sweet filth into my ear. He nipped my earlobe, then murmured, "Relax. We have all night."

The anxiety that had been building released suddenly, tension dissipating like smoke.

His nose nuzzled behind my ear, inhaling my scent as his hips ground against my ass, following the rhythm I'd set as I rode the toy. I wanted to touch him, mount him, ride him until we were both crying each other's names.

Every moment he'd stared at me with that particular intensity, every time he'd touched me with reverence, every word he'd just spoken—it was everything I'd needed and wanted, without knowing I needed or wanted it.

The orgasm began to crest, building like a wave. My legs began to shake, my entire body trembling. Rowan was my anchor in this delirium of pain and pleasure, the only solid thing in a world gone liquid and strange.

I wanted more. Wanted him inside me. I was desperate, frustrated, but I knew this wasn't the moment to ask for that.

Yet I knew he would give me everything if I only asked.

"Rowan, I want to—"

"You are safe. It is okay, Violet. Let go." He reassured me, twisting my nipples and sinking his teeth into my shoulder with just enough pain and pressure to tip me over the edge.

My heart seemed to explode as the orgasm ripped through me, tearing a scream from my throat. Rowan's hand covered my mouth, muffling the sound, his own drawn-out "fuck" whispered next to my ear as my body convulsed.

My eyes rolled back. Every muscle spasmed, and all the tension leaked from me as I melted into him.

Bliss. Pure, uncomplicated bliss.

The toy dropped from my nerveless hand, still vibrating against my ass as we both lay there panting. Rowan was breathing hard, his length pressed firmly between my cheeks, but he made no move to seek his own relief.

His hands traced my curves once more—gentle now, almost reverent—before he slowly began to withdraw them.

"Wait," I murmured, not ready to lose his touch.

"Shh, I have you." He grabbed the toy, turned it off, and slid off the bed.

My skin was no longer feverish, but goosebumps rose at the loss of his body heat. I heard his footsteps padding across the floor, then returning. His touch was soft and careful as he reached for me.

"Do you want to use the restroom?"

It was so considerate that I couldn't help the laugh that escaped. "Yes, thank you."

His hand traced a pattern from my neck to my hip bone, the touch absent-minded. I didn't know if he was even conscious of it until he felt me shudder in response. "Sorry," he said as he helped me stand, ensuring I could walk.

My legs felt shaky but functional. I used the restroom, hyperaware of the mess between my legs, and realized I needed to shower. There was no avoiding it.

As I washed my hands, Rowan entered the bathroom and tossed the soaked towel in the hamper. I did my best not to stare at the hard lines of his chest, at the well-defined muscles there, knowing it would rekindle the heat within me. "Do you want to rinse?" he asked.

Focus, Violet. "Yes, I feel gross."

His tone was filled with adoration when he said, "You look divine."

The compliment caught me so off-guard I loosed a tiny gasp. We stared at each other across the bathroom—him shirtless, me completely naked, his cock still visibly hard and tucked into his waistband. I saw his thick head poking out above the elastic, flushed and glistening.

It was the sexiest thing I'd ever seen, and I wanted to wrap my lips around it.

No. This has to be a one-time thing.

"I really should rinse," I said weakly, and fled into the shower. It was a massive glass enclosure with a rainfall head and multiple jets. *For when four people need to simultaneously shower, I suppose.*

Hidden among the steam and spray, I let myself breathe. I took a full shower, relishing in the water running down my body. When I rinsed between my legs, I hissed at how swollen and sensitive I still felt. A small part of me wished I'd asked for his cock instead of the toy.

It's fine, I told myself. *Orgasm achieved. Crisis averted. You can rest now.*

I did feel exhausted. With the all-consuming need for an orgasm satiated, I was left limp and drained... but better. I was hopeful the drug's effects had dissipated.

I finished quickly and stepped out to find Rowan waiting with a towel, ensuring I could walk without falling. I almost wanted to tell him to stop coddling me, but when I saw him still flushed and visibly hard in his sweats, desire flared again.

I shoved it down ruthlessly.

"How do you feel?" he asked.

"Tired but better."

"Let me help." He scooped me up and carried me back to the bed, where he set me down and dried my hair.

The normalcy of it felt surreal after our moment of shared intimacy. His fingers shifted through my tresses, a reminder of how his touch grounded me.

He kissed my shoulder once more—a slip, it seemed, because he stilled immediately. He mumbled, "Sorry," then gestured for me to lie down.

That was the second time he'd apologized to me in less than an hour. It unnerved me. It felt unlike Rowan to be so apologetic. *He's worried that he took advantage of me*, I suddenly suspected. I hoped I was wrong, because the truth was that Rowan had been nothing short of amazing.

Fresh sheets covered the bed. I realized he'd changed them while I'd been in the shower. I slid under the covers and looked at him expectantly. Rowan turned off the light and moved towards the door.

"Wait," I said.

His shadow stilled in the doorway. "Yes?"

"Can you," I paused, uncertain how to ask. "Can we sleep together?"

"I think that would be unwise." His voice was careful, measured.

"I meant rest. Close our eyes. *Literally* sleep."

"Oh."

"It's okay, Rowan. I don't think you're particularly lucid right now with the absence of blood in your brain."

His laughter rumbled softly through the darkness between us. "This is true. Are you alright with that?"

"Being cuddled after the best orgasm of my life?" I patted the mattress, the sound carrying across the room. "Yes. Come on. I won't bite."

Rowan slid in beside me, and I heard him mutter under his breath. "I would honestly welcome being bitten right now."

But he didn't push me for anything.

I turned to my side, and Rowan followed, wrapping his arms around me until I was encased in his warmth. His nose nuzzled against the crook of my neck as he inhaled my scent.

"Is this okay?" I asked.

"No, this is not okay." His lips pressed against my neck. "This is perfect." His length was nestled against my ass, but he made no demands.

For once, I felt relaxed and unbearably sleepy. "Rowan." I yawned, my eyes already drifting closed. "You promise you're okay with... this?"

He was quiet behind me, but I felt his breath hot against my shoulder. "I will never be okay with *how* this came to be. Someone harmed you. There will be retribution for that."

Retribution. The way he said the word, with such an icy certainty, filled me with a contradictory feeling of comfort and dread.

Rowan continued. "But am I okay with *this*?" he asked as he squeezed me against him. "Gods, yes, Violet. You are... everything."

His words slid warm down my chest into my belly, and I smiled. I wrapped my arms around his, where they rested across my ribcage.

"Thank you, Rowan."

"Anything for you, *volchok*."

And I fell asleep to his words, feeling safer than I had in two lifetimes.

Chapter 22

Rowan

Violet was curled onto her side, back pressed against my chest, one hand tucked beneath her cheek. Her breathing had finally evened out—deep, rhythmic, the kind of sleep that spoke of genuine rest rather than drug-induced unconsciousness. The fever flush had faded from her cheeks, leaving her skin its natural warm caramel in the dim amber light I'd left on. I needed to see her, needed to confirm she was truly safe, unable to tear my gaze away.

Her dark hair spread across the white pillow, the red streaks catching light in shades of burgundy and crimson. The thin sheet covering her had slid down, exposing the curve of her hip and the lean muscle of her thigh. She looked peaceful. Younger, somehow, without the sharp wariness she wore like armor when awake.

Exquisite

The word settled in my chest, undeniable.

I'd been watching her for the better part of an hour, telling myself it was necessary. That I needed to monitor her breathing, her temperature, any sign the drug was still wreaking havoc through her system. That I was being vigilant, protective, responsible.

But that was only half true.

I simply wanted to look at her: memorize the slope of her nose, the fullness of her delicate lips, the soft curve of her ear where I'd whispered filth that made her come undone in my arms.

What have I done?

The question circled through my mind like a wolf stalking prey, relentless and hungry.

I'd touched her. Held her while she brought herself to orgasm. Whispered obscene encouragement in her ear—things I'd never said to anyone, things I hadn't known I was capable of saying—while she'd ground her ass against my aching cock and soaked my sheets with her release.

I've never been so ravenous for someone. Ever. Not in fifty years of my previous life, nor in the five years since my reincarnation.

In the Wastelands, I'd been scarred, my face carved up by violence and survival. My body had been a roadmap of every mistake I'd made, every fight I'd barely survived, every desperate choice that had kept me breathing another day. Women didn't look at men like me with desire unless they were paid, a luxury I could barely afford the few times I partook. Intimacy required vulnerability, and vulnerability meant death in a world where everyone was looking for a weakness to exploit.

And then there had been Faelin. I'd loved Faelin—loved her with a fierce, protective intensity that had driven me to make deals I couldn't cover, to trade years of my freedom for medicine that came too late. But that love had been pure in its simplicity. She'd been like a little sister, precious and bright in a world of rot and ash. I'd wanted to protect her, to give her a chance at something better than the brutality of the Wastelands.

This was different. Foreign. *Terrifying* in its intensity.

Looking at Violet made my chest tight and my cock hard. Forced me to clench my hands out of an urge to touch and claim and possess. A raging inferno burning that would consume me if I wasn't careful.

And it had...

I'd held Violet's trembling body while she'd used a toy to chase relief.. I'd cupped her breasts and twisted her piercings and told her she was perfect while she'd fallen apart in my arms. And when she'd screamed my name, her body convulsing with the force of her orgasm, I'd felt something crack open in my chest—something I'd kept frozen and buried for decades.

Did I do the right thing?

The question gnawed at me, sharp teeth tearing at soft tissue.

Her body had turned into an endless pit of desire by succubus blood. Yes, she'd said the words—*I'm clearheaded enough to know what I'm asking*—but had she been? Truly? Could anyone give their honest consent while burning from the inside out, while pain and pleasure blurred into something indistinguishable?

I replayed the moment in my mind, picking apart every detail like I was on the hunt.

"I don't want to be alone, but I don't want to force you into anything you don't want."

Her words. Clear. Articulate. Concerned for my consent even while her body was on fire.

"Can you touch me? It doesn't bother me. I feel safe with you. I want you to touch me."

Her permission. Explicit. Repeated.

I'd watched her body's responses—the way she'd arched into my touch without hesitation, the way she'd spread her legs wider when I'd commanded it, the way she'd ground herself against me with desperate hunger. She hadn't frozen. Hadn't flinched. Hadn't shown any of the signs I knew to watch for, the tells that indicated someone was enduring rather than enjoying.

She wanted it. She wanted me.

But had she wanted *me*, or had she just wanted relief from agony?

The distinction mattered. It *really* fucking mattered.

My gut twisted with guilt that felt like swallowing broken glass. I should have said no. Should have left the room entirely, let her handle it herself despite her pleas for me to stay. That would have been the honorable choice. The safe choice.

But she would have suffered alone. The drug would have tormented her for hours—Jules had said as much—and I would have abandoned her to that torment rather than risk crossing a line I couldn't uncross.

Which is worse? Helping her while she is compromised, or leaving her to suffer?

I didn't have an answer. I wasn't even sure there was a right answer.

What did I know? I'd denied myself any personal, physical pleasure. Kept my hands away from her cunt despite desperately wanting to feel her slick heat, to slide my fingers inside her and curve them exactly how I knew would make her scream. Kept my cock trapped in my sweats even when every ravenous animalistic instinct had screamed to bury myself inside her and fuck her until neither of us could remember our own names.

I'd only touched where she'd explicitly given permission—her breasts, her waist, her shoulders. Nothing more. I'd helped her reach orgasm so she could rest. That was all. Nothing more.

Keep telling yourself that.

The thought came bitter and mocking, because I knew the truth buried beneath my rationalizations. Yes, I'd wanted to help her. But I'd also wanted to brand myself into her memory so thoroughly she'd never look at another man the same way.

Possessive. Protective. Both truths coexisting in the same breath.

So much for keeping boundaries. I'd told Levi nothing like this would happen. Promised him I'd keep her safe, keep my distance, treat her like a ward and nothing more.

Fuck Levi.

I hadn't been lying when I'd made that promise. I'd genuinely believed I could watch over her without wanting her. At the time, I honestly didn't think of Violet as anything other than a spoiled pain in the ass princess.

Which she is, I reminded myself.

But... she'd come to be so much more than that, and I wasn't about to flog myself over circumstances I couldn't have predicted. Besides, Levi was an asshole who'd spent years treating me like a villain. He could handle a little disappointment.

The guilt over consent, though? That lingered like smoke.

I needed to move. Needed to do something other than spiral through the same thoughts on an endless loop.

Violet's breathing remained deep and even, her body relaxed in genuine sleep. She was safe. I could leave her for a few minutes.

I slipped out of bed with practiced silence, my feet finding the wood floor without a sound. My body protested—muscles stiff from holding still for hours, my cock still painfully hard and straining against my sweats, the waistband digging into sensitive flesh. The bathroom marble was cool against my bare feet as I started the shower, twisting the knob to its coldest setting. I stripped off my sweats, still damp with her sweat and mine.

Cold water hit my back, and I gritted my teeth against the shock of it. Ice straight from some glacial stream, stealing my breath and prickling my skin with a thousand tiny needles.

My cock remained stubbornly hard, jutting forward despite the temperature that should have killed any arousal. I stared down at it, half-tempted to take myself in hand and find relief in a few quick strokes.

But the thought of Violet walking in to find me with my hand wrapped around my cock – stroking myself furiously while I was meant to be watching over her – stopped me. Heat rushed through me then. Despite the cold water, embarrassment and arousal twisted together in a way that tightened my balls.

No. I knew I should not leave her alone for longer than necessary. I couldn't risk her waking to find me gone, potentially panicking, hurting, or needing help that I wasn't there to provide.

And frankly, I'd survived unimaginably far worse pain than blue balls. The Wastelands had taught me to endure broken bones, infected wounds, and hunger that turned your stomach into a gnawing maw of agony. Aching balls were nothing. Barely registered on the scale of suffering I'd weathered.

I scrubbed quickly with pine-scented soap, the smell sharp and earthy. The water sluiced down my body, over muscles still tense with unresolved want, circling the drain in a miniature whirlpool.

I shut off the water, dried with efficiency rather than care, and pulled on fresh sweats and a clean white shirt. My cock protested being confined again, but I ignored it. *Discipline. Control.* I'd built a life on both.

When I slipped back into the bedroom, Violet hadn't moved. Still curled on her side, still breathing deep and steady, still heartbreakingly beautiful in the dim light.

I eased back into bed beside her, careful not to jostle the mattress. She made a small sound—wordless, content—and shifted slightly closer to my warmth. I let myself relax into the pillows, watching her in the amber glow, and felt my eyes grow heavy.

Sleep came easier than I'd expected, dragging me down into darkness.

I woke to the sound of pain.

Small, breathless sounds that pulled me from sleep with the efficiency of an alarm. My eyes snapped open, immediately searching for the threat. The room was darker now—the bedside clock reading 6:27 in harsh green digits. Morning, but barely. Pale gray light was just beginning to filter through the windows, dawn still an hour away.

Violet was awake beside me, her face twisted with discomfort, her hands hovering over her chest like she wanted to touch but was afraid to.

"Violet?" I pushed up on one elbow, concern sharpening my voice. "What is wrong?"

"My nipples are on fire," she said through gritted teeth, her breathing shallow and quick.

My blood turned to ice, cold and immediate. *Side effects. The drug is still in her system.* "Is it the succubus blood? Are you experiencing symptoms again?"

"The *what*? No." She looked at me like I'd grown a second head. "It's not the drug, you paranoid asshole. I just got them pierced two weeks ago. You're not supposed to play with them for like six months after."

The guilt that slammed into me was immediate and crushing. "Fuck. Violet, I did not know. I am so sorry, I should have known better, I should have been more gentle, I should have—"

"Rowan," she cut me off, a smile tugging at her lips despite the pain tightening her features. "How the hell would you know the first thing about proper pierced nipple aftercare?"

She was right, but it didn't stop the tide of guilt swelling within me. "I should have asked you." The words came out stiff, formal, weighed down with self-recrimination.

"I asked you to touch me," she said, her tone gentler now. "I *needed* you to touch me. You think I was worried about piercing aftercare when all I could think about was fucking you?"

Her words dug deep into the darkness I was struggling to keep at bay. "That does not absolve me of—"

"Oh my god, stop." She laughed, the sound pained but genuine. "You're really gonna beat yourself up over this? I practically begged you to play with my nipples, and now you're acting like you committed a crime."

Despite everything, I felt my mouth twitch towards a smile. "I hurt you."

"Yeah, well, it was worth it." She shifted, wincing. "Though I'm definitely paying for it now. I need a cold compress and saline wash, or these things are gonna be angry for days."

I was already moving, sliding out of bed with purpose. "I will get these things."

"Saline solution, if you have it. If not, I can make some with salt and water. And something cold—ice pack, frozen vegetables, whatever you've got."

I headed to the bathroom, my mind cataloging supplies. I kept a first aid kit under the sink—a remnant of survival instincts that refused to die even in this comfortable life—and I knew it contained saline solution. The freezer had ice packs I used for training injuries.

Two minutes later, I returned with my arms full: spare shirt, saline spray bottle, clean soft washcloths, two gel ice packs wrapped in thin towels so they wouldn't be too cold against her hurting nipples.

Violet had sat up against the headboard, still nude, the sheet pooled around her waist. Morning's pale light painted her in shades of pearl and rose, highlighting the swell of her breasts and the angry redness around both piercings. The barbells looked embedded in dried bloody tissue, the skin puffed and tender.

I did that.

"Alright," I said, settling beside her on the bed with my supplies arranged on the nightstand like surgical instruments. "Walk me through this."

"I've got it," she said with a laugh.

"*Nyet*. Please let me fix what is my fault."

She looked at me for a moment, contemplating something before she shrugged. "Fine. If it'll stop you from hovering like a guilty mother hen. . ."

"Thank you. It will."

"It's not complicated." She gestured to the saline bottle. "Just spray it on, let it sit for a minute, then gently pat dry. The cold compress will help with the swelling after."

I picked up the saline bottle, reading the label with the same focus I'd once used to identify which plants in the Wastelands were edible and which would kill you in minutes. Sterile saline solution. 0.9% sodium chloride. Wound irrigation and cleaning.

This is just wound care. Clinical. Simple.

"Ready?" I asked.

She nodded, and I saw the way her breath quickened slightly. Anticipation or nervousness, I couldn't tell.

I angled the bottle and sprayed her right nipple first, the mist settling on inflamed skin. She drew in a sharp breath, her body tensing, but she didn't pull away. I watched the solution bead on her skin, watched it run down the curve of her breast in tiny rivulets that caught the light. I willed my cock to not respond.

"Does it hurt?" I asked, my voice rough.

"Stings a little. But it's helping, I think." She glanced down at herself, then back up at me. "You can do the other one."

I repeated the process on her left nipple, hyper-aware of my hands' proximity to her skin, of the way her chest rose and fell with each breath. Her breasts were fucking perfect—I could admit that even as I tried to maintain a clinical detachment. Full and round, sitting high despite their size, the kind of curves that artists spent lifetimes trying to capture. Her skin was soft, supple, warm beneath my careful touch when I steadied her with one hand while spraying with the other.

But I compartmentalized those observations, shoved them into a box labeled *not now*. She was in pain. Pain I'd caused. That was what mattered.

"Let it sit for a minute," she instructed, her voice steadier now.

I waited, counting seconds in my head, watching the saline work. After sixty seconds, I picked up one of the clean washcloths—soft white cotton that smelled of lavender—and gently patted her right nipple dry. The touch was feather-light, barely there, but she still drew in a quick breath.

"I am sorry."

"You're fine." She watched me with an expression I couldn't read. "I told you I can do it myself."

"*Nyet*," I repeated. "I am the one who hurt you."

"So dutiful," she said, a smile playing at her lips. "Anyone ever tell you that you take responsibility way too seriously?"

"Frequently." I moved to her left nipple, repeating the gentle patting motion. "I ignore them."

She snorted, then winced at the movement. "Of course you do. God forbid Rowan ever half-ass anything."

"There is no point in doing something if you are not going to do it properly." I set aside the damp cloth and reached for the ice packs.

"Is that your life motto? Because it explains so much about you." Her tone was teasing now, the pain clearly easing enough for her smart-ass mouth to return.

"It has served me well thus far." I unwrapped the first ice pack from its protective towel and held it up. "This will be cold."

"Yeah, that's generally how ice works." But there was affection beneath the sarcasm, warmth that tightened my chest.

I pressed the ice pack gently against her right breast, careful to center it over the inflamed piercing. She sucked in a breath, her body tensing, then slowly relaxing as the cold did its work.

"Is that better?" I asked.

"Yeah. Much." She looked down at my hand holding the compress, then back up at my face. "You know you don't have to keep apologizing, right? I'm not mad at you."

"You should be." I applied the second ice pack to her left breast, mirroring the placement. "I should have asked about your piercings. Should have been more careful."

"Rowan." She reached up and caught my chin, forcing me to meet her eyes. "I asked you to touch me. *Begged* you, actually."

"That is not the point—"

"That's exactly the point." She released my chin but held my gaze. "You helped me. You could've fucked me. God knows I would've let you. . . but you didn't. You kept boundaries and respected my body—my *consent* when most people wouldn't have. So stop beating yourself up over my sore nipples."

The casual way she said it—*you could've fucked me*—sent heat rushing through my body despite my best efforts at control. My cock, which had finally started to soften during the clinical piercing care, immediately responded.

Treacherous bastard.

"How are you feeling otherwise?" I asked, desperate to change the subject before she noticed my body's reaction. "The effects of the drug, I mean. Do you feel any lingering symptoms?"

She considered, her brow furrowing slightly. "No. Actually, I feel fine. Better than fine, honestly. Like it just. . . worked its way out of my system."

"Good." Relief washed through me, genuine and profound. "That is good."

"Yeah." She shifted the ice packs slightly, adjusting their position. "Which means I should be totally fine for my shift tonight at Oubliette."

And just like that, the moment of peace was shattered.

My jaw clenched hard enough to make my teeth ache. Every muscle in my body went taut, coiling with renewed tension. My voice was firm when I said the word, "No."

She tilted her head to one side and stared at me with a confused look. It was as if she didn't comprehend why I objected to her returning to the place she'd been slipped something less than eight hours ago.

"No." I threw my hands up, exasperation bleeding through every movement.

Disappointment stooped her shoulders, pulling them down like gravity had doubled its weight on her frame. But her voice held firm, unyielding as winter stone. "I'm sorry, Rowan. I have to go back."

The finality of those words, leaving no room for negotiation or argument, reminded me viscerally of Faelin in her last moments—that same grim determination, that refusal to bend even when bending might have saved her life. The memory cut sharp and cold, a blade between ribs I thought had scarred over.

An awful pit opened in my stomach, yawning and dark.

"Violet, you were drugged last night." I kept my voice level, reasonable, even as frustration clawed at my restraint like a caged animal. "You cannot possibly expect me to stay silent about this. I will not tell your father, but I sure as hell will not allow you to walk back into that place tonight, or *any* night."

We still had hours before her next shift at Oubliette. Hours I fully intended to use to convince her this path was madness. But the stubborn set of Violet's jaw, the way her chin tilted up in defiance even as disappointment curved her spine, told me I wouldn't be able to convince her without laying some truths bare.

Truths I wasn't certain I was ready to expose. Truths that might shatter whatever fragile trust we'd so recently built between us.

"Violet, listen. I do not understand why you are so determined to return there. If money is truly your goal, then surely there is a coffee shop nearby where you could apply. A bookstore. Hell, a boutique in the shopping district below us. Anywhere that does not involve a club full of—"

I caught myself before saying too much.

She shook her head as she said, "I have to be *there*." Her breathing quickened, shallow and tight. Her heart rate increased. I heard it rabbiting against her ribs, feeding the predator inside of me and urging me to circle closer.

Her physiological changes led me to my next question, spoken with a calm I absolutely did not feel. My own heart hammered in my chest, but I forced my voice to remain level, gentle.

"Violet, what exactly is in Oubliette that you cannot find anywhere else?" I reached for her hand where it fisted in the white sheets, and covered it with my own. Her skin was warm, no longer feverish but still carrying heat. I remembered her confession from last night, about being coerced, about touch being a minefield of triggers and trauma. This was safe ground. Permitted contact. "Please. I need to understand."

A shadow crossed her face like a cloud passing over the sun, and it pained me to feel so powerless against whatever demons haunted her. In the morning light streaming through the windows, illuminating every detail in brutal clarity, I watched her body go taut with tension. Every muscle coiled like rope about to snap, her spine straightening against the ligneous headboard, her free hand clenching and unclenching in the bedsheets in an unconscious rhythm.

Whatever this is, it goes far beyond my fears for her safety.

She teetered on some invisible edge, and I recognized the haunted look in her eyes from my previous life—that same look of those fools who'd ventured beyond the furthest edges of the Wastelands and into the Chittering Dark.

I squeezed her hand, feeling the delicate bones beneath warm skin. "I am here for you, Violet. Let me help you."

Her mouth opened, then closed. Her throat worked as she swallowed. For a long moment, she simply stared at me with those hazel eyes that shifted colors in the changing light—more gold now, less green, like autumn leaves before they fell. I watched the exact second resignation crossed her features. Her shoulders dropped, the tension bleeding out of them. Her jaw unclenched. Something fundamental shifted in her posture, as if she'd been holding herself together through sheer force of will and had finally decided to let go.

"Alright." The word came out barely above a whisper.

The fluttering anxiety in my chest eased slightly. *Thank fuck.*

She looked into my eyes and said, "I'm hunting a man."

My cock twitched despite the gravity of the moment. *Well, that's oddly promising.*

I waited for her to continue, keeping my expression carefully neutral. I'd learned in my first life that people revealed more when you gave them silence to fill. Her brow pinched when I didn't react as she'd apparently expected—no shock, no horror, no attempt to talk her out of it.

"You don't have anything to say to that?" Suspicion colored her voice.

I shook my head. "You have never given me reason to doubt you, Violet."

Disbelief flickered across her face, quickly followed by something that looked dangerously close to affection. She narrowed her eyes into a scowl that didn't quite hide the softness beneath. "Why are you so perfect, Rowan?"

"Oh, please." I couldn't stop the dry smile that tugged at my mouth. "We both know how 'perfect' we are around each other. Let us skip the charades."

She gave a conceding nod and, to my disappointment, pulled her hand away from mine to put on the spare shirt. The loss of contact felt more significant than it should have. She hugged her knees to her chest, ice packs now forgotten, curling into herself and looking smaller. Younger. More fragile than the fierce creature who'd danced on that stage, who'd ground against me last night while I whispered in her ear.

"He's someone who hurt me." Her voice came out steady despite the tremor I could see running through her hands. "No—he *broke* me in ways I can't explain. Ways I'm not ready to explain."

Her hazel eyes found mine, holding my gaze with an intensity that felt like a physical touch. I held her stare, admiring the way morning light lit her caramel skin, catching gold in the undertones and painting her in warmth. The way those hazel eyes sparked with flecks of amber and green and something that looked like barely contained rage.

"Is he the one you fight in your nightmares?" Surprise and shame danced across her face as she turned away quickly. I waited for a moment before I prompted her. "Answer my question, Violet."

She let out a long sigh. "Yes."

So he dies. "Then I will kill him for you." The words came out in an exhale, purging the anxiety that had been coiled in my chest since she'd first mentioned Oubliette.

Startled eyes opened to meet mine as relief washed through me, cool and sweet as spring melt. *Her demon is mortal. A man. Just a man.*

Men, I could hunt. Men I could track through cities and across state lines. Men I could corner in dark alleys or expensive penthouses. Men I could string up and bleed dry without losing a single second of sleep.

If it had been a vampyre lord with centuries of accumulated power, or a petty god lounging in divine indifference—that would have been infinitely more complicated. That would have required planning, resources, and knowledge I was still gathering about this timeline's supernatural hierarchies. Regardless of the length of time, I would have burned covens and hunted demons for her.

But a man? A man who'd hurt her? That was as easy as breathing.

She made a disgruntled sound, somewhere between a laugh and a scoff. "Don't act like you've killed before. Besides. . . it's not that easy, otherwise I would've done it already."

Oh, volchok, if you only knew.

She shifted against the headboard, the wood creaking softly under the redistribution of weight, and sighed. The sound carried exhaustion and frustration in equal measure. She closed her eyes, dark lashes creating crescents against cheeks still faintly flushed from last night's fever. "I don't need you to fix my problems, Rowan. I've had enough of men doing what they *think* is best for me."

Dangerous words from such a fierce *volchok*. Words that would have sent most men scrambling to prove themselves, to assert their dominance, to override her clearly stated boundary.

I am not most men.

I scooted closer, angling my body so I had to look up at her. Rested my head in the crook of my arm, deliberately making myself smaller, less threatening—not an easy feat given I was six-foot-five, and two hundred ten pounds of muscle, but body language mattered. Perception mattered. One of her complaints she'd voiced before, in sharper moments, was feeling overpowered by my presence.

"Violet, you told me this man hurt you. . . but is there more?" I waited, and I knew the answer when she stilled. "So this man touched you without your consent." It was not a question. My voice came out calmer than I felt, but beneath that manufactured quiet, possession and anger simmered like magma under the earth. Waiting. Building pressure. "That is enough for me. You may be under my protection, but you are still your own woman. You are my equal in all ways, and I value your input." I stopped, letting the words sink between us. "Violet, you are free to hunt him in the way you think is best. I am simply here to remind you that your current approach is flawed."

She cracked open one eye and peeked down at me, her gaze assessing. "Oh, really?"

I nodded, fighting back a smile. "A little humility is an important skill to learn."

She laughed then, genuine and warm and completely unexpected. The sound filled the quiet bedroom like light filling darkness, chasing shadows into corners. "And you have *so* much of it, Rowan."

My breath caught in my chest, trapped somewhere between my lungs and my throat. I loved the way her laughter sounded. In my room. In my bed. With me. The intimacy of it, the casual domesticity, felt more dangerous than anything that had happened last night.

Fuck.

I looked towards the wall behind her, focusing on the dark television screen mounted there, willing myself to breathe steadily against the returning hardness in my sweats. My cock had barely softened since last night, and her proximity—the scent of her skin combined with the memory of her body arching into mine—was doing absolutely nothing to help.

"I am yours to use, Violet." I forced the words out past the tightness in my throat, meaning every syllable with a ferocity that surprised even me. "If you do not want me to tell your father or Charlie what is happening, then you need to trust me. Let me help you hunt this man properly."

She fisted the sheet tighter, her knuckles going white with pressure. The tendons in her hand stood out in sharp relief against her skin. After a long moment where I could practically hear her internal debate, she gave a tight nod.

"It's complicated, but I'll do my best."

I shifted to sit beside her, both of us leaning back against the wooden headboard that was still faintly warm from where our bodies had pressed against it hours before. We stared at the opposite wall where the darkened television screen reflected our images back at us—two figures side by side in rumpled white sheets, our breathing the only sound breaking the heavy silence.

The quiet between us was not uncomfortable, but weighted with things unsaid. I heard the building settling around us, the faint hum of the heating system, and distant traffic from the street below. My heightened hearing picked up her elevated heart rate, the slight hitch in her breathing that suggested she was gathering courage for something.

"There's something else I need to tell you. Something that's happened to me," she started, her voice smaller than I'd ever heard it. Uncertain in a way that Violet never was. "And it's going to sound... impossible. Insane, maybe. You're probably going to think I'm delusional or need psychiatric help or—"

"Violet—" I tried to interrupt, to reassure her.

"Just listen, okay?" She cut me off, still not looking at me. Her gaze remained fixed on some point across the room, as if meeting my eyes would steal whatever courage she'd scraped together. "Let me get it out before you react. Before you decide I'm crazy."

I nodded, even though she wasn't watching. "I am listening."

She took a deep breath. Her hands twisted in the sheets, wringing the expensive cotton like she was trying to strangle it. Whatever secret she carried, I could tell it was heavy.

My mind immediately spiraled through possibilities, each scenario worse than the last. *She has discovered the supernatural world on her own. She has been attacked by a vampyre in some dark corner of campus. Hunted by a werewolf who caught her scent. Seduced by a siren who tried to drown her in promises. Marked by something ancient and hungry that I cannot protect her from.*

The thoughts crashed through my skull like an avalanche, burying rational thought beneath layers of protective instinct and mounting dread.

"I'm not *just* the twenty year old Violet you grew up with," she said. "I *am* her. But I'm also... older. With memories from a different life."

The world opened beneath me.

I felt the actual physical sensation of freefall, of solid ground dissolving into void, of everything I thought I understood about reality restructuring itself into impossible new configurations that my mind struggled to map.

My heart stopped. Actually stopped for one horrible second before slamming back to life with enough force to make my ribs ache. I knew—with the bone-deep certainty born from my own impossible experience—that she was telling the truth.

We are the same.

The realization detonated in my chest like a bomb, scattering every thought I'd been trying to hold together. Whatever fears I'd harbored before—the supernatural world reaching out to grasp at her from beyond the veil—*this* was so much worse.

Chapter 23

Violet

I remembered everything from last night. Every touch. Every whispered command. Every shuddering breath he'd drawn when I'd ground against him.

But now was not the time to dissect what we'd done, what lines we'd crossed, what it meant that I'd fallen apart in his arms while he'd held me together.

"I'm not really twenty," I started, feeling my pulse echo in my ears like a drum. My body still sang from last night's pleasure, muscles loose and sated in a way I hadn't felt in either lifetime. "I lived before. In another time, another body."

The words felt like pulling shrapnel from a wound—necessary, agonizing, leaving me raw.

"I was nine when I was abducted. Thirty-three when I was murdered." I hesitated, struggling for words that could possibly contain the enormity of what I was trying to explain. "Then I woke up here. Younger. Safe with my family somehow. I thought I was free."

The room was quiet except for our breathing as the world continued around us—distant traffic humming below, the building settling, the whisper of wind against glass. I felt foolish trying to explain something that sounded ripped from science fiction, but I didn't know how else to begin.

"But waking every day, wondering if this life was a dream..." My voice cracked, and I forced myself to continue. "Struggling with nightmares that felt more real than the sheets I woke up in. I couldn't ignore the possibility that the man who destroyed me might still exist in this timeline. That he might be hurting other girls the way he hurt me."

Rowan remained still beside me, his presence solid and grounding. I looked towards the darkened television screen, noting how much taller he sat compared to me even slouched against the headboard. His white-blonde hair was tousled from sleep, sticking up in places where my fingers had tangled through it hours ago. His pale eyes looked unearthly in the morning light filtering through the windows—blue-gray like winter ice, like frozen lakes that held entire worlds beneath their surface.

I clenched my thighs together, remembering his hands on my body. Patient. Careful. *Reverent.*

Everything I had never been able to feel with Edward. Everything the few high school boys I'd dated behind Daddy's back had failed to provide—clumsy fumbling in backseats, more concerned with their own pleasure than mine.

"My daddy. . ." I stopped, shaking my head. "No. Charlie. Shit." I took a ragged breath. "I don't know how to begin explaining the family situation."

Rowan's hand found mine, his fingers lacing through mine with gentle firmness. "I am aware of your father's and Charlie's situation. Their rebirths."

I gasped and turned to face him, but his gaze remained fixed forward on our reflections in the black mirror of the television. "How. . .?"

Rowan sighed, the sound heavy with its own weighted history. The way his attention stayed fixated on the screen led me to believe he was searching for the right words, mapping out his explanation before speaking.

"It is complicated," he said finally. "But it does sound similar to what you have experienced."

"And you believed them?" Hope fluttered in my chest like a bird testing damaged wings, perching on my soul with insidious claws that dug deep. "You believe *me?*"

"Of course I do." He said it as if it were the most obvious thing in the world, as simple as stating water was wet or fire burned.

The certainty in his voice sent a jolt through me, relief coursing through my veins like cool water after burning. He believed. He didn't push or pry into the impossible mechanics of rebirth, didn't demand explanations I couldn't provide, didn't look at me like I needed psychiatric intervention.

He simply waited for me to continue. Let me exist in my truth without requiring me to defend it.

I couldn't help how instinctively I yearned for him in that moment—this man who accepted the impossible because he'd apparently witnessed his own impossibilities.

Rowan continued, unaware of my internal struggle. "Not all things in life have to make sense, Violet." He flexed his jaw, the muscle jumping beneath his skin. "This life, this world. . . it is not as simple or safe as most people believe. There are monsters and events beyond mortal understanding."

Yeah, no shit. Me, daddy, and Charlie being prime examples of that.

His low voice had turned sober, weighted with knowledge that sat heavy on his shoulders. He forced a flat smile that didn't reach his eyes. "Some monsters are mortal, like the man you are hunting. Others are not."

"Monsters. . ." I breathed, my mind racing. "Mortals and. . . what?"

Since waking up in this fucked-up charade of a second life, I had tried desperately not to dwell on the cosmic mechanisms behind my rebirth. Tried to focus on the practical—finding Edward, making him pay, protecting others from his particular brand of evil. But someone close to me this entire time apparently held answers to questions I'd been too afraid to ask.

"I want to understand," I said, surprised by how much I meant it.

He snorted, a sound caught between humor and resignation. "I do not fully understand it myself, but. . ."

We sat side by side, staring at our reflections on the television's dark screen. His thumb began to caress my wrist slowly, the repetitive motion sending delicious pulses of residual pleasure through my core. The touch was absent-minded, almost unconscious, as if his body sought connection while his mind worked through how to explain the inexplicable.

"There are beings out there who like to play with the lives of mortals, Violet." His voice dropped lower, intimate despite the heavy subject. "Some are the typical stories meant to scare children—vampyres, shifters, demons. But those stories hide truth beneath layers of lies and exaggeration."

"You mean like the ones you used to tell us?" I thought back to family camping trips, Rowan spinning tales around crackling fires while Charlie and Levi listened with indulgent smiles. Stories of shifters and ancient vampyres, of folklore so obscure I'd tried looking them up in libraries later and found nothing. I'd always assumed it was Rowan and Charlie bonding over shared interests, invented mythology they'd created together.

"They are real," he said quietly. "Just like the gods mortals once worshiped. And they are *bored*, Violet."

"Bored?" My heart hammered in my chest, the word seeming too small, too mundane for what he was describing. How could gods be *bored*? How could boredom justify ruining lives, stealing futures, playing with human souls like chess pieces?

But Rowan was not the type to joke, especially not when I'd barely confessed my own existential crisis iceberg.

"Your rebirth, your previous life. . ." He looked at me then, his eyes creased with a pain I wasn't comfortable witnessing. Too raw. Too honest. "It was probably because of a god's decision. Or their mistake." He reached out, cupping my cheek with his free hand, his thumb stroking slowly across my cheekbone. "And the wrath that has led you down this path of hunting your abuser. . . I am sorry, Violet."

My breath snagged in my throat. The air felt suddenly too thick to pull into my lungs. "You're sorry?"

His thumb continued its gentle path across my skin, the touch grounding even as his words threatened to unravel me. "Your pain. Your loss. Your tragedy—you surviving twenty-four years of abuse you should never have endured. . ." He broke off and leaned forward, pressing a kiss to my forehead. The tenderness of it, the softness, made my eyes sting. "You did not deserve it, Violet. It was never your fault."

The thing about emotions you've pushed down for so long, buried beneath survival instincts and the brutal arithmetic of staying alive another day—eventually they resurface, rearing their ugly heads in places you least expect.

Guilt and remorse for the life I'd lived, for the girl I'd been, crashed into me like a tsunami. The thoughts I'd carried for years in my previous life, thoughts that had become mantras I'd whispered to myself in dark rooms while strange hands violated my body: *It's your fault. You didn't listen. You trusted the wrong person. You deserve this.*

"No, I didn't listen to Daddy's warnings..." The words tumbled out, frantic and broken. "I met someone I shouldn't have trusted, I met him at the warehouse, I was so stupid—"

Rowan stopped me, his hand tightening on my cheek. "In your previous life, you were a child who trusted someone who did not deserve it. It was not your fault what happened then. It is still not your fault now."

And just like that, the endless dam of emotions I'd been holding back broke.

Tears flooded down my cheeks, hot and unstoppable. Words escaped me entirely, stolen by sobs that tore from my chest like they'd been living there all along, waiting for permission to emerge.

I was pain given form. I was loss wearing skin. I was the nine-year-old girl crying in a warehouse, begging and screaming for her mommy and daddy until her voice gave out. I was the teenager learning that her body was currency, that men would pay for access to her flesh, that screaming only made them enjoy it more. I was the twenty-year-old who'd stopped crying, stopped begging, stopped hoping for rescue because hope was a luxury she couldn't afford.

I was the forgotten wails echoing beneath a hidden moon as I was sold to the man who would methodically destroy every piece of who I'd been before ending my life with the same casual indifference he'd shown throughout.

I was Edward's pet. His property. His favorite broken toy.

And now I'm not.

The realization crashed over me with the force of revelation. *I am not his anymore. I am free.* Then my sobs intensified, wracking my body with violent tremors.

My hands reached for Rowan instinctively, and he wrapped me in his arms without hesitation. He pulled me against his chest, one hand cradling the back of my head while the other pressed against my spine, holding me together while I fell apart.

He whispered words of affirmation I wasn't sure I believed, his voice a low rumble against my ear. "You are loved. You are safe. You are with me."

He nuzzled into my hair as the wails began in earnest—animal sounds I didn't recognize as coming from my own throat, grief so profound it had no language.

I was empty, pouring years of rage and frustration and shame and terror into him. My fists pounded against his chest, beating against solid muscle, needing to hit something, to hurt something the way I'd been hurt. He merely held me tighter, absorbing every blow without flinching.

"You are strength," he whispered into my hair. "You are fire, Violet. You may have broken, but you are the metal that has been reforged in flame. You are the weapon you have become now."

The words shouldn't have helped. Shouldn't have penetrated the storm of grief consuming me.

But they did.

I drowned in memory and present simultaneously—smelling the warehouse's mildew and Rowan's pine scent, feeling Edward's hands and Rowan's gentle hold, hearing my own screams and Rowan's steady heartbeat against my ear.

I was drowning, and Rowan was my anchor. He led me both into the deep abyss of my endless sea of pain and simultaneously towards the light of salvation, refusing to let me drown alone in either.

I didn't know when it began—couldn't pinpoint the exact moment—but the truth of it crashed into me in relentless waves.

I had always felt safe with him. Even when I'd antagonized him, pushed his buttons, dared him to retaliate—I'd never once feared his response. He was my pillar, holding me with unwavering strength and those icy eyes that always seemed to see straight through every defense I'd constructed.

"Rowan." I gasped his name, searching for something—air, grounding, *him*.

I clutched at his shirt, my skin suddenly on fire again. But this wasn't the drug-induced fever from last night. This was something else entirely.

"Rowan, I need..." I struggled to articulate what was happening, my body responding to his proximity, his scent, the safety of his arms with a desire that felt overwhelming.

He tightened his embrace, one hand stroking down my spine in soothing repetition. "Shh, *volchok*. I am here. Whatever you need, you only need to ask."

The endearment slipped out so naturally, as if he'd been calling me that for years.

The fire surged through me, hot and unrelenting. I began to shake, but not from grief this time. The agony of emotional pain was being replaced by wildfire, desire coursing through my veins like molten metal.

It should feel wrong. I'd just confessed the horror of my previous life, sobbed in his arms like a broken child. My eyes were swollen, my face blotchy, my nose running.

And yet.

He'd accepted me. Accepted the impossible nature of my rebirth without question, already familiar with Levi and Charlie's situation. He'd led me through my breakdown with a calm, steady presence. He was everything I'd lacked in my other life—patience where Edward had been cruel, gentleness where I'd known only violence, choice where I'd had none.

I craved him the way the earth craved spring after endless winter, the way life and death danced in their eternal cycle. The world had been twisting and turning towards this moment of acceptance and absolutes, and I was done fighting it.

I shoved hard against his chest, expecting resistance.

To my surprise, he let me push him back against the headboard. His eyes were dark, pupils blown wide, and I recognized that look—wildfire to match my own.

We stared at each other, the silence pregnant with implications neither of us was willing to voice first. I trailed my gaze down from his blown pupils to his lips, watching his mouth with rapt fascination. My tongue darted out to wet my own lips, and I watched his eyes track the movement.

I wanted to taste him. Needed to.

He must have felt it radiating from me because he started to protest, his voice carrying a low warning. "Violet. . ."

Don't. Don't ruin this with logic or reason or regret we might feel later. I silenced him with a searing kiss.

He groaned into my mouth, his hands immediately moving up to tangle in my hair. I felt it then—the truth of us. We were an inferno together, unstoppable and consuming. Tongues and lips clashing, teeth scraping, neither of us holding back. We were fire and ice attempting to devour each other, each trying to melt or freeze the other in equal measures of passion that felt dangerously close to worship.

I grabbed his shirt and pulled him over me, wrapping my legs around his waist. He made an approving sound deep in his chest as I felt the hard length of him press against my core through the thin fabric of his sweats.

It was glorious. Sinful. Not nearly enough.

I couldn't get enough of him—his taste (mint and something darker), his scent (pine and clean male musk), the solid weight of him settling between my thighs.

"We should talk more—" He tried to inject reason into the chaos, pulling back enough to search my face.

"Fuck now, talk later." I gripped the hem of his shirt and lifted it off him, raking my nails down his firm torso.

He was beautiful. I loved the way his muscles rippled underneath my fingertips, the way his abs contracted when I scraped across them, the small sharp intake of breath when my nails found his nipples.

"Violet." His voice came out strangled, somewhere between a plea and a warning. "Your body is reacting from opening up and sharing your trauma with me. That combined with last night—"

I nibbled his jaw. "Don't fucking *psychoanalyze* me right now, Rowan. I want you."

His breath hitched. "I will not last long after last night. We should not do this when you have been so upset. There is more we should discuss—"

I bit into his shoulder, my teeth sinking into the junction where his neck met muscle. His body quivered, and he went silent.

When did I gain so much power over him?

The realization was intoxicating, headier than any drug. He showed me his desire freely, without restraint or shame, and I wanted to bathe in it.

"I am choosing this, Rowan." I released his shoulder, admiring the perfect impression of my teeth in his skin. "I want you to fuck me."

I felt him shudder, his whole body trembling against mine. "*Nyet*, wait, Violet. I might—"

I reached down and cupped him through his sweats, enjoying how hard and thick he felt against my palm. His cock jumped at the contact, and I couldn't suppress my smile.

"I want your cock in me, filling me to the brim." I stroked him slowly, feeling him throb and thicken. "I want to feel your balls slap against me while you—"

He shuddered again, more violently this time, and I felt moisture gather near his head, soaking through the fabric.

I looked down, then back up at him, surprised and delighted. "Did you just—?"

"Fuck." He glared down at me, but there was no real anger in it. "Now you have done it."

His infuriating smirk played at his lips despite the flush staining his cheeks, despite the small sheen of sweat gathering at his temple.

"Did you?" I asked again, wanting to hear him say it.

He let out a low laugh that I felt vibrate through his chest and into mine. "I challenge any man *not* to after spending an entire night with you, followed by you whispering filthy things in their ear while gripping their cock." He shuddered again, his eyes closing briefly. "It has been hell and bliss in equal measure."

I couldn't help the way my body responded—nipples going tight and aching, the throb between my legs blooming into a need I couldn't control. "Can we keep going?"

"Of course." His eyes opened, darker now, pupils eclipsing the pale blue-gray. "Though I might need to tie you down to keep you reigned in. You are fucking dangerous."

My breath caught. "Does that upset you?"

"You are perfect, Violet."

My heart clenched at the words, at the raw honesty in his voice. I squeezed him once more through the damp fabric of his sweats, eliciting another groan that shot straight to my core.

Addicting. This is addicting.

"Then tie me up, Rowan."

The look he gave me was enough to bring me to my knees had I not already been laying beneath him. Heat and hunger and something that looked dangerously like devotion.

"Violet, I do not think that is wise." But the desire burning in his eyes contradicted his words, uncoiling a part of me I'd thought had died with my previous body.

"I trust you." The confession tumbled out in a rushed frenzy, desperate and honest. "I want you to. I *need* you, Rowan."

His gaze traveled down my body slowly, deliberately, leaving my mouth dry and my pulse thundering. My nipples peaked beneath his gaze, and I watched his tongue dart out to wet his lips.

He wanted me. The evidence was written across every line of his body, every labored breath, every minute tremor in his hands.

I can't get enough of that look.

"Please." I begged, past pride or shame. "I'll be good. I'll listen to every command."

His breath shuddered out of him, and he closed his eyes like he was in pain. "Fuck, Violet. If we do this, you really cannot act up. You will need to trust me completely."

I slid my hands along his torso, torturously slow, mapping every ridge of muscle and plane of skin until my hands wrapped around the back of his head. His hair was silk between my fingers, finer than it looked.

"Violet—" he started, the warning lacing his tone.

I gripped his hair and brought his head down to mine. Steel eyes widened in surprise as I bit at his lower lip, tugging it between my teeth.

"I want you to tie me up and fuck me stupid, Rowan." I held his gaze, letting him see every ounce of desire and trust and need burning through me. "You'll do this for me, won't you?"

He released a breathless, "Yes."

I smiled against his mouth. "Good."

I kissed him then, and he met my fire with ice—a slow, deliberate dance of tongues as he tamed my wildfire with patient, methodical strokes. Taking control. Claiming dominance. Showing me exactly who would be leading this dance.

Yes. Finally.

"Take off your clothes," he commanded against my lips.

I obliged immediately, sitting up to peel off his shirt I'd been wearing. He stepped away from the bed, and something in the corner caught my eye—my bag.

A devious smirk played across my face as an idea formed.

When Rowan returned—gloriously, magnificently naked, his cock already hardening again despite having just come—he stopped mid-stride.

I was nude as he'd commanded, yes. But I'd also pulled out my spare black stockings from my bag and wore them for him, the mid torso tights hugging my legs. I'd positioned myself in the center of the bed, legs spread wide in shameless invitation.

"I thought I said to get naked." His voice had gone rough, his eyes locked on where the stockings ended near my navel and bare skin began.

"I thought you might enjoy these." I traced one hand down my body slowly, over my breast, across my stomach, stopping just before reaching where I knew he was desperate to stare.

He took a deep breath, his chest expanding. He closed his eyes and nodded, looking like a man struggling for control. "Very much so. Do you mind if they tear?"

He watched me stretch my other arm over my head, my back arched and breasts lifted, as my hand continued its path past my navel. I shook my head, watching his breath quicken, as I lowered my hand to tease myself with my fingers. "Not at all."

"Fuck, Violet." He crossed to me in two strides, the cerulean rope dangling from one hand. His cock twitched, thick and flushed and already leaking again.

I felt gloriously unhinged, knowing I was breaking him down piece by piece.

"Do you like what you see, Rowan?"

"Yes." The word came out grated, forced through clenched teeth. His eyes trailed down my body in a touch that felt physical, hot and possessive. He dropped to his knees beside the bed, rope coiling at his feet. "Can I?"

I widened my legs further, knowing exactly what he was asking. "Touch me, Rowan. I'm yours."

He let out a long, drawn-out groan and buried his face between my legs.

The stockings went up to my torso, but his tongue found my center as if there were no barrier at all. He pressed against me, broad strokes of his tongue running the length of my covered slit, and I let out a moan that echoed off the bedroom's high ceilings.

"Oh god, Rowan. That feels so good."

He gripped my thighs, his fingers digging into soft flesh as he widened my legs even more. The stretch burned perfectly, and then my heels were hooked over his shoulders, my body completely opened to him.

I was on display—aching and needy and desperate—and he fucking knew it.

"You look so gorgeous like this, Violet." He nipped at the stocking covering my inner thigh, his teeth grazing the sensitive skin beneath. "Spread open for me. Dripping."

"You like making me beg, don't you, Rowan?" My voice came out breathless, wrecked already.

More teeth, and I felt the stocking tear. Cool air hit newly exposed skin. "Want me to punish you when all you deserve is praise and rewards for being so fucking perfect?"

I whimpered as his thumb moved to circle my clit through the ruined stocking, the wet fabric creating delicious friction. I could feel how drenched I was, my arousal soaking through the black nylon.

"Please, Rowan. Tie me up and show me how good I've been."

He chuckled, the sound vibrating against my inner thigh and causing me to shudder. "You always know exactly what to say to get your way, do you not, my *volchok*? Showing me your teeth when all you really want is to be fucked senseless."

"Yes," I pleaded, past any pretense of pride. "Just for you. I need you to."

I felt the stocking rip more—a decisive tear—and then two fingers slid inside me without warning.

I nearly vaulted off the bed, my hips lifting, a moan tearing from my throat that was half pleasure, half shock. He was thick, his fingers stretching me, curving immediately to find that spot inside that made stars burst behind my eyes.

"Such a good *volchok*." His voice was pure gravel now, wrecked and wanting. "Move against my fingers."

I didn't need his urging. I was already moving, my body dancing with a want that felt all-consuming. He thrust into me with steady rhythm, his fingers crooking on each stroke, his thumb finding my clit and circling with maddening precision.

The orgasm built fast, racing towards me like a freight train. I couldn't help the way his name tore from my lips in ragged pants. "Rowan, I'm close—"

He removed his fingers abruptly, leaving me empty and gasping.

"Wait, no. Why?" I pleaded, my voice breaking.

"Someone asked for rope." He stood, leaning over me to shove his fingers into my mouth. "And I want you to come on my cock, not my hand."

I choked as he pushed them deep enough to make my throat convulse, my body struggling for air. But I took it, tasting myself on his skin—salt and musk and something uniquely mine.

"Good *volchok*s get rewarded when they listen." He removed his fingers slowly, and I gasped for air. "Now sit up and be still."

I nodded mutely and sat as commanded, my body thrumming with anticipation.

He tilted my head up to look at him, and slowly—deliberately—licked the fingers he'd used inside me. My eyes fluttered, my body going molten as I watched him taste both my saliva and arousal like it was the finest delicacy he'd ever encountered.

"Fucking delicious," he muttered, confirming my thoughts.

He leaned forward and began the tie, his movements deft and confident. The rope was soft against my skin—not scratchy like I'd expected, but smooth. He worked with practiced efficiency, wrapping and knotting, his breath warm against my collarbone as he concentrated.

I relaxed into his touch, into the ritual of it.

He paused at one point, assessing his work, then moved behind me to finish. I felt strong arms wrap around my chest as he pulled me deeper into the bed, positioning me exactly how he wanted me.

Then teeth sank into my shoulder—a sharp, claiming bite that pulled a moan from somewhere deep inside me.

The pain was hot and unrelenting and exactly what my body craved. I cried out, the sound echoing off brick and glass, as he pulled back and gently ran his tongue over the mark he'd left. My legs quivered, the orgasm that had been building threatening to crest if he continued this perfect torture of pain and pleasure.

"One more tie. Be patient, *volchok*."

I let out a whimper as he kissed my temple, the tenderness at odds with the bite mark throbbing on my shoulder.

He moved back in front of me and began working on my hands, lifting them above my head. He was careful of the small tattoo on my forearm—a pair of yin and yang snakes wrapped around a moon. "I would wrap this if I could, but for now, this will keep you still." He secured the rope to something above me—the headboard, I realized—and moved out of the way to assess his work.

I squirmed slightly, testing the restraints. Despite being bound, I was comfortable. The rope held me firmly but didn't bite. My arms were positioned in a way that didn't strain my shoulders. My legs were free to move.

As always, he'd been careful with me.

He stood beside the bed with a hungry look in his eyes—his gaze like hot trails of desire raking across my skin—as he slowly palmed himself.

I rubbed my thighs together, bucking my hips in wordless plea. "Rowan, don't leave me waiting."

He looked down at me with half-lidded eyes, his hand still moving over his length in slow, deliberate strokes. "Oh? Tell me, how badly do you want it?"

Oh god, how the tables have turned.

"Why don't you taste me again, Rowan?" I opened my legs for him in invitation, relishing how wet I felt—arousal dripping down my thigh onto the bed below me.

I'd always been self-conscious about how wet I got, convinced something was wrong with me. Every partner in this life had commented on it, some with appreciation, others with discomfort. But now? Now I reveled in it. Reveled in knowing I was soaking his expensive sheets with evidence of exactly how much I wanted him.

"Shove your tongue in me, Rowan." The words poured out uncensored, unfiltered. "Spit on me. Tell me how good I've been before you slide your cock into me."

I couldn't help how sublime the words felt, how right.

"I want to be spread open and used by you."

"Fuck, Violet." His hand moved faster against his cock—thick, flushed dark at the head, a bead of moisture glistening at the tip. "You have got a filthy mouth on you."

My eyes were glued to his length, cataloging every detail. The prominent vein running along the underside. The way it curved slightly upward. How it bobbed with each breath he took.

I want that inside me. Now.

"The safe word is *red*," he said, his voice taking on that commanding edge that made my core clench. "*Yellow* if you are feeling unsure and I will slow down. I will not risk hurting you, so you had better use them if needed. Do you understand?"

"Okay." I was aching for him, barely able to form words. "Complaints against my mouth?" I asked, suddenly unsure of myself.

He raised an eyebrow. "I love how filthy you are. Though I might use a ball gag if you keep talking, else I might embarrass myself again."

I shook my head vigorously, the motion limited by the rope. "Rowan, the fact that you came is the hottest fucking thing ever. I just regret it wasn't down my throat."

He let out a pained groan and crawled onto the bed, his thick cock jutting towards me in a way that made me clench with anticipation. "I need you to stop talking, or I *will* find that gag. Be the good girl you claim to be."

He positioned himself between my spread legs, his hands sliding up my thighs. He gripped my hips and lifted me, angling my body so that his face was inches from where I desperately wanted his cock inside of me.

My weight was supported entirely by his hands and the rope, the position leaving me completely vulnerable.

He inhaled deeply and closed his eyes, a look of pure bliss crossing his features. "Fuck, you smell so fucking delicious. I have not been able to get your scent out of my head since I first saw you at the shower."

Butterflies erupted in my belly, a swarm of them taking flight. "Really? That long ago?"

His tongue darted out—quick and precise against my clit—and I cried out, the sensation electric.

"Yes, really, Violet." He punctuated each word with another lick, another stroke, driving me out of my mind. "Everything about you is dangerously fine-tuned for temptation."

He ran his tongue down my slit in one long, languid stroke that left me shuddering. "Your taste is like a pomegranate from Tartarus. I would eat every morsel willingly, bind myself to your domain for eternity."

His tongue circled the hood of my clit in maddening patterns, and I felt my orgasm slowly building again, coiling tighter with each pass.

"You smell divine, enough to drive men into rut with how promising you are." His voice vibrated against sensitive flesh. "It makes me want to fill you with my cock and drown you in my come until you cannot remember any name but mine."

His words pushed me closer to the edge, and my eyes fluttered back as he continued his assault. His tongue entered me then, pushing past my folds with unrelenting pressure. I tightened around him immediately, my body begging for release, for something more, for *him*.

"And this. . ." His tongue thrust deeper, and I keened. "This perfect cunt is exactly what every man dreams of. Soft, warm, tight." He pulled back slightly, and I felt his breath hot against my entrance. "You are perfect the way you are, Violet. Every inch of you, inside and out." His voice dropped even lower, commanding and dark. "Which is why you will not come until I am buried deep inside of you. You *will* wait for me, Violet."

Fuck, he knows exactly what he's doing to me.

I was near delirious at this point, feeling the orgasm crest and hover, my body shaking from the effort of holding it back. I couldn't help it—I started begging.

"Please, Rowan. Please fuck me. Fill me up. I can't hold it—"

My hips dropped as his hands repositioned, gripping my hip bones hard enough to bruise. He angled me, lining himself up, and then slammed inside in one brutal thrust.

The orgasm broke immediately, crashing over me with the force of a tidal wave. I heard him let out a string of curses as he began to fuck into me with an intensity that made the first orgasm bleed into a second.

I cried out his name over and over, the syllables breaking apart into incoherent sounds, riding the waves of my second release.

"Fuck, you take me so well, my little *volchok*." His voice was ragged, wrecked, barely human. I could feel the tension of his orgasm building as his cock thickened inside me, stretching me even further.

"Yes, yes, please—"

"I am going to fill you up, Violet." His words were accentuated by his thrusts that hit something deep within me that made me see white. "Is that what you want?"

Sweat glistened between our bodies, the scent of sex and salt thick in the air. He leaned down, his teeth finding my breast, the flesh catching and tugging. I felt another orgasm building impossibly fast, brutal in its intensity. Too soon, but my body wouldn't listen.

"Yes, I want it. I want you to fill me."

He lifted my leg, pressing my calf against his face, his fingers leaving marks where they gripped. "Fuck, this pretty pink cunt belongs to me now."

"Yes," I gasped, feeling him hit deeper from this angle, bruising my cervix with ruthless thrusts. "Don't fucking stop, Rowan. I'm all yours."

Pain and pleasure mixed in a feral cocktail of need between us until his body went rigid, every line of him reflecting honed perfection as he thrust deep one final time. A guttural groan tore from his throat, and I felt him pulse inside me, heat flooding my core.

The sensation pushed me over the edge again, my third orgasm ripping through me as I cried out his name as pain and pleasure tore through me.

He kissed me then, capturing my scream with his mouth. Our tongues clashed as we rode each other's releases, his hips still moving in small, grinding circles that prolonged every aftershock.

When he finally broke away, we were both breathless, gasping like we'd run miles.

We stared at each other, chests heaving, and I couldn't help it—a giggle bubbled up from somewhere deep inside. The absurdity of it, the perfection of it, the sheer unexpected *joy* of it.

Rowan caught it too, his mouth curving into a coy smile. We sat there—him still buried deep inside me, me still tied and trembling—laughing and smiling at each other like idiots.

It was freeing in a way I couldn't articulate.

He kissed the inside of my calf, his lips soft against sweat-dampened skin. "Are you alright?"

"Yes," I breathed, enjoying the fullness of him still inside me. "That was..."

I trailed off, unable to find adequate words.

He raised a brow, a smirk playing at his lips. "Acceptable? Amazing? Borderline rapture?"

"Perfect." I laughed at the word, realizing how often we'd used it to describe each other. But it felt fitting. "My brain is not working right now."

He shifted carefully, his hands gentle as he helped lower my leg. He slid out slowly, and I let out an involuntary whimper at the loss.

"No..."

He chuckled, warm and affectionate. "I cannot leave the ropes on you for long, *volchok*. It is not safe."

I pouted—full lips and everything, the expression exaggerated and childish.

It seemed to catch him off guard because he smiled and leaned down to kiss my nose. "Patience is not your virtue, is it?"

"I thought that was obvious." I blew off hair that had fallen on my face, unable to adjust with my hands tied. "What does that word even mean? *Volchok*?"

He stood and began untying me with the same care he'd used to bind me, ensuring he massaged each spot the rope had touched. "I could tell you, or I could let you learn on your own."

"I'm sure it's derogatory, whatever it is."

"It means 'little wolf.'"

"Oh." I felt foolish. "So, it's an affectionate pet name?"

He hummed to himself but didn't answer, the sound smug and amused, as if confirming my guess. The last of the rope fell away, and I sat up, feeling sore in all the right ways. Muscles I'd forgotten existed made themselves known, a pleasant ache that spoke of being thoroughly used.

Rowan sat on the edge of the bed, his hands carefully assessing my wrists, my arms, checking for any rope burn or circulation issues. "Can I carry you to the shower, *princess*?"

The word sat differently this time—not mocking or dismissive, but affectionate. Earned.

I threw my hand out dramatically, tilting my head up with exaggerated haughtiness. "You may."

He grinned, genuine delight crossing his features. "Why, thank you."

He gathered me into his arms, carried me into the shower, and set me down gently on the built-in bench. He turned on the water, testing the temperature with his hand before adjusting it warmer. Steam filled the space, carrying the scent of his soap, which I was learning to love on him.

He helped me shower with the same methodical care he'd shown while tying me, washing every inch of me with gentle hands. Shampooing my hair that had me moaning all over again. Soaping my skin. Rinsing me clean.

I yawned, exhaustion finally catching up with me, but I felt well-sated. Boneless. *Happy.*

Standing wrapped in a big fluffy towel afterward, having him rub me down and tend to me like I was precious—it was everything I'd wanted without knowing I'd wanted it.

And it was dangerous. Because I was not worth the pain I would bring him. My path would lead him down a blood soaked road that he did not deserve by loving someone like me.

A girl could get used to this. . . but I can't, I thought solemnly. *This can't happen again.*

Chapter 24

Rowan

"When were you going to tell me?" I hissed the words, careful not to wake Violet in the bedroom. She had gone back to sleep in preparation for tonight's shift after I had sworn I would wake her up in time to get ready.

My call to Charlie was the first in many days, and I had promised him an update on Violet's situation. But right now, fury burned through my veins like acid, and the careful diplomacy I usually maintained with my adoptive father evaporated like morning dew under desert sun.

I felt blindsided. Betrayed. And in the wake of Violet's confession—her truths laid bare between tear-stained sheets—I felt vile for not having my own honesty to offer in return.

How could I tell her about my rebirth when I didn't even know she carried the same impossible weight?

Charlie's voice carried a note of apology that did nothing to cool my rage. "Levi made me swear not to say anything, Rowan. I gave him my word."

"I do not care about your word to Levi." The words came out sharp enough to cut. For once, our relationship shifted from father and son into something else—two men on opposing sides of a decision that had left Violet vulnerable and alone with knowledge that could have killed her sanity. "She confessed to me that she was reborn. That she holds memories of a life where she was abducted as a child, then murdered at thirty-three. Are you telling me that information was not important enough to share?"

Charlie took in a breath, the sound ragged and pained. Then another, like a drowning man surfacing. "She refused to tell Levi and me what type of life she lived before. We assumed certain things, hoped we were wrong, but she shut us out completely." I heard the strangled quality in his voice as he battled with his own agony, his own helplessness in the face of Violet's suffering. "Rowan, we did not *know*. She never told us the extent of what happened."

"Neither did I until she broke down in my arms." The memory of her sobs, her fists beating against my chest, her body wracked with grief so profound it had its own gravity—it threatened to drag me under even now. "Are you telling me I am supposed to be comfortable leaving her here at this school?"

Silence stretched across the line, heavy and damning.

Charlie's voice, when it finally came, held a tremor of fear I had never heard from him before. "Did you find something? Is she in immediate danger?"

I gripped the phone tighter, my knuckles going bone white. I was unsure how much to relay when Violet had begged me not to reveal the whole truth—her hunt for Edward, her dancing at Oubliette, the drug. . . So I went another route, offering a truth that was public knowledge.

"There was a murder at the school. Surely you have seen the news?"

"I did, but. . ." He paused, and I could practically hear him choosing his words with deliberate care. "Was it one of *them*?"

The way his voice shook—part disbelief, part shock, part hope that I would say no—nearly had me laughing. Still the cynic, it appeared. Still hoping the supernatural world would leave our family untouched despite evidence to the contrary.

"I do not know yet, but I am investigating." I kept my tone measured, professional, even as rage and protective instinct churned beneath the surface.

"If it is, Violet needs to leave that campus immediately. Are we clear?"

Violet's face flashed through my mind—her expression tortured and defiant when she'd said, "*I've had enough of men doing what they think is best for me.*"

Ah, fuck. She is not entirely wrong.

"Wait." I forced my voice to remain steady, to not betray the internal war I was waging. "Violet is an adult, Charlie. More of an adult than any of us want to admit, given her previous life's experience. She needs to decide what to do with her future, but she needs to be aware of the dangers if she chooses to stay."

Charlie's voice turned hesitant, uncertain. "Rowan, I do not know if Levi will—"

"Then you handle him." I cut him off, injecting steel into my tone. "He holds you in high enough regard to leave you alone with Sloane. We both know *that* means he trusts you more than any other living person."

I waited for Charlie to process the implication, to understand I was calling in a debt of trust.

Finally, he said, "Okay. Do you plan on telling Violet? About your past life?"

The question burned at me, reminding me of what a coward I was.

I did not know if Violet would find solace if I told her of my reincarnation. Despite her knowledge that both Charlie and Levi had been reborn like her, she never opened up to either of them about what she'd suffered during her first life.

Then, if I were to tell her of my own complication of being in a completely *different* body? I was afraid she would reject me or believe that I was mocking her. Just as I was forced to do—over and again these past five years—with Charlie and Levi, I would have to spend time proving my first life to her.

"No," I said. "I will tell her when I am ready. Charlie, when you have time, look into something called the *Pax Tacere*. It might be related to things happening here. I will reach out if anything changes." The words came out commanding and final.

We said our goodbyes—brief and awkward, the conversation having stripped away our usual easy rapport. I ended the call and stared at my phone's dark screen, seeing my reflection distorted in the glass.

It had been nearly three weeks since the night I first found Violet outside Oubliette's entrance, all defiance and desperation wrapped in an ebony cocktail dress. Three weeks since I'd watched her dance for the first time and felt something fundamental shift in my chest, some tectonic plate of my carefully constructed emotional landscape cracking under pressure.

Fourteen days since I first felt her cunt clench around my cock as I whispered filth in her ear—since I first heard the sounds she made when she came apart in my arms.

After I'd taken her back to her dorm—after we'd fucked with a desperation that had left us both shaking, after I'd tied her up and learned she trusted me with her body in ways she'd never trusted anyone—something between us had shifted.

Violet was more guarded than ever, refusing to let me back in. She'd rebuilt her walls higher and more vicious than before. While she had never verbally said it was a '*mistake*', it fucking felt like she thought that way. Despite my pleas, she stalked the shadows of Oubliette each night, searching for her monster with a single-minded focus that left little room for us to discuss the intimacy we'd shared. Each night I watched her dance was a reminder of the dangerous games she played between the veils.

Our days were filled with loud notes—her hurled barbs and bratty retorts designed to provoke, my cold counters and visceral threats I'd meant in my bones—sharp enough to cut, and driving us apart.

Other days were filled with quiet notes—how much closer we stood, how lightly our fingertips brushed together, how often we'd reach out to grace a brief touch on an arm—that would set our blood singing so sweetly, we had to force ourselves to walk away.

So we'd fallen into a complicated rhythm, alternating between forbidden desire and frustrated anger, that pulled at us both. Yet, somewhere between her venom and my control, we'd created a space neither of us admitted to needing—a dance that simmered beneath our skin and occasionally erupted into arguments that left us both breathless.

Hopefully, this would not turn into one of those arguments.

"Are you sure you want to do this?" I asked Violet as I stood in her dorm room.

"Bring you to class?" Violet clarified, shoving textbooks into her bag with more force than necessary. The canvas bulged, overstuffed with the evidence of her academic dedication. "Professor Wright's instructions for today were, 'bring a friend to traumatize,' as he put it. He even booked a larger auditorium to accommodate the extra bodies. I believe it's his way of making up for having to postpone his guest speaker."

"Guest speaker?"

"Yeah," she said as she struggled to zip her bag closed. "A colleague of his who studies and writes about the occult. Thorngood or Thornwood or something? Whatever. A lot of the kids were looking forward to his lecture."

Given the nature of this guest speaker's studies, I had to admit that I, too, was disappointed, and I'd only just found out about him. "Why postpone then?"

"Well, given the higher than normal number of unsolved *murders* this semester," she said, "I think the school decided to postpone having a famous professor give a lecture on the occult until after Halloween."

"That seems oddly prudent of the school." I kept my tone light, but the observation was genuine.

Twenty-one days since the murder. Twenty-one days without answers, without arrests, without any indication that the campus police or Atlanta PD had a single lead. The investigation had gone cold, and students were beginning to relax back into their routines despite the curfew still in effect. Charlie had also not been able to find much of anything on the *Pax Tacere* the vampyress mentioned.

"Ah, yes, the other variable that seems to complicate my peaceful school life." Violet's tone dripped sarcasm as she balanced the overstuffed bag on her shoulder, her body tilting slightly under its weight. "*Allegedly*, the school administration believes things are safe now." Even her voice held disbelief, the words flat and unconvinced.

The dark circles under her eyes, faint but present, served as evidence of too many late nights at the club combined with maintaining her pristine grade point average. *She has been ploughing like a horse*, I thought as I reached out to lift her bag from her shoulder. "Allow me, *volchok*."

She raised an eyebrow. "Oh? Is this some new chivalrous manservant duty you feel obligated to start doing?"

"Obligated?" I asked as I opened the door for her, and lowered my head in a mock bow. "It brings your servant joy to be of assistan—"

She cut me off with a playful punch to my stomach that shouldn't have set my skin on fire the way that it did. "Come on," she said as she marched out the door, "let's get this over with."

The walk to her class was insightful in ways I hadn't anticipated. I enjoyed surveying the campus architecture with the eyes of someone who'd spent a previous lifetime cataloging potential shelter, potential weapons, potential escape routes. Ancient walls of stone and slate rose around us, some buildings dating back over a century. Old tapestries still hung in certain corridors—faded medieval scenes depicting stories of rage and death, religious iconography mixed with mythology that most students probably walked past without a second glance.

We crossed a sun-drenched courtyard where oak trees provided scattered shade, their leaves rustling in the warm October breeze. Students clustered on benches, textbooks open, taking advantage of the pleasant weather. The scent of cut grass and approaching autumn hung in the air—earth and decay and the promise of coming cold.

We entered a large lecture hall through heavy wooden doors that creaked on old hinges. The room was designed in classic academic style—tiered seating arranged in a semicircle facing a podium and chalkboard, the space able to accommodate maybe two hundred students. Violet chose a seat in the back row, as far from the podium as physically possible while still remaining in the room.

I settled beside her, immediately cataloging exits as I set her bag down. Two doors at the back where we'd entered. One at the front beside the podium, likely leading to faculty offices. Windows along the left wall, too high to be practical escape routes, but possible in an emergency. The room's acoustics would amplify sound, making quiet conversation difficult.

The space simmered with unspent energy, students filtering in with unusual enthusiasm for what I'd assumed would be a dry philosophy course. I listened to their whispered conversations, picking through the noise with my enhanced hearing.

"Professor Wright is supposed to be amazing..."

"I heard he makes you question everything you believe..."

"Sarah took this last semester and said it changed her entire worldview..."

"Sucks that Professor Thornwood bailed..."

"Did you see that Thornwood video? The one where he's talking about demons..."

Violet leaned towards me, her shoulder brushing mine, as she whispered in a conspiratorial tone, "Do you suppose Professor Thornwood knows about the world beyond your veil?"

I knew that part of her was asking in jest, but a small part was asking in earnest. She still did not believe everything I had told her about the supernatural world—the *real* world, as it was—but I could tell that she *wanted* to believe. As I sat and pondered her question, I recalled the conversation we'd had when I first explained what little I knew of supernaturals.

"You're telling me vampyres are real." Violet had stared at me from across my kitchen table, her hazel eyes narrowed with suspicion and disbelief in equal measure. *"Actual vampyres. Not just stories."*

"That is what I am telling you." I had done my best to keep my tone matter-of-fact.

She'd laughed, the sound slightly manic, and shook her head. There was, I'd suspected, a hint of disbelief in that movement.

"I am serious, Violet." I'd leaned forward, needing her to understand. *"The world you think you know is a veil hiding what truly exists beneath. Vampyres. Shifters—werewolves, werecats, other forms. Demons of various hierarchies. Gods who walk among mortals playing their games. Creatures from every mythology you've ever read, existing in spaces just beyond human perception."*

Her silence pushed me forward. *"There are four reigning families, Violet. We must take care to never run into one of them. The most dominant family being Wallachia in the pharmaceutical industry."*

Her skepticism had warred with something else. Perhaps the fact that she'd already caught a glimpse of the impossible through her rebirth? I couldn't have said for certain.

"And you know all of this... how?" she'd asked.

"Because I have encountered them. Survived them. Learned to identify them." I'd held her gaze. *"The bartender at Oubliette? Andy? I suspect he*

is a siren. I can hear the water in his lungs when he breathes, like the ocean never quite left him."

"You're insane."

"*Perhaps I am, but for other reasons.*" I'd shrugged. "*Besides, insane does not imply incorrect. Regardless, you will be more careful now, will you not?*"

She had been. Grudgingly. But without evidence—without me somehow convincing a vampyre to bare fangs or a shifter to sprout fur—I couldn't prove anything to her definitively. She relied on my word, which in itself felt significant given the fucked-up rebirth card she'd been dealt.

"Perhaps," I whispered my reply, my breath moving the hairs near her neck, "Thornwood has had his own experiences with the supernatural world, and that is the reason *why* he has devoted his time to occult studies?"

She nodded, thoughtful as a flush crept on her face.

I looked around the room and assessed the class. Roughly one hundred fifty students, their heartbeats creating a symphony of rhythm around us. Steady pulses, normal respiration, the scent of caffeine, stress, and cheap body spray.

"Professor Wright should be here any minute. . ." someone said from a few rows down.

"You mean *short king*?" Her friend giggled as she threw out an elbow teasingly.

As if summoned by his name, the door beside the podium burst open with dramatic flair.

A man strode in with a hop to his steps, all theatrical energy and barely contained enthusiasm. He was younger than I'd expected—maybe mid-forties—with round wire-frame glasses and a burgundy velvet blazer over plaid navy dress pants. He waved to the room with both hands, his grin wide and genuine. "Students! What a glorious day! Thank you to those of you who brought your partners as instructed."

He dropped a battered leather briefcase on the desk with a heavy thud, pulled out his lecture notes, and turned to the chalkboard. His handwriting was surprisingly elegant as he wrote in large, sweeping letters:

Plato's Euthyphro Dilemma

I shifted in my seat, unable to suppress a small smile. "Oh, this will be good."

A favorite topic of Charlie's and mine during long evenings when I was being homeschooled. I was curious to see how Professor Wright would approach it.

"What—" Violet started, but Professor Wright turned back to face the class and began speaking with the energy of someone who genuinely loved his subject.

"As you all know, philosophy and religion are often intertwined in fascinating, complicated ways. In keeping with this week's theme of moral foundations, we are diving into Plato's classical problem." He tapped the chalkboard with his chalk, leaving small white marks. "So, students, here is your question: Is something good because God commands it, or does God command it *because* it is good?"

Murmurs rippled through the classroom, students leaning towards their partners.

"And we needed to bring friends for this?" Violet asked, genuinely confused.

"I want you to turn to your partner," Professor Wright continued, his voice carrying easily through the space, "and explore this question together. What better way to bond than to discover your fundamental differences or surprising similarities? Create a Venn diagram with your answers, see where you overlap and where you diverge." Even from our distance, I could see Professor Wright waggle his eyebrows with theatrical mischief. "Let the philosophical chaos commence!"

Violet turned to me, clearly put out by the assignment. She pulled out a sheet of notebook paper and a pen, drawing two overlapping circles with quick, efficient strokes. I watched her work, noting the way her hair fell forward as she concentrated, the way light from the windows caught on her crimson streaks and turned them to fire. I fought the urge to brush her hair away from her face, to tuck it behind her ear just for an excuse to touch her.

"So. . ." She tapped her pen against the paper. "Thoughts?"

I crossed my arms over my chest, settling back in my seat, enjoying her discomfort with this assignment. "You tell me first."

She rolled her eyes—a full, exaggerated rotation—and wrote next to the left circle two words in large bold letters.

No God.

"There is no God," Violet said. "Therefore, by default, morality is not tied to some type of divine command. We create morality through social contracts and our shared survival needs."

"Interesting." I leaned forward, reading her neat handwriting. The letters were precise, controlled, each one perfectly formed. "And where does that leave room for absolute moral truths?"

"It doesn't. Morality is relative to culture, time period, and circumstances. What's 'good' in one context might be 'evil' in another."

"Then explain this," I said as I leaned forward. "If gods exist—and they *do*, Violet—and they created the concept of morality to benefit themselves, then what is 'good' is defined by whoever holds the most power at any given time. Divine command theory, but applied to polytheistic reality where gods war with each other and use mortals as chess pieces."

She stared at me, considering my words, her brow furrowing. "Okay. But if gods determine morality without any external standard of goodness, then how do we know their commands are inherently good? What if they're just... powerful and wrong?"

I smiled, feeling the familiar thrill of intellectual sparring. "We do not know. That is precisely the problem. Does a god's omnipotence mean His commands *create* morality, making anything He decrees automatically good by definition? Or does His nature—His supposed goodness—mean He only commands what *is already* good by some external standard?" I paused to watch her process before I continued. "And which God are we even discussing? The Christian singular God? The Greek pantheon? The Norse? Egyptian? Hindu? Each tradition has different answers."

She huffed, clearly frustrated but engaged. "Well, this is annoying."

She raised her hand, and Professor Wright noticed immediately. He wove through the rows of seats with surprising agility, arriving at our desk with an expectant smile. "Yes, Miss Shaw?"

"Are we focusing exclusively on the Christian God for this exercise, or are other theological frameworks acceptable?" She asked, her tone respectful but carrying an edge that suggested she already suspected the answer.

Professor Wright's eyebrows rose with evident delight. "A fabulous question indeed!" He turned to me, assessing. "What say you, Mister. . .?"

"Monroe," I said. "And I would argue that Plato's Euthyphro dilemma originated in ancient Greek polytheism, where multiple gods with conflicting wills created obvious problems for divine command theory. It was not until Christianity and other monotheistic religions attempted to apply it that it became a significant philosophical challenge—because one God means one will, theoretically removing the problem of competing divine commands."

Professor Wright actually clapped his hands together, the sound sharp and delighted. "Oh, might we have a student of religious studies among us?"

I shrugged, keeping my expression neutral. "Hardly. I simply think the application of moral beliefs, regardless of their religious background or origin, creates the foundation for who we are as individuals."

"So you believe morality is not defined by divine command, but by personal experience and rational choice?" He leaned against our desk, genuinely interested now.

"I believe those with innate kindness are a rare blessing in a world carved from blood and bone," I said carefully. "Whether that kindness originates from a divine spark or human compassion matters less than the kindness itself."

"Is it really so hard to just be a good person?" Violet asked, bringing both our attention to her.

Her question hung in the air, simple and devastating in its directness.

"No, I do not think so," I responded, meaning every word. "I think those who choose kindness despite the world's cruelty and social norms are the closest thing to divinity we will ever witness."

Professor Wright cleared his throat, looking slightly moved. "Well said, Mr. Monroe. Thank you for attending today."

"Thank you for allowing me to sit in on your class."

"Ah, yes." Professor Wright straightened, addressing the room again. "Given the rising tension on campus, I thought permitting students to bring someone they cared for would ease their discomfort rather than forcing them to partner with classmates they might not know."

He moved on to another group, leaving his words hanging between us.

I glanced at Violet, who had fixed her gaze on her paper with sudden, intense focus. A faint blush crept up her neck, staining her cheeks with color.

"'Someone they cared for', huh?" I kept my voice low, intimate.

She turned a deeper shade of pink and mumbled something about not knowing anyone else on campus well enough, though we both knew Alice came to mind as an alternative.

But she chose me.

I settled deeper into my seat, watching her pretend to take notes while actually just drawing small spirals in the margins of her paper. Enjoying seeing her this way—somehow balancing exams and essays and sleepless nights at Oubliette, pushing herself against the world's hunger for her while maintaining her grades with obsessive faithfulness.

After another twenty minutes of philosophical debate around us—Professor Wright facilitating discussions with the skill of someone who genuinely loved watching minds wrestle with impossible questions—he dismissed the class.

"Well, that was fun," I said, gathering Violet's books while she shoved papers into her bag.

"Better than studying together?" She shot me a look, one eyebrow raised.

"This was more insightful than when we studied for your Psychology exam and listed all the qualities I shared with an Antisocial Personality Disorder diagnosis." It had made for an entertaining game, cataloging the ways in which each of us was fundamentally damaged by our respective traumas.

"Insightful?" She added her final notes to the diagram we'd created—a Venn diagram that showed surprising overlap in our moral reasoning despite arriving from different theological starting points. "I suppose it was."

Pride blossomed in my chest as I watched her. Having never been given a proper education in my previous life, I'd taken to it voraciously in my early years with Charlie homeschooling me. But seeing Violet bent over her notes, her mind sharp and engaged, left a fierce satisfaction burning through me.

Though beneath that satisfaction, fear and hope warred within me. Fear that she would eventually realize she didn't truly need my help, that she could hunt Edward alone, that she would sever the fragile connection between us. Hope that she was—maybe, just maybe—beginning to trust me, to rely on me, to need me in ways that went beyond practical protection.

The thought of her pushing me away left an icy ache beneath my ribs.

I told myself it was about keeping her safe, about fulfilling my obligation to Charlie and Levi.

I was becoming quite accustomed to lying to myself like that.

"There. Done." She gathered her diagram and books, noticing other students making their way towards the front to submit their work. "I think we can turn this in and escape?"

I waited while she organized her materials, then followed her down the tiered steps towards the podium.

"I found a celiac-safe restaurant nearby we could try," I offered as we joined the line of students waiting to submit their assignments. "Are we visiting Hyacinth after this, or would you prefer to get food first?"

I watched her lips purse as she considered, the small movement drawing my attention to her mouth. "I wouldn't mind trying a new place. We could try to invite Jules to join us again? As long as they have something other than a regular bun. I still haven't found anything remotely close to a decent gluten-free option in this city."

"You are in luck." I stepped closer as the line moved forward. "This place apparently has some of the best gluten-free options in Atlanta. If you are willing to try something new. It is called Cooper—"

I stopped mid-sentence.

The musk of a shifter hit my enhanced olfactory senses like a physical blow—wild and earthy, carrying undertones of fur and forest and something fundamentally *other*. My nostrils flared as I inhaled more carefully, tracking the scent to its source.

Instinctively, I listened.

There you are.

A female, a few students ahead of us in line. Her heartbeat was wrong—too fast, running at roughly one hundred sixty beats per minute even while standing still. The rhythm was steady but elevated, as if she'd just finished sprinting or was preparing to fight.

Shifter. Definitely a shifter.

Violet said something I didn't quite catch, her voice distant and muffled beneath the sudden hyperfocus of my hunter instincts activating.

I needed a better look at this woman. Needed to see her face, assess the threat level, determine if she was the one I'd been searching for.

The she-shifter was maybe five-nine or five-ten and slender, her frame suggesting speed over strength. Dirty blonde hair fell in waves past her shoulders, catching the afternoon light streaming through the windows. She wore a long cream-colored sundress that brushed her ankles, paired with a fitted denim jacket and combat boots. The boots were interesting—black leather with multiple chains wrapped around the ankles, the metal glinting with each step.

"Rowan, are you okay?" Violet's voice was suddenly closer, concerned. Her hand touched my arm, warm through my shirt sleeve.

I startled, jerking my attention back to her. "Hey, yes. Give me one second."

I stepped out of line, moving with purpose towards the front. I needed to get closer to the shifter, needed to confirm what my senses were telling me. I shouldered past a pair of students, and as I closed the distance, another scent hit me beneath the wild musk.

Blood.

Metallic and iron-sharp, the scent of fresh blood clung to her despite obvious attempts to wash it away. Not her blood, I'd wager—it smelled far too strong, was far too much. Someone else's blood. Recent. Within the last twelve hours, I estimated.

Found you.

I picked up my pace and was almost to her, almost close enough to see the side of her face. She turned slightly as I reached for her, and I nearly caught a glimpse of—

A hand grabbed my arm and yanked me backward with surprising strength.

"Rowan!" Violet's voice carried an edge I rarely heard, sharp. She threw an apologetic look to the students I'd bulldozed past. "Sorry! He's not cutting in line, I promise."

She pulled me back towards our original position, and my opportunity vanished as the blonde shifter submitted her assignment and left through the front door. The scent of blood and wild things faded with her departure.

Fuck.

"Violet, that was important." I kept my voice low, aware of the students around us pretending not to eavesdrop. "I was trying to see her face." I knew then my mistake.

"Going to talk to that girl was *important* to you?" Her cheeks were flushed, bright spots of color high on her cheekbones. Her eyes flashed with temper.

Jealous. She was jealous, and it was simultaneously infuriating and adorable.

"I did not mean important in that way—"

"Then how *did* you mean it? What was that?" The line moved steadily until she stormed towards the front, our diagram clutched in her hand like she was envisioning choking me. She slapped it on Professor Wright's desk with more force than necessary, ignoring his cheerful, "Thank you, Miss Shaw!" and marched towards the exit.

I followed, catching up to her in the hallway outside the lecture hall.

"I can explain," I started.

"Oh yeah?" She whirled on me, her bag swinging with the momentum. "Kind of like you can explain why you had a brand-new sex toy in your closet?"

I stopped in my tracks, genuinely confused by the conversational whiplash. "What?"

"The toy, Rowan." Her voice pitched lower, conscious of students passing us in the corridor as we moved towards a secluded corner. "The purple one you so conveniently had available when I needed it. Care to explain that?"

This is what she is focused on?

"I do not understand what you are asking, Violet."

She stepped closer, crowding into my space, her finger poking my chest with each word. "I don't know what weird fantasies you had about picking up college students, but you *never* explained why you just *happened* to have an unopened toy ready to go."

We were hate-whispering at this point, our bodies inches apart, her breath hot against my chest.

"That was two weeks ago. . ." I started, then reconsidered. "Never mind. Violet, do you really want to have this conversation right now? In the middle of a hallway?"

"Yes." She crossed her arms, her jaw set in that stubborn line I'd come to recognize as immovable.

We were at the end of the corridor now, with enough space between us and other students that our lowered voices wouldn't carry.

"For someone who is actually thirty-three years old," I said, letting my voice drop to something dangerous, "you do realize that acting bratty in the middle of campus will not save your ass from a spanking when we get home?"

The threat did little to deter her. If anything, her eyes brightened with challenge.

"Says the guy refusing to answer my questions."

Ha.

The truth was far more mundane and somehow more damning. I'd merely wanted to learn a suspension tie that incorporated toy placement, challenging myself to master the technical aspects. The toy had been a necessary component for practicing the tie's mechanics on Marie Antoinette.

Now the image of Violet wrapped in my cerulean rope, unable to escape, helpless as she was brought to orgasm after orgasm, bloomed in the dark corners of my mind with vivid clarity.

"You think I am looking for potential partners when I am occupied watching a *bratty princess* every night?" I let skepticism color my voice.

"Your cock did not seem to mind *this bratty princess* when it came all over your pants for me." She deadpanned, rising to the challenge without hesitation.

Fuck, I loved this about her.

The verbal dance between us filled a hollow space inside me I'd never noticed existed until she'd crashed into my life. Her vicious words struck against my weathered defenses, my calculated responses catching her when she thought herself untouchable. Each clash left me feeling raw, exposed in ways I hadn't experienced since my rebirth. When her hazel eyes narrowed, and her chin tilted upward in pure defiance, my chest seized with possessive hunger that bordered on feral.

"Fine." I leaned down, bringing my mouth close to her ear. Near enough that my breath stirred the small hairs at her temple, close enough to smell her shampoo—floral and sweet. "I was working on suspension ties that require strategic toy placement for maximum effect. Happy now?"

She blinked up at me, her pupils dilating slightly. "You mean. . . with the rope?"

I nodded, letting my lips brush against the shell of her ear as I spoke. "Yes, Violet. You wrap the toy in rope and tie it directly against your clit where you cannot dislodge it. Then you are suspended in the air, completely at its mercy. Unable to move, unable to escape. Orgasm after orgasm until you are left a filthy, desperate mess of need and pain."

I pulled back just enough to watch her reaction. Her breathing had gone shallow, her lips parted, a flush spreading down her throat.

"I was planning to get a larger toy for the full tie, but I wanted to practice with a smaller one first on Marie." I held her gaze.

She nodded wordlessly, her tongue darting out to wet her lips. "And the girl?" Her voice came out smaller now, uncertain. "The blonde?"

I sighed, weighing truth against necessity. "She looked like someone I knew. Or perhaps not. I am not certain." Mixing truth with lies, the way I'd learned to survive in my previous life.

"Someone you liked?" The question carried hesitance, vulnerability she rarely showed.

Jealousy looked lovely on her—the way her shoulders tensed, the way her eyes searched my face for deception, the slight downturn of her mouth. I wanted to tease her more, to draw out this moment of her caring enough to be jealous. But something in her expression stopped me.

"Not liked romantically." I kept my voice gentle, honest. "Just possibly important. But it does not matter now. She is gone, and I have no way to track her." I stepped closer, eliminating the space between us. "Only you matter, Violet."

Her eyes lit up despite her obvious attempt to suppress the reaction, a spark of pleasure she tried to hide behind a scowl. She muttered a small apology about being "hangry," her stomach choosing that moment to growl audibly.

I admired her features in the hallway's fluorescent lighting—the exhaustion pulling at her eyes, the determination in the set of her jaw, the way she held herself despite being tired enough that most people would have collapsed.

She is a goddamn beast.

A fierce, protective, and dangerously possessive urge coiled inside me like a snake preparing to strike. My hands itched to shield her from every threat, every hardship, every person who'd ever hurt her or might hurt her in the future.

Which meant I needed to hunt down that shifter. The smell of blood on her meant a kill, and a kill on campus meant a possible connection to the unsolved murder. But I doubted the shifter would hunt during daylight hours. Predators like that preferred darkness, the cover of night when humans felt most vulnerable.

Let us wait. For now, I need to feed my volchok.

I wrapped my arm around her shoulders, feeling her lean into the contact despite her earlier prickliness. "Let us get you fed. And if you want. . ." I let the offer hang, watching her eyes flick up to mine with renewed interest. "I can show you that suspension tie I mentioned."

Her breath caught, and I felt her body respond—a small shiver, her heartbeat kicking up, the faint scent of arousal beginning to bloom beneath her perfume. "Really?" She tried to sound casual and failed spectacularly.

"Really." I steered us towards the exit, already planning the evening in my mind. "But first, food. Then Hyacinth. Then I will tie you up and make you scream my name until you forget every other word in your vocabulary."

Her laugh rang out in the corridor, bright and genuine and absolutely perfect.

"Deal."

Chapter 25

Violet

*P**retty sure I had said never again, and yet here we are*... The rope held my body like a lover's embrace, tightening in subtle ways when I shifted my weight on the edge of Rowan's bed. Each movement sent the cerulean fibers pressing deeper into my skin—not painfully, but with enough pressure to remind me I was wrapped, contained, held.

Safe.

The word whispered through my mind unbidden, and I pushed it away. Safety was an illusion, a pretty lie people told themselves. But the rope... the rope didn't lie. It simply was.

"How does it feel?" Rowan's voice came from behind me, soft and low, carrying that particular quality that made my spine straighten involuntarily.

I was in a sheer sleeveless black bodysuit, bound in blue rope that wrapped around my chest and torso in an intricate diamond pattern I couldn't fully see. The tie started above my breasts, crisscrossing over my ribs and around my back in what felt like dozens of carefully placed loops. My arms were free—for now—and my legs dangled off the bed's edge, feet barely touching the hardwood floor.

Rowan knelt beside me, his piercing eyes tracking my face with unnerving focus. He wore dark grey sweats and nothing else, his chest bare, his white-blonde hair slightly disheveled from where he'd run his fingers through it earlier. The energy in the room simmered—thick and charged, electricity waiting for a spark.

"It feels oddly comforting." I heard the surprise in my own voice. "Relaxing, even."

His mouth curved into a small smile, genuine and unguarded. "The Hishi Karada wraps around your body to mimic a hug. The pressure triggers your parasympathetic nervous system—tells your body it is safe, that you can rest."

I tested the bonds carefully, shifting my shoulders. The rope held firm but gave slightly, adjusting to my movement without biting. "And you learned this... how?"

"Books. Practice. Trial and error on Marie Antoinette." He reached for more rope coiled beside him on the bed—the same cerulean blue, soft and smooth beneath my skin. "I can show you more ties if you are interested."

"I am." The admission came easier than it should have. "Especially the one you mentioned. With the toy."

His eyes darkened, pupils dilating slightly. "Ah, you mean the basic crotch rope tie altered to allow a toy?"

"Yes." My voice came out breathy, and I watched him register the change with predatory satisfaction.

But he didn't move to begin that tie. Instead, he began wrapping more rope around my torso, adding to the existing pattern. His movements were methodical, practiced, each loop placed with deliberate precision.

"I need to finish this one first," he said, his breath warm against my shoulder as he worked. "Then we can discuss more advanced applications."

"Why bother finishing the tie?"

He scoffed. "Shibari—also known as Kinbaku—celebrates the body," he explained, his fingers gliding across the patterns along my ribs. "Every knot is designed to enhance, to display, to honor the art of what it holds. It would be sacrilegious to not at least attempt to finish the tie, Violet."

My cunt purred at the thought, but I remained calm. "I don't like waiting, Rowan."

"I am aware," he said drily. "Tell me, do you know the differences between Shibari and Hojōjutsu?"

I shook my head. "No, but I have a feeling you're about to tell me."

He smiled at that. "Hojōjutsu was a precursor to modern-day handcuffs. The knots are designed to dig into pressure points and apply stress to joints. It was meant to break the body. With Hojōjutsu," he whispered into my ear, "It is time that becomes the torturer."

"Oh. Interesting history lesson." I waited until he'd made several more passes with the rope before I spoke again. "So are you going to tell me about the girl from class?"

His hands stilled for a fraction of a second—barely noticeable, but in our time together, I'd learned to read his microexpressions.

"What about her?" He resumed his work, threading rope beneath an existing loop.

"Don't play dumb, Rowan." I tried to turn my head to look at him, but the rope's positioning made the movement awkward. "You were totally fixated on her like she was... I don't know, someone important."

"She might have been."

"Might have been what?" Frustration bled into my tone. "An ex-girlfriend? Someone you fucked? Someone you *wanted* to fuck?"

"None of those things." He tugged the rope tighter—not painfully, but enough to make his point. "And you are being a brat."

"Then tell me who she was." I refused to let this go, jealousy coiling hot and ugly in my chest. I hated the feeling, hated that I cared enough to feel it, but I couldn't seem to stop. "You don't just chase random women through academic buildings for no reason."

"Unless they are avoiding their bodyguard like *someone* I know." He moved around to face me, his expression serious now. Gone was the playful dominance, replaced by something harder. More cautious. "She was not a woman I knew personally." He held my gaze. "But I believe she may be connected to the murder on campus."

The jealousy evaporated instantly, replaced by sharp focus. "Connected how?"

Rowan sighed, moved back behind me, and returned to his work with the rope. I felt him creating a new anchor point at my back, his fingers brushing my spine with clinical efficiency. "I do not know. Not yet. Hence why I wanted to speak with her."

"That sounds like bullshit."

I couldn't see his face, but I heard the scowl in his voice. "Why would I lie—"

"If you wanted her number, at least be *man* enough to admit it instead of—"

"*Tfu!* You are not listening with your ears or thinking with your head. You are listening to your gut and thinking with your heart," he said as he tightened a knot for emphasis.

"Don't turn into a fucking fortune cookie to avoid admitting the truth! Why were you checking her out?"

The rope tightened again. Not enough to hurt—it actually felt incredible—but enough that I felt his frustration through the ropes. "I already told you. She may be connected—"

"And I already told you *bullshit*," I growled the last word, my throat raw with anger. "Stop fucking lying to me."

He tightened the rope even more. "I would not lie to you, Violet. But I need to hunt down—"

"Hunt down?" I laughed as I said it. It was a cruel laugh, incredulous and dismissive. "You're not the police, Rowan."

"The police will be clueless to catch this thing, and it *will* kill again unless—"

"This *thing*? What do you mean by *thing*, Rowan?"

His hands stilled. I felt some slack loosen the knot he was working on before he moved back around to face me. "Promise me you will not overreact to what I am about to tell you."

"I can't promise that. I don't know what you're about to say."

"That is fair. Give me a moment to think, please." He moved back behind me and continued securing the knot he'd been working on. It took a long while for Rowan to finish his knots before he moved to stand in front of me in silence.

I had experienced some heavy silences in my first life. After I'd been catfished and kidnapped at nine, there was the frozen and terrified silence of that first night I'd spent blindfolded, bound, gagged, alone, and cold.

The still silence that radiated from Rowan was heavier than either of those. It felt as if he were shouldering the weight of the world with that silence and waging a war within himself on how to break that silence.

I took a tiny breath and said, "You just said you would not lie to me. Unless that was a lie... please tell me what you meant and what you're thinking."

"I would not lie to you," he said with a nod. "The woman from class was not entirely human, Violet. She was a shifter."

I blinked at him, processing the words. "A shifter? Like... like a *werewolf*?"

"Perhaps. Or another type of shifter. I could not determine her specific animal without closer proximity."

"Okay." I forced myself to remain calm. "Let's say I believe you. How do you know she was a shifter?"

"I could smell her." He said it matter-of-factly. "Shifters have a distinctive musk—wild, earthy, carrying notes of whatever animal they can become. And I could hear her heartbeat. It was running at approximately one hundred sixty beats per minute while she was standing still. No human's resting heart rate runs that fast."

I stared at him. "Smelling her seems invasive, but you could *hear* her heartbeat... from across a crowded lecture hall?"

"Yes."

"That's not possible, Rowan."

"It is possible when you have enhanced hearing." He returned to his work with the rope, apparently unconcerned by my skepticism. "You have heard those urban legends about people being *changed* from nearly a decade ago? The extremely rare and bizarre side effects from a pharmaceutical drug? How some allegedly underwent odd mutations?"

"Of course I've heard stories, but those are all... I mean, they're just tabloid bullshit."

"You are going to have a hard time believing me about all I have to tell you if we cannot get past this," he said with frustration. "How can I prove this to you?"

I shifted on my knees, testing the bonds. The rope held firm, my arms secured behind me, the cerulean fibers wrapping my torso in a familiar embrace I'd grown to crave. I faced his bedroom door from my position on the bed.

"I don't know, Rowan. It just sounds—"

"Wait here," he said as he headed towards the door.

"Where are you going?"

He didn't answer, just opened the door to his bedroom and walked out into the hall. "Say something. Whisper it."

This is ridiculous. But fine. I'll play along.

"This is stupid," I whispered, barely putting any voice behind the words.

"This is stupid," he called back immediately, his voice carrying easily from wherever he stood.

I blinked. *Lucky guess. Has to be.*

"Go further away," I said.

Footsteps retreated down the hallway, followed by silence. "Okay," his voice echoed from what had to be the kitchen. "Try again."

I dropped my voice to barely a breath. "You can't possibly hear this."

"You cannot possibly hear this." His response came back without hesitation, and I heard amusement coloring his tone even from that distance.

My heart kicked up, pulse jumping in my throat. *No. There has to be an explanation. He's bugged his room.* That was it. Hidden microphones somewhere near me, and he was wearing wireless earbuds.

Except I was only in a bodysuit, which couldn't hide any device. And from my position facing the door, I saw his discarded shirt on the floor, his jeans folded over the chair. No pockets to hide electronics. No earbuds were visible when he'd been standing in front of me moments ago.

"Close the door," I called out. "Go into the hallway and close that door too."

"Violet, I am in nothing but sweatpants."

"So? This will only take a second."

"As you wish, *volchok*."

He came back to close the bedroom door, then I heard his muffled footsteps retreating. I felt more than heard the front door close. I sat in silence for a moment. My pulse hammered loud in my ears, my breathing shallow and quick. The rope pressed into my ribs with each inhale, grounding me.

This is insane. This is absolutely fucking insane. But a part of me—the part that had already accepted my own impossible rebirth—whispered that maybe, just maybe, the world was stranger than I'd allowed myself to believe.

I licked my lips. Dropped my voice to the barest whisper, so quiet I could barely hear myself. "Rowan... I want you to fuck my slutty mouth and choke me with your thick cock."

Silence.

My heart raced, heat flooding my face despite being alone. The words hung there, filthy and desperate and true. I waited, counting my own panicked heartbeats.

One. Two. Three. Four. Five.

Nothing.

Finally. Finally, I stumped him.

Relief and disappointment warred in my chest. Relief that he wasn't actually some superhuman freak. Disappointment that—

The bedroom door opened.

Rowan stepped through, his pale eyes locked on mine with an intensity that stole my breath. He crossed to me in three strides, each step deliberate and predatory. When he reached the bed, he bent down, bringing his face level with mine.

"I will not shout that for the neighbors to hear." His voice had gone rough, gravelly with want. "But I would be happy to oblige your request, *volchok*."

The bottom dropped out of my stomach.

"You—" I started, my voice strangled. "You heard that?"

"Every word." He straightened, and I tracked the movement with wide eyes. "Every filthy, desperate word."

"That's not possible." But even as I said it, I knew I was lying to myself. "You bugged the room. You have—I don't know, hidden microphones or—"

"Where would I have hidden them on you, Violet?" He gestured at my bound form. "You are wearing practically nothing. I am wearing practically nothing. No earbuds. No phone. No device to hear you with except my own two ears."

I opened my mouth. Closed it. My mind raced through possibilities, desperate for a rational explanation that would let me cling to the world I understood.

There wasn't one.

"You really heard me," I said finally, the words coming out smaller than intended. "From the hallway. Through two closed doors."

"Yes."

"That's..." I struggled to process it, this fundamental shift in what I thought was possible. "That's not normal, Rowan."

"I know." He moved behind me, and I felt his fingers resume their work on the rope. "But it is real. And it is how I knew that woman in class was not human. How I know when you are nervous, or angry, or," his voice dropped lower, intimate, "when you want me."

Heat flooded through me despite the creeping unease. "What do you mean?"

"Your heart." His hand pressed against my back, right over where my heart hammered against my ribs. "Right now, it is beating at approximately one hundred beats per minute. When you are calm, it runs closer to fifty. When you are nervous, around seventy. When you are angry with me—which is often—it spikes to one hundred and ten."

His fingers trailed up my spine, following the rope's path. "And when I touch you like this, when you want me, it races. One hundred and twenty, perhaps one hundred and thirty. I can hear the exact moment desire takes over."

I shivered, goosebumps racing across my skin. He could hear all of that. Could track my body's responses in real-time, could know what I felt before I even admitted it to myself.

"That's..." I searched for words, my thoughts tangling. "You can hear everything."

"Not everything." His hand settled on my shoulder, warm and steady. "But enough. Heartbeats. Breathing patterns. The rush of blood through veins if I am close enough."

"So you've just been... listening to me? This whole time?"

"Not deliberately invading your privacy, if that is what you are asking." He came back around to face me, kneeling so we were eye level. "I cannot turn it off, Violet. My enhanced hearing is always there. But I can choose what I focus on, what I pay attention to. I have taught myself how to lower or increase the sensitivity of my hearing. Otherwise? I would go crazy."

"And you pay attention to me." It wasn't a question.

"Yes." No hesitation. No shame. "I pay attention to you because I care whether you are safe, whether you are afraid, whether you are in pain." His hand cupped my face, thumb stroking my cheekbone. "And because when your heart races like it is now, I know you want me as much as I want you."

My breath caught. Because he was right—my heart *was* racing, my pulse thundering in my throat, my body responding to his proximity and his words and the knowledge that he could hear every single physical tell I had.

It should have felt invasive. Violating. Like he'd been spying on me without permission.

But instead, it felt... intimate. Known. Like he saw parts of me I'd been hiding and didn't flinch away.

"You really can hear my heartbeat right now," I said softly.

"One hundred and twenty-four beats per minute and climbing." A smile tugged at his lips. "You are aroused, Violet. Your body gives you away."

"That's..." I shook my head, trying to organize my thoughts. "That's creepy, Rowan."

"You are not the first person to tell me that," he said with a small laugh, the sound warm despite the heavy conversation. "Well, you wanted to know how I identified the shifter. This is how."

I swallowed hard, acutely aware of my naked vulnerability in front of him. The rope held me but didn't hide me, and knowing he could literally hear my body's responses to him left me feeling exposed in ways that had nothing to do with nudity.

"So the girl..." I forced myself back to the original topic. "You think she killed that student?"

"I think she might have been involved, yes." His expression turned grim. "She smelled of blood, Violet. Fresh blood. Not her own—too much of it, too strong and it was within the last twelve hours."

The implication settled over me like a shroud. "And you were going to... what? Confront her?"

"Identify her. Follow her if possible. Gather information." He shrugged. "But you pulled me away before I could get close enough to see her face clearly."

Guilt pricked at me. "I thought you were flirting with her."

"I know." He smiled, no trace of recrimination. "Your jealousy was apparent."

"I wasn't jealous."

"In the classroom, your heart rate spiked from seventy to one hundred and twenty in a few seconds. You were very much jealous, *princess*."

I wanted to argue, but he'd literally monitored my cardiovascular response in real-time. There was no point in lying.

"Fine. I was jealous." The admission tasted bitter. "Happy now?"

"Oddly, yes." He returned to his rope work, and I felt him making final adjustments. "Though I would prefer you simply ask me questions rather than assume the worst."

"That's rich coming from you." I couldn't help the edge in my voice. "You assume the worst about everything."

"Because I have learned that assuming the worst keeps you alive." He tied off what felt like a final knot, then stepped back to assess his work. "But I am trying to be better. With you."

The vulnerability in those last two words tightened my chest.

"Have you had any luck at the club?" He changed subjects with the smoothness of someone deliberately redirecting. "Finding information about your target?"

I considered lying, keeping my cards close. But he'd been honest with me about his hearing. The least I could do was return the favor.

"I've heard whispers about something called the Second Circle." I watched his face carefully. "Dancers talk about it like it's some kind of exclusive club *within* the club. But nobody will give me details."

Every muscle in Rowan's body went rigid. His eyes—previously warm with affection and desire—went cold and hard as winter ice.

"Second Circle." He repeated the words like they tasted foul. "You need to stay away from that place, Violet."

"Why? What is it?"

"Nothing you need to concern yourself with." His tone had gone flat, final. "If dancers are mentioning it, they are either trying to recruit you or warn you away. Either way, you do not go there. Ever. Are we clear?"

I bristled at the command in his voice. "You can't just tell me to avoid something without explaining why."

"I can, and I am." He crossed his arms over his chest. "The Second Circle is not a place for mortals who value their sanity and souls. That is all you need to know."

"But—"

"No." The word came out sharp enough to cut. "This is not a negotiation, Violet. You do not go near the Second Circle. You do not ask about it. You do not accept any invitations if they are extended. Promise me."

"I am not a child, nor do I need protecting." I yanked away from him, my breathing shallow.

"Violet, you need to—"

"Don't tell me what I need. If Edward is connected to the Second Circle, I plan to figure out why." I snapped.

Rowan's expression was tight. I'd never seen him like this—genuinely frightened beneath the authoritative exterior. Whatever Second Circle was, it terrified him in a way shifters and murder apparently didn't.

"There's something else," I said finally. "Two vampyres have been... persistent. At the club."

"Vampyres?"

"I mean, I don't know if they're *actually* vampyres." I rushed to clarify. "But based on what you've told me about these... *supernaturals* as you call them? They match the description. Pale. Beautiful in that uncanny valley way. They don't breathe regularly—I've watched them. And they've been trying to get me to go to a private room with them for the last week."

"Them." Rowan's voice had gone deadly quiet. "As in plural. *Two* vampyres?"

"Twins, I think. Or at least they look identical. Both male, dark hair, heterochromic eyes." I shrugged, trying to appear unconcerned despite the unease that crawled up my spine whenever they watched me dance. "I've been declining, obviously. But they're getting more insistent."

"Names." It wasn't a question.

"They haven't given me names. Just keep calling me *'beautiful girl'* and saying they want to *'taste'* me." I rolled my eyes. "Very original."

Rowan was across the room before I could blink, his phone in his hand. "We need to identify them, and I need to know if management is aware they are hunting dancers."

"Hunting?" The word sent ice through my veins. "Rowan, they're just customers. Creepy customers, but—"

"Vampyres do not simply *watch*, Violet. They do not show persistent interest without intention to feed." His jaw clenched hard enough that I could see the muscle jump. "And twins hunting together is significantly more dangerous than a single vampyre. They coordinate, trap prey between them, making escape nearly impossible."

"I haven't agreed to go anywhere with them."

"Good. You will continue to refuse." He looked up from his phone, and the expression on his face was pure lethal promise despite the tension between us.

He cared. Possibly more than he should. Definitely more than I deserved.

"Okay." I kept my voice calm. "I promise I'll stay away from them, but not from the Second Circle."

Some of the tension bled from his shoulders, but his expression remained serious. "Thank you." He set his phone down and returned to me, his hands gentle as they cupped my face. "I know you can take care of yourself, Violet. You are one of the strongest people I have ever met. But you are also mortal and breakable, and vampyres are neither of those things. Promise me you will not take unnecessary risks."

"I won't make a promise I can't keep," I said with a sad smile, "especially if it involves Edward."

He sighed before he kissed my forehead—soft, gentle, completely at odds with the violence simmering beaneath his skin—then stepped back. "The tie is finished." He gestured at my bound torso. "Do you want to see?"

I nodded, and he produced a full-length mirror from beside his closet, angling it so I could see my reflection.

My breath caught.

The rope created an intricate pattern across my chest and ribs—geometric shapes mixed with organic flow, the cerulean blue stark against my light caramel skin. It looked like art. Like I was the canvas and he was the painter, and together we'd created something beautiful from vulnerability and trust.

"The Hishi Karada. Also known as the Rope Dress. You can wear it underneath clothing," Rowan said, his voice soft with pride.

"It's beautiful. I feel. . . held."

"You are held, *volchok*." He moved behind me, his hands settling on my bare shoulders. "And you are safe. Always safe with me."

The word echoed in my mind again—*safe*—and this time I didn't push it away.

His hands began to move, sliding from my shoulders down my arms with deliberate slowness. Not the clinical efficiency of rope work, but something else entirely. Something that made my skin flush and my breath quicken.

"Rowan. . ." His name came out uncertain, a question and a plea.

"Do you want me to stop?" His palms glided back up, over my shoulders, down to rest just above the rope at my collarbones.

"No." The admission was immediate and honest. "But this is probably a bad idea."

I let my head fall forward, giving him better access. His fingers dug deeper, finding knots of stress and methodically releasing them. Pleasure radiated from each point of contact, washing through my body in waves that left me boneless and pliant.

"Oh my god," I breathed. "Why does that feel so *good*?"

He chuckled, the sound vibrating through his chest and into my back where we touched. "You do not take rest days, Violet. Between dancing, riding Hyacinth, and Jiu-Jitsu, you are constantly using your body. I am surprised you have not collapsed from exhaustion."

His hands moved lower, following the line of the rope down my spine. Each vertebra received individual attention—press, release, move to the next. Clinical and sensual in equal measure, the dichotomy making my head spin.

One hand trailed to the back of my neck, fingers threading through my hair before gripping firmly at the base of my skull.

I gasped, my neck arching instinctively, baring my throat in a gesture of submission that should have terrified me. *I never thought I'd be okay with a man having this kind of control over me.*

But this was different. This was Rowan. And somehow, that made all the difference.

"You watch me so closely," I managed, my voice rough. "It's almost creepy how much attention you pay."

"Almost." His breath ghosted across my exposed throat. "But you like it."

I wanted to deny it, to maintain some shred of pride and independence. But his other hand had found the bandage on my thigh, where my snake and roses tattoo was still healing. The slight pressure through the protective covering sent jolts of sensation racing through me.

"You don't know me..." My protest was weak and unconvincing.

He laughed. It was a genuine laugh, the sound warm and infectious. "I know you better than you think, *princess*." His fingers traced the edge of the bandage carefully, avoiding direct contact with the healing ink beneath. "Does it hurt?"

"I'll survive."

His hand left my thigh and came back in a light slap—not hard enough to truly hurt, but sharp enough to send competing signals of pain and pleasure singing through my nerves.

I cried out, my hips jerking forward involuntarily.

"Not what I asked." His voice held amusement and warning in equal measure.

"Don't get soft on me now, Rowan." I fought to keep my breathing steady. "I use the pain to stay focused. To remind myself that I'm here, that this is my body to use how I want. Not because someone else commanded me to."

"And yet you take orders *so well* when I give them." The note in his tone suggested he saw straight through my defenses.

"Maybe I need a better handler."

"Maybe you need to stop being a brat."

His grip in my hair tightened—not yanking, but firm enough that I felt thoroughly caught. I couldn't suppress the gasp that escaped, couldn't hide the way my thighs clenched together, couldn't disguise the arousal flooding through me.

I wanted this man to use me, call me his filthy *volchok*, and it scared me. I'd never imagined—never in either life—that I would be okay with a man exerting authority over me. After Edward, after years of being commanded and controlled and treated like property, I'd sworn I'd never submit to anyone again.

But this wasn't submission. Or maybe it was, but it was submission I *chose*. Power I *gave* rather than power that was taken.

The difference felt cosmic.

"Then it's no fun, Rowan." I managed to inject challenge into my voice despite the way my body trembled.

"Must you always be pushing boundaries?"

"If you can't take it, then let me go."

He leaned down, and I felt his lips press against my collarbone—soft, almost chaste. The gentleness of it contrasted sharply with his grip in my hair, and the juxtaposition made me dizzy.

"And leave you alone to fend for yourself?" His mouth moved along my shoulder, trailing kisses that felt like brands. "I think not."

My neck was beginning to ache from the angle, and somehow I knew he was aware of it. Reading my body's signals, monitoring my comfort, ensuring he pushed right up to my limits without crossing them.

"I am capable of taking care of myself." But the words lacked conviction.

His teeth found that spot on my neck—the one he'd discovered weeks ago, the place that made my brain short-circuit, and my cunt clench with need—and grazed it with just enough pressure to make me whimper.

"You are, Violet." He released my hair, both hands moving to massage where he'd held me. The relief was immediate and exquisite. "Fuck, you are very capable."

His palms worked the sore muscles with practiced skill, and I melted under his touch.

"But when you are with me. . ." He pulled back, and I felt him shift position behind me. "Let me take care of you."

My heart stuttered in my chest. Full-body shivers cascaded through me, raising goosebumps across every inch of exposed skin.

"Oh god." The word came out shaky, overwhelmed. "Why was that so hot?"

I felt his smile against my shoulder blade before I saw it. When he moved back around to face me, that tantalizingly smug expression I'd learned to love was firmly in place.

"Because you want me." He eased me down and settled between my spread thighs, his hands resting on my knees. "You just do not want to want me."

The truth of it hung between us, undeniable and terrifying, cementing the weeks I had tried to deny myself the truth he had so casually spoken aloud.

His hands began to move again—starting at my feet this time, fingers trailing from the top of my arch, around the curve to my heel. Achingly slow, deliberately torturous, each touch sending sparks up my legs.

I watched him work, cataloging every detail. The concentration on his face. The way his white-blonde hair fell forward, catching light from the bedside lamp. The flex of muscle in his forearms as his fingers wrapped around my ankles, applying pressure that made me shudder.

"The crotch tie I mentioned earlier," he said conversationally, as if we weren't both acutely aware of the sexual tension thick enough to choke on, "Is relatively simple in construction. You add an adjustable loop that changes size depending on the toy being used."

His hands roamed higher, massaging my calves with firm strokes that felt professionally therapeutic and erotically charged simultaneously.

His thumbs pressed into the muscle just below my knees, working out tightness I hadn't known existed. "The toy sits directly against your clit, held in place by the rope. You cannot move it. Cannot escape the sensation. Just constant, unrelenting stimulation until—"

"Until I come apart." I finished for him, my voice barely above a whisper.

"Until you come apart," he agreed.

His hands reached my thighs—carefully avoiding the bandaged tattoo—and gripped with that familiar strength I'd told myself to forget. Told myself I didn't crave.

I'd lied to myself about a lot of things.

My legs spread wider involuntarily, my body making decisions my brain wasn't ready to endorse. His hands moved roughly up my sides now, all pretense of massage abandoned. No more therapeutic massage—this was pure possession, pure claim.

He sank deeper between my thighs, his torso pressing against my core. I could feel him—hard and thick against my wet heat through his sweats—and I wanted those clothes gone. Wanted him inside me. Wanted to feel that delicious stretch, that perfect fullness.

When his fingertips applied pressure along my ribs—right where the rope sat—I nearly came apart from that alone. This was pure desire, raw need, both of us caught in the gravity of wanting each other.

"Rowan. . ." His name came out desperate, pleading.

"I know, *volchok*." His mouth found mine, and we kissed like we were drowning. Like we could breathe each other in, and somehow that would be enough oxygen.

Tongues clashed. Teeth scraped. His hands tangled in my hair while mine gripped his shoulders, nails digging into muscle.

We were the storm-driven sea and the crumbling bluff it loved to ruin—every crash between us eroded the line where he ended, and I began—and I never wanted it to stop.

He pulled back suddenly, both of us panting. His eyes were wild, pupils blown so wide that barely any blue-gray remained visible.

"We cannot do this." The words came out strained, pained.

Reality crashed back in. "What?"

"Jules." He closed his eyes, jaw clenched. "We promised to meet her for dinner before your shift. If we do this now—if I start fucking you the way I want to—we will not have time to do it properly."

Frustration and arousal warred within me. "Rowan—"

"No." He opened his eyes, and the hunger in them nearly undid me. "You deserve better than a rushed fuck because we lost track of time. You deserve to be thoroughly wrecked, Violet. And that takes hours I do not currently have."

His hand cupped between my legs—not penetrating, just resting there with possessive certainty. I was soaked, and we both knew it.

"So you are going to wait for my cock." His voice dropped into that commanding tone that made my cunt clench. "You are going to sit through dinner wet and wanting, knowing exactly what I plan to do to you when we get back here tonight. And then—only then—will I fuck you until you forget every name but mine."

I whimpered, my hips trying to grind against his hand despite knowing he was right.

"Do you understand, *volchok*?"

"Yes." The word came out broken, desperate.

"Good." He removed his hand, and I actually whined at the loss. "Now let me get you out of this rope before we both do something we will regret."

He began untying me with the same methodical care he'd used to bind me. Each knot released slowly, each loop of rope removed with delicacy.

And with each section that came free, I felt an unexpected sadness.

The pressure eased. The embrace loosened. The sensation of being held—truly held—faded with every inch of cerulean fiber that unwound from my body.

It felt like a lover's hug ending too soon. Like safety being peeled away layer by layer, leaving me exposed to the cold reality of a world that didn't care if I lived or died.

By the time the last rope fell away, I felt bereft.

Rowan noticed—of course, he noticed—and pulled me into his arms. Skin against skin, his chest warm against mine, his hands stroking down my bare back with soothing repetition.

"I know," he murmured against my hair. "I know it feels like a loss. But the rope will be here when we return. And so will I."

I buried my face in his shoulder, breathing him in. Pine and clean male musk and something that was uniquely Rowan.

Mine, some possessive part of me whispered. *He's mine. For now.*

"Come on, *princess*." He pulled back, brushing hair from my face with gentle fingers. "Let us get dressed and go meet Jules. The sooner we finish dinner and your shift, the sooner I can bring you back here and make you scream."

The promise in his voice sent heat flooding through me all over again.

"Fine." I stood on shaky legs, my body still humming with unfulfilled desire. "But you're buying me extra fries for this torture."

His laugh followed me as I gathered my clothes, rich and warm and absolutely perfect.

And despite the frustration thrumming through my veins, despite the ache between my thighs that wouldn't be satisfied for hours yet, I found myself smiling.

Chapter 26

Rowan

"How much do you know of the veil and the world that lies beyond it?" Jules asked as she stared at the burger and fries on my plate.

Her question broke the chewing silence at our table. It had taken us weeks to convince her to meet with us outside of Oubliette, away from prying eyes and ears. She had been nearly the same ever since Violet had been drugged, bubbly and warm, but she refused to discuss anything while within the walls. She met all of our questions and inquiries with deflections.

"Another time."

"Not now."

"Catch you later."

Her elusiveness had been infuriating.

However, she had also been absolute in her efforts to ensure Violet stayed safe. That was, I assumed, in no small part due to me threatening to burn the place down if she didn't inform her 'clients' to not eat the staff.

The proprietor sent Violet roses as an apology as well. It was a large bouquet that nearly filled the doorway of her dorm. I would have tossed it in the trash had Violet not objected.

When neither of us answered her question, Jules continued, brushing back her loose tresses. "After you were drugged, I assume Rowen informed you a little on... the nature of things?"

Violet stiffened next to me, her food mid-bite as she eyed us both warily. "Partially? Why don't you fill us in? It has been several weeks now. . ."

Jules nodded. "You were slipped something exceptionally rare. Neither Succubi nor Incubi blood is allowed to be sold, and it is traditionally only shared with trusted partners due to its addictive nature."

"That did not stop anyone from slipping it into her water," I grumbled before finishing a fry.

Jules ignored my jab. "Regardless, the symptoms are typically alleviated through shared energies or auras. Solo practicing does little to subdue the symptoms."

"Auras?" Violet asked.

Jules's voice took on the cadence of Professor Wright. "Auras are the energy fields surrounding all living things. Think of it as our life force, or an indicator of our vitality. A person can share their aura in a multitude of ways, but the primary method is through physical contact." She motioned us closer and lowered her voice. "Incubi and Sucubi feed on sexual energy. . . They are creatures of lust and desire. Therefore, alleviating the symptoms of their blood would require auras in that heightened sexual state."

Violet's face turned bright red. "Oh, the colors I saw. Good to know. How do *you* know so much about all this, Jules?" She was quick to change topic despite the glare I sent her way. She hadn't mentioned anything about seeing auras.

That made Jules pause. "I work closely with the proprietor, Damien, on both sides of the veil. My skills, while currently dormant, are often sought after."

I had to ask the obvious question. "These sought-after skills you speak of? What is it that you specialize in?"

Jules laughed. "I suppose fortune reading could be one way to look at it? Honestly, sweetie, I'd rather not go much more into it right now."

I didn't like how much she kept hidden, but I took what little she would give us.

As I pondered what question to ask Jules next, she shocked Violet and me when she said, "By the way, Damien wants to meet you both tomorrow night."

My interest shifted from learning more about her to what she'd said. Beside me, Violet stiffened, her heart rate spiking. Our words collided in unplanned unison.

"Why?"

"Are you serious?"

After our voices crashed together, Violet laughed—real and unguarded at our stumbling—and her face lit up in a way that caught me unprepared.

My heart clenched, any earlier tension melting like the first thaw after an endless winter.

I gestured towards her with mock formality. "Ladies first."

Her eyes locked with mine, that familiar spark of challenge flashing green and gold, before she mimicked my exaggerated gesture back at me. "Please, age before beauty."

The comeback forced a smile across my face. I nearly laughed at the eerie accuracy of what she had unintentionally said. *If you only knew just how much older I was.* I grabbed a fry and chewed with deliberate slowness, holding her gaze, making a show of taking my time. "If you insist."

But beneath our verbal dance, my body had shifted to high alert. The proprietor. Damien.

I narrowed my eyes on the petite blonde across from us. "Why does he want to meet?"

Jules shrugged, her shoulders shifting beneath the soft pink sweater she wore—meant to hide the lingerie beneath, though on Jules it only made her stand out more. "He did not explain why, aside from wanting to show you two Second Circle."

Violet leaned forward, elbows on the table, energy sparking off her like static electricity. Her eagerness was palpable. "Second Circle?"

Fuck. Second Circle was where I had met my demon, followed by my ill-fated quest for the book. I definitely did not want Violet venturing there alone.

My response overlapped with Violet's question: "I do not think that is wise." As she asked, "Is that the underground club I see people disappear into?"

Jules shook her head with a small laugh, more to herself than us. "Easy, you two." She paused, her expression shifting to wry amusement. "Meeting needs and desires is the proprietor's particular skill, after all. Second Circle is where desire is made manifest."

Despite Violet's excited squeal, the way Jules said those words left me feeling like there was more she could not—or would not—say. Before I could press her, she pushed back her chair. The legs scraped against the diner's tiled floor, the sound making my teeth clench and muscles tense.

"It's getting late, and I need to head back." She stood, gathering her purse. "See you for tonight's shift?"

I looked at my unfinished burger, felt a moment of frustrated hunger, then wiped my hands on my napkin and rose. "I will escort you back."

I need to question Jules about Damien without Violet around. I want to know as much as I can about him before we meet.

Violet's offended look was immediate, her mouth twisting in a pout that almost made me laugh. "You are going to leave me here alone?"

"Yes." I headed towards the door with Jules.

"What if somebody kidnaps me while you are flirting with Jules?" She called after me.

When I turned back, I was not surprised to see rebellion flashing in her eyes. *As predictable as sunrise, her temper.*

I gave Violet a firm look—*stay*—and headed outside with Jules.

The diner sat only a block from Oubliette, nestled on the far side of the shopping district. Chic in its retro design, all chrome and vinyl and neon signage promising burgers and shakes. I felt confident leaving Violet alone as long as she stayed within those walls, among witnesses.

Jules walked beside me, her silence heavy, her thoughts clearly tangled around Damien's message. The night stretched wide and empty above us, moonless—the kind of black that predators favored. The promise of fall teased the lingering residue of summer as a breeze whispered between buildings. It was colder than previous nights, autumn finally claiming its territory.

"Did your friend make it home safely?" I asked, keeping my voice soft.

Jules tensed, clearly taken aback. "Yes, after a long night of hedonism, she finally crawled back home."

I chuckled at the image. "Back to her master's domain, you mean?"

"Prejudice does not look well on you, Rowan." She hugged herself against the chill, her arms wrapping tight around her middle.

My skin crawled with caution, hairs rising on the back of my neck the way they did when danger lurked close. The leather of my jacket creaked as we walked. I counted the soft, rapid flutter of Jules's heartbeat beside me—one hundred twenty beats per minute, far too fast for a casual stroll. Her pulse had spiked when she spoke of Damien earlier and had not settled since. The rhythm was quick and irregular, a frightened bird trapped in her chest. The scent of her cotton-candy perfume mingled with the sharp tang of sweat beneath it, fear's signature fragrance.

"For what it is worth," I said, glancing at her, "I never thanked her for helping with Violet. Or you."

She shrugged, the gesture small and almost dismissive. "I care for my girls like my own. Like family."

"And yet that same family swims amongst the waters of sharks unknowingly."

Jules sighed, the sound heavy with resignation. "I do not expect you to understand the balance, Rowan."

"No, I do not think I will. Not when it threatens those I care for."

"Folly is perennial, and yet the human race has survived." She quoted Russell as our steps echoed down the alley across the street from Oubliette, the club's neon sign visible in the distance.

I started to respond when two figures rounded the corner. They slinked down the alley towards us, their strides fluid and unnatural. The absence of heartbeats confirmed what I feared even before I saw their faces: vampyres. My ears strained against the silence where their pulses should have been, that void of sound more alarming than a growl. As they neared, their skin gleamed like polished alabaster under the distant streetlights.

"Jules, stay near me." My voice left no room for argument. She startled at the command before she pressed into my side, her breath coming fast and shallow.

"They shouldn't be hunting, much less so close to Oubliette."

"Well, it seems they do not give many fucks, do they now?" I snapped, already mentally preparing for a fight.

Once the pair drew closer, I recognized them. The twins from the club. Their heterochromia gleamed in the streetlight with an unnatural luminescence that human eyes didn't possess. The soft scrape of their shoes against the pavement created an eerie rhythm.

"Well, well, well," the twin to my right said with a grin, his voice as smooth as polished glass. "Louis, what is this we have stumbled across?"

The twin to my left, Louis, raked his gaze over me, measuring, dismissing, then speaking with a faint curl of lip. "René, I do believe this is that grim guard dog of the newest girl. What was her name?"

René made a show of pretending to remember as he tapped a slender finger to his temple. "Alexis, I believe?"

Violet's stage name. Relief flickered through me that they didn't know her real name. It was a small mercy in a world that rarely offered any.

"I want no trouble," I said as I raised my hands, the universal signal for passivity and truce. I inhaled deeply. The night air was thick with the stench of nearby garbage and the scent of distant rain. I hoped they would leave us alone and fuck off to their coffins.

They did not.

The twins' grins grew in unison as they took a few steps away from each other, then started to circle us. I could handle myself against these bloodsuckers, but Jules... She was breakable, as fragile as spun glass in a storm. I didn't think I could take them both while also protecting her.

"*Pax vobis ambobus sit*," I said as I pushed Jules back and kept myself between her and the twins. *Peace be with you both*, in Latin. From my previous life, I knew there were some long-lived vampyres who respected the ancient language despite its ties to Christianity. Such a greeting was meant to dissuade the undead, a respectful and subtle way to show fealty.

René edged further to my right as surprise flashed across his face. His raven-black hair spilled down his back like oil as he cocked his head, birdlike, studying me as though he were deciding which part of my throat to tear out first. "Did you hear that, Louis? This guard dog speaks."

"It's an impressive bark," Louis said as he stepped closer to my left. He combed a hand through his equally long hair. "But we have no interest in a dog's tricks. Where is your master, little guard dog?"

"Not here," I said flatly as I lowered my hands. I felt the violent tension rising and knew we were about to come to blows. I shoved my hands deep into my jacket pockets.

"Yes," René said with a hunger in his voice, "that we can see. But *where* is Alexis? She always looks so delicious on that stage... we were thinking of having a taste."

At that, any desire I'd harbored to resolve the encounter peacefully snapped like a frozen branch. My lips peeled back in a snarl as the words tore out, guttural and unrestrained from a primal darkness within me. "You will never touch her, *chudovishche*."

Their smirks died, faces hardening to marble. Whether they spoke Russian or not, they didn't need a translation to know I had called them a *monster*.

Behind me, Jules's breath hitched, a frightened rabbit heartbeat hammering against my back. The twins' eyes tracked the sound, nostrils flaring at the scent of her fear. I saw their fingernails flashing into claws as they bared their elongating fangs. The alley suddenly felt too narrow.

In a blur, they lunged.

Against a single vampyre, even a very young one, an unprepared and unarmed man stands little chance of survival. Against two, in a dark alley, in the middle of the night, while simultaneously trying to protect a friend? It would have been certain death.

For an unprepared and unarmed man.

Thankfully, I was neither of those things.

In my previous life, silver was one of the most valuable commodities mortals traded. I had thought it so bizarre when I was reborn into a world where people cared so much about gold. It did not make sense to me that gold would be so expensive, while silver was downright cheap in comparison. It did not make sense... but I was grateful for it.

It made buying powdered silver quite affordable.

I yanked my hands from my pockets, tossed a fistful of silver dust directly into Louis's face, and was rewarded with the sounds of his eyes sizzling and his voice screeching. I tried the same on René, but he ducked aside, and the silver cloud wafted over where his head would have been.

Stupid old man, I cursed at myself. I was out of practice. It *had* been years.

Predictably, René swiped his hand at my face, so I caught his wrist. My hand was still coated in silver dust, and I felt his flesh bubble and give—like squeezing warm wax. I twisted the wrist and yanked his arm down, slamming my other silver-dusted fist into his face as he swung his free arm at me.

I had to release him and step away, his claws swiping where my throat would have been. He looked at me and I laughed at his face; there was a perfect imprint of my fist seared into his broken cheek, the skin there sizzling as if from a chemical burn.

I spared a glance over my shoulder to see Jules safe, pressed against the wall of the alley, looking mortified. Louis was still down on his knees to my left, shrieking in agony while clutching his eyes. I knew he would start to heal soon. I needed to finish his brother before that happened.

"You have something on your face," I said with a laugh. I gestured to my own cheek with one hand, as if I were showing a friend where they had an embarrassing speck of food, while I stuck my other hand back in my jacket.

"I will drink you dry and have pigs eat your corpse, dog!" René juked to my right, then my left, tempting me to throw another fistful of silver dust that he would dodge.

This dog has done that trick already. Time for a new one.

I tossed another fistful of silver dust towards him. He dodged, dashed towards me, closed the distance, and he was very nearly upon me when I ignited the road flare.

I slashed at him with the flare like it was a dagger, the flames cutting through the air between us, and he swiped at me with his claws. There was a flurry of exchanges. I came away bloody. He came away burnt. We were at a stalemate. He couldn't commit to lunging at me and sinking his teeth into my throat, out of his fear of the flare. I couldn't commit to grappling him and holding my fire to him, out of my fear of the fangs.

There will be no escape for you two. Not after tonight. I knew that if I did not end them, then they would just come back with more of their coven and look to settle the score. I could not let that happen. Not when they had threatened Violet.

"Rowan!" Violet's scream, shrill and broken, cut through my thoughts. I heard her panicked terror, and I looked over my shoulder towards the source of her voice.

It was enough. The twins struck in tandem, a pair of perfect hunters. *Vampyres, ever the opportunists.*

Louis tackled my legs while René grabbed my arm that held the flare. We were all falling together when he bent my wrist backwards. There was a sickening crunch, a bloom of pain, and then the flare clattered to the pavement. My back slammed into the ground, the wind shoved out of me. I reached up with my free hand and drove a silver-dusted thumb into René's eye; I was rewarded with him howling before a wet popping sound—like a water balloon bursting.

Louis's eyes had either healed already, or he was blind fighting. Either way, he yanked my hand away from his brother's face and pinned it to the pavement. René followed suit. Each of the twins had an arm now, and regardless of how hard I struggled and thrashed and heaved, it was futile. I could not have broken free of their vampyric strength any more than I could have lifted a mountain.

In unison, they locked their jaws onto my throat and drank.

White-hot agony ripped through me and tore a cry from deep in my chest. Fire blazed throughout me. . . followed by fear.

This fear is not for you, I thought once more.

My strength failed. My vision narrowed, black edges crawling inward until all I saw were the tops of their pale foreheads bobbing up and down as they drank my blood.

Then, right before I lost consciousness, I saw the craziest goddamned thing.

Violet leapt onto Louis's back, wrapped an arm around his neck, and had him locked in a rear-naked choke.

A blood choke. Ha. That's funny.

Chapter 27

Violet

Rowan leaving me alone in the diner left a sour taste in my mouth.

I should be good and wait. He's only with Jules. I wasn't worried about Rowan and her hooking up. Not when he had practically confessed to me. That was not the cause of the unease I felt as I watched them walk off. I didn't actually know the reason I felt so worried, but I hurried to pay the bill so I could follow after them.

Settling the tab took longer than it should have, giving Rowan and Jules a bit of a head start. As I rushed out the door, the cool night air blasted against me and pebbled my skin. I was about to turn the corner when I heard an inhuman shriek.

My heart nearly stopped, but I ran like hell towards that sound. I had no idea what I expected to find, but Rowan wielding a road flare and fighting one of those creepy twins from the club was *not it*.

"Rowan!" I called for him as I ran. I wanted him to know that I was there, that I was coming, that I had his back, that he wasn't alone.

Then the idiot turned to look at me, like he forgot he was in the middle of a back alley brawl.

What happened next... I wasn't prepared for what happened next.

I expected the three of them to wrestle around on the ground: punching, kicking, grappling. Maybe one of the twins would pull out a knife. I saw Rowan gouge out an eye, and I winced from the scream that followed.

What I was *not* prepared for was discovering that vampyres really did exist by watching two of them bite down on Rowan's throat.

The world tilted. My mind rejected what my eyes insisted was real: twin mouths latched onto Rowan's neck, their faces transformed into something predatory and wrong. Not metaphorically predatory. Actually inhuman, with features that had shifted into angles that shouldn't exist on a human face.

I didn't think. Thinking would have paralyzed me. Instead, I let muscle memory take over, launching myself at the nearest twin's back. My arms snaked around his throat in a perfect rear naked choke, my bicep pressed against one carotid, forearm against the other. My legs wrapped around his waist, heels digging into his hips for leverage.

Ten seconds or less. That's all it took to put someone out when you cut off blood to the brain. I'd practiced the choke dozens of times on the mats and always secured the nearly immediate tap from partners who didn't want to black out. The science was simple: compress the carotid arteries, stop blood from reaching the brain, lights out.

I squeezed harder than I ever would while rolling on the mat, putting every ounce of strength into the hold. My bicep burned. My forearm ached. Almost as if it were staged, the sky opened up, and it began to downpour. I counted in my head as I waited for his body to go limp.

One Mississippi. Two Mississippi. Three Mississippi.

He didn't even notice I was there.

Four Mississippi. Five Mississippi. Six Mississippi.

His throat felt wrong under my arm. Too cold. Too hard. Like trying to choke marble wrapped in silk.

Seven Mississippi. Eight Mississippi. Nine Mississippi.

He kept feeding. The wet, sucking sounds continued. Rowan's blood ran down the creature's chin, mixing with rivulets of rain, dripping onto the alley floor into water and rotting garbage.

Ten Mississippi.

Nothing. No slackening. No tap out. No sign he even felt my arms around his throat.

Eleven. Twelve. Thirteen.

My arms shook with effort. Sweat mixed with rain, making my grip slip. The vampyre reached back with one hand, casual as swatting a mosquito, and grabbed my wrist. His fingers were ice against my skin.

He pulled my arm away from his throat like I was a child playing at violence.

The strength in those fingers defied reason, defied physics. I'd grappled with men nearly twice my weight, learned to use leverage and technique to overcome raw power. But this wasn't human strength. This was something else entirely, something that made all my training worthless as a paper airplane in a hurricane.

"Please," I gasped, abandoning technique for desperation. "Please stop. You're killing him."

The vampyre's twin pulled his mouth from Rowan's throat long enough to laugh. He looked at me with his one good eye. Blood painted his lips, turning his teeth into crimson daggers. "That's rather the point, love."

I tried to wrench free, to throw myself between them and Rowan, but the one holding my wrist yanked me off his back and tossed me aside. I hit the alley wall hard enough to drive the air from my lungs. My vision sparked white, then gray, then cleared.

The road flare had rolled into a gutter and was being swept away in a river of sludgewater. As the flickering red light faded, I saw how pale Rowan had become. His skin looked like snow, his lips tinged blue, his eyes rolling back to show only white as he fought to stay conscious.

I scrambled forward on hands and knees through the garbage and water. "No! Please, stop!"

I knew this feeling. This helplessness. This watching something terrible happen while being too weak to prevent it. In that other life, Edward had kept me ignorant and isolated specifically so I would feel this way. So I would know, bone-deep, that resistance was pointless. That I was nothing. That my struggles were entertainment at best, annoyance at worst.

And that part of me watched Rowan die and knew the same truth: *I am powerless.*

Rain began to slice down harder in razor sheets, cold and sharp against my skin. It plastered my hair to my face, mixed with tears I hadn't realized were falling. The vampyres kept feeding, their throats working as they swallowed, and swallowed, and swallowed.

Arms wrapped around me from behind before I could throw myself at them again. Small arms, but strong as steel cables. Jules. I hadn't heard her approach, but suddenly she was there, holding me back while I thrashed and fought and screamed.

"Don't," she whispered harshly against my ear, though her voice trembled. "Don't get closer, sweetie. They'll take you too."

"I don't care!" I tried to elbow her in the ribs, stomp on her feet, throw my head back into her face—every technique I'd learned for dealing with a rear grapple. But Jules had positioned herself perfectly, her chin tucked against my shoulder, her body angled to avoid my strikes. "Let me go! Jules! Let me go, they're killing him!"

"I know, sweetie. I know." Her voice broke on the words. She was crying too, I realized. Her hot tears mixed with rain on my shoulder. "But you can't stop them. Neither can I."

The feeding sounds grew wetter, more obscene. Rowan's hands, which had been pushing weakly against the twins' shoulders, fell to his sides. His head lolled back to the pavement.

"Rowan!" My scream shredded my throat. "Please! Please, somebody, help him!"

The alley stank of garbage and blood and rain. Somewhere, a cat yowled. Somewhere, people were living their normal lives, eating dinner, watching television, completely unaware that the world contained monsters who could drain a man dry in an alley.

Rowan's eyes found mine across the space between us. Still conscious, somehow. Still aware enough to see me struggling, failing, breaking apart. His lips moved, forming my name without sound. An apology, maybe. Or a goodbye.

That's when the air changed.

It happened between one heartbeat and the next: the temperature dropped ten degrees, the rain eased, the distant streetlamps flickered. A scent drifted through the alley that overpowered the garbage and blood. It reminded me of jasmine, lavender, and warm summer stones.

The twins released Rowan immediately, their heads snapping up like wolves scenting a larger predator. One of them actually whimpered. The sound was so incongruous with their previous dominance that I stopped struggling in Jules's arms.

They dropped to their knees in the filthy alley water, heads bowed so low their foreheads scraped the ground.

"Mistress," the one-eyed vampyre gasped.

A woman I least expected stepped from shadows that shouldn't have been deep enough to hide within. She moved like liquid poured into the shape of a person, each step deliberate and graceful.

"Natalia?" I whispered.

She was still just as beautiful as when I'd seen her last, but in that moment, she was also terrifying. The rain made her dark skin look like polished onyx, and turned her snow white hair into a darker grey. She wore a bubblegum pink tube top and a skirt that should have looked cheap, but instead looked like she was slumming for fun—playing at being a college party girl. Thigh-high stockings completed the outfit, making her legs seem impossibly long in combat boots.

Dear god. She's not human either.

"You stopped. How disappointing," she said, a lilt to her voice that I had once found alluring. Now it sent shivers of icy fear throughout me. My stomach turned. She'd been watching. Watching while they fed. Watching while I begged. Watching while Rowan died.

She glided past where Jules still held me, close enough that I caught more of her scent: not just jasmine and stone but something else, something that made my body scream warnings. She knelt beside Rowan, studying him.

"This one. . ." She reached out with one perfectly manicured finger, not quite touching the blood running down his throat. "This one, I was considering having for myself."

The phrasing made me want to vomit. *Having him.* Like he was a vintage wine or an expensive meal. A thing to be consumed at leisure.

The twins exchanged terrified glances. "Forgive us, Mistress Natalia," One-Eye stammered. "We didn't know you had claimed him."

"I had not." She tilted her head, hair sliding over one shoulder like water. "Not yet. But I was. . . interested. Especially when he offered to help me. And now you've gone and broken him."

Rowan's chest barely moved. Each breath looked shallower than the last. Blood bubbled at the corner of his mouth. I'd seen enough death in my previous life to recognize its approach.

Before I could think better of it, I spoke. "Please." My voice came out raw, destroyed by screaming. "Please, can you save him?"

Natalia's attention shifted to me with the weight of a physical blow. Her eyes were so dark blue they appeared black, and looking into them felt like falling into a bottomless well. "Save him? Why would I do that?"

"Because..." I swallowed. "Because he's no good to you dead."

She laughed, soft and genuinely amused. "Oh, little fighter. Death is hardly an impediment to my desires. Some things are actually more cooperative afterward."

The casual mention of her cruelty, delivered with such nonchalance, forced bile to rise in my throat. But I pressed on. "I'll do anything," I begged. "If you save him, I'll do anything you want."

Jules's arms tightened around me, a warning I ignored.

Natalia turned back, one perfect eyebrow arched. "A*nything*? Do you understand what that word means to someone like me?"

No, I don't. How can I? But I don't care. "He doesn't deserve to die. He was only walking Jules home. To keep her safe. If you want payment, if you want... entertainment? Then take it from me. Please. You would do the same for Alice, wouldn't you?"

"Violet, no," Jules whispered.

Natalia's demeanor changed then. Her spine straightened, and the look of amusement on her face turned to fury as she approached with slow, measured steps. The twins scrambled back and away from her, still prostrated in the filthy water. She stopped just outside of arm's reach, studying me with her impossibly bottomless eyes.

"You should take care using her name in my presence." Her voice was cold as stone, but I heard the hidden meaning. *Don't you dare bring Alice into this.* She continued. "You would trade yourself for him?"

"Yes."

"You would suffer for him?"

"Yes."

"You would die for him?"

"Yes." No hesitation. No calculation. I was astonished at how true it was.

She smiled then, and I understood why the twins feared her. It wasn't her beauty or power. It was the complete absence of anything recognizably human in that expression. It was like seeing a spider smile.

"How tediously romantic," she said with a yawn. She glanced back at Rowan, who had gone still except for the barest rise and fall of his chest. "Though I confess, I'm curious what kind of man inspires such devotion."

She moved towards him again, and this time she did touch him, fingers pressed to his throat where the twins had fed. Rowan didn't react. He was beyond such things now, balanced on the knife's edge between life and whatever came after.

"Still warm," she mused. "Still technically alive, though barely. The twins have always been such greedy feeders."

"Please," I whispered. The word was all I had left.

Natalia's hand remained on Rowan's throat for a long moment. Then she stood, brushing imaginary dust from her skirt.

"No," she said simply.

The word slammed into me. I sagged in Jules's arms, all fight leaving me at once. Rowan was going to die. I was going to watch him die. And there was nothing, *nothing* I could do about it.

"However," Natalia continued, and hope sparked painfully in my chest, "I might be able to be persuaded..." She gestured to the ground at her feet. "Crawl to me, little fighter. Crawl over here and lick my boots clean. Show me how much his life means to you."

Heat flooded my face despite the cold rain. Crawl and lick. Crawl through the garbage and blood and filthy water, then lick away the same from her feet. Debase myself for her amusement while Rowan died inches away.

I knew this game. I knew the pleasure some took in humiliation, in making you complicit in your own degradation. Edward had been a *master* of it. He'd make me thank him for things that broke me. He'd made me beg for things no sane person would ever actually want. He'd made me perform countless sexual acts with a zeal and eagerness I didn't feel.

This bitch may be some ancient vampyre badass, but Edward was a world-class grandmaster sadist. She's got nothing on him.

I pulled away from Jules to drop to my knees, but her grip tightened. She anchored me to stand with her. "No," she said quietly, "I refuse to allow you to bend to her whims. The *Pax Tacere* be damned. You let me handle this." Then, with a formality I'd never heard from the bubbly, ditzy Jules, she practically shouted, "I greet you, Natalia, Little Mistress of the Wallachia family."

The words rang in the alley with a weight I didn't understand. The barest recognition of the name flickered in my mind, then I recalled Rowan explaining the world of the supernaturals. *"There are four reigning families, Violet. We must take care to never run into one of them."*

Wallachia. . . one of those four reigning families had been named Wallachia.

Well, shit.

Jules released me and stepped forward, dropping into a perfect curtsy; the formal etiquette of it looked ridiculous in an alley filled with soaking wet garbage. In the same formal tone she used before, Jules said, "Your men broke etiquette after he declared peace in the old tongue. This was a flagrant violation of the *Pax Tacere*."

The change in Natalia was instant and terrifying. The lazy amusement vanished, replaced by something ancient and angry. Her eyes flashed gold—literally flashed—like sunlight behind stained glass. "Is this true?" She asked the question so quietly that I barely heard her over the rain.

One-Eye raised his head slightly, trembling. He cupped his hands up towards Natalia, lips trembling, as if he were begging for salvation. "He. . . he spoke the words. But he is a nobody! He is—"

"A *patron* of Oubliette," Jules interrupted, still holding that perfect curtsy. "As well as a guest of the Second Circle. In fact," she emphasized her next words, "these two were meant to meet *Him* tomorrow."

Natalia's demeanor flashed from quiet anger briefly to panicked terror, before whipping into an incendiary rage.

It dawned on me that when Jules said, *"Him,"* she must have meant the proprietor of Oubliette, Damien. That realization did not, however, help me understand what was happening. I couldn't process the politics and protocols playing out while Rowan bled on the pavement. But I did understand power, and the power dynamics had just shifted completely. Despite Natalia being of the Wallachia family—and despite that apparently being a big deal—she seemed beside herself at the thought of angering some nightclub owner.

Then Natalia disappeared.

At least, that's what it looked like. In truth, she moved faster than my eyes could follow. One moment she was standing still looking at me and Jules, then the next she had One-Eye by the throat, lifted off the ground as if he weighed nothing. His feet kicked uselessly in the air. One of his arms hung limp and broken at his side. Fear weighed heavily within the alleyway, coating the twins in a sheen of sweat that mirrored the droplets of rain. Even from a distance, I saw his eyes wide and his chest heaving in gulping gasps of air.

I think I'm about to find out if vampyres can piss themselves.

"You fed on a patron of Oubliette?" Each word was precisely enunciated and as cold as a winter wind. "On a *guest* no less? You broke our *peace* with the Second Circle?"

One-Eye tried to speak but only managed a gurgle. One of his hands clawed at her grip, drawing no blood despite his inhuman strength.

"Mistress, please!" The other twin begged for his brother's life on his knees in the filthy water.

Natalia wrapped her free hand in One-Eye's long black hair, gathering it like reins. Then she *swung him*. His body became a weapon, a living flail that slammed into his brother with a wet thud.

"Holy shit," I muttered, caught between fear and amazement as Jules remained stoic. It was as if she were immune to the violent display of power.

Meanwhile, Natalia shouted while she swung repeatedly. "You." Thud. "Fed." Thud. "On." Thud. "A guest." Thud. "Of his?" Each word was punctuated by swinging one brother into the other.

One-Eye sobbed, begging between impacts, his broken arm flopping uselessly. The one on the ground being beaten tried to crawl away, but Natalia followed, relentless, using one twin to bludgeon the other.

I couldn't breathe. Couldn't think. The casual violence of it, the way she wielded an entire person like a weapon, triggered every trauma response from my previous life. I craved Rowan then, his safety, his calming presence, his gifted hands tying me up.

And he's dying while this is happening.

The twins were both sobbing now, inhuman creatures reduced to weeping children, pleading in languages I didn't recognize. Blood ran from split lips and broken noses, but still Natalia continued, methodical and cold despite their quivering bodies.

"Please!" The twin on the ground managed between hits. "Mercy! We beg your mercy!"

"*Mercy?*" She paused, holding the hanging twin still for a moment. His hair was wrapped so tightly around her fist that patches had torn from his scalp. "You would have me show you *mercy* when you've potentially started a war with someone even *my father* would pay obeisance to?"

She brought One-Eye down one more time, harder than before. Both twins screamed in harmony, a sound that would live in my nightmares forever. Then she dropped the one she'd been holding, letting him splash into the standing water beside his brother. They lay there gasping, sobbing, trying to crawl towards each other, but too broken to manage it.

My body wanted to run, to hide, to make myself small and unnoticeable. But Jules's hand found mine, and she squeezed, either in warning or in comfort, to keep me anchored and still.

Natalia turned back to us, not a speck of blood on her despite what she'd just done. "The Wallachia family will pay recompense for this failure. Tell your master he may name his price."

Jules finally straightened from her curtsy, and when she spoke, she sounded nothing like the Jules I knew. "As you command, Mistress Natalia."

The white-haired vampyre looked at Rowan one last time, something like regret flickering across her perfect features. "A waste. He would have been... a formidable ally."

She turned and walked towards the twins. They cowered before her, too injured to flee, as she reached down and grabbed fistfuls of hair: a twin in each hand. Then she walked towards a shadowed corner of the alley, dragging the kicking and screaming twins behind her like luggage.

Then she was gone. *They* were gone. As if the darkness were a doorway, she stepped into the shadows without breaking stride and vanished. Only the scent of jasmine lingered, already fading in the rain.

Jules let out a shuddering breath. "Oh, thank god she left. Quick, we need to get him inside."

Inside. Inside where? Rowan was barely breathing anymore. The rising and falling of his chest had slowed while monsters played politics over his corpse. I dropped to my knees beside him, hands hovering over his body, afraid to touch and confirm what I already knew.

"He's going to die," I whispered. The words felt unreal in my mouth.

"He sure is," Jules said, "*If* we don't get him inside Oubliette." She crouched down next to me. "Come on, sweetie. We need to move him. We need to get help. We need..." Her voice trailed off as she looked down the length of the alley towards Oubliette.

I forced myself to tear my eyes away from Rowan to follow her gaze.

There was a man standing at the entrance to the alley. Oubliette was visible over his shoulder. He stood in a perfect circle of light from a streetlamp over his head, almost angelic. *No, not an angel.* Deep down, I knew. Mere men didn't look like that. Men didn't have features carved by some deity's fevered dream of temptation. Men didn't cause you to forget how to breathe simply by existing near you. Men didn't cause the filthiest fantasies to flash through your mind while your closest and dearest friend bled out at your feet.

Desires made manifest, Jules had said, and I didn't understand what she meant the first time I met him. But now, the words resounded within me as I watched him approach, dressed in a suit the color of crimson. His dark hair swept back from a face that was all sharp angles and dangerous beauty—features carved in warm bronze, with gilded eyes that somehow held depths of light even from a distance.

As he approached, his footsteps measured and unhurried, I whispered, "Is that who I think it is?"

"That," she said with reverent awe and relief, "is Damien."

Chapter 28

Rowan

It had been a long time since I had felt Death's grasp. Not the brush of it during a fight, or the fleeting flirtation of it during a fall, but the true weight of it—the heavy, soundless presence that filled lungs and heart like cold water.

Even when faced with the inevitable, my thoughts turned to her. Memories of the fight flickered through the domain of in-between before me, then met silence. Was she okay? Did they hurt her?

Time passed slowly, or maybe not at all, as I waited in the silent domain of a vast, endless corridor. I found myself desperately missing her. Her scent, her voice, the way she filled a room with defiant warmth even when she was angry at me. Memories of her anchored me, flickering faintly like candlelight seen through glass, reflecting off the obsidian walls of my prison.

Memories of Charlie—the man I considered to be the closest thing to a father figure I'd ever had—rushed to the surface. His laugh, his cleverness, the way his hand would grip my shoulder to offer comfort or counsel. All of it threaded through me as I drifted, feeling the beat of my heart slow... then falter... then slip like sand between fingers.

I am dying, and it feels more... final this time.

Behind me stood a Grim. Not the caricatured skull-faced figure from stories, but something far older and more patient. Taller than any mortal, its form wrapped in smoke and shadow that billowed without wind, edges fraying into nothing before reforming. The cloak—if it could be called that—seemed woven from the absence of light itself, drinking in what little illumination existed in this place. Its face remained hidden within the depths of that hood, though I sensed the weight of its attention.

In its skeletal hands, it held a scythe. The blade gleamed iridescent black, catching colors that had no names, its edge impossibly thin—the kind of sharpness that could sever more than flesh. The weapon stood upright like a horizon line at my back, patient as stone. The Grim didn't move. It didn't speak. It simply waited, its mission inevitable.

I knew what it was: not my executioner, but my escort.

Was this really the end?

I stood, feeling light and ethereal. The space around me wasn't a void so much as a corridor: endless, smooth, similar to Oubliette's polished interior. My fingertips traced the slippery walls, and warmth seeped from them into my touch.

I should move... but to where?

Deep down, I knew. To Violet.

I walked because there was nothing else to do, my bare feet slapping softly against a floor that shouldn't exist. No air, no wind, no scent. Simply endless time and nothing.

More memories of Violet flashed through the darkness, reflecting off obsidian in broken stories of our mingling lives. Her face—angry, then smiling—echoed within the walls like shuttered film.

I miss her. The ache of knowing I might never see her again rose beneath the hollow emptiness of my ribs, where my heart remained quiet. Even without my heightened hearing, I knew I was teetering on Death's threshold.

Then, from a distance, I saw it. A golden silhouette, faint at first but growing more solid the closer I came. A door, impossibly out of place in the endless black.

Curiosity got the better of me. I turned to the Grim, my voice hoarse and cracked as it carried over the distance. "You will not mind if I go take a look, right?"

Silence answered. Its billowing hood remained unmoving, scythe upright and glinting with those strange, nameless colors.

I laughed softly, the sound thin and strange in this place. "No, you will not mind."

So I walked.

Each step towards the door felt heavier than the last, like wading through unseen dark water. My footsteps echoed softly against nothing, but as I neared the golden shape, another noise began to sound faintly—a wet, dull rhythm, like flesh striking stone.

The door stood tall and narrow, carved from something that reminded me briefly of the solidified light I'd seen after using Jules's portal in Oubliette. It looked solid, indestructible, yet simultaneously ethereal—as if I could pass my hand through it and find resistance and emptiness both. Intricate etchings covered its surface: spirals, dagger-points, cups spilling liquid, snakes coiled around blades. The largest and most elaborate carving was in the center—a chalice bearing twin daggers crossed like wings.

And engraved upon that chalice were the words *Lavernai Pocolom.*

A shiver ran through me, echoing between my bones. The words were ancient and foreign, yet my tongue ached as though it had once spoken them. Familiar and daunting in equal measure. The faint gold outline of the door pulsed slowly, like breath. It was then I realized the door was alive.

As I stared, I heard something. The briefest of whispers.

"Rowan."

I reached out, fingers trembling, feeling a strange pull. The Grim stayed where it was—seemingly miles away now, unmoving—a shadowy silhouette at the edge of the dark, endless corridor.

The door pulsed again, golden light spilling faintly into my palm. For a heartbeat, it felt warm. Then cold. And beneath the whisper of my name, another voice curled like smoke.

"Will you choose, Rowan?"

I glanced up, suddenly aware I was not alone. An ethereal wisp of shadow and smoke sat above the gilded door. Even from where I stood, I could see the faint outline of Her form—the physical embodiment of transition between Life and Death made manifest in Her features.

Half Her face was breathtaking: raven-black hair framing youthful beauty, skin pale as moonlight, one crimson eye that held the warmth of every sunrise. The other half was a polished white skull—clean bone gleaming in the golden light, an empty socket where the second eye should have been. The division ran perfectly down the center, as if someone had drawn a line and declared: *here ends life, here begins ending.*

I knew Her.

"Death," I said as I raised my hand. "I greet you. Again, it would seem."

"Enter or fade?"

Her whisper thickened until it wasn't just in my head but in my bones, thrumming like a second pulse. The golden door pulsed with the unspoken words, light swelling in slow, deliberate breaths. I looked from Her to the door then back. "Death, I do not understand what you ask of me."

She merely watched while perched atop the door.

I tried another approach. "What is this door?"

"A choice."

Simple words for a complex situation. I glanced once more at the etched lines, as if staring would reveal the hidden meaning I sought. "Is this a way back home?"

"A way away from me."

Her words held no malice, but I heard the underlying message. To walk through this door would be to deny Her path. To refuse the finality of it all. "I cannot leave her," I whispered.

Death's form spilled onto the floor before me, startling me as Her inky shadows billowed out and filled the space with Her presence. Face to face now, I was unable to determine where I should look—torn between the youthful features on one side and the polished skull on the other. She tilted Her head, soft waves of raven silk spilling across Her crimson eye and empty socket both.

"You escaped my grasp once."

Her voice was almost curious, soft as the shadows that danced around Her. I pressed my hand to my chest, feeling the silence where my heart should beat. "*Da.* I did. Once."

"You seek to escape once more."

I shook my head. "I would welcome you with open arms, Eternal One." I hesitated. "But it is not my time. Not yet."

To think I dare to argue with Death herself.

"What is a shepherd without its flock?"

She asked the question as She began to circle me. I was momentarily reminded of the vampyress before Death's billowing, glacial shadows curled around me. Is this why Death was often described as frigid? Her very presence may have been cold, but there was warmth in Her words.

"Death is absolute. We are the beginning and the end of all things."

It was an all too familiar comfort I wish I knew. "I know this to be the truth. But even the Fates have staved off Death when it was meant to be."

She stopped her circling and stood, scrutinizing me—or so it felt—yet her face remained impassive.

"Even gods, both known and forsaken, yield to Me. Why is it the folly of mortals to flee from the truth of things?"

I didn't know how to answer that question. I doubted I ever would.

"Enter or fade? Make your choice."

She turned back to the door and pointed with one pale, skeletal finger.

Life or Death, I mused. But my choice was made. I stepped forward, icy wisps trailing behind me as I neared the door. Violet's name echoed deep within my being, and the faint memory of her kiss, her warmth, her laughter propelled me forward. My hands hovered inches from the carved gilded chalice, trembling. Cold bled from it—a void that wasn't empty, yet could never be filled. My fingertips tingled as though dipped in ice water.

I faltered. Every instinct screamed at me to pull back, to accept the quiet end, to allow nature to run its course. The balance that existed in all things—especially between Life and Death—weighed heavily on me. I had already defied Death once before, and though She stood near, I did not want to incite Her wrath. I *should* let the Grim take my soul to where it belonged.

Wherever the hell that is... I'm dying to find out.

The terrible joke brought a smile to my face. Violet would have laughed at that. She shared my dark sense of humor.

Once more, images of her face flared in my mind, and I thought of her defiance, her stubbornness, her fury. I remembered her voice—shrill and breaking through chaos as teeth tore into me.

"Rowan!"

The last of my restraint shattered.

"I will not fade," I whispered to no one but myself, though Death stood as witness. My voice cracked like brittle ice. "I will not fade while she still needs me."

The chalice seemed to lean towards me, its etched daggers of crimson glinting like a predator's teeth. The pulsing light quickened. I pressed my palms flat to the chalice sigil, and Death's words slithered within me, grasping the last of my hesitation with icy fingers.

"Fade you shall not."

Heat exploded up my arm, searing and freezing simultaneously. Pain reverberated within me, as if I were being unmade and remade all at once. The carvings writhed beneath my hand, shifting like snakes. The weight of thousands of names, thousands of souls, pressed into me, through me, around me.

Behind me, the Grim moved for the first time. Its scythe tipped forward in what might have been acknowledgment, the iridescent blade catching impossible light before the entire figure faded like smoke on the wind.

Death stood passive and calm, Her mismatched face—beautiful and skeletal both—reflecting the gilded light of my choice. Her crimson eye and empty socket both bore into me with equal weight.

"The sun will greet you once more. You will rejoice and dance in her warmth. That is what Life brings."

She lifted Her hand, palm upward, and a scale appeared between Her fingertips. It looked weightless yet impossibly heavy, tilting slowly to one side.

"But heed this warning: pain will taint your path, filling your soul with remorse. For your choices, you will weep, Rowan. The Forsaken have no place among the living. But know, your suffering will yield to triumph, and what once perished shall rise to hunt."

"Wait—" I cried out as the door unlatched with a sound like flesh tearing, silencing my words.

So long as she is safe. The thought burned through my resolve. *If it means her salvation, I would die and relive an eternity of beginnings and endings for her.*

Death nodded, as if She'd heard my unspoken vow.

And then, with a sound like a million mouths inhaling at once, the door swung inward.

Gold light poured through, swallowing my vision. The corridor, the Grim, Death Herself—all dissolved into radiance so bright it had weight, had texture, had *sound*. I felt my body unraveling, threads of self coming loose and reweaving into patterns I couldn't comprehend.

Heat flooded through me, but nothing like the searing pain of touching the chalice. Instead, it was more like the warmth of the summer sun on winter skin. My lungs expanded, though there was no air to breathe. My heart—silent for so long—stuttered once, twice, then caught rhythm like a drum remembering its beat.

Sensation returned in a rush: the phantom press of rope around ribs, the ghost of Violet's lips against mine, the sharp bite of autumn wind, the wet copper taste of blood, the sound of rain, the scent of jasmine and rot and *life*.

I fell forward, unable to know if I was falling or rising, or both at once. Violet's name burned on my tongue, a prayer and a promise and a plea all woven together. The golden light swallowed me whole.

Chapter 29

Violet

Damien scooped Rowan off the pavement as if he weighed nothing and headed back towards Oubliette, with Jules and me rushing to keep up. Everything about the proprietor defied logic, defied reason. He was mesmerizing, his presence a gravity that held my gaze. It felt absurd to notice how beautiful he was as he carried Rowan's dying body, but it was also impossible to look away.

If I'd had a single moment to grasp the hilarity of seeing Rowan in a princess carry, I would have snagged a picture as ammunition for later. After he awoke.

If he ever wakes.

That thought lashed through me like a whip. I had no idea if Rowan would live. No idea if whatever had just happened in that alley—*being attacked by actual vampyres*—had taken too much from him. If the pale blue tinge to his lips meant he was already gone, just a body that hadn't figured it out yet.

Jules hooked an arm under mine, half-carrying me into the club as my legs trembled. My body decided it was done cooperating, done pretending I was fine, done holding it together. Every muscle shook as if I'd run a marathon.

Romeo opened the door expectantly—his massive frame filling the doorway, face carved from stone and just as expressive. He didn't ask questions. Didn't react to the blood painting Rowan's throat, to the way my hands shook, to Jules's tear-streaked face. He simply stepped aside, a silent sentinel to horrors he'd probably witnessed a thousand times before.

How many people has he seen carried through these doors?

Instead of moving straight towards the main floor—toward witnesses, towards normalcy, towards the comforting lie that the world made sense—Damien turned a sharp left. He followed the wall until it rounded over to the bar and led towards the back area, away from prying eyes and questions I couldn't answer.

I caught sight of Andy tending bar. His face blanched when he saw Rowan being carried, body slack in Damien's arms like a broken doll. Andy looked like he wanted to speak—his mouth opened, throat working—but thought better of it. Survival instinct, maybe. Or experience. He'd been at Oubliette long enough to know when to keep his mouth shut.

Not a soul dared to approach us.

Good. I don't have words for what just happened.

I expected Damien to take us down the hallway lined in burgundy velvet that led towards his office, but instead, he walked right past it to a set of stairs I'd never seen before. We descended those spiraling stairs down into the club's hidden heart. The air changed with every step—thicker, warmer, carrying scents that made my hindbrain scream warnings my conscious mind was too exhausted to process. Incense, sex, something copper-sharp that could have been blood or fear or both.

Faint moans drifted up from below, but they weren't only sounds of pleasure. There were moans of pain, of surrender, of euphoria, of sorrow—the sounds of people discovering *exactly* how much they could take before breaking. The quiet rasp of whispers felt like a thousand confessions brushing my ears at once, secrets whispered in darkness by people who thought no one was listening.

My fingers tightened around the iron banister, steadying myself against vertigo that had nothing to do with the stairs. The metal was cold beneath my palm—grounding and solid—to remind myself that I was real, that *this* was real. I focused on the certainty of cool iron pressed against my skin, because everything else felt like a fever dream.

At the bottom of the stairwell was a heavy-looking door, wrought from blackened metal set into the stonework of that deep underground basement. There were words inscribed on the door in a language I didn't recognize. Despite its anachronistic appearance, the door was automated—it swung open as Damien approached with Rowan in his arms.

It was in *that* moment the absurdity of the situation struck me. "Jules, what are we doing? Rowan needs a doctor. He needs to be taken to a hospital. Where are we going?"

"Sweetie," she said without slowing her pace or turning to look at me, "I am going to need you to trust me and Damien. I know that's going to be hard for you, but please. . . we are going to do our best to help your friend. Now, be mindful as you step through the door."

Anger seeped into my bones then, its fiery heat a reminder of what feeling powerless was like. My words struck out. "Where are you taking him? Why are we—"

My chest seized. Stepping through the threshold, past the heavy dark doors, struck me with an intense dizziness as my world shifted. My clothes were suddenly dry, and even Jules looked refreshed. Shit, what was that?

As she held me steady, Jules said, "Easy there, sweetie. Entering this place can be hard on you the first time, especially if you aren't in the right state of mind."

My thoughts were thick, but I was still able to ask the obvious. "Where are we? What is this place?"

"*Mi gatita*," Damien called over his shoulder, "it brings me pleasure to welcome you to my Second Circle. Although I do obviously wish you were here under more *auspicious* circumstances."

Second Circle? I made it. The thought was a bitter one. I had hoped to uncover the entrance of this place, to see if it was even real. I was convinced Edward was frequently within the Second Circle—convinced *that* was where he'd hidden himself away.

And there were plenty of places to hide.

Long straight hallways of polished obsidian stretched out in three directions—before us, to our right, to our left—and those halls were lined with a diverse variety of doors. The scope of it seemed impossible. The corridors shrank to small pinpricks of darkness on the distant horizon, with both sides of the hallways littered with doors. Between each door were torches of blue-tinted flames, giving off a clean and brilliant light without any hint of smoke.

"What happens behind those doors? What would I find if I opened them?" I asked, suddenly afraid to know the answer. I struggled to keep my senses, but the rage inside gave me the strength to poke at the world I was entering.

"It's complicated," Jules replied as we kept walking.

I realized then that I didn't want to know. Couldn't afford to wonder. My brain was already fracturing under the weight of too many impossibilities: vampyres existed, Natalia was one of them, Alice might be too, Jules knew far more about all of this than she should, and I was following a nightclub owner into his secret sex dungeon as he carried Rowan's dying body.

Oh god... Natalia is a vampyre.

That thought was relentless, and it unsettled me in ways I couldn't articulate. She'd been in my dorm room. She'd seemed *normal*—bitchy and beautiful and perhaps a little cold. But cold in the way college girls were so often cold, not in the way monsters were outright cruel.

And she *was* cruel. Heartless. She'd stood in that alley and watched the twins drain Rowan. Watched me fight, beg, scream, and break myself against their indifference. Watched like it was entertainment, like we were performances staged for her amusement. Asked me to debase myself at her feet for her pleasure.

All of that *before* she'd brutalized the twins with violence so casual it bordered on comedy.

Is Alice a vampyre, too? The question ate at me. Sweet and kind Alice. Alice, who seemed so demure and thoughtful. If her story about the two of them growing up together and sharing a wet nurse was to be believed, then it was certainly possible. If Alice was also a vampyre, if she'd been lying to me all that time, it would be just one more lie built on foundations of bullshit and blood—

Can't think about that now. Focus on Rowan first. Everything else later. Besides, I laughed at the absurdity of the thought, *things can't get much worse, right?*

As we continued down the hall, we passed doors of wood, of frosted glass, and of shimmering metal. I opened my mouth to ask how much further we were going when a wind rose from nowhere—no vents, no open windows, just a fierce wind buffeting against us. It fluttered our clothes, pulling at fabric with invisible fingers. My hair lifted, strands catching in my mouth, and I tasted copper and salt.

Damien stopped at a pair of tall doors carved from crimson wood. Like the previous doors we walked through, these too were automated and opened before him. The sound the doors made as they swung open was like a sigh of relief. Like a welcome.

The room was a gothic study out of a movie or dream. Shelves lined with ancient books climbed the walls, spines cracked and faded, titles I couldn't read in languages I didn't recognize. Some looked older than anything I'd seen, even in university archives, covers of vellum and leather and possibly human skin, binding knowledge I was willing to bet should have stayed forgotten.

A great fireplace hissed with green and blue flames that threw shadows across a wide oak desk scattered with papers. Upon the desk, serving as a hideous paperweight, sat a large bust of a boar-faced man with massive tusks. The scent of cinder and wine clung to the air throughout the room, thick and almost narcotic, making my head swim.

This is where Damien really works, not the office upstairs.

Damien crossed the room with unhurried grace, each step measured and deliberate, laying Rowan onto an immense settee. It was wine-dark velvet, a piece of furniture that probably cost more than my entire tuition.

Rowan looked small on it. Fragile. Two things he'd never been in all the years I'd known him.

Don't die. Please, don't die. Not like this.

"I will get something for the blood," Jules murmured. Her voice was steady, but I caught the tremor beneath it, the hairline cracks in her composure. She darted off through the door, leaving me alone with Damien.

He was bent over Rowan, unbuttoning his torn shirt with long, deft fingers that moved with practiced efficiency. Stripping away blood-soaked fabric, revealing pale skin painted with violence. The wounds were ghastly: strips of missing flesh near his neck and arm, clawed marks that had gone to the bone, meat and muscle exposed in ways that made my stomach lurch.

I'd seen worse in my previous life. I'd *experienced* worse. But this was different.

This was Rowan.

"Is he still alive? Can you help him?" My voice sounded thin and thready, like it was coming from very far away.

"He very well might live, but whether or not he wakes is far more uncertain." Damien's tone was even and conversational. He sounded as if he were discussing what he'd had for lunch and not Rowan's mortality.

My throat closed. Acid burned the back of my tongue. *Uncertain.* That word shouldn't exist in a world where I'd clawed my way back from death itself, where I'd been given this second chance.

"What can we do? What can *I* do?"

This time, Damien's eyes met mine. They were gold, yes, but a shade so dark they reflected the blue firelight, framed by impossibly long lashes. He was beautiful in ways that made my core clench and rushed heat through my body. I caught the scent of wine and cinder on his skin, something spicy and dangerous and intoxicating.

Stop. Don't look at him like that. Don't feel that. Rowan is dying, and you're getting wet over this guy.

"Ah, sweet *gatita*," he said, "I am afraid that there is little either of us can do for him right now. It is faint, but I can feel the presence of a Grim waiting beside him."

"What does *that* mean?"

Jules reappeared, balancing a basin and a cloth. She knelt across from me, movements quick and practiced like she'd done this before, cleaning wounds with a tenderness that belied her efficiency. Her hands were steady, even though I could see tears tracking down her face, cutting through makeup and leaving pale trails.

How many times has she done this? How many dying people has she tended to?

"*Gatita* means kitten," Damien said as he stood, tossing Rowan's shredded shirt into the blue-green flames. The fire hissed like a living serpent, sparks jumping high enough to make me flinch. The shirt didn't burn so much as dissolve, fabric turning to ash and acrid smoke that made my eyes water.

"You know that's not what I meant." The limited Spanish I knew from my family made it simple enough to follow the pet names he seemed to assign people. Now he was just pissing me off.

He rubbed his wrist, thinking aloud. "A Grim is a sort of *chaperone* of the soul to Death's realm. Most mortals have no clue how to find their way in the ever-expansive afterlife, so a Grim is often sent to offer guidance and assistance." He sighed. "I must confess that I did not expect this to happen."

I strode to Damien's side, desperation finally spilling over. My hands were shaking. My whole body was shaking. "You explain like *I'm* supposed to know what that all means. Tell me, how can we save him?"

I'll do anything. Trade anything. I already offered myself once tonight, and I'll do it again. Just save him.

Damien began to speak, mouth opening around words I desperately needed to hear when Jules's astonished voice said, "Look!"

I spun, heart in my throat, and watched the impossible happen.

Rowan's bare chest glowed faintly, like a dying ember fighting to rekindle. Gold light seeped through his skin—illuminating veins and arteries in a network of brilliance—as his wounds knit together. *Knit* is the closest word I can use to describe how his bite marks, slashes, and gashes weaved themselves closed. It was as if time ran in reverse, wounds fading away as though they had never been. His breathing steadied, deepened, and became the strong, even rhythm I'd heard thousands of times.

He's alive. Oh, thank god, he's alive. "Oh my god," I whispered as I perched beside him. My shaking hands hovered over his knitted flesh. I was desperate to touch him, but also afraid to. "How?"

Damien was suddenly next to me, the warmth of his body radiating between us. He hadn't crossed the room; he had simply appeared. "A god indeed," he said, amused. "Though *which* god is an interesting question, *mi gatita.*"

We both stared at the faint glow pulsing under Rowan's skin. For the briefest moment, a word shimmered across his collarbone, written in gold light before vanishing like breath on glass: *Lavernai.*

A small gasp escaped Jules and me both.

"Was that word important?" My voice seemed to echo in the cavernous study as Rowan's chest rose and fell steadily, a rhythm that made my heart stutter in disbelief. I couldn't breathe fast enough, couldn't think straight enough to process the miracle before me.

He's healing. He's actually healing. This is real. This is happening.

Damien's gaze sharpened, all humor gone. "Well, it would appear that he does bear the *mark* of a god."

Confusion laced my words. "What?"

"No," he mused to himself, ignoring me. "This seems to be *more* than simple divine intervention at play here."

I opened my mouth to ask Damien what he meant, but stopped when I saw Rowan's pale blue eyes flutter open. They were unfocused, as though he were trying to remember where he or *who* he was.

Then they locked onto mine.

"Are you hurt?" His voice was raw, ragged, barely a whisper, but it was like a chorus in my ears.

My knees gave way as my vision blurred, and I fell forward, throwing my arms around him without thought. "Am I hurt?" My voice was thick. "I thought I'd lost you." I choked on my tears as I buried my face against his neck, inhaling the scent of him—sweat, blood, pine, life. "I thought. . . I thought you—"

The words died. I couldn't finish them. Couldn't articulate the abyss that had opened beneath me when those twins latched onto his throat, couldn't explain the way my world had narrowed to the wet sound of them feeding, couldn't describe the same sense of helplessness I had only ever felt one other time before. A kaleidoscope of pain echoed through my entire being despite the relief I felt at the insistent beating of Rowan's heart, which seemed to match my own fervent pace.

At the end of my first life, the fear, desperation, and hopelessness of Edward killing me? That amalgamation of feelings. . . watching Rowan die in front of me felt the same.

"I am here," he murmured, voice hoarse yet resolute. He wrapped an arm around me, his hand trembling slightly as it pressed against my back. "I am here."

I couldn't stop crying. The tears flowed freely now, hot and unrelenting. My body shook against his, desperate to anchor him to me, to make sure he was truly, undeniably real. Every second I'd feared he was gone replayed through my mind, and as I processed that he was here—alive and safe—relief burned through me like a wildfire.

"You can't do that to me again, Rowan," I whispered, voice breaking as I pressed my mouth to his neck. I felt his heartbeat against my lips, steady and strong. "You don't get to call me reckless ever again. Not when you nearly died brawling with *vampyres* in a back alley. Don't ever do that. Not again. Not ever."

I can't watch you die. I cannot. I've buried too many pieces of myself already.

His free hand lifted slowly, brushing my hair back from my tear-streaked face, his touch gentle but grounding. "I will not make a promise I cannot keep, Violet." He said with a lilt of humor, using the same phrase I had used against him from what seemed like ages ago.

"Hypocritical ass." I half laughed, half sobbed, and hugged him tighter. My fingers dug into his skin as though holding him could make the last moments of fear vanish, could rewrite history so I never had to watch blood pour from his throat, never had to hear those wet, obscene feeding sounds, never had to taste that bitter flavor of helplessness again.

"I was so scared," I admitted, shivering against him. The confession felt like peeling off my skin, exposing raw nerve endings to air. "I don't even want to think about. . ." I trailed off, the words not needing to be said.

Don't make me survive losing you. I can't. Not after everything.

Rowan's lips pressed briefly against the top of my head, a soft promise. "I am not going anywhere. You have my word."

Liar. Everyone leaves eventually. Everyone dies or betrays or decides you're not worth the trouble. That's what I learned with Edward.

But I wanted to believe Rowan. I wanted to believe *in* Rowan. I *needed* to believe both in him, *and* in this life I'd learned to share with him.

"Well," Damien said, "I am an avid and enthusiastic fan of happy endings, especially when those endings are between lovers. However, I have never been a fan of *deus ex machina* in my stories. I find the involvement of a god to be rather. . . offensive." His voice cut through the warmth of our moment, smooth and teasing. His tone was laced with an amusement that felt inappropriate given we'd just witnessed what seemed like a miracle.

Rowan stiffened beside me, muscles going rigid beneath my hands. I looked up to see his gaze sliding between Jules and Damien, sharpening into that hunter's focus I'd seen a handful of times. The look that said he'd identified a threat and was calculating how to survive it.

"A demon?" Rowan's voice was low and dangerous, stripped of the gentleness he'd just shown me. He pushed himself up to sit. "No, a *High Demon*. Why is there a High Demon here?"

High Demon? What is a High Demon? How is that different from a regular demon? Are there rankings? Hierarchies?

Too many questions. My brain couldn't process them fast enough, couldn't catalog the information flooding in faster than I could sort it.

"You mean Damien?" I turned my tear-streaked face to stare back at the proprietor of Oubliette, unsure of what Rowan saw that I was missing. To me, Damien looked like a man. A beautiful man, yes. In fact, so beautiful it was unsettling. But still just a man.

Damien's smile faltered a fraction before he composed himself. "Well, you've certainly lost quite a lot of blood just now. I imagine you are feeling rather confused and—"

"Why is there a High Demon here?" Rowan repeated.

"Oh, come now," Damien said with an air of disbelief. "I know I *do* look devilishly handsome. But in case you weren't aware, High Demons are a rather rare sight. Not nearly common enough for one to stumble across you in a back alley during an evening stroll."

My stomach dropped. Rowan's glare did not waver. "Do not mock me, demon. Though you are the first I have met, I know that your kind bears a mark to distinguish you from lesser demons."

That seemed to grab ahold of Damien's attention. "Fascinating," he said with a toothy smile and an arched eyebrow. The shift in Rowan's attitude ratcheted up the tension in the room, but Damien kept his tone casual. "And do tell me, what *mark* would that be?"

"Your two hearts."

For the first time, Damien froze. Humor drained from his expression, replaced by a dangerous calm that accentuated the firelight flickering against the walls, as if the fire itself feared him. "I would wager you'd been blessed by Godsblood to be able to discern my two hearts with nothing more than a glance." He laughed as if he'd told the punchline to a joke nobody else understood. "So, what gift were you given, then? You can see through my flesh and into my chest as if I were made of glass? Peruse through the thoughts in my head and read them at your leisure like a book?"

Rowan's eyes narrowed as he said, "I can hear one heart beating in your chest while the other beats in your lying tongue."

His tongue? How does that work?

I saw it then—the shift in Damien's posture, the faint tightening of his jaw, the flash of anger in his golden eyes. His body became a coiled spring, a sheathed blade, a marauder about to pounce. The weight of his fury pressed down upon all of us in the room like a storm gathering overhead, and even Jules—normally so composed and confident—cowered before him.

Fear curled through me, icy and sharp. We were in a room with someone who could end us in an eyeblink. I didn't know how I knew this, but I could feel it in the very depths of my bones. Damien was beyond dangerous.

And yet...

Rowan's presence emboldened me, and—whether it was true or not—gave me the feeling that we could face anything together.

He's insane. We're both insane. This was going to get us killed.

But maybe I didn't care. Maybe after spending my entire first life making myself small and quiet and obedient just to survive, I was done with simple self-preservation. Maybe I was ready to burn if it meant burning brightly along with someone I trusted.

Damien stepped closer, slow, deliberate, each footfall measured like a count towards execution. I held my breath. The firelight danced across his sharp features, his eyes locked on Rowan's, each measuring the other with the weight of predators deciding if the fight was worth it.

The quiet pressed down, almost unbearable, broken only by the soft crackle of the fireplace. I clutched Rowan's arm, holding him close, knowing that whatever came next, he wouldn't yield easily—and I wouldn't let him face it alone.

"I do wish you had not said that aloud, *chico valiente*. You owe me a great boon for what you have forced me to do," Damien's voice cut through the silence like a razor, his words as solemn as a eulogy.

The nickname caught me off guard. Brave boy? What was he talking about? A boon? That's medieval shit. Fantasy novel shit. Not real-life shit.

Except apparently it was real life now. Apparently, everything was real: vampyres and demons and gods and grimoires and resurrections.

Jules stepped close with her hands clasped together over her chest. There were tears in her eyes, and her voice cracked, sounding desperate and hopeless as she begged, "Wait! Please! I promise never to—"

Then everything changed.

Chapter 30

Rowan

Damien's hand struck Jules in the chest—punched through Jules's sternum like it was wet paper, then yanked her heart out. It looked as easy for the High Demon as plucking a flower.

The sound was from a twisted nightmare that I'll never un-hear. Organic and hollow—ribs cracking, tissue tearing, blood splattering. The worst was the wet sucking noise of her heart being ripped from her chest. Jules didn't scream. She didn't have time. Her eyes went wide, mouth forming a perfect 'o' of shock, and then she was falling.

Crumpling.

Gone.

One moment she'd been speaking—alive, present, her heartbeat steady in my ears. The next, silence. That vital rhythm snuffed out like someone had blown out a candle.

I'd barely caught the motion; it was little more than a blur of movement. Damien's hand, clutching Jules's heart, was already back at his side by the time I registered what happened.

Too fast. Far too fast.

I'd seen death before. Lived with it. Even died myself—twice now it seemed—before coming back. I'd watched Nightbeasts tear through human flesh like wolves through deer. Watched hypothermia turn skin blue-black and brittle. Watched starvation hollow out eye sockets until nothing remained but animalistic desperation.

But this? This was new.

The casual brutality of it, the effortless murder of someone who'd done nothing wrong, the callous snuffing out of a light as bright as Jules's... I reached out, gripped Violet's hand, and squeezed her as tight as I could without hurting her. I knew the shock and hurt that must have been rippling through her.

Every muscle in my body locked down, rigid and overwhelmed with a feeling that only came over me from watching the innocent die. That feeling was not fear. I'd crossed that threshold years ago, died twice already, and knew what waited for me beyond that horizon. Fear was a luxury for people who hadn't already stared into Death's face.

This was rage, blinding and hot. Pure, crystalline, murderous rage born from decades of watching predators devour prey and being too small, too weak, too *late* to stop it.

"You..." The word scraped out of my throat like broken glass. I couldn't finish the sentence. Couldn't find the word adequate for what he'd just done, what he was. "*Chudovishche.*"

The word felt insufficient. Weak. But it was all I had in that moment.

"How astute." Damien stood there, his fingers dripping crimson, and reached into his breast pocket with his clean hand. Drew out a white silk handkerchief, began wiping blood off with the casual air of someone cleaning off paint after an art project. Each stroke deliberate. Unhurried. The red stained the pristine fabric in spreading blooms.

"The location of a High Demon's second heart is our most closely guarded secret. Knowing that secret is akin to having my life in your hands." His voice was soft and conversational, as if he were discussing the weather rather than the murder he'd just committed. Those gilded eyes caught the firelight and gleamed with an unsettling luminescence that was utterly inhuman. "You should think well before you speak again."

The threat landed with the accuracy of an arrow to the heart. It had not been loud nor theatrical. But it was the most sincere threat I've ever been given, all the same.

Damien walked to the fireplace and tossed the blood-soaked handkerchief into the flames. The silk caught immediately, curled black, then disintegrated into ash and memory.

Every survival instinct I'd honed over my lifetime in the Wasteland screamed at me to bow, to submit, to recognize the apex predator and make myself small. This thing wearing a man's face could end me as easily as he'd ended Jules. My heightened hearing couldn't save me. My tracking skills wouldn't matter. He was speed and violence wrapped in expensive suits and honeyed words.

But Violet was still breathing beside me, her pulse hammering in my ears, her hand trembling in mine. Knowing she was there, that I was responsible for keeping her safe, made supplication impossible.

"So, you plan to kill us now as well, High Demon?" My voice came out low, barely more than a hiss, but it cut through the crackling fire and the terrible silence Jules's death left behind.

"Oh, *chico valiente*," Damien said while waving his hand, "I don't believe there is any need for further violence. I know the secret location of my hidden heart is safe with the two of you."

I scowled. "Why in the name of any god would we keep your secrets after you have killed our friend?"

Damien's lingering gaze slid to Violet, paused, then back to me. His eyes looked focused. Calculating. "I need you both to understand something about the situation we find ourselves in. I have made it an *artform* to only surround myself with individuals whom I find singularly interesting, useful, entertaining, or some combination of those three. I've known Jules since a time before your ancestors climbed down from the trees and stood upright. Throughout the millennia together, I have come to cherish her company more than most. *That* is why I gave her a swift and painless end." He took a deep breath. "I would not be inclined to do the same for either of you should my secret leave this room. I would visit upon you both—with a joyous and childlike glee—a holocaust of suffering that neither of you is capable of imagining, despite the horrors you have each seen throughout your lives. Are you both understanding me?"

In my peripheral, I saw Violet nod. I felt compelled to do the same.

"*Maravilloso*," Damien said as he spread his hands and smiled.

At the sight of him looking so insufferably smug and triumphant, everything I knew of demons flashed through my mind in a rush. Granted, everything I knew could fit in my back pocket and still leave space for my wallet. Still, there was one thing I felt nearly certain of.

Nearly.

Fuck, this is going to be a gamble.

"I suppose," I said, "you have more to offer us than simple threats, demon?"

Damien's smiling face froze, his whole body still. "Would you prefer complex threats?"

I sighed, as if bored with the conversation. "I would *prefer* that we agree to some terms. You mentioned that I owe you a boon, then you give us conditions for our silence. As far as I am concerned, my silence can serve as my boon, and we can be done with each other."

"Ah," he said, "I see where you wish to take this. You're even more knowledgeable than Jules let on. Am I to assume you wish to forge a contract then? Make our arrangement *official*?"

"Rowan," Violet asked, her voice tinged with sorrow and fear, "what's he talking about?"

I turned to look at Violet. "He is a demon. They live to make deals. To bind mortals within convoluted contracts. It is in their nature."

"*Si*, your man is correct there, *mi gatita*. But if we are to be honest with one another, who *doesn't* love a good deal?" Damien turned from us and looked towards a bust upon his desk before he said, "Ciriatto, would you be kind enough to bring me a pot of coffee and remove Jules, please?"

The statue didn't respond. I wasn't sure how I would have reacted if it had.

Damien moved to the leather chair behind his desk, the blue and green fire roaring behind him, and settled into the plush seat with the languid grace of a cat claiming sun-warmed stone. He gestured for us to sit in the two chairs in front of his desk.

Where did those come from? I knew I'd been distracted—coming back from the dead could do that to a person, I supposed—but how had I not noticed the two chairs in the middle of the room?

Violet cocked her head. "Those weren't there a second ago."

"You are very observant," Damien said as he gestured again for us to sit. Once we had, he continued. "Now, you must understand, you are negotiating from a place of weakness. Aside from the overwhelmingly obvious fact that you are entirely at my mercy here in Second Circle beneath my nightclub, there is the slightly less obvious truth that this tragedy is entirely your own fault. After all," he said and pointed a slender finger at me, "you shared secrets that were not yours to share. You spoke carelessly in the presence of others. You *forced* my hand."

My jaw clenched so hard I feared I'd break a tooth. "Bullshit."

"And as I explained to you both earlier, I am *quite* fond of Jules. I have been for literal ages. Not only is she a singular companion, dare I go so far as to call her a friend, but she helps me run many of my Oubliettes. She is, in a word, *irreplaceable*." He clucked his teeth and shook his head, the very image of dejected sorrow. "Such genuine sweetness in a person has always been, and I do believe always will continue to be, exceedingly rare. I shall miss her terribly."

"*You* killed her," Violet and I said in unison. From her, the words were a hot venom she nearly shouted in anger. From me, the words came out icy, flat, dead. In that same cadaver, tone I said, "Her death will rest on your conscience. Not mine."

"Oh, on the contrary." Those golden eyes fixed on me, ancient and merciless. "You were the one who created this situation that necessitated her death. It was your thoughtless carelessness. Therefore," he gestured between us, "*you* owe *me* recompense. As I said, a boon would be appropriate. A favor of my choosing, to be called upon whenever I should require it."

I laughed. Couldn't help it. The sound came out harsh and bitter, scraping against the elegant room like nails against silk. "You are insane if you think I will give you anything. You are nothing more than a murderous demon. Jules's death is your fault. It was your *choice* to kill her. There is no world where I owe you aid or recompense for your own bloodlust."

Damien smiled. The expression was beautiful and terrible at once, a glimpse of something vast and hungry wearing human features like a poorly fitted mask. "Oh, but you will help me, *chico valiente*. Both of you will." He leaned back, crossed one leg over the other. "Because I am the only way you will ever find Edward Fitzgerald."

The name slammed into me—a sledgehammer to the stomach.

Beside me, Violet went rigid. Her pulse spiked—I heard it, that sudden acceleration, the rabbit-quick panic of prey recognizing the carnivore's scent, and I knew she was thinking exactly what I was.

How? How does he know that name? How could he possibly know about Edward? I'd been careful. Violet had been careful. We hadn't spoken that name in public, hadn't given anybody, either within Oubliette or outside of it, any reason to connect us to Edward.

What else does he know? That question ricocheted through my skull, spawned a dozen more. Did he know about Violet's previous life? About her rebirth? Did he understand what she was, what we *both* were?

Then an even more important—far more terrifying—thought occurred. *What impossible terms will Violet agree to if this High Demon can actually deliver Edward to her?*

As Violet and I sat there considering how to reply to Damien's question, the door to his study opened. A seven-foot-tall boar-faced demon squeezed into the room carrying a silver tray with a pot and a cup of white porcelain. Fifty years from my first life of seeing truly weird shit all over the Wastelands greatly helped me keep my composure in that moment.

Violet did not have that experience.

"Ohmyfuckinggodwhatthefuckisthat?" She scrambled out of her chair and away from the new demon.

There was a heartbeat where nobody moved or said anything before the boar-faced demon replied, "Coffee."

"Ciriatto," Damien addressed the boar-faced demon, "thank you. You can place it right here on the desk. And if you would be so kind as to take Jules's body back to her room? I'll see to her after I have finished with this meeting."

Massive and silent, the demon's pig-like face was as blank as fresh snow. He set the silver tray in front of Damien, then turned to Jules. He lifted her as if she weighed nothing.

No, as if she means nothing. As if her death means nothing.

She was nothing more than a broken thing to be disposed of. Her head lolled back, arms hanging loose, blood still dripping from the cavity in her chest. The demon's expression never changed. He simply carried her towards the door, her body swaying with his measured steps.

My stomach twisted. Bile burned the back of my throat. I turned from the sight of Jules being carted away like a sack of meat and took several deep breaths. *This is what gods and demons and all the rest of the supernaturals do. They take and take and take all that they can, just because they can.*

The room pressed in around me. I focused my senses on my surroundings in an attempt to ground myself, to not let my fury and sorrow take control. Shelves climbed towards the shadowed ceiling above, each packed with ancient tomes—their spines cracked and faded. Many titles I recognized, even from this distance: *The Sixth and Seventh Books of Moses, Pseudomonarchia Daemonum, The Lesser Key of Solomon.* Forbidden texts I'd only heard whispered about in my previous life, now casually displayed like trophies.

The scattered paperwork on Damien's desk was covered in sigils penned in ink that shimmered faintly in the firelight. I recognized some of those as well: binding circles, warding marks, symbols from random grimoires. Others were older, stranger, pulled from traditions I didn't know. The air smelled of coffee, cinders, and red wine, heavy enough to taste. My hearing picked up the hiss and pop of the fireplace and, beneath that, the steady thrum of Damien's two hearts.

One in his chest where it should be. One in his tongue where it shouldn't.

He leaned forward, all dangerous elegance: skin the color of burnished earth catching firelight, hair swept back to reveal a face too perfect for mortality, eyes molten amber that seemed to peel me apart. The scent of him rolled over me—cardamom, sandalwood, something faintly carnal.

"Now, where were we?" Damien poured coffee into his delicate porcelain cup, the stream of dark liquid smooth and controlled. "I believe you two were processing your shock over how I knew you were hunting a man named Edward Fitzgerald, *sí?*"

I felt Violet's hand tighten in mine, heard her breathing change—faster, shallower. Her heart hammering in her chest sounded like it was trying to break free.

She wanted Edward dead. Needed it the way I'd once needed warmth in the tundra, needed it with a desperation that eclipsed reason and self-preservation. Vengeance was her north star, the fixed point around which everything else orbited.

If Damien was offering her a path to Edward's throat—

Fuck.

She'd take it. Of course, she would. She'd make a deal with this demon wearing human skin, would bind herself to him with obligations and boons, and walk straight into whatever trap he'd carefully constructed.

Because revenge mattered more than safety.

Because some scales needed balancing, even if it cost everything.

I'd spent fifty years learning when to run, when to fight, when to make deals with devils. And every instinct I possessed was screaming that this was the kind of bargain you didn't walk away from. The kind that followed you like a shadow, collected its due with interest, left you wondering when the other shoe would finally drop.

But Violet?

Violet was already leaning forward, her voice steady despite the chaos I could hear in her pulse. "You can deliver him to me?"

And there it was.

The moment she stopped asking *if* we should deal with this demon and started negotiating *terms*.

I watched Damien's smile widen, watched those golden eyes gleam with satisfaction as he sipped his coffee. "But of course I can, *mi gatita*. And I am confident that I already know the answer to this next question, but I *do* want to hear it directly from your lips." He paused and sipped his coffee. "*Why* does someone gifted by the God of Time want to find Edward Fitzgerald?"

God of Time?

Things were still hazy—my mind struggling to catch up with being resurrected, with the golden door I saw, with Death herself releasing me, with Jules's sudden murder—and Violet answered before I could, her voice steady where my own was not.

"Vengeance," was all she said.

The word thrummed through the room like a loosed arrow. It struck me in the chest as well—an echo, a kinship I couldn't unfeel. Her heartbeat spiked. I heard it clearly, hammering against her ribs.

Damien clicked his tongue, amused. The sound was sharper than it should have been, almost metallic. "*Mi gatita*. . . how primitive." His smile was too perfect for how dangerous he truly was. "You seek vengeance upon a man for pain he rendered upon you in a different life?"

He knows too much. How does he know about Violet's rebirth?

I tensed, bare skin prickling with cold despite the heat from the fireplace. My eyes moved to Violet, and I saw her hand clench—knuckles white, tendons standing out like bowstrings. The fracture showed behind her resolve, hairline cracks in stone about to break. She glanced at me quickly, searching for something, then turned back to him.

"Both lives are me," she said, voice taut as wire. "The joy I've experienced in this life does not erase the pain he caused me in my previous life."

My heart hammered against my sternum. "Violet, we can surely find another way to get to Edward." The words were fire on my tongue, ash in my throat. "He *killed* Jules."

Her breath hitched—I heard it catch, heard the wet sound of tears she was holding back. "I know he did." She turned to me, and her eyes held a haunted shadow I recognized. This was a side of her I had barely glimpsed, seen glimmers of beyond the youth she portrayed. She looked like someone who had seen death countless times. Someone, I realized, like me. "But I have to hear him out, Rowan. If he can get me closer to Edward—"

"At what cost?" I asked.

"At *any* cost. Part of me feels as if," she paused and struggled for the right words, "as if killing him is the reason I am here. The reason I was given this second chance."

I squeezed her hand. "Violet, you do not know that."

"And neither do you," she snapped. "How could you? You know so much about this supernatural shit we're in," she said as she waved her hand around the room. "But you don't know how or why I was reborn. It had to be for a reason. Just... forget it. You wouldn't understand."

Damien chuckled, the sound resonating in his chest in strange harmonics. His two hearts beat out of sync with each other, creating a rhythm that hurt my head if I focused on it too long. "I imagine he would understand better than most. He is, afterall, grappling with his own form of reincarnation."

Violet's eyes widened in disbelief, her expression pained. Her pulse jumped. "What?"

Shame poured from every pore—I could smell it on myself, sharp and acrid, mixing with the cinder-wine air. I looked away from her, focusing on Damien. "Demon," I said with malice, "that was not your secret to share."

He set his coffee cup down and placed his hand over his chest in mock surprise. "Oh? Did I thoughtlessly share a secret of yours aloud? Did I carelessly let slip something you would have much preferred to keep quiet? I cannot *begin* to fathom how that must feel."

"It's true?" Violet asked. The hurt in her voice matched the pain on her face.

I opened my mouth to answer her, but Damien spoke first. "*Sí*, it's true, he never told you, shame on him. Now you two handle it on your own time." He waved his hand dismissively. "Let us return to the topic at hand—writing up a contract for how we are going to all help each other get what we want."

My patience thinned like ice over deep water. I shifted forward in my chair. I could not stand idle while he toyed with her. "Violet, we can find another way."

She turned on me, heat rising in her cheeks. "There is no other way. I've searched Oubliette for weeks and haven't been able to find even a whisper about him."

"But you cannot enter a contract with a High Demon." A tang of fear rose beneath my ribs into my mouth.

"The contract was your idea! Why did you even bother bringing it up if we weren't going to do it?"

I ran a hand through my hair and took a breath. "I suspected he planned to kill us to keep the secret of his hearts safe, and *I* was the one who was going to enter a contract with him to prevent that. Not us. Not you." I looked her in her eyes. "I have had some experience with this sort of thing."

Violet's eyes widened—betrayal hitting her like a physical blow. Her breathing went shallow. "Oh, so entering contracts with demons is *something else* on your resume? Is that *another* secret you hid from me?"

"Violet, I did not hide—"

"Bullshit! When I told you about my previous life, you didn't think to mention you'd gone through the same thing?"

"It is not the same—"

"Do you know how alone and crazy I've felt ever since I was reborn?" Time seemed to slow. Guilt and fear tangled together within me as blood roared in my veins.

"Violet, please! Charlie and Levi refused—"

"*They* already told you before I did? Are you serious?"

"What? No, listen."

But she wasn't listening, and I feared this miscommunication would be the death of her.

Her hands clutched into fists. She turned her furious gaze to Damien, and I heard her decision before she spoke it—heard it in the way her heartbeat steadied, in the way her breathing deepened with resolve. "I will give you anything," she said.

My heart dropped. The fire hissed.

Damien's grin widened, predatory and pleased. He leaned forward to pick his coffee cup back up. "But what if the thing I want is not yours to give?"

Confusion crossed Violet's face for the briefest beat until Damien's gaze slid past her and straight to me. *This will not end well.*

"The thing which I seek," he purred, and I felt the words vibrate through me, "lies buried in your boyfriend's chest right there."

The words washed over me like ice water. Cold spread from my sternum outward, numbing my fingers and toes. I felt something shift within me: tightness shrinking around my ribs, pressure building behind my breastbone, as if my heart had suddenly grown twice its size.

"No," Violet whispered, barely audible even to my enhanced hearing. My blood turned to ice as she spoke, her voice breaking. "You can't have him."

Damien laughed—dark and indulgent, like espresso poured over cream. The sound echoed strangely in the room, bouncing off leather-bound spines and polished wood. "Oh, I don't want him, *mi gatita.*" His amber eyes gleamed in the firelight, pupils expanding and contracting like a cat's. "No, not him. I seek what's buried *within* him."

Everything in me went taut, my muscles coiling and jaw clenching hard enough that my teeth ached. I tried—and most likely failed—to not let my terror show.

Damien's voice was syrupy and slow, each word deliberate, as his attention moved back to Violet. "My offer is a simple one. You seek a man. I know where he is. I know how to get to him. I know the desires that drive him, the sins that sustain him. But. . ." he trailed off as his gaze shifted to me, raking me up and down—slow, appreciative, invasive. "But such knowledge requires payment."

"I don't understand," she said. "What is it you *want* from me? From Rowan? What do you mean buried inside of him?"

Damien's gaze was still on me as he said, "There is something buried within him. Some type of artifact or relic that has become entwined with his soul. Now, I cannot discern precisely *what* this artifact is nor how in the names of the Nine it got there, but it very much *feels* as if it's connected to The Library somehow."

The Library.

Memories rushed forward like a waterfall. The mythical halls of The Library, the luminous golden tome I'd stolen from there, my hapless and hopeless run through the Wastelands to escape the Library's Hunter, all ending with that Hunter's blade sliding between my ribs.

Violet's voice was still tinged with anger. "Rowan, do you know what he's talking about?"

The fire spat mockingly as the silence stretched between us. Eventually, I nodded. "Somewhat. I do not know anything about an artifact, but I am familiar with The Library."

"Familiar with The Library," Damien echoed, then laughed. "You say something so outlandish with such casual flippancy, as if you were discussing popping into a gas station."

Violet said, "I am assuming we're not discussing a regular library and this is more 'supernatural beyond the veil' shit?"

I nodded again, still staring at the demon. "Why do you want access to The Library?" I asked, voice flat.

Damien's eyes widened, and I caught a glimmer of genuine surprise flicker across his face. Both of his hearts beat in perfect unison for the briefest moment. "*Why?* It is *The Library*. It has been the source, seat, and storage of all that has ever been known or will yet to be known since before the dawn of time." He spread his hands as if the answer were obvious, fingers catching the firelight. "Why would I *not* want to go there? Why wouldn't anyone?"

Fair point to a stupid question.

A thought hit me then. "If you seek The Library, why not use a portal to get there? A door like the one Jules used?" I thought back to the night Violet was drugged—the knowing void peering into me, the feel of being hooked and yanked through that endless emptiness, the swirling iridescent lights taking shape and gaining solidity. "Surely a High Demon as ancient as you claim to be must have a portal door like this one?"

Damien's expression darkened, just slightly. Both hearts stuttered, then resumed their irregular rhythm. He poured himself more coffee, and the dark liquid caught the green-blue firelight, turning it into something that looked like liquid shadow. "Because to reach The Library through a conventional *portal door*, as you call it, one must pass through The Lighthouse." He took a slow sip. "And The Lighthouse Keeper is rather... wroth with me."

"Wroth," Violet repeated, skepticism sharp in her voice. "You could just say angry. What did you do?"

Damien's smile was all teeth, white and sharp in the firelight. "That, *gatita*, is a story for another time." He took another sip, savoring it. "What matters right now in the course of our negotiations is that I cannot go by way of The Lighthouse, which means I must find an alternate entrance. And that," he pointed to my chest, "I do believe will be the key to unlocking that entrance."

I felt the trap closing—heard it in the way the room's ambient sounds seemed to contract, in the way even the fire's crackle became expectant. "So, you want to rip this thing out of my chest, then?"

"No," he said as he shook his head and set down his coffee cup. "I mean, I certainly *could* tear you to pieces and hope whatever relic has bound itself to your soul doesn't get destroyed in the process. However," he said with another ingratiating smile, "that is a rather barbaric solution to a uniquely elegant situation."

I scoffed. "Well, thank the *gods* you are not a barbarian, demon."

"Despite how unfortunate the circumstances under which we have met were and regardless of what you may think of me, I am typically *not* a violent individual. Indeed, I would much prefer to find a path forward where we can *all* get what we desire."

What I desire is that you never killed Jules. I nearly spat that thought out in anger before the demon continued his sales pitch.

"There is the Strega of the First House," he said, lifting his coffee cup. "She is the owner and landlord of the Den of Nine Sins. She knows the oldest of the old ways, possesses the ancient magics gifted only to mortals, and walks the forgotten paths. Not only can she safely remove that relic from your chest, but she can identify how it can be used to get to The Library."

Strega of the First House. The title felt familiar, as if I'd read it somewhere long ago. I sat there, combing through my memories to place where I knew the word from.

"Why not go ask her yourself?" Violet asked, voice tight with suspicion.

Damien laughed with genuine amusement. "Ah, *mi gatita*, if only it were so simple. Her house is. . . hungry for me. I cannot set foot inside that place without paying a price I am unwilling to pay."

The way he said *hungry* made my skin crawl as if we all knew it was not a metaphor nor an exaggeration. I asked, "You want us to go in your place?"

"Precisely." He set down his coffee cup with a soft *clink* against the silver tray. "You return to me with that relic currently residing within, you along with the knowledge of how to get to The Library. In return, I shall give you Edward Fitzgerald's location along with every sordid detail of where he hides, who protects him, and how to end him."

Violet's hands trembled. The war in her played out in her heartbeat: desire and fear, vengeance and cost, all fighting for dominance as her pulse pounded. "You said that Rowan owed you a boon because he forced you to kill Jules," she said. "How does any of this absolve him from that?"

Damien smiled even wider. "Oh, you are such a sharp one, *gatita*. Don't worry your pretty little head on your boyfriend's behalf. We'll draw up a contract, put all of this in writing, and make it official. We can specify the conditions under which he shall be absolved from owing me recompense then. So," he purred as he leaned forward, "Do we have a deal?"

I looked at Violet and held my breath as I waited for her reply.

Chapter 31

Violet

*D*o *we have a deal?*

Damien's question hung in the air like smoke from a funeral pyre—thick, choking, impossible to escape. His amber eyes caught the firelight, patient as a cat watching a mouse decide which direction to run, knowing it didn't matter because all paths led to the same place.

This is it. This is my chance.

Damien was offering the answer I'd been clawing towards since the moment I was reborn. *Edward.* His location. His habits. His hiding places. Every single detail I needed to make him bleed the way he'd made me bleed, to hear him scream the way I'd screamed into pillows and gags and empty rooms that echoed with my silence.

I tasted it, the copper tang of his blood on my tongue. The salt of his fear in the air. The bitter-sweet satisfaction of watching realization dawn in his eyes as he understood—finally, *finally* understood—that the nine-year-old girl he'd shattered and sold and rebuilt into merchandise had grown teeth sharp enough to tear out his throat.

All I have to do is risk Rowan's life. That's all.

Just Rowan. Just the boy I'd grown up with, shared a childhood with, had a thousand memories of. Just the boy who'd grown into a man who made me feel safe, seen, whole, and cherished. Just the man who'd died while protecting those he cared for.

And what did he do when he came back from the dead? His first impulse had been to shield me from whatever fresh hell was unfolding. Rowan was the only person in the supernatural shitshow my life had become who I trusted, one of the only people who looked at me like I was actually *worth* protecting.

But it hadn't been enough. Jules's death still reigned, her empty eyes now another weight of memories to the ones I bore watching Edward kill the other girls in his ownership. . . all the while knowing my time would come one day. I would never forgive the demon for what he did, but he was the one who held what I wanted.

The pressure in my chest built, squeezed, and made breathing feel like work. Jules's body—wherever they'd taken it—probably wasn't even cold yet. That massive pig-faced nightmare demon had only just carried her out, her arms swinging loose and head lolling back. And already Damien sat there sipping his goddamn coffee like murder was just another Friday night expense to be written off in whatever ledger demons kept.

Now he wants to gamble with another life. With Rowan's life.

I felt the weight of Rowan's hand wrapped around mine. His fingers were long, his grip strong enough to anchor me but loose enough that I could pull away if I wanted. He wasn't holding me captive in his grip. He was just there. Present. *Real.* His hand was the only comforting thing I could grab hold of in a room that smelled of smoke, wine, and blood—the coppery aftermath of Jules's murder. It was a scent that clung to the air like cloying perfume, sweet and organic and wrong.

I focused on Rowan's thumb as he traced small circles on the back of my hand. The gesture was unconscious, automatic—comfort offered without thought because that's who he was beneath all the cynicism and anger. He was someone who'd appointed himself my protector without asking. Someone who'd shadowed me and guarded me because he'd decided I was worth defending.

He was also someone who'd hidden the truth about his own rebirth while I drowned in the isolation of mine.

The thought burned through me again, acid-hot and vicious. All those weeks of feeling insane—of wondering if I was the only one walking around with two lifetimes bleeding into each other like watercolors in rain, of thinking I was losing my mind—and he'd *known.* He'd been through the exact same cosmic screw-up and never said a word to me.

He knew before I told him. Daddy and Charlie told him. Of course they did. That's why they sent him here to babysit me. Two men whom I thought I could trust with anything had shared my secret behind my back while I was still trying to figure out if I was crazy or not.

And Rowan had just. . . what? Decided I didn't deserve to know he understood? Decided to let me suffer alone while he played cryptic bodyguard and tracked my movements like I was prey he couldn't quite decide whether to protect or study?

How dare he?

But also—

He died for me tonight.

The image was seared into my brain like a brand—his body on the ground of that dirty alley, blood mingling with rainwater as it spread out beneath him like a blanket. The sight of it—not dripping but *flowing*, pulsing out with each weakening heartbeat until there was more of him on the ground than in his veins. His eyes went distant, unfocused, the way an animal's eyes went when they stopped fighting and slipped away to wherever souls went.

Yet he'd come back. *Somehow.*

And now this perfectly sculpted demon, this eerily sexy *thing* wearing human skin like a bespoke suit, wanted to send us to some mysterious Strega—whatever that was—who could supposedly extract something from Rowan's chest or soul or whatever. . . *without* killing him in the process.

Because demons from the stories I knew were all *so highly regarded* for their honesty and concern for human welfare. Because I could totally trust that a deal with this demon wouldn't end with Rowan bleeding out on another floor while I held his hand and felt his pulse stutter and stop again.

My throat tightened. Anger, gratitude, grief, and anxiety all coiled together into a knot I couldn't untangle. The swirl of emotions stuck in my throat, as jagged as broken glass.

I didn't understand half of what Rowan and Damien discussed—lighthouses and libraries and relics bound to souls—but it was obvious that Damien was offering to deliver Edward to me in exchange for our help. . . help that would endanger Rowan.

This is it. This is my chance.

Twenty-four years as Edward's pet. Twenty-four years of learning that my body wasn't mine, that pain was currency, that survival meant becoming whatever shape he needed that day. Dancer. Doll. Decoration. *Thing.* Merchandise with a pulse and wet holes.

My memories from my first life were crystal-clear and inescapable. And now I had a chance to make the man responsible for that lifetime of suffering pay. But at what cost?

I felt Rowan's hand gently squeeze my own and looked into his pale blue eyes. He stared at me before giving me the slightest nod. I realized he'd been quietly waiting for me to answer Damien's question, and that I'd frozen while pondering. *He isn't rushing me*, I realized. It wasn't an impatient squeeze. *He is reassuring me that he's here. That he'll support whatever choice I make.*

He would die for me.

He *had* died for me.

But would I let him die for my vengeance?

The answer should have been easy and immediate. Edward Fitzgerald *deserved* to suffer. He *deserved* to bleed.

But did Rowan?

His thumb kept moving over the back of my hand in those small circles.

No. No, he does not, I thought as I loosed an explosive exhale.

Even if it meant never finding Edward. Even if it meant carrying this hatred for the rest of this second life. Even if it meant the scales never balanced and the universe never corrected its cosmic error of letting that monster keep breathing, keep touching, keep destroying.

Rowan was alive. And I was choosing—*actively choosing*—to keep him that way.

We'll find another way. The thought echoed in my skull, desperate and determined in equal measure. *We'll hunt Edward without demon contracts, mysterious artifacts, or whatever the hell a Strega is.* It would be harder and slower, but it would not involve gambling with lives I couldn't afford to lose. Not after losing Jules. I knew I could not bear another.

I lifted my chin, met Damien's molten-amber gaze—those eyes that saw too much, knew too much, promised too much—and let my voice cut through the smoke-thick air. "No. No deal."

The word shattered the silence in the room like a stone through a window.

Damien's eyebrows rose—genuine surprise flickering across features too perfect to trust, too beautiful to be fully human. He set down his coffee cup with deliberate care. "No?" His voice was velvet wrapped around steel, curiosity sharpening the edges. "How exquisitely unexpected, *gatita*. And here I thought vengeance was your heart's one true desire, the very thing that you *lusted* after more than all else."

"It is." My voice came out flat, hard, no room for negotiation.

"And yet," he gestured between Rowan and me with one elegant hand, "Here you stand, choosing *him* over your need to avenge the pain of a life un-lived—"

"I lived it," I spat.

"Yes," Damien said with a smile, "you did indeed. And I can *smell* the coppery scent of bloodlust wafting off of you. I can *taste* the nectar of your desire over how much you thirst to rip Edward to pieces, then shred those pieces into ribbons." Damien's eyes flashed a brilliant gold as his smile grew even wider. "Your lust for revenge, for violence, for pain is... *delicious*."

"Thanks?" I said, not knowing how else to reply.

"However," Damien said as he raised a hand, "I must caution you, *gatita*. I feel it is rarely ever in an individual's best interest, either in the long term or the short, to act against their base nature. We have these instincts, urges, compulsions, and desires for a reason, *si*? To ignore them for overly long is to do so at great peril."

"Yeah, well... I've had a lot of practice at *not* getting what I want. A whole lifetime of it, in fact. Besides," I said as I looked at Rowan and squeezed his hand back, "some things are even more important."

"Oh, *mi aves fénix*... how very romantic." His smile was all teeth and knowing amusement. "Or perhaps this is just foolish. I confess, I do not possess the foresight to tell which."

I said nothing. Couldn't trust my voice not to shake, not to reveal how close I was to changing my mind, to grabbing his offer with both hands and damn the consequences.

His knowing smile told me that he enjoyed my moral struggle like a fine wine. "Tell me, *mi gatita*, does your boyfriend know what you are sacrificing for him? Does he understand the weight of the gift you offer with your refusal? Does he understand just how much you *lust* for the blood of this man?"

"That's no one's business."

"Oh, but it is." Damien leaned back in his chair, crossing one leg over the other with casual grace. "Everything that happens within my domain is my business. Every choice, every sacrifice, every delicious moment of indecision." He picked up his coffee cup again, inhaled the aroma, and sipped. "And you, *gatita*, are positively *aching* with indecision right now."

Rowan's grip tightened on my hand while the other clenched into a fist. "We're leaving," I said over my shoulder as I turned to leave. "No deal. No contract. No help finding Edward. We're done."

"*Hold*," Damien said, but the word sounded. . . odd? The tone and timbre of his voice sounded off, sounded heavy. It was spoken as neither a request nor a command, but more of a simple statement of fact.

We stopped walking away and turned to face him.

Damien set his coffee cup back down before he stood. "There is still the rather significant matter of the boon he owes me for the death of my good friend Jules," Damien said, pointing to Rowan. "I would be remiss if I did not insist upon *something* in recompense for such a tragic loss."

"*Tfu*! As I told you once before, High Demon, you may have my silence as a boon. You will get naught else from me." Rowan took a step towards Damien, placing himself between me and the demon. "If you are unhappy with that offer, then strike me down and be done with this farce."

You idiot! My pulse thundered in my ears as the image of Damien's hand ripping Rowan's heart out swam in my vision. The thought of his body crumpling to the floor, the same as Jules's, like a puppet with its strings cut, impaled me with a spike of fear. I knew Rowan was fearless to a fault, but even he had to recognize that whatever the hell a demon like Damien was capable of, this was neither a fight he could win nor a person he could intimidate.

Unless...

Unless Rowan knew Damien wouldn't risk the relic that seemed so important to him. Unless he was willing to gamble his life—possibly *both* of their lives at this point—on the assumption that Damien needed him alive to find his way to some lighthouse. Whatever that place was.

Damien studied us for a long moment. I felt his amber eyes peeling me apart layer by layer. Then he let loose a full-throated laugh that filled the study with its rich warmth. The sound bounced off leather-bound spines and polished wood, seeming to come from everywhere and nowhere.

"Very well, *chico.*" He picked up his coffee cup and raised it in our direction before taking another slow sip of coffee. "You may both leave the Second Circle. For now." The implication hung heavy—*but you'll be back.*

Just like that.

No threats. No bargaining. No attempt to sweeten the deal or point out everything I was throwing away. Just... his permission. Like I'd asked to be excused from a dinner party rather than walk away from the only solid lead I'd had on Edward's location in weeks of searching.

My muscles trembled with exhaustion and spent fear, but I forced them to hold steady. Forced myself to straighten my back and keep my chin up. I wouldn't give him the satisfaction of seeing me crumble. Wouldn't let him see how much walking away from this was costing me.

My legs nearly betrayed me as I turned and walked towards the door. The adrenaline crash hit like a truck—hours of terror, revelation, murder, and resurrection all caught up at once. Jules's death. Rowan's secret. This entire negotiation with a demon who killed as easily as breathing and smiled while doing it.

Rowan shuffled beside me, and I knew he had to be in agony—the slight hitch in his movement, how he cradled his wrist, the tremble in his limbs. Pain flashed across his face, and I could only imagine how his body must have felt after coming back from being dead.

Being resurrected wasn't the same as being healed, I suppose. He'd been beaten, slashed, and bitten tonight before being drained nearly entirely of blood. His wrist was barely functional, badly swollen. He was running on pure stubborn willpower combined with his obsessive compulsion to protect me.

And I almost traded him to a demon.

The thought made bile rise in my throat, acid-sharp and bitter enough to water my eyes. As we neared the door to the study, I sniffled at the thought of losing him to Damien, which prompted him to check on me.

"Violet, are you okay?" he asked, timbre low and hoarse.

"Honestly? No, I'm not." I released an exhausted sigh, crossing over the plush rug. "But I don't think anybody *would* be after the night we've had. I'm still pissed at you, by the way."

"For dying?"

"No, you idiot," I said. "That you've already lived a life before..."

Rowan reached for the handle to the study's door as he said, "Well, my reincarnation is not *exactly* the same as yours, Levi's, and Charlie's. It is—"

"Ah, I nearly forgot," Damien's voice called out behind us.

Every muscle in my body locked down. *Here it comes. The twist. The double-cross. The revelation that we can't simply walk away from a High Demon after declining his offer.* Surely there would be consequences for wasting Damien's time—for rejecting him.

I turned slowly, Rowan's hand still gripped in mine like a lifeline.

Damien moved around his desk with that liquid grace that made the mundane act of walking look like a dance, as if his feet barely touched the ground. He approached us with measured steps, each one deliberate and unhurried, stopping close enough that his scent wrapped around us both.

Again that smell of smoke and red wine, but now there was also a hint of coffee, sandalwood, and something distinctly *carnal*—the scent of sex and sin and a pleasure so intense it rolled off him in waves and saturated the air like an intoxicating fog. Part of my brain screamed to run, while another part begged for him to come closer.

The heat from his body reached me even from two feet away, fevered and inviting and wrong. He extended his hand towards me, palm up, fingers long and elegant and still faintly stained with Jules's blood that no amount of silk handkerchiefs could fully cleanse. The stains were russet-brown now, dried in the creases of his skin, under his perfectly manicured nails.

"May I please have your hand, *gatita*?" His voice was honey and smoke.

The phrasing was polite. Courteous, even. The tone of someone asking permission rather than demanding compliance.

But I had a feeling that nothing about Damien was truly a question. Just opportunities to consent to things he'd already decided would happen.

I hesitated, every instinct screaming *don't touch the demon*, but the combination of curiosity, exhaustion, and the sheer weight of the past hour won out. "Why?" I heard myself ask.

"I have a gift to bestow upon you. You may consider it my own version of recompense for how this evening's events have played out... regardless of *who* may or may not have been at fault."

Rowan squeezed my hand. "Violet? We do not accept gifts from demons. Let us go."

I knew he meant well and that he understood a whole helluva lot more about all the supernatural shit we'd found ourselves in. But I was still mad as hell at him.

Against my better judgement, I reached my hand out and placed it in Damien's. The warmth radiating from his palm against mine was shocking. *No, not warm. Hot, like he's all fire inside.* His flesh was impossibly soft, no calluses, no scars, perfectly maintained in the way that came from never doing manual labor, never struggling, never bleeding for anything.

His fingers closed gently around my wrist, turned it over so my hand was palm up. The pad of his thumb traced a line from my palm to my pulse point, the touch impossibly delicate, as if he was savoring the moment. His skin against mine sent heat crawling up my arm and made my pulse spike beneath his fingers.

Then he pressed down.

Heat flared beneath his touch—not quite burning or painful, but *intense*. Like liquid gold poured directly into my veins, spreading up my arm in waves of sensation that stole my breath and kicked my pulse into a gallop. It was pleasure and pain braided together so tightly they became indistinguishable, building to a crescendo that felt obscene in its intimacy.

The heat spread up my arm, across my shoulder, down my spine. My skin flushed hot, then cold, then hot again. Every nerve lit up like Christmas lights, oversensitive and overwhelming.

Oh my god, was the most intelligible thought I could manage.

My knees went weak. Heat pooled low in my belly, slick and urgent and completely wrong given the circumstances. Rowan had died, had come back, had lied to me. Jules was dead. We were in a demon's study in the basement of a nightclub. I should not be getting aroused—should not be biting back a moan—while this *thing* pretending to be human caressed me.

But my body didn't care about what it *should* do.

The sensation peaked as a white-hot, nearly overwhelming, and delicious pleasure-pain. My toes curled, and my breathing came in shallow gasps—sounding far too close to the noises I made during sex—before the feeling faded. As Damien lifted his fingers from my skin, I was left with a throbbing heat in my wrist.

I yanked my hand back, cradled it against my chest, and looked down.

On my inner wrist, where Damien had pressed down with his thumb, an intricate and gorgeous golden snake glowed. Coiled and sinuous, its body wrapped around itself into a heart-shaped knot. The lines were delicate, artful, exquisitely rendered. I squinted at it to see that each scale had a level of minute detail that was breathtaking.

He had tattooed me. Without permission. Without warning. Without asking if I wanted to be permanently marked by a demon's power, branded like property, claimed in a way that went deeper than skin.

Anger bubbled up, and I burst out, "How dare you—"

Rowan reached out to take my arm. "What did he do? Did he hurt you? Let me see."

"Calm yourself, *chico*. The pain was pleasurable for her, of *that* I can promise you," Damien said with a low laugh.

Rowan bristled. "Fuck you, demon—"

"It is a gift freely given from me to you, *mi gatita*." Damien's voice was velvet soft and filled with satisfaction in every syllable. He looked pleased with himself. Smug. "It is for when your pride inevitably crumbles when you realize that you *do* need my help... help that only I can provide." He paused, smiled wider. "All you need to do is simply whisper my name with intention, with a real *longing* for me, and I will hear you. Regardless of where you are, regardless of how much time may come to pass, regardless of how *desperately* you come to regret denying my offer of assistance tonight," he said as he bowed his head slightly. "Whisper my name to the snake, and I will come."

The tattoo pulsed once against my skin—warm, possessive, claiming—then settled into stillness. I still felt it there. Not painfully, but *present*.

I stared at the golden snake coiled upon my wrist, at the delicate lines that formed runes within its scales. It *was* beautiful. Objectively, undeniably beautiful. It was the kind of ink I'd have gladly paid *serious* money for if I'd seen it in a portfolio at Inkwell or Sacred Skin or any of the other parlors I'd visited since my rebirth. It was the kind of art that made other people stop and ask where you'd gotten it done, who the artist was, and how long it took.

Despite that I didn't choose this tattoo, despite that I knew I *should* have felt violated for Damien essentially branding me without my permission... I loved it.

And damn him for knowing that I would.

Damien returned to his desk and settled back into his chair. He picked up his coffee cup, inhaled the aroma with the appreciation of a connoisseur, took a slow sip while watching us over the rim with those too-knowing amber eyes.

We turned towards the door again. Rowan's hand found mine, his grip steady despite the exhaustion I heard in his breathing—shallow and controlled, the breathing of someone in pain and trying not to show it. The slight tremor in his fingers said his body was running on fumes.

Again, Damien's voice stopped us from leaving. "It is a long walk from here to *wherever* you two are headed. Would you like for me to conjure up a door, *mi aves fénix*?"

The question stopped me mid-step. I turned, certain I'd misheard. "What?"

Rowan said, "If there is no cost to such an offer." His voice was cautious, suspicious in the way that came from decades of learning that nothing was ever free. That generosity from the powerful always came with strings attached, hooks buried in the gift, prices that didn't reveal themselves until you were already bleeding.

"It seems your dearest boyfriend did not tell you how gods and demons travel, *gatita*." He made a small gesture with his hand—barely a flick of his fingers, casual as someone swatting a fly—and reality just. . . *shifted*.

One moment, there was only a wall next to us. The next moment, there was a door.

Heavy oak that looked centuries old, dark enough to be almost black, with grain visible in the firelight like muscle beneath skin. Iron hinges hand-forged and ancient, the kind of metalwork that belonged in museums or castles or places where history had weight and blood.

Just a door that absolutely, definitely, had *not* been there a second ago.

My stomach dropped. The floor felt unstable beneath my feet, as if the ground itself had betrayed me by allowing this impossible thing to exist. The air pressure in the room changed—subtle but noticeable, like my ears needed to pop, like we'd suddenly gained or lost altitude.

"Huh," was all I could say.

"Think of a place you have been," Damien purred. "It must be a *place*, not a person nor a time, and it must be a place you *desire* to go. Then?" He waved his hand. "Open the door and walk through."

I thought of all the places I could have gone. I needed somewhere to retreat to, somewhere to feel safe, somewhere I could process the overwhelming deluge of this night's events.

Home? As in my parents' house, my childhood home, my bedroom. I still thought of that as home, and why wouldn't I? I hadn't even been at college for a full semester. But then I thought of Daddy, how he would worry and wonder and pepper me with questions as to why I was home.

Dorm? It was where I'd spent most of my nights since being reborn, where I'd spent so much time plotting and planning my vengeance against Edward. But Alice might be there, which would mean that Natalia might be there, too.

Rowan's? In the short time since we had become lovers, we had made so many memories in his place. In his bedroom, specifically. I knew that I would feel safe there. But I was still pissed at him, and as childish as it might have been, I didn't want to give him the satisfaction of picking his apartment as my refuge.

Then it hit me, and I realized there was only one place in all the world I could go in that moment to settle my heart and calm my mind. It wasn't even a question, and I felt ridiculous for even entertaining any other destination.

Before I could question it further—before I could demand clarification on how the door worked or refuse Damien's offer—I thought of where I wanted to go, grabbed the handle, and opened the door.

And I saw grass.

Familiar grass, autumn-brown and damp with the recent rain, stretched out in a field I knew intimately. Had ridden through dozens of times. Had jumped fences in. Had spent hours grooming and training in. Whenever this second life felt too heavy to carry, when the only thing that seemed to make any sense was the rhythm of hoofbeats and the simple joy of speed and movement and freedom.

The Shademore Equestrian Center.

The stables.

Hyacinth.

The intense warmth of Damien's study collided with the cold night air beyond the door, creating a fog that rolled across the grass. The field was empty, dark except for the distant lights from the stable buildings casting yellow-warm glows that didn't reach this far.

Yes, I thought, realizing that somehow the door had known I wanted—*needed*—to ride Hyacinth. Only rushing through the fields on my baby could help me forget everything, even if only for a moment.

Rowan started to ask, "Is that—"

A soul-wrenching sound tore through the air, a scream shattering the silence. High and piercing and *wrong*—the kind of sound that reached down into your guts and activated every prey instinct evolution had instilled over millions of years. Not a human scream, but unlike any sound I'd ever heard an animal make. It was a sound of terror and pain braided together into a noise that I knew would haunt my nightmares until the day I died.

It came again, closer and more panicked.

"No," I whispered as horror ripped into my chest, stole both my breath and balance. My heart stopped, then slammed into overdrive, pulse pounding in my ears, drowning out everything else.

My horse.

My *baby*.

He was screaming.

I ran.

Didn't think. Didn't plan. Didn't slow from Rowan shouting my name behind me, his voice sharp with warning and fear. I just *ran*—through the impossible door, through the space that shouldn't exist between Damien's study and the fields behind the stables.

My hands hit earth as I stumbled through, as momentum and portal-physics and my own desperate speed sent me sprawling. Grass met my palms—cold and damp and *real*. Blades tickled between my fingers, bent beneath my weight. The ground was soft, yielding, saturated from earlier rain that had turned the equestrian center into a swamp of mud, grass, and horse shit.

The impact jarred through my wrists, up my arms, into my shoulders. Pain sharp and immediate that grounded me, proved this was real, proved I wasn't hallucinating or dreaming or trapped in some nightmare my brain had conjured.

The smell hit me next. Wet earth and manure and autumn decay—leaves rotting in piles by the fence line, grass turning brown as winter approached, the particular organic stink of a stable that never quite left even when you were fifty yards away. Compost and hay and horse sweat and leather and the sweet-sour smell of grain.

And beneath it all—

Blood.

The night air slapped me cold and sharp, stealing the breath from my lungs. My exhale came out as visible mist, the temperature having dropped into the low forties while we'd been in Damien's study. Cold enough to make my fingers ache, my ears burn, my breath catch.

I scrambled to my feet, legs shaking from exhaustion and terror. The grass was slick beneath my feet, treacherous, threatening to send me sprawling again. My clothes soaked through at the knees where I'd landed, cold water seeping into fabric and prickling my skin.

The field stretched out before me, dark and empty except for—

There.

Fifty yards away, at the edge of the tree line where the manicured equestrian grounds gave way to wilderness and state forest, I saw him. Hyacinth's form looked diminutive against the *thing* stalking him. His copper coat was stark against the darkness like a beacon, like a target, catching the moonlight that filtered through the clouds. His head was thrown back, neck arched, ears pinned flat against his skull in terror.

He screamed again—that same piercing sound that turned my blood to ice water and activated every protective instinct I'd ever had.

And then I saw the wolf.

My brain refused to understand what I was seeing. It was too large. Twice the size any wolf should be, probably four hundred pounds of muscle and fur and nightmare. Its coat was midnight-black with patches of dark grey, thick and coarse, standing up along its spine in a ridge that made it look even bigger. The fur seemed to absorb the moonlight rather than reflect it, like the creature was made of concentrated shadow.

Its eyes glowed. Actually *glowed* a yellow-green. Even more frightening than their luminescence was the intelligence in those eyes, seemingly human in their focus and intent.

Rowan's words echoed in my memory, his voice quiet and certain. *"She smelled of blood, Violet. Fresh blood."*

The shifter he'd warned me about, the murderer, possibly a girl in my philosophy class. This had to be the thing that killed that student.

And now it has cornered my horse.

"Leave him alone!" The words tore out of my throat, raw and desperate and utterly useless.

I was too far away. The wolf didn't even turn, didn't acknowledge my presence at all. It just circled Hyacinth with the patient confidence of a predator that knew its prey had nowhere to go, that understood cornering and fear and the sweet anticipation of the kill.

Hyacinth's sides heaved with exertion and terror. Sweat darkened his coat, made it cling to the muscles beneath. His nostrils flared wide, red-rimmed, breathing hard enough that I could hear it from here—the harsh exhales of panic, the kind of breathing that came before hearts gave out from sheer terror.

I ran harder, legs burning with effort, lungs screaming for air in the cold night. Each step felt like moving through water, time stretching and compressing wrong, the distance refusing to shrink fast enough, no matter how hard I pushed.

Move, move, fucking MOVE—

The wolf lunged.

The motion was liquid speed and brutal economy, covering the fifteen feet between them in a heartbeat—explosive violence that clutched my lungs, ceased my breathing.

Long curved claws flashed in the moonlight like black knives. They raked across Hyacinth's side and made a sound like tearing wet fabric.

Bright red bloomed across his chestnut coat.

Blood. So much blood. It poured from the gashes in his flank, four parallel lines carved deep into muscle, soaking his coat and dripping onto grass already dark with rain. The scent hit me even from that distance—copper and salt and iron, the particular metallic tang of blood that I'd smelled a thousand times in training accidents and injuries but never this much at once.

Never this *much.*

Never *Hyacinth's* blood.

The sound he made wasn't the whinny of pain from a cut leg or the protest of a horse being tasked to do something uncomfortable. This was *agony*. Raw, visceral, the sound of an animal dying and knowing it, but fighting anyway because the body didn't know how to do anything else. His front legs pistoned upward, a thousand pounds of terror and survival instinct. One hoof connected with the wolf's snout, a solid impact that sounded like a baseball bat hitting a side of beef—hollow and meaty.

The wolf yelped and stumbled back, shaking its massive head. Hyacinth spun as if to flee. The wolf recovered and lunged again, but Hyacinth delivered a powerful hindkick—the wolf was caught midair by a pair of horsehooves. The sound of hooves striking the wolf's skull thundered like a shotgun blasting a wooden barrel.

The impact echoed across the field, sharp and final. The creature *cried*—a sound too human for the body it came from, full of pain and outrage and surprise, almost like a child's wail of betrayed hurt.

Then it turned and ran. It disappeared into the tree line in a blur of dark fur and glowing eyes, leaving only the scent of wet dog and musk and something chemical.

I was still ten yards away when Hyacinth crumbled.

His legs folded beneath him—first the front, joints buckling like they'd been cut, then the back following in slow motion. He went down in a heap of red blood and wrong, wrong, *wrong*. The sound he made wasn't a scream anymore; it was a long, low, guttural moan, a soft noise for the broken and the dying.

No, god no, please.

His moan turned wet and gurgling. The sound of lungs filling with blood, of a body shutting down system by system, of consciousness fading like light through closing shutters.

"No, no, please," I managed through sobs.

Tears blurred my vision, turned the world into watercolor streaks of darkness and brown and red. So much red. The grass beneath him was already saturated, crimson spreading outward in a pool that caught the distant stable lights and turned them rust-colored.

My boots slipped in mud and blood as I got nearer. Each step splashed, sent droplets flying. The smell was overwhelming now—copper thick enough to taste on the back of my tongue, sweet and metallic and nauseating.

I crashed to my knees beside him, hands reaching for his neck, his head, searching for some way to help, to fix, to *stop this*. His coat was soaked—blood and rain and the cold sweat of shock making him slippery beneath my fingers. Warm. Still warm. Still alive even though he shouldn't be, even though the amount of blood spreading beneath him said his heart was still pumping even as his body was failing.

His eyes found mine. Brown and liquid and beautiful, framed by lashes that were matted with blood now. But the light was already fading at the edges, awareness dimming like someone was slowly turning down a dial.

He knew me. Still recognized me despite the pain, despite everything. His ear flicked towards my voice, the small movement taking effort that cost him.

"Please, baby, please don't—"

My hands found the wound. Four parallel gashes torn through his flank, each one deep enough that I could see the layers—skin, fat, muscle, and oh god—

His bowels hung out.

Intestines grey-pink and glistening, spilling from the cavity in his belly where the wolf's claws had ripped him open. They steamed in the cold night air, still warm, still technically alive even as the rest of him was dying. The membranes were intricate and complex, and never meant to see air.

Blood pulsed from torn arteries with each weakening heartbeat. Not spraying anymore—the pressure wasn't high enough—just welling up and spilling over, adding to the pool beneath him.

I sobbed. Deep, shuddering, wracking sobs. The sound tore out of my chest, grief and horror and helplessness all woven together into an atavistic animal noise I didn't recognize as coming from me. It sounded raw and primal.

Footsteps behind me. Running steps splashing through blood and mud. Rowan's voice was sharp with shock and grief that matched my own. "Violet! Are you hurt?"

He dropped beside me, his hands immediately moving to Hyacinth's belly, trying to hold—to what? Put the organs back? Stop the blood? Keep his intestines from spilling further onto the saturated grass?

There was too much. Too much damage. Too much red soaking into the earth and running over our hands and seeping into our clothes as we tried uselessly to stem the tide, to hold back the inevitable with nothing but desperation and willpower.

Hyacinth made another sound—softer, wetter, gurgling. His breathing became labored, each inhale a titanic struggle. His sides heaved, ribs standing out in sharp relief beneath blood-soaked hide. Foam flecked his muzzle—pink-tinged, blood-mixed—and his tongue lolled slightly, going pale at the edges.

I stroked his neck, his mane, and felt his pulse against my palm growing weaker with each beat. *Thump... thump... thump...* Each one fainter than the last, the rhythm stuttering, failing.

"Please, baby," I choked, "please don't leave me."

His eyes were still on mine. Still aware. Still *there* enough to recognize me, to know that I was here, that he wasn't dying in this cold field alone. His breathing slowed, his pained moans of suffering quieted, and a silence—silent save my hysterical sobbing—began to settle over us.

Then Rowan's shout shattered that gathering silence. "Damien!" His voice cracked on the name, desperate and furious. His hands were still pressed to Hyacinth's belly, fingers slick with blood. *"Demon!"* He screamed it louder, rage tearing his throat. "I will sign your contract! I will visit your damned Strega! I will get you into The Library! *But save this damned horse!"*

Hyacinth's breathing changed. Became shallower, more ragged. His pulse beneath my palm was barely there now—just a faint flutter, inconsistent, failing.

No no no no—

"Damien!" Rowan screamed again, louder. "Rip the fucking relic from my chest! Tear it out! Kill me if you have to! *Just save him!*"

The offer hung in the cold night air, terrible in its sincerity. Rowan was offering himself. He was willing to die if it meant saving a horse.

This horse. My horse. For me.

Because Rowan understood. He knew that losing Hyacinth would shatter parts of me that would never recover from his loss. He cared enough about me, my health, and my happiness to make that offer.

He cared enough to die for me. *Again.*

I was too broken to process it properly. Too shattered by the sight of Hyacinth dying beneath my hands, too overwhelmed by the sheer volume of blood and the wet sounds of his labored breathing and the knowledge that I was watching another thing I loved slip away.

But somewhere beneath the shock and grief, I felt it.

Gratitude. Love. The knowledge that Rowan would sacrifice anything—had *died* for me already tonight—and was willing to do it *again.*

My peripheral caught movement at the portal door we'd come through. Reality rippled like a heat shimmer, and the air distorted as Damien stepped through with the casual grace of someone taking an evening stroll through a garden rather than a muddy field full of horse shit.

He strolled across the field towards us, unhurried, taking his time. He took in the scene with those amber eyes that saw everything and felt—what? Amusement? Satisfaction? Sympathy?

I couldn't tell, and I didn't care. I could only hold Hyacinth's head as his lifeless body grew colder. I begged—aloud, internally, or perhaps both—for this to be a nightmare, for this to not be happening.

Please god, please. I can't lose my baby.

"Demon, I will pay whatever boon you deem appropriate." Rowan's voice was raw, stripped of everything except desperate sincerity. No pride. No bargaining. "If it is within your power, save this horse."

Damien stopped a few feet away, careful not to step in the spreading pool of blood. He tilted his head, studied us with a look of curiosity as if trying to understand human attachment, human love, human grief.

His smile was a crescent moon on a cloudless night. "Very well, *mi aves fénix*. Let us discuss the terms of our contract."

Epilogue

Violet

"And this," I murmured, brushing blood from my knuckles against the glossy sheen of my coat, "Is where we will pause." Edward's head lolled forward, his breath ragged and wet. The bruises across his skin were already deepening from the rope, flesh discoloring as time slowed around him. He wasn't dying quickly. No, that would've been merciful. He was unraveling, inch by inch, as was evident by the puddle of piss now below him.

Rowan stood against the wall, arms folded, his face unreadable but his eyes fixed on Edward with a detachment that chilled me. He had seen bodies rot, had seen death claim people in crueler ways than most could stomach. He knew what was coming—how Edward's body would swell, how the nerves would scream until finally, mercifully, they gave out.

I exhaled, stretching as if from nothing more strenuous than a rehearsal, then slipped the heavy overcoat from my shoulders. Underneath, crimson silk clung to my skin, shimmering like fresh blood beneath the low light. A slinky, shiny red slip that gleamed with every movement, paired with black heels that clicked across the concrete floor.

My uniform of power and decadence.

"I'm due on stage in a few minutes," I said to Edward softly, almost like a lover whispering a promise.

He didn't stir. His head lolled again, spit sliding down his chin. I crouched, tapping his cheek with a manicured finger. No response.

My patience snapped, and I slapped him sharply across the face. His head jerked up, eyes rolling until they finally locked on me. Anger burned there, diluted but alive.

"Be a good boy and wait for me," I crooned, patting his head as if he were nothing more than a dog.

Rowan came forward then, his presence filling the room with a quiet gravity. He extended his arm, the picture of composure even here in the stink of fear and blood. I took it with ease, rising gracefully.

The door creaked open wider, and Ciriatto stepped in, the boar-faced demon who prowled the Second Circle. His gaze flicked to me, then to Rowan, then finally to the half-conscious figure roped to the chair.

Edward's eyes shot open so wide I thought they'd burst from his face. He kicked and writhed against his restraints, yelled his muffled screams into his gag, and looked near to tears with fear.

Ciriatto stared at him for a moment before turning to me. "First time?"

"Seeing a demon?" I asked with a laugh. "I imagine so. How can I help you, sir?"

"He asked me to tell you that the girls have been looking for you," Ciriatto said. His voice was low and respectful, though his eyes gleamed with an unspoken understanding.

I smiled, sweet and sharp, leaning briefly into Rowan's side. "I imagine he was worried I would lose track of time having fun down here, but we were actually just leaving. Would you be so kind as to take care of our guest? He needs to stay alive for the remainder of our love play."

Ciriatto's curled, the sharpened teeth between his tusks gleaming. "With great pleasure."

I didn't look back. Didn't need to. The sound of Edward's gagged screams and Ciriatto's lumbering steps towards him were enough.

Rowan's arm tightened around mine, steady and grounding. He bent his head to press a kiss against my temple, a gesture that was both intimate and a declaration of our relationship.

As the door shut behind us, the muffled beat of music from above began to thrum louder, a reminder of the stage waiting for me. The world of velvet, smoke, and sin welcomed us back as the basement—and Edward's final hours—faded into the shadows behind us, awaiting me to finish my story.

Thank You

Thank you, my beloved chaos *lectores*[1], for picking up this book and taking the leap of faith to check out an indie author. It really means the world to me.

I truly hope Fated Rebirth gave you a much needed escape and just so we're clear... there is *so much more* where that came from. The love poured into world building is equally important and with each story, a little more is revealed in the symbiotic relationship of the mortals and supernaturals while gods play mafia in the background intent to rule through the currency of worshippers.

I do want to give a fair warning, though: my catalog is a wild ride in the best possible way. I write across a broad spectrum of romance, from completely unhinged monster smut to sweeping dark romantasy epics with a sprinkling of contemporary. The common thread? High heat, powerful emotions, unapologetic characters, and happily-ever-afters every time.

If you'd like to continue our relationship (because consent is key) along with gaining access to bonus smut, spicy artwork, and info on my other projects, come find me at www.renormist.com.

Additionally, Newsletter subscribers get first access to:
- free bonus content
- spicy art drops
- early updates

---

1. readers

- exclusive Second Circle request forms where each quarter, I pull one subscriber's prompt and write a custom short story.

And lastly, your TBR is probably overflowing (same), but if you're not sure what to pick up next, here are a few options:

☐ **Dark PNR/Fantasy – A Second Circle Series**

Captured Prey, A Primal Play Novella is part of the Second Circle Entry series, told in third-person POV. Each story explores desire, inhibition, and awakening in richly sensual worlds. Often pairing mortals with monsters, love and hunger intertwine as things that go bump in the night steal your heart...and possibly your soul. Seductive. Sinister. What are you waiting for?

☐ **Dark Contemporary – Star-Cross'd Fates Series**

One More Chance is an emotional, second-chance marriage-in-crisis romance told entirely from a deeply flawed but redeemable male POV. A story of betrayal, regret, and the brutal climb toward forgiveness when love tries to survive the damage of the past. Here, you are given a glimpses of how one god's choice led to mortals' souls being trifled with and how those mortals move forward given a chance to fix their mistakes in a contemporary setting.

Audible available as well!

Before We Belong is a slow-burn, why-choose contemporary romance that explores redemption, vulnerability, and the courage to redefine what love and belonging can look like. Perfect for readers who crave emotional depth, found family, and forbidden love threaded with sensuality and heart.

*Coming soon! Subscribe to my newsletter to get access when it drops for Pre-Order

Once again, thank you again for taking this adventure with me. I hope we meet again between the pages soon.

ACKNOWLEDGEMENTS

I'd like to thank my editors, all of them, for your undying patience with this story. I could not have gotten here without your help.

To all my readers who support me, thank you. Meeting you and talking with you has given me so much joy. I am naturally an introvert though I can act like an extrovert, so events wear me out. But meeting everyone has been a gift in itself.

Thank you to my friends and family. I didn't think I would ever get far with this, and yet here we are.

And lastly, I want to thank my library. The only safe place for me to escape growing up, and for the world it opened up to me. So many authors influenced me and I would run out of room listing them.

ABOUT THE AUTHOR

Reno is an aspiring indie author on a mission to fund her cat's lavish lifestyle. She writes high-heat contemporary, fantasy, and dark(ish) romances that explore kink, desire, and the complexities of love for characters thirty-five and older.

Drawn to the unconventional, Reno crafts worlds where fantasy and passion collide — where gods, mortals, and monsters (both the spicy and unspicy kind) come alive on the page.

She has a soft spot for full-body tattoos, tragic villains, and stories that blur the line between sin and salvation. To stay up-to-date on exclusive content, head over to www.renormist.com and sign up for the newsletter!

Made in the USA
Middletown, DE
05 March 2026

29307141R00219